BROKEN KNIGHTS

GIFTED ACADEMY BOOK FOUR

MICHELLE HERCULES

INFINITE SKY PUBLISHING

Photography: Michelle Lancaster
Models: Meika Woollard & Lochie Carey

Editor: Theresa Schultz
Proofreader: Hot Tree Editing

Paperback ISBN: 978-1-950991-60-0

CONTENTS

PROLOGUE
XAVIER

Saturn's Bay – Six and a Half Years Ago

The club's grand opening was only a week away, but Xavier couldn't find an ounce of excitement or motivation. It was a miracle he had been able to keep the project rolling while his thoughts were consumed with worry over the disappearance of Paul's daughters, his nieces. If he could, he'd abandon everything and go in search of them.

He actually did go to Hawk City as soon as he heard the awful news that his brother and sister-in-law had been brutally murdered by Neo Gods agents. But at the time, Daisy and Rosie had been staying with a distant relative. He should have known the arrangement was temporary. He should have intervened. But fear his enemies would find out about his connection to Paul kept him from getting involved. And now the guilt ate at him.

A gorgeous Fringe was performing on the brand-new main stage, but Xavier saw nothing as he stared ahead with a closed fist covering his mouth. In his other hand, he nursed a glass of whiskey, neat.

His phone's screen lit up a second before the device vibrated on the table, bringing Xavier back to the present. The call was from an unknown number, which prompted him to answer right away.

"Xavier speaking."

"I've found them," said a female voice he hadn't heard in years.

Jodie Fallon was someone from Xavier's past he wished he could forget. She had only brought misery to his family, and he was convinced Paul's death was somehow linked to the woman. He hadn't asked her for help, so the fact that she knew who he was looking for made his entire frame tense.

"I didn't realize you were looking," he replied.

"Of course I was searching for them. They're Will's nieces too."

"Don't you dare speak his name," he hissed through clenched teeth.

"You're never going to forgive me, are you?"

"No."

Xavier heard a heavy sigh on the other end of the line, but that didn't change how he felt. Jodie got his older brother Will killed, then married the Idol responsible for his death.

"Hate me all you want, but don't let your feelings get in the way of saving your nieces."

He stood suddenly and made a beeline to his office at the back of the club. This was not a conversation he should have out in the open.

"I'm not. Give me a second." Once the door was safely locked, he continued. "Go on. Where are they?"

"Chatterton. A few days ago, they slept in a homeless shelter. But they haven't returned. My contacts believe they're living in an abandoned train station downtown."

Xavier's hand curled into a fist, and then his entire body

seemed to freeze. The rage he had carried deep in his gut his entire life threatened to burst through.

"They're living on the streets?" His voice was low, and it cracked at the end.

"I'm afraid so, Xavier," Jodie replied.

He had mastered controlling his emotions a long time ago, but today he was having a hard time keeping them concealed. Daisy and Rosie were the only family he had left. He was born south of the border and forced to grow up fast when his parents ditched him at an orphanage at the age of five. He ran away from the nightmarish place as soon as he could, coming to the country by hiding in the trunk of John Rodale's car.

When the Norm found him, instead of calling the police, he gave Xavier a place to stay, and then, much to Xavier's surprise, the man adopted him later. And now Xavier was repaying that act of selfless love by letting his own nieces fend for themselves in a dangerous city.

"I know you don't trust me, but I can get them to a safe location," she continued.

"No! Absolutely not. You're already too involved. I don't want to sic your despicable husband on the girls."

"I've been careful. Jonathan knows nothing," she gritted out.

"Like he knew nothing about Paul?"

"Paul got killed because he had a big mouth. I tried to warn him, but he wouldn't listen to me."

"Just stay away from them, Jodie. I mean it."

"As you wish."

She then told him the address, which Xavier jotted down in illegible scribbles on the first piece of paper he could find—the back of an envelope.

He was just about to fold the note and stick it into his breast pocket when a knock came at the door.

"Come in."

"Sorry to interrupt, Mr. X, but you have a visitor," one of Xavier's bodyguards announced.

"I don't have time for visits, Leonardo. I'm heading out."

The burly bodyguard was shoved to the side and a tall blond man entered his office, commanding Xavier's attention immediately. Apprehension took hold of Xavier, and at once, he projected his powers to the max. He was only a level six Fringe, but thanks to his ability as a Morph, he could pretend to be a level ten Idol. And Xavier needed to appear stronger than he was, for standing before him was not only a level fifteen Idol, but also one of the leaders of the Knights, a clandestine organization committed to protecting Fringes and Norms from the oppressive hand of the Idol race.

Leonardo made to remove Gunther Silverstone by force, but Xavier lifted his hand to halt him. "It's fine, Leo. You can go now."

Silently, he nodded before shutting the door. Silverstone remained where he stood, watching Xavier with dispassionate curiosity.

Xavier sat down, getting comfortable in his chair. It was all a show. Every nerve in his body was crackling with electricity, and all his muscles were stiff. "How can I help you?"

"Xavier Rodale. You're a hard man to find."

Xavier narrowed his gaze and clenched his jaw. Very few people knew his last name. "What do you want?"

"Do you know who I am?"

"I've seen your picture in the social pages of the newspapers."

The man smiled tightly. "Let me rephrase. Do you know who I work for?"

Xavier leaned forward, keeping the glower in place while his brain scrambled to find a situation where he might have slipped up, where the likes of Silverstone would suspect the nature of his gift. When he couldn't think of any, he replied, "You're part of the Knights."

The man finally walked forward and then pulled up a chair. When sat down, he seemed relaxed, which only made Xavier tenser.

"That's right."

"Why were you looking for me?"

"I have an offer for you."

"I'm not interested. I have no desire to get embroiled in your illicit activities." Xavier began to stand up, ready to escort the arrogant Idol out of his office.

"Really? I thought you would be more sympathetic to our cause after we prevented the Neo Gods from murdering your nieces in cold blood."

At once, Xavier froze. He thought he had been careful, but apparently not, since Silverstone knew about Daisy and Rosie. He sat back down, feeling leery and on edge. He had to be careful about his next words.

"What do you know about them?"

"We know their current location. As a matter of fact, we have been keeping tabs on their movements for a while."

Son of a bitch, Xavier thought.

"Why?"

"Let's just say I have a vested interest in keeping them safe."

Fury erupted from the pit of Xavier's belly. He had left his nieces alone in order to protect them, but it seemed his sacrifice had been in vain. Leaning forward, he slammed his open palms on his desk. "You stay the hell away from them."

Silverstone narrowed his cunning eyes. "You should be thanking me. If it weren't for my agents, they'd be dead by now. You do know what happens to pretty girls who wander far from home."

Xavier's stomach twisted savagely. He was young when he left the south, but he remembered the atrocities and violence against young girls and women who didn't have anyone to protect them. His head felt heavy all of a sudden, so he dipped his chin, closing his eyes for a moment.

"I'm not trying to rub salt in your wound. I'm offering my help. I can take the girls from the streets and place them in a safe house until you're ready to claim them."

Xavier lifted his head to stare Silverstone in the eye. He was usually a good judge of character, but he was having a hard time figuring out the Idol in front of him.

"What do you want in return?" he asked through clenched teeth.

"I want you to come work with me."

Xavier's eyebrows shot up while his blood ran cold. "Why?"

"Because I could use someone with your *special* skills."

Fear gripped Xavier's insides, twisting them in a merciless vise. His heart pounded against his rib cage as he stared at the Idol. "My special skills?" he asked finally.

"I know what you are, Xavier."

Xavier's stomach bottomed out, and the instinct to flee took over. He would do it if his nieces' lives weren't on the line.

"And you still want me to work with you?"

"Yes. I'm not like the majority of Idols. I don't destroy people out of fear. And I know your kind has been hunted to near extinction."

"Then you know why I can't work for you and risk discovery."

"You won't be discovered. No one will know about your association with the Knights besides me, not even the other members."

"Do you want me to work for you as a spy?"

"Precisely. In exchange, I'll personally see that your nieces are kept safe."

Xavier passed a hand over his face, feeling like there wasn't much he could do. Silverstone had him cornered.

"Jodie Fallon knows about them too. She offered me the same thing you did, to keep Daisy and Rosie safe."

"I know."

Xavier wasn't surprised. He knew Jodie better though, and that didn't give him comfort. People would say to trust the devil you know, but in his experience, that was a load of crap.

"I don't trust either of you, but Jodie less so."

"I take it you refused her offer."

"I did. I was on my way to rescue the girls myself when you showed up."

"Do you think now is the right time to bring children into your life?" Silverstone glanced at a promotional poster for Unearthly Desires.

Xavier clenched his jaw while gripping the edge of the desk so tight, his knuckles turned white. He knew he wasn't in the least prepared. If he brought Daisy and Rosie into his life right now, he might be putting them in even more danger.

He let out a resigned sigh. "No. I need more time."

"Then let me help you." Silverstone leaned forward eagerly.

"What do you want with them?"

"I have a theory. It might be nothing, but I believe one of your nieces is destined to save the world."

"They're Norms. How could they possibly do that?"

Silverstone pierced Xavier with a hard stare. "You should not underestimate the power of Norms."

A great sense of shame took over Xavier. He knew better than anyone else what a simple Norm could do. His own adoptive father, with one act of kindness, had made a deep impact in his Xavier's life. He had saved him.

"I accept your offer, but I'll give you this warning. If you or any of the Knights harm my nieces in any way, I *will* come for you."

The corners of Silverstone's lips twitched upward. "I expect nothing less from you."

1

DAISY

My body is numb, my mind is whirling, and yet I can sense Rosie's stare burning a hole through my face as I pack my suitcase.

"What?" I ask without glancing in her direction.

"You haven't said much since we got back."

"Perceptive," I mumble.

She walks over and sits on the edge of my bed. "How are you feeling?"

"I don't want to talk about it." I shove a piece of clothing in the suitcase without bothering to fold it.

"You can't blame yourself for what happened to Rufio."

I whip my face toward her. "Really? I can't blame myself? I'm the one who took away his powers, Rosie. Who else am I going to blame?"

"His father. The one who forced you to do it."

Shaking my head, I look away. "He used me, but that doesn't absolve me. I should have fought harder."

She lets out a loaded sigh. "Seeing Rufio reduced to a

powerless Norm didn't make me happy like I thought it would. I've always wished that fate on every single ruthless Idol I met. But I don't feel an ounce of satisfaction. Instead, I feel sorry for him."

Even knowing Rosie's statement is a breakthrough for her, it makes me mad as hell.

"Don't ever let him know you pity him," I warn through clenched teeth.

A pregnant silence descends over us. I shouldn't have lashed out at her, but I can't help the anger that's swirling in my chest. The immense guilt smothering me is wrapped in barbed wire. It cuts deep as it suffocates me. I have to find a way to restore Rufio's powers, but I don't know where to begin.

Then a light bulb flashes above my head. The antique book I got from Gifted Academy's librarian. I never returned it to her. It's still in my dorm room. I'm not sure if it has the answer I'm looking for, but it's a start.

My phone rings loudly, making my heart lurch inside of my chest. It must be one of my boyfriends, and right now, I can't talk to them.

"Are you going to get that?" Rosie asks.

"Nope." I turn around and head to the bathroom. I've already packed everything from there, but I need to hide from Rosie's prying eyes.

When I'm halfway there, she says, "It's Andromeda."

I stop in my tracks, furrowing my eyebrows. *Why would she call me now? Did something happen?* I retrace my steps and grab my phone from Rosie's hand.

"Hello?"

"Hi, Daisy. It's Andy. Are you still in Hawk City?"

"Yeah, but not for long. We're heading to the airport as soon as everyone finishes packing. What's up?"

"I hate to do this to you, but I need your help."

I notice the tension in her voice, which raises all kinds of alerts in my head. "What happened? Are you okay?"

"I can't explain over the phone. Can you meet me in person?"

"Yeah. Are you in the dorm building?"

"No, I'm a block away from Paragon Academy. I'll text you the address. And please, don't tell your boyfriends. My problem is of the... sensitive variety. Definitely not something I want to share with a bunch of guys."

I wasn't planning on telling any of them, but Andromeda's remark sure as hell makes me curious. I wonder if her problem has anything to do with Stephan. I know Principal Fallon wants to return to Saturn's Bay as soon as possible, but she can wait a little longer. Andromeda has saved my ass countless times. I'm not going to turn my back on her now.

"Okay, don't worry. I'll be there in a few."

When I end the call, Rosie stares with a question in her gaze. "What happened now?"

"Andy needs my help with something. I'm going to meet up with her."

She stands. "Can I come? I don't want to be alone right now."

"Sure. But promise me you won't be rude to her."

A blush creeps up Rosie's cheeks while guilt shines in her eyes. "I know I've been acting like an ungrateful brat lately. I see now that I was wrong to put every Idol in one bucket of evil."

"Yeah, you were wrong," I reply, though not to be mean. I'm done sugarcoating things for her. "But I'm glad you can see that now. Better late than never, right?"

She lifts her gaze to mine. "Right. Well, if we want to sneak out without a security detail, we'd better get going. I'm sure one or all of your boyfriends will be here any minute."

Rosie isn't wrong. No sooner do we step foot in the hallway

than I sense Morpheus and Bryce getting near. They must be inside the elevator.

"We need to take the stairs," I say.

We break into a run. If I can sense them, they can probably sense me as well. *Crap*. That won't leave me much time to find out what Andromeda needs.

By the time Rosie and I reach the ground floor, her breathing is coming out in bursts.

"Shit. Why are we running?"

"I sensed Bryce and Morpheus nearby. They're probably on their way here."

"What are they? Bloodhounds?"

"Something like that. Come on. Let's go."

We race out of the gates of Paragon Academy, following the directions I typed into my phone. It leads to an intersection where there are more commercial buildings than residential homes. Restaurants and small convenience stores are still open and bursting with activity. The directions lead away from the busy pedestrian traffic into a narrow alleyway between buildings. Soon, the cacophony from the street behind us fades away.

Rosie steps closer to me, pulling on the sleeve of my jacket. "Are you sure you have the correct address?"

I check Andromeda's text again. "Yes."

"This doesn't seem right."

A sense of dread licks the back of my neck, giving me goose bumps. I'm getting a bad feeling about this too.

Something small crashes ahead of us, making my heart leap up to my throat. Tense now, I focus on my powers, letting them flow freely through me.

"Andy?" I call.

Someone steps from the shadows, and my heart expands in relief when the small streetlight shines over Andromeda's lavender hair.

"Hey, Daisy, thanks for co—" She stops abruptly as her gaze settles on Rosie. "Why is your sister here?"

"Uh, you said not to bring my boyfriends. I didn't think you would mind Rosie."

"I'm not here to be a brat. I swear," she says.

Andromeda drops her chin for a second. At the same time, her chains fall from her wrists and circle around her. "I really wish you had come alone."

She throws her arms forward, launching her deadly weapons in our direction. Rosie screams, and I'm too slow to block Andromeda's attack. Her chain wraps around me faster than I can blink, squeezing me like a boa constrictor. She yanks both Rosie and me forward, and trapped like that, we both fall on the dirty ground.

"What the hell! Why are you doing this, Andy? I thought you were my friend."

She glances in my general direction, her blind eyes cold and hard. "I'm sorry it has to be this way, Daisy, but I don't have a choice. I just wish you hadn't brought your sister with you."

I struggle against my constraints, but it's futile. *Shit.* There's only one option. I have to use my Unmaker gift against her. I don't know why it hasn't been triggered yet. I haven't learned to control it, after all.

I focus on the energy in her chains, using it as a guide to the source of Andromeda's power in her core. But when I try to pull it into me, I can't. *Damn it.* She's stronger than I am. No wonder my powers weren't triggered automatically.

"Andromeda!" a male voice yells from behind us. "Let them go at once."

"Walk away, Soren. This doesn't concern you."

A gust of wind flies by me, colliding with Andromeda a second later. Her chains slacken right before they release Rosie and me. Quickly, I jump back to my feet and reach for Rosie.

Andromeda is distracted now by Soren, so that's our chance to run away. But I can't leave him.

"Go, Rosie. Run back to the school and get the guys."

"What about you?"

"I have to help Soren."

Rosie races toward the end of the alley, and I whirl around, trying to find an opening. Soren is moving so fast that he's nothing but a blur. The same can be said of Andromeda's chains. They're like golden flashes of light.

If I can't take away her powers, I have to try to slow her down. I stretch my right arm, palm facing forward, and will Andromeda to stop moving. The air ripples in front of me, and a moment later, Andromeda's movements become sluggish. She glances at me in slow motion, her long hair whipping in front of her face.

Soren, who is unaffected by my slow-motion trick, takes the opportunity to shoot her in the neck with a tranquilizer. Seconds tick by. All I can hear is the sound of my heart racing. Finally, her eyes roll back in their sockets and she collapses, unconscious.

Breathing heavily, Soren spares a fleeting glance at Andromeda's crumpled form on the ground before he turns to me. "Are you all right?"

"Yes. I can't believe she attacked me." I walk over. "Do you think she was somehow forced or brainwashed to turn against me?"

Soren opens his mouth to reply, but his attention switches to a commotion behind me.

My boyfriends are here.

"Daisy, are you okay?" Bryce pulls me into his arms, crushing me against his chest.

"I'm fine."

"What happened to Andromeda?" Morpheus asks.

"She turned against me. I don't know why."

"I do," Soren replies. "She's a Neo God spy."

"What?" we all ask in unison.

The sound of tires screeching nearby draws our attention to the main street. A black SUV has parked at the mouth of the alley, blocking the way. Mr. Silverstone exits the vehicle, sporting a grim expression on his face. I expected to see Stephan with his father, but it seems the man came alone.

Rufio stops next to me but leaves enough space between us that it feels like a chasm. His eyes remain trained on Andromeda when he says, "If she's a Neo God spy, she's not working for my father."

At once, the Silverstones turn to him. "How do you know?" Soren asks through a frown.

"The man is too arrogant. He'd never, ever recruit an Idol with a disability, no matter how powerful they were. Which means she must be working for someone else."

"That's something we have yet to confirm," Mr. Silverstone replies. "Soren, would you take the girl to the car?"

"Where are you taking her?" I ask.

"Don't worry about Andromeda. She's our problem now."

Morpheus steps into Soren's path. "Hold on." He lifts her limp right arm and, through slits, inspects her hand.

"What are you doing?" Soren asks.

"I sensed something peculiar."

Mr. Silverstone steps closer. "What, son?"

"The mark of a demigod."

"You've got to be kidding me," Rufio blurts out, stepping away from us. My body angles to follow him, but I catch myself. I don't dare approach him, even if it's to offer comfort.

"So not the island god," Phoenix pipes up, wide-eyed.

"Island god?" Soren raises an eyebrow. "What are you talking about?"

"Don't mind Phoenix," Bryce replies, frowning at his friend.

Morpheus releases Andromeda's hand and then glances at

Mr. Silverstone. "I'd like to be present when you interrogate her."

He jerks his head back. "I don't think that wi—"

"I must insist." Morpheus's shadows make an appearance, circling only around his wrists. But no one with a pulse can miss the threatening aura that surrounds him now.

"If you're staying, shouldn't we all?" I ask.

"No. We have to get back to Saturn's Bay ASAP," Bryce replies.

Rufio has his back to us, and since he remains quiet, I don't know what his thoughts are on the matter.

"Bryce is right, Daisy." Morpheus looks at me. "You should return. I'll get back home as soon as I can."

He leans closer and then kisses me on the cheek. My face becomes hot in an instant, but I try my best to keep my reaction from showing.

I watch them go without saying another word. My heart is wound tight again. Andromeda's betrayal was a blow, but I suspect there's more to the story than meets the eye. I hope Morpheus is able to uncover the truth.

"Damn. I can't believe we didn't suspect anything," Phoenix mutters.

"Did you guys notice Stephan's absence?" Rufio finally speaks. "Don't you think that was odd?"

"Totally." Phoenix nods.

"Yes, it was strange. But discussing the matter in a dark alley is not going to help us." Bryce turns to me. "Come on, Daisy. Let's head back. I've had enough of Hawk City."

2

MORPHEUS

The atmosphere inside the car couldn't be tenser if it tried. I'm riding shotgun, and Soren is in the back seat with Andromeda. We've been on the road for about five minutes, and no one has said a word. I'm usually the quiet one, but I can't keep my mouth shut any longer.

"How long have you known she was a spy?" I ask.

Mr. Silverstone's grip on the steering wheel tightens, matching the hard clench of his jaw. "We should wait until we arrive at a secure location to talk about this."

"Are you afraid your own car is bugged?"

"I'm not taking any chances."

"Where's Stephan? I'm surprised he didn't come on this tag-and-bag mission."

"My son is not dealing well with the truth about the girl. He'll come around."

Of course. It was obvious there was something going on between Stephan and Andromeda. If they were involved romantically, Stephan would take the blow the hardest. But I'm only making assumptions, and that leads to nowhere. I need facts. But as much as I'd like to keep grilling Mr. Silverstone, I don't want to waste my breath. He'll only talk when he's ready.

It takes another twenty minutes to arrive at a house in the suburbs of Hawk City. Not exactly where I imagined the Knights' secure location would be. Mr. Silverstone parks the van in the garage, and only when the door is shut does Soren exit the vehicle with Andromeda in his arms. She's still out cold.

"What did you do to her?" I ask.

"Tranquilizer. The effect should wear off soon," Soren replies.

I follow them inside the house and quickly realize this is not a secret hideout. This is Mr. Silverstone's home.

"Uh, I thought we were taking her to a secure location," I say.

"This is it. Our headquarters in the city has been compromised," Mr. Silverstone replies.

"Compromised how?"

"We had a mole." Soren takes Andromeda to a large room I can only assume is his father's office. He lays her on the leather couch and then pulls up a chair in front of the desk.

"You're not going to detain her? She's a spy."

Mr. Silverstone walks around the desk and takes a seat as well, looking mighty casual about the whole deal. Something isn't right here.

"What the hell is going on?" I ask.

"Relax, kid, and take a seat." Mr. Silverstone points at the vacant chair next to Soren's.

"No. I won't fucking relax. Andromeda ambushed Daisy in a dark alley. I need answers."

I sense the darkness uncoiling in the pit of my stomach, churning as it gains strength. I have better control of my powers now, but it's still linked to my emotions.

Calmly, Mr. Silverstone links his hands together, leaning

forward as he rests his forearms on the desk. "Fine. It was all a ruse."

"What do you mean? Is she a spy for the Neo Gods or not?"

I glance briefly at Soren, who is staring at a random spot on the desk. His expression is somber, closed off. The fact that he's not tossing out cocky remarks as he usually does is troublesome.

"A few months ago, Andromeda came to me. She was recruited by the Neo Gods when she was fairly young, duped into propaganda that's far from the truth. Like many other Neo God members, she regretted her decision immensely, but once you take the pledge, it's almost impossible to get out."

Finally, I begin to get a clearer picture. "She's working as a double agent, isn't she?"

"Well, yes, but the information she's been giving to the Neo Gods is mostly harmless to us. However, we know now that there's dissent among their ranks, and that's something that can greatly benefit us."

"Rufio was right. She isn't working for his father."

"No. But it seems the son of a bitch who has her on a leash is far worse than that Kent asshole," Soren spits out.

"You said you felt something in the alley," Mr. Silverstone continues. "You believe Andromeda was marked by a demigod?"

I swivel on my chair to glance at her. My gaze drops to her hand, but what I'm searching for can't be seen by the naked eye. The demigod signature is there, underneath her skin, almost dormant. Normally, I shouldn't be able to sense it, like I couldn't sense the mark Phoenix's disgrace of a father used to control him. *Why can I sense Andromeda's when it's not even active?*

She stirs in her sleep, and her eyelids begin to tremble. Her eyebrows furrow, but she doesn't wake up. Instead, she begins to move restlessly on the couch, turning her head from side to side as if she's having a nightmare.

"What's happening to her?" I ask.

Mr. Silverstone stands and walks over to the couch. "I don't know."

Andromeda reaches for her right hand, letting out a screech of pain. The mark of the demigod flares up in an instant, becoming a hot beacon of energy to me. It's probably still invisible to everyone else though. Her noises become louder and laced with agony. Mr. Silverstone drops next to her and tries to wake her by shaking her gently.

Soren jumps from the chair, body tense as he watches the scene unfold. A cloak of uneasiness has wrapped around him. I can sense it without even looking in his direction. I'm not sure why I can tune into the emotions in the room like that. It's never been one of my abilities. But I push those details to the background. The longer I watch Andromeda struggle, the surer I am that I know the identity of the demigod who marked her. His signature feels familiar somehow.

"Move aside," I say as I walk over to the couch.

Mr. Silverstone glances at me with eyes that are rounder than before. His surprise is obvious, but at least he doesn't offer resistance and moves away from the girl.

I take his spot, crouching as well, and then grab Andromeda's hand. I'm not surprised that her skin is burning up. My guess is that's exactly what she must be feeling right now—like her hand is on fire. I close my eyes, blocking out all external sounds so I can focus on the energy emanating from her mark.

I sense the will of the mark's creator, strong and malicious. I try to block it, stop the pain it's inflicting on Andromeda, but the harder I try, the further I'm sucked into the dark chasm of the mark's power. I can't let it trap me in that void. I unleash my shadows, letting them envelop my body in a protective barrier. I sense the antagonizing energy diminish, but before it vanishes completely, I hear the sound of wicked laughter in my head. It makes my skin crawl. I'm still holding Andromeda's hand when the laughter ceases, but a voice speaks in my mind.

"Hello, brother."

My eyes fly open, and I let go of Andromeda's hand. Immediately, bile pools in my mouth while my stomach clenches painfully. I drop onto my ass, breathing hard as I try to grapple with what just happened.

"Are you okay, dude?" Soren asks.

I don't answer right away, and while I attempt to recover my voice, Andromeda opens her eyes and glances at me. Her eyes are unseeing, and yet I can still feel the weight of her stare.

"You stopped him," she whispers.

"I'm not sure what I did."

"Stopped who?" Soren looks from me to her.

"The Neo God who controls me." She sits up.

I get back on my feet, still jittery from the battle I waged in the nether. "Did you know who he was when you pledged your life to him?"

"Do you mean did I know he was a Neo God?"

"No. Did you know he was a demigod?"

The blood drains from Andromeda's face, turning her complexion even paler than before. "Nathaniel is a demigod?"

"If that's his name, then yes, he's a demigod."

Her shoulders sag forward. "Now everything makes sense. No wonder he wasn't worried about Daisy using her Unmaker powers against him."

"Why would a demigod pose as an Idol and join the Neo Gods?" Soren asks. "It makes no sense."

I pass a hand over my face. "I don't know. But not all demigods are created equal. Some have limitations."

I acquired this knowledge once I learned about my lineage. The thought is bitter, but my lingering feelings of low self-esteem are not important right now. What the demigod said is. He called me "brother," and I don't know what to make of that statement. He can't be a lost sibling, which only leads to one conclusion: he was messing with my head. But to what purpose?

Andromeda throws her legs to the side of the couch but remains seated. She massages her right hand while keeping her chin dipped low.

"He wants Daisy," she says.

Fear and anger mingle, forming a cold dagger that pierces my chest. All Neo Gods are gunning for her now that they know she's the Unmaker. But adding a demigod to the list of people who want to harm Daisy only makes everything worse. Maybe Nathaniel is working for the island god. *Fuck!*

"He's not touching a single hair of hers," I grit out.

"He doesn't want to kill her. He's collecting powerful Idols."

"What for?" Soren asks.

"I don't know. He never told me."

An idea springs into my head. But first I need to know what the Knights want to do about Andromeda's boss. "What was your plan?"

"The only people who know Andromeda is a Neo God are those in this room and Stephan. I haven't disclosed her double agent status to the rest of the Knights, and I intend to keep it that way."

It's a smart move. The fewer people who know about it, the less likely it is her cover will be blown.

"He doesn't know Andromeda was captured, right?" I ask.

"I don't believe so," Mr. Silverstone replies, glancing in Andromeda's direction.

"He doesn't know. It's why he was punishing me. He does that when he thinks I'm blowing him off."

"But he knows now that I helped you," I say. "So you're going to bring me to him."

She lifts her chin, piercing me with such an intense stare

that it almost feels like she has X-ray vision. "And you think he's going to welcome you with open arms without retaliation?"

"He won't retaliate."

"What makes you so sure?" Soren asks.

"She said he collects powerful Idols, right? You're looking at one."

Soren snorts. "Cocky much?"

Andromeda tilts her head to the side, narrowing her gaze. "You're not an Idol."

Soren whips his face to hers. "Come again?"

She ignores him and keeps staring at me. "You've been masking your powers all this time. You're a demigod."

3
_____

DAISY

My mind is still whirling as I board the small private jet. Andromeda being a spy makes no sense to me. She saved me countless times; she even killed a Neo God, for crying out loud. And there's no way that encounter in the alleyway was planned. Something isn't right, but unfortunately, staying in Hawk City for another day to find out the truth wasn't an option. Principal Fallon was eager to return to Saturn's Bay as quickly as possible. I hope Morpheus can get to the bottom of it.

The tension inside the plane is so thick, it's smothering. I'm sitting next to Bryce, and Phoenix is across from me, but neither speaks much. Principal Fallon is in the seat across the aisle, presumably sleeping. I honestly doubt it. I wouldn't put it past the woman to pretend to be asleep so she could eavesdrop on our conversation. Too bad she's out of luck and no one is talking.

Rosie and Toby are sitting behind me, and Rufio took the farthest seat from us as possible. He's in avoidance mode, but as painful as it is, I'm glad. I still can't look him in the eye. There's no amount of excuses or pleas for forgiveness that can make things better.

I thought we would strategize during the flight, but perhaps Principal Fallon doesn't think it's safe to talk about the Knights and the Neo Gods in public. The Knights are still considered criminals. Terrorists, even.

My chest becomes tighter when I finally have the time to think about the implications of the events of Hawk City. The guys and I were probably caught on camera fighting that gang of Fringes. Does that mean we're wanted by the authorities now? One of the Neo Gods was Hawk City's chief of police. All Bryce's father has to do is make a call and we're doomed.

I gasp out loud, earning Bryce's, Phoenix's, and Rufio's attention. My gaze locks with his for a fleeting moment, but Bryce's hand on my arm draws my eyes away from Rufio's cold stare.

"What is it, Daisy?"

"What do you think is going to happen now? Is your father going to send the police after us?"

Bryce rubs his jaw. "I don't know what he'll do. I think we should lie low for a while and wait for him to make the first move."

"No. We're not hiding," Principal Fallon chimes in.

I knew she wasn't asleep.

"What do you propose we do? Return to Gifted Academy as if everything were normal?" Rufio asks angrily.

"Yes. That's precisely what we should do right now. Going into hiding will set us back months. Staying visible will force your father to show his hand sooner."

"You mean use Daisy as bait," Phoenix retorts angrily.

"I'm not afraid of him," I say.

Bryce squeezes my hand. "We know you aren't, but he already managed to capture you once. We can't be too careful."

"He's not going to catch me unguarded again."

Rufio stands suddenly and pierces me with his intense blue eyes. "As long as you have weaklings attached to you, you'll always be in danger."

"What's that supposed to mean?" I frown, not liking his insinuation.

"He's talking about me," Rosie pipes up. "If Toby and I hadn't been captured, then you wouldn't have been put in that situation."

"That's bullshit, Rosie!" I yell, frustrated.

Rosie stands from her seat as well and walks to mine. "It's not bullshit, and you know it."

"And now you have another weak link. Me," Rufio deadpans.

Twist the dagger in my chest harder, why don't you?

"Bryce could always try to turn Rosie into an Idol." Phoenix shrugs.

Rosie's green eyes widen. "Over my dead body."

"I guess someone still hates us." He chuckles.

She crosses her arms and pouts. "I don't hate all Idols anymore, but that doesn't mean I want to become one."

The airplane hits a pocket of turbulence, which forces everyone to return to their seats. But the atmosphere around us is still permeated with the heaviness of spoken *and* unspoken words. I don't know what to make of Rufio's statement. Was he trying to break up with me? My eyes burn just thinking about it. I love him with all my heart. I can't bear to think that he'd want to leave me, but at the same time, I wouldn't blame him if he did. I took away his powers, after all.

The plane shakes again, more violently than before. My heart leaps up to my throat as my pulse quickens. I clutch the armrests in a vise hold and try not to let the panic set in. But when the plane drops suddenly, Rosie and I scream.

"It's okay, Daisy. It's just a patch of bad weather," Phoenix tries to reassure me with a smile.

It would have worked if there weren't another drop, followed by more shaking.

"What the hell is going on?" Principal Fallon pulls up the window shade just in time for us to see lightning strike the sky, revealing a cluster of angry clouds quickly approaching our small plane.

"Oh my God," Rosie whimpers behind me.

The pilot says something over the speakers, but I barely make out his words over the loud pounding in my ears. We're all looking out the windows now, and with each new strike of lightning, the plane seems to shake harder.

"The sky was supposed to be clear all the way to Saturn's Bay. This isn't a normal storm," Principal Fallon mutters.

"It's not. It's the island god," Bryce declares.

A loud boom outside draws another scream from me. I hear Rosie whimper, and then Toby tries to calm her down. I wish I could tell her everything will be okay, but I'm gripped by terror too. This is my second time flying, but I've seen plenty of plane-crash movies. If this small jet gets hit by a lightning bolt, it's game over for us. There's no amount of Idol power that can save us.

The nose of the plane dips suddenly at perilous angle. The pilot shouts something over the speakers. Maybe he's telling us we're going down. I don't know because I'm screaming.

"Daisy! Daisy!" Bryce shakes me, turning me around. "I need you to calm down."

"I can't," I sob through my tears.

"Leave her alone, Bryce. Can't you see she's in distress?" Rufio yells from his seat.

"I can't have her lose her mind now. We all need to work together if we want to keep this plane from crashing."

"Bryce is right," Principal Fallon chimes in. "I'll focus on the wind, but I need Daisy to slow down our descent. Can you do that?"

"I-I don't know."

Phoenix leans forward and grabs my hands. "You can do it, babe. I have faith in you."

His eyes are shining with intensity. It's not until I feel the panic release its grip in my heart that I realize Phoenix used his gift to help me. I'm calmer, but not calm. However, now I can concentrate on my power and attempt to make time move slower around the plane. The loud whizzing noise begins to fade, and the sense that we're plunging to our deaths lessens.

My erratic breathing returns to normal, but too soon. The noise of the propellers stops, and the lights in the cabin flicker until they go out completely.

"What happened now?" Rosie shrieks.

"Son of a bitch. He cut the plane's power off," Rufio grumbles in the darkness.

"That's your department, Bryce," Phoenix says.

"I'm on it."

I avoid looking at him, afraid if I do, I'll lose focus and the plane will start to drop like a bomb again. But I feel Bryce's powers blaze next to me, and then I can see it when his body flares up like a supernova. A moment later, the engine restarts and the lights return.

No one speaks for the longest time. I don't dare to pull my powers in, but I know if I keep the plane moving at snail pace, we'll never make it back to Saturn's Bay before we run out of fuel.

"Is he gone?" I ask.

"I don't sense his presence anymore," Bryce grits out.

I let go of my powers then, sinking into my seat and closing my eyes. I've never sustained the slow-motion trick for this long before, and now I feel drained.

It's another minute or so before someone nudges my arm. I blink my eyes open lazily, coming face-to-face with Rufio, who is leaning over me. I sit up straighter in an instant.

"Are you okay?" he asks.

"Yeah."

"You weren't moving." He takes a step back.

"I think I pushed myself to the limit."

He doesn't reply, and his expression doesn't change from the cold mask he's wearing. I can't begin to understand what's going on inside his head.

"I'm going to check on the pilot." Principal Fallon heads for the cockpit.

Rufio returns to his seat, leaving me filled with doubt.

"Don't mind my brother," Bryce whispers in my ear. "He's never dealt with change well. He'll come around."

Bryce is trying to make me feel better, but all he did was make me angrier at myself. I have to bite the inside of my cheek to avoid snapping at him. I can't take my frustrations out on him. It's not fair.

Principal Fallon returns, sporting a frown that can only mean she's the bearer of bad news.

"What now?" Bryce asks.

"Barring any more natural disasters, we should make it back to Saturn's Bay in one piece."

"That's good news," Phoenix says. "Why the sour puss expression, then?"

Principal Fallon narrows her eyes to slits. "Now that the worst has passed, I'd like to know who the island god is and why he tried to take our plane down."

4

———

DAISY

When we finally land at the private airport in Saturn's Bay, my mind feels bruised and sore, as if my brain had been in a fighting ring the whole night. It wasn't only the ordeal of trying to keep the plane from crashing that made me feel so wretched, it was the exhaustion of witnessing Principal Fallon pressure and coerce her sons and Phoenix into talking about the island god. But no matter what tricks she used, they wouldn't tell her a thing.

She exits the plane first, practically breathing fire from her nose. I stay back, choosing to deboard the plane last. But before I even get down the steps, I hear more shouting and arguing. *For fuck's sake. What now?*

I hurry out and see the source of the woman's displeasure is my uncle Xavier. He was in Hawk City with us but chose not to catch the same flight as we did. So wrapped up in my problems, I didn't stop to consider his reasoning for not wanting to fly with us. I'm sure I'll find out now.

Principal Fallon stops talking when Xavier's attention lands on me.

"How did you get here before we did?" Rosie is the one who asks.

"I left a couple of hours earlier. I had arrangements to make."

"It was all for nothing, Xavier. Daisy is coming back to Gifted Academy with me."

"What is this all about?" Rufio asks.

"Daisy and Rosie aren't safe at Gifted Academy. They never were, much less now that Daisy's identity as the Unmaker is unveiled. I'm taking them to a secret location," Xavier replies.

"That's absurd." Principal Fallon scoffs. "We can't let the Neo Gods force us into hiding. I discussed this topic on the way here with the boys and Daisy. We all agreed that the best we can do now is act like nothing is amiss."

"No. We didn't all agree." Rufio takes a step forward. "I think Daisy and Rosie should go with Mr. X."

"What about Toby?" Rosie asks, clutching her boyfriend's arm tight.

"I'll be okay, sweetheart." He smiles at her.

"I'm all for keeping the girls safe," Phoenix pipes up.

"This wasn't what we agreed on, Xavier," Principal Fallon grits out. "I need access to Daisy at all times. We're at war!"

"Sorry, Jodie. That's out of the question. Daisy will be there to assist the Knights when it's needed, but she won't be at your beck and call."

"Do I have a say on the matter, or are you going to make all the decisions for me?" I butt in, sick and tired of everyone discussing me like I'm a prop, an object.

"Of course you have a say, darling," Xavier replies in a much softer tone.

I glance at Rosie, so small and frightened. And then I seek Phoenix's, Bryce's, and, last but not least, Rufio's gazes. This doesn't feel like I'm making a decision about my safety. It feels like they're making me choose between my family and the men I love.

"This place you're taking us, is there room for the guys too?"

Xavier's eyes reveal surprise before he's back into business mode, cold and calculating. "Yes. They can come too."

"No! I won't allow it. Bryce and Rufio are coming with me," Principal Fallon snaps, displaying a loss of control for the first time ever.

"Mother, you can't force us to do anything," Bryce replies calmly. "But I'll return to Gifted Academy with you."

My heart sinks. I can't believe Bryce is choosing to go back with his mother. He looks at me, an apology filling his eyes. Then he moves on to glance at Rufio. "You should go with Mr. X, brother. It's not safe for you at school anymore."

When I thought Bryce couldn't hurt me anymore with his words, he sucker punches me in the stomach. And worse, I have to take in the pain without making a peep. First of all, he's not doing it on purpose, and second, he's right about Rufio. Powerless, he'll be easy prey to the other kids. I'm sure he made quite a few enemies while he was at the top of the food chain. I can't believe his mother isn't even considering that. She's a hateful bitch.

My decision is clear.

"I'm not returning to Gifted Academy. And I want Rufio, Toby, Phoenix, and Morpheus to come with us."

Phoenix walks over and casually throws his arm around my shoulder. "Babe, I'll go wherever you go. I never liked school anyway."

At once, my powers flare up, and I begin to pull his powers into me. *Damn it!* I can't keep letting this foreign magic run amok. I step away from his embrace before it's too late.

"You're coming with us, right, Toby?" Rosie looks up, eyes full of hope.

He tenses on the spot, and his face twists into a guilty

expression. "Eh, as much as I would like to come, I have to return to school. The upcoming war hasn't distracted me from my goal. I want to become a doctor, and for that, I need a proper education."

"At least someone is thinking," Principal Fallon mutters, much more composed now.

Rosie's crestfallen expression makes my heart ache for her. But she recovers quickly and puts on a brave face. "I understand, Toby."

I glance at Rufio, hoping to catch his eyes again. I'm upset that Bryce feels the need to return to Gifted Academy, but he can take care of himself. If Rufio doesn't come with me, I'm going to spend my living hours consumed with worry that something terrible will happen to him. I don't trust his mother one bit.

"Rufio, are you coming with me or not?" Principal Fallon asks.

He raises his chin, staring defiantly at her. "Not."

Her eyes seem to sparkle with rage, but the moment passes, and then she just stares at him with dispassionate boredom. "Very well. I guess it's only Bryce and me, then." She whirls around and heads for her car that's parked in the hangar.

Bryce walks over and stops in front of me. He captures my face between his hands and leans down. "Please don't be mad at me, my love. I know what I'm doing."

"I wish we didn't have to be apart. So much is changing, and fast. The world is more dangerous than it was before." My eyes fill with tears, and I don't try to hide them.

"I know. But we can't let my mother loose like that. Someone has to stay close to monitor her movements." Bryce moves closer to my ear. "She can't be trusted."

My blood runs cold. It's one thing for me to suspect Principal Fallon has a hidden agenda, but for Bryce to feel the need to spy on her? That rings all kinds of alarm bells in my head. "If she's not to be trusted, then why did Mr. Silverstone partner up with her?"

"That, you'll have to ask him. I don't know."

He leans closer and kisses me tenderly at first. But I throw my arms around his neck, rising on my tiptoes to deepen the kiss. I don't know when I'll see Bryce again, so I need to get my fill of him, of his love, to hold me over. My cheeks are wet when we break apart.

He wipes my tears with his thumbs and whispers against my lips. "I love you."

"I love you too," I reply in a choked voice.

He steps back and then glances in Phoenix's direction. "Don't let anything happen to her."

"You know I won't."

On the way to his mother's car, Bryce stops next to Rufio and whispers something in his ear. I can't hear the words, but Rufio nods in response.

While I was saying goodbye to Bryce, I missed Toby's departure. He's already by Principal Fallon's car. Rosie is a sobbing mess, hiccupping. I make a motion to go to her, but Rufio beats me to it. He squeezes her shoulder and says, "He'll be fine. He's an Idol now."

Rosie nods and then wipes her runny nose with the sleeve of her jacket. The moment is surreal, which explains my dropped jaw.

"Come on, people. We've lingered here long enough," Xavier calls our attention.

With sluggish steps and morose temperaments, we board his SUV. Rufio asks to ride shotgun, which feels like another jab against me. Rosie ends up sandwiched between Phoenix and me since I can't be near him without sucking his powers. As soon as Morpheus returns from Hawk City, I'm resuming my training. This succubus deal can't go on for much longer.

"Where exactly are we going?" I ask Xavier.

"You'll see when we get there."

"You're not going to make us wear blindfolds, are you?" Rufio asks.

"No. Why would I do that?"

"My father made us wear blindfolds when he took us to his Neo Gods' lair."

"We've established that your father is a major asshole. Please don't put me in the same league as him."

"I think we all got the short stick when it came to parents," Phoenix mutters, reminding me that he may pretend everything is fine, but one can't simply erase years of trauma and torture in a few weeks.

I wish I could grab his hand, offer some kind of comfort. But all I can do for now is keep my distance and pray I don't end up unmaking him too.

5

MORPHEUS

I laugh without humor. "You must still be under the effects of the tranquilizer. I'm not a demigod, my father was."

Andromeda twists her face into a scowl. "I know you're not lying. But you're wrong."

Soren and his father are both gawking at me with renewed interest, which only serves to grate on my nerves.

"Quit staring! I'm not a demigod. Don't you think I'd know if I were one?"

"It depends. Like you said in that alleyway, not all demigods are created equal. It seems you were talking from experience," Mr. Silverstone replies.

"I wasn't." I pull my hair back, yanking at the strands. "The gods left this world many centuries ago. There's no chance one came back to sleep with my mother."

"Are you sure your mother is your mother?" Soren asks.

Without a second thought, I raise my arm, sending a dose of terror his way. He clutches his chest while his eyes bug out. Darkness swirls in my core, growing exponentially with my anger. I'm not sure how long I'd keep torturing the guy if it weren't for Andromeda's chain wrapping around my wrist and yanking back.

Soren lets out a gasp, leaning his hands on his knees. "What the fuck!"

"Don't ever talk about my mother," I grit out.

"He didn't mean it as an insult, dumbass." Andromeda removes her chains from around my arms but doesn't stand from the couch.

"How do you know what he meant or not?" I spit back.

"It was an honest question," Soren pipes up. "Maybe your parents adopted you."

As quick as it came, my anger deflates. I rub my face, glancing at a random point on the far wall. "I'm not adopted. I look like my mother. And I heard my parents arguing about my conception. My mother wanted an Idol child so badly that she cheated on my father. I've always assumed she was able to summon a demigod to sleep with her, but maybe I was wrong." I shake my head. "No. That's not possible. If I were a demigod, I wouldn't have spent most of my life at the mercy of my powers."

"What do you mean, son?" Mr. Silverstone asks.

"The shadows. They used to take over my body. They've almost managed to kill me a few times. My mother had to procure a special bracelet set to keep them contained."

Mr. Silverstone's gaze narrows. "Hmm. It's possible that those bracelets did more harm than good. By suppressing your demigod powers when they manifested, your Fringe lineage became stronger."

"How did you finally learn to control them?" Andromeda asks.

"Daisy destroyed my bracelets by accident. Then I had to learn or die."

The conversation ceases for a moment. There's been a lot of new information to process. I'm reeling from the possibility that I might be a demigod. If it's true, then I could maybe defeat the island god and free us all from the stupid promise we made him.

Andromeda hisses, breaking the silence. She's clutching her right hand, bending forward. "Fuck. He's back again."

"What can we do?" Mr. Silverstone takes a step forward, watching her as if he truly cares about her well-being.

"Nothing. That son of a bitch wants to talk to me. Most likely to ask why I failed to bring Daisy to him tonight like I had promised."

"Where's your phone?" I ask.

"Here." Mr. Silverstone hands me the device. "We kept it to support our former plan, which was to keep Andromeda prisoner to buy us more time."

"That doesn't help her with the torture," I retort.

"I know. We were working on a way to remove that mark from her."

"Bryce and Rufio had a block in their heads, which was also the work of the Neo Gods. Only Daisy was able to remove it from Bryce."

"I don't think Daisy can help me," Andromeda grits out. "If Nathaniel is a demigod, then surely his mark is beyond the skills of the Unmaker."

Her phone rings with an ominous sound that makes me question the girl's taste.

"That's him," she says.

"What are we going to do now?" Soren looks at his father.

"We can't let him keep punishing her." I give her the phone. "Answer him."

She presses the screen, silencing the abhorrent noise. "What do you want now?" she asks her jailer.

"Don't you 'what' me," an angry voice retorts loud enough that we can all hear it. "You were supposed to bring me the Unmaker. That should have been an easy task for you."

"Daisy didn't come alone. I had to fight all her boyfriends at once. I almost didn't escape."

"Somehow, I have a hard time believing you. But you met someone else tonight, didn't you?"

"Yes." She turns in my direction. "He tried to help me."

"The Unmaker must be on her way back to Saturn's Bay already. We'll get her later. I want you to bring me your new friend."

The small hairs on the back of my neck stand on end. Anticipation gives me a stomachache. This person, no matter how awful he is, might have answers about my heritage that I can't ignore. I sense the Silverstones change their demeanor as well. They're anxious for this encounter too, but for different reasons.

"I think I can arrange that. Where should I meet you?"

"I'm having a small get-together at my house tonight. Bring him as your guest."

Andromeda twists her expression into a glower. "Are you kidding me? You're throwing a party?"

"Well, I thought you would be bringing me a great prize, so I wanted to celebrate. I can't kick everyone out now. What would your parents say?"

Andromeda's face seems to drain of blood. Her eyebrows furrow in a stern line. "Fine. I'll be there in half an hour."

"Oh, and dress accordingly, darling. You don't want to stick out more than you already do."

The call goes silent, but Andromeda seems frozen in time.

"Why was Nathaniel talking about your parents?" I cross my arms.

She finally wakes from her stupor and sighs. "He's a sneaky weasel. He tricked my father into becoming his business partner. It wasn't enough that he got me to pledge myself to his disgusting cause and put a torture device on me. He also had to bring my folks into the picture. You know, for extra leverage."

"What are we supposed to do now? Let Andromeda go, just like that?" Soren turns to his father.

Mr. Silverstone rubs his chin, staring hard in her direction. "That wasn't the plan, but letting Andromeda return to the Neo Gods' fold will work to our benefit. We need more information."

"What about him?" He points at me.

"What now?" I frown.

"The Neo Gods know about your involvement with the Knights. You can't simply waltz into their domain as if you weren't the enemy."

"Don't worry about me. If Andromeda is right and I'm a demigod, I can handle whatever those motherfuckers throw at me."

"I'll keep Morpheus safe," Andromeda declares, amusing me to no end. I chuckle and immediately pick up on her irritation. "What's so funny? You don't think I can protect you?"

I raise my hands, palm up. "I believe you. I didn't mean to offend."

"Whatever. Let's get going. Nathaniel is not a patient man. If I don't arrive at his stupid party when I said I would, he's going to make my hand burn again."

"Fine. I can't linger in Hawk City for much longer anyway. I have to get back to Daisy."

Andromeda bites her lower lip. "On a scale of one to ten, how pissed off do you think she is at me right now?"

"I don't think she's angry at you. Probably shocked. But once she learns the truth, it'll be fine."

"No. Under no circumstances are you to tell anyone else about Andromeda," Mr. Silverstone pipes up.

I give him a droll stare. "No offense, sir, but I'm not lying to my girlfriend or my friends."

He opens his mouth to no doubt argue with me, but

Andromeda butts in. "I'm with Morpheus. Daisy is an ally. She needs to know I didn't betray her."

Mr. Silverstone stares at the ceiling and lets out a heavy sigh. "This is what I get for dealing with a bunch of teenagers."

I fight the urge to roll my eyes, but Soren doesn't. Our gazes meet, and some kind of understanding exchanges between us. I still think he's an ass, but maybe we can find a way to work together in peace.

I glance at my casual clothes. "I'm not changing to attend a Neo Gods party."

Andromeda snorts. "And you thought I was going to?"

6

RUFIO

Hollow. That's how I feel. I never understood what my powers meant until I was stripped of them. They were an intrinsic part of me, and now I'm not even sure who I am anymore. My identity was linked to my abilities, and now that they're gone, I'm nothing. Vapor.

I've been avoiding Daisy. I don't want her to see that I'm an empty shell, not the man she fell in love with. The old Rufio would hate her for what she did, vow revenge, but there's not a smidge of animosity in my heart toward her. The ugly feeling is reserved for the real villain in this story: my father and the other sycophants.

It would have been easier if I had gone with my mother, but I can't bear to stay away from Daisy. Honestly, I don't know how Bryce was able to make that decision. He has his reasons, and I can't begrudge him for what was no doubt perceived by Daisy as a traitorous move.

The place Mr. X brought us to is a beach house near Echo Cove. I questioned his choice. The house is the furthest thing from what a secret hideout should be like. It's right smack in the middle of one of the busiest destinations in Saturn's Bay. Hiding in plain sight is Mr. X's strategy.

Nonetheless, it's a comfortable house with plenty of rooms. I don't even have to bunk with Phoenix, something I was totally expecting. As soon as we arrived, Mr. X offered us food, but I refused and retired immediately to my new quarters. I wasn't hungry despite not having eaten anything in hours.

It's already morning, but since no one was able to shut their eyes on the flight here, the first order of business was to catch some z's. If only I could shut my eyes and relax. The queen-sized bed looks inviting enough, with its fluffy pillows and soft sheets, but I'm too restless to fall asleep.

I wait until I don't hear a sound in the hallway and slip out. If I can't sleep, then I might as well do a little exploration. The beach house is spacious and light. Big glass windows give anyone in the house an unobstructed view of the ocean. It was the first issue I pointed out to Mr. X. Any onlooker from the beach would be able to see us as well. I forgot that Mr. X wasn't born yesterday though. Those windows are mirrored from the outside.

I walk closer to them, losing track of time by just watching the waves crash against the turf and then slowly recede back. It wasn't that long ago that Daisy almost drowned in those waters. I was able to save her then, but if anything were to happen to her now, I'd be useless. A boulder sits on my chest, caving it in. I meant what I said to her. I'm another deadweight attached to her ankles, dragging her down. She won't let go of her sister, under-standably so, but she should cut me loose. She doesn't need me.

I flatten my palms against the glass, leaning forward until my forehead meets the smooth surface. "Fuck. What am I going to do?"

"Rufio?"

Warmth spreads through my chest, easing the heaviness.

Daisy's voice is like a caress against my bruised heart. I almost think she's just a figment of my imagination. I didn't sense her approach, after all. But when she stops next to me, understanding dawns on me. I've lost my sensitivity to auras along with my powers. An elephant would have been able to sneak up on me and I wouldn't see until it was right in front of my face.

"You couldn't sleep either, huh?" she continues.

Wordless, I push myself off the window and turn around, ready to leave. But she grabs my arm, halting me. "Don't go. Please."

"What do you want from me, Daisy?" I ask without making eye contact.

"I want you to look at me, for starters."

With a heavy exhale, I do as she asks. And like a sandcastle, my heart crumbles into a pile of dust. Her beautiful hazel eyes are filled with regret and guilt, which only makes me feel worse.

"Stop that," I say.

"Stop what?" She releases my arm.

"Stop feeling guilty for what you did. It wasn't your fault." She takes a step back, but I can still see her lips quiver. "Damn it, Daisy. Don't you dare cry on me."

"Quit telling me what to do or how I should be feeling!" With a jerky swipe of her arm, she dries off a rogue tear that escaped her eye.

I turn away, pulling my hair back hard until it hurts. I welcome the pain. "I can't deal with your torment on top of everything."

"Please don't shut me out, Rufio. I'm hurting too, and there's nothing you can do about it." She steps closer and places her hand on the middle of my back. "I'll find a way to restore your powers, even if it's the last thing I do."

I pivot on the spot, reaching for her arms. "I won't allow you to risk your life for me, Daisy. You've done enough."

She winces at my words, and I don't understand the reason. What I'm asking her is not that farfetched.

"I know I've done plenty. I unmade you."

Fuck. That's what she thinks I meant?

I cup her cheeks between my hands. "No. That's not it. You've helped us plenty. You've risked your life to save us even though none of us deserve it."

"Shut up. Don't say that. And I already told you that you can't order me around. If I want to risk my life to save yours, I will."

"Why are you so stubborn?" I press my forehead against hers, breathing in her sweet perfume.

The heady scent goes straight to my head, making me dizzy, but not because she's stealing my powers. There's nothing left for her to take. I'm unsteady for different reasons. My craving for her has not diminished. If anything, it's grown exponentially, and now there's nothing deterring me from claiming her. I bring my lips to hers, prying them open hungrily. It's been too long since I could kiss the girl I love like this, and I plan to savor every second of it.

Daisy curls her fingers into my shirt, bringing me closer to her. Her tongue mingles with mine with the same urgency. I run my fingers through her hair, grabbing a fistful of the strands and tilting her head to the side so I can devour her mouth thoroughly.

She releases my shirt to circle my waist with her arms. An enticing moan escapes her lips, spurring me on. My entire body is on fire, even my bones. My cock is pressing hard against my jeans, and I've been without sex for so long that any little friction could be my undoing.

No. I can't lose control of my body like that. The only way my cock is going to explode is inside Daisy's sweet pussy.

I pick her up and with urgent steps and veer for the nearest couch. I'm too lost in my lust to make it to my bedroom. Everyone is asleep anyway. We're all alone. Daisy sits on the couch and, without letting go of me, pulls me on top of her. I fit snuggly between her legs, but my jeans are in the way.

"Hold on." I jump back to my feet, then remove the pesky barrier as fast as I can—which, considering I no longer have enhanced Idol speed, isn't fast enough. I push the bitterness aside. I can't let it sour this moment.

Daisy is wearing soft flannel pj's that provide easy access for my greedy fingers. I drop on my knees and then tug on the elastic waistband with my teeth. She threads her fingers through my hair, arching her back.

"Rufio, please don't torture me like that."

"I'm not trying to be mean. I just want to taste you first. It's been so long."

I pull her pants down, but not all the way, only enough to reveal her simple cotton panties. I kiss her pussy over the fabric, then lick her down the middle, drawing a whimper from her. *Fuck.* I'm not going to last long like this. My balls are already tight, ready for release.

Just one taste.

I pull the fabric aside and immediately place a kiss right above her clit. Her hips buckle, but I keep Daisy in place so I can have a better sample. I lick her bundle of nerves with a long and slow swipe of my tongue. She makes a disgruntled sound in the back of her throat, then slings her arm across her face.

Shit. She's close. I can feel the tension in her legs; I can sense the small tremors that are already running through her body. I keep on pleasuring her even at the risk that I might pull a kick-draw move. If it happens, I'm sure I'll recover fast.

"Rufio, oh my God. I'm going to come."

Yes you are, babe.

I suck her clit into my mouth, lapping at her sensitive nub, which is exactly the nudge she needs to break apart under my tongue. Her cries are muffled by the pillow she placed over her head.

Damn it. I wanted to see her face all flushed from pleasure.

When her body becomes lax on the couch, I crawl back up until my face is level with hers. I yank away the pillow that's hiding her postcoital beauty and gaze down with a lazy smile on my lips. She stares back with hooded eyes, and then her mouth splits into a satisfied grin. Her cheeks are still a pretty pink color.

"Hi," I drawl.

"You said you just wanted a quick taste."

"True. But you know me, I'm such a glutton for you."

With a rotation of my hips, I nudge her entrance with the tip of my erection. Daisy opens her legs wider and brings her knees up. I try to go slowly to prolong the sensation, but she's too slick. Besides, it seems my dick is in command now. A tremor ripples down my back when I'm completely inside of her. I close my eyes for a brief moment, fighting the wave of pleasure that's threatening to sweep me under too soon.

Daisy captures my face between her soft hands and brings me down for a long, delicious kiss. Fuck restraint. I'm not going to last long if I move at a snail's speed. I pick up my pace, and soon I'm pistoning in and out of her like the sex-deprived man I am now. Her kitten moans mix with my grunts. I'm trying to keep the noise down, but I feel too good, and being quiet is quickly turning impossible.

"We're going to wake the entire house," she whispers against my lips.

"I don't care."

"Oh shit." She tenses underneath me.

I stop moving and lean back. "What's wrong?"

"We forgot protection. There hasn't been time for me to get on birth control."

With a curse lodged in my throat, I close my eyes. "I don't have any."

"I don't want you to stop."

I open my eyes again, immediately getting lost in hers. "I can pull out."

"Okay."

"Okay," I repeat, then claim her lips again.

The brief pause didn't do anything to diminish my libido or help me last longer. Not even a minute later, I'm unable to fight my own body. I pull out as fast as I can, then hide my face in the crook of her neck and cry out as I empty myself on the couch. I don't move from my spot for several beats while Daisy and I try to catch our breaths. It's not until she tenses that I lean on my elbows.

"What is it?"

I hear a groan nearby, which propels me to sit up on high alert. When I see who made the noise, I don't know if I should be embarrassed or fucking angry.

"Phoenix!" Daisy hisses. "Were you spying on us?"

He steps out from behind the column that did a half-assed job of hiding his large frame. He's only wearing a pair of sweatpants, and his hands are crossed in front of his crotch.

Son of a bitch.

"Were you jerking off in the shadows, you perv?" I ask.

He frowns, staring daggers through his eyes at me. "I did not have voyeuristic intentions when I came to the kitchen to grab a glass of water. It's not my fault you two decided to get it on in the living room. You should be glad it was me who caught you and not Mr. X."

Daisy puts her pants back on in a hurry, then fixes her pajama shirt. *Damn.* I didn't even get a chance to play with her gorgeous tits.

"You should have made yourself known." She glowers at him and then scurries back to her room.

"Thanks a lot, asshole," I growl.

Phoenix's eyebrows shoot to the heavens.

"Why are you mad at me? I'm the one who should be pissed."

"Oh yeah? Why is that?" I shove my legs back into my jeans while keeping my glower in place.

"You just got the sweetest pussy on the planet when the best I can do right now is jerk off while I watch."

"At least you've still got your powers."

He winces, and then pity quickly shines in his eyes. *Damn it.* I shouldn't have gone there.

"Don't look at me like that," I snap.

"What the hell is going on here?" Mr. X walks into the living room, sporting the mother of all glares.

"Nothing. Absolutely nothing."

I head back to my room, feeling worse than I did before I came out here. I'll have to clean the mess I left on the couch later. Hopefully, no one will notice. Yeah, I got to be with Daisy, and it was amazing, but making love to her didn't fill the hole in my chest. I don't think anything ever will.

7

BRYCE

The drive back to Gifted Academy campus is quiet, but not more pleasant because of it. Mom can be just as aggravating when she's not speaking. Her closed-off expression and the hard clench of her jaw tell me she's thinking of a plot to get her way. She's seething that Mr. X swept in and pulled the rug from right under her feet. And I'm so fucking glad he did. It's one thing for me to agree to my mother's scheme. I'm doing it with my eyes wide open. It's a different story to let her use Daisy for her wicked plans.

Mom parks in front of the main school building, but she maintains her gaze on the street when she finally breaks the silence. "I expect to see you and Toby in class today."

The clock on the car's dashboard flashes six thirty. There won't be time for a quick nap. I'm fine, but poor Toby looks worse for wear.

"Sure thing, Principal Fallon." He gets out of the car, but I don't move to do the same. I can sense my mother wants to say more to me.

"We need to commence recruiting ASAP. Start with the low-level Fringes. They'll be more motivated to join the cause."

Bitterness pools in my mouth. The reason those poor kids will be easy prey is the constant bullying that my mother allowed to happen under her watch. It's possible she knew about my gift of Idol creation all along. But how?

"You let them suffer at the hands of the stronger students on purpose, didn't you?"

"You're talking gibberish. Why would I do that?"

"To have those students exactly where you wanted them. Desperate for a way to fight back."

"You speak as if I knew you would develop the ability to create Idols."

I whip my face to her. "Didn't you?"

She meets my stare without flinching. "Of course I didn't know. Go on now. I have to get to work."

Yeah, like I believe your lies.

I get out, but before I close the door, I lean in. "Oh, I forgot to mention this earlier. Your assistant, Bethany Walkers, is a Neo God."

Mom's eyes grow rounder. "How do you know?"

"She had the same odd glint in her eyes as a Neo God woman I met in Hawk City."

Who disappeared in the crowd once the tide turned on her. The memory makes me bitter. Amanda was working for my father there. I wonder if she'll follow him here.

By the time I get onto the curb and grab my bags, Toby is already halfway toward his dorm building, which is not the same as mine. I run to catch up with him, reaching the guy in seconds.

He jumps back, startled. His head must have been stuck in the clouds if he didn't hear my approach.

"Shit, Bryce. You startled me."

"Sorry. I want to ask if you'd like to move in my apartment. Now that Rufio and Phoenix aren't returning to school, I have two spare bedrooms."

"What about Morpheus? Do think he'll join us or choose to stay with Daisy?"

"Honestly, I don't know. I'm sure that if he decides to return, he won't mind you moving in."

Toby rubs the back of his neck, then glances away. "Hmm. Can I think about it?"

Damn. I didn't expect him to hesitate like that. I wonder if he's afraid of me or something.

"Yeah, of course. Take your time. I guess I'll see you later, then."

As much as I'd like to brush off Toby's response as being of no consequence, I'm still annoyed by it when I reach my floor. The feeling changes to something completely different when I walk in front of Daisy's old dorm room. My heart squeezes so tightly in my chest that I can't breathe right for a moment. My steps falter, and then I completely freeze and stare at her door.

The spell is broken when a door at the end of the corridor bangs shut. Three seniors, all high-level Idols, are walking toward me. They're all wearing their school uniforms, even though class won't start for another hour. I veer for my apartment, crossing paths with them. At first, I don't think they'll let me pass. They're projecting their powers to the max. I also can't miss their aggressive stance aimed at me.

"Is there a fucking problem?" I ask, leveling up my powers too. *I can play this game all day, suckers.*

"No, no problem at all. *Yet,*" one of them sneers.

I laugh without humor. "Seriously, after all these years attending the same school, now you decide to test your luck?"

"Your days of supremacy are over, Norm-lover," the second idiot spits out.

I curl my hands into fists, trying my best not to fall for their baiting. I could take these three bullies easily. They're powerful but no match for me. I just don't want to deal with the aftermath, which will include more one-on-one time with my mother.

I snort. "Whatever."

Using my telekinesis, I shove them out of my way as hard as I can. The idiot who spoke last hits his shoulder against the wall and lets out a growl. *Oh, goodie.* I triggered his gift, which is the ability to shift into some kind of beast. No wonder his nickname is Monster.

"You'll get what's coming for you, as—"

I snap my fingers, cutting off his tirade. The gesture is only for show—my mind is all I need to bend the air around the guy's throat to do my will, which is to block his airways. Not all telekinetics are able to do that.

"You were saying?" I ask.

One of his friends lifts his arms, displaying steely knives instead of fists. "Let him go."

"Are you for real? Do you think you can harm me with those pitiful makeshift weapons?"

Monster boy is turning purple, and his other friend doesn't seem inclined to help. I let him go, sick of the whole scene already.

"Run along. Your presence is nauseating."

The three clowns scurry away with their tails between their legs. I watch them disappear around the corridor, and then I enter my apartment. My stomach is still a mess. I wasn't kidding when I said I was nauseated. But it wasn't because of them, per se. This whole situation sickens me. The constant power struggle, the need to be superior, the oppression of the weak. And there's more violence and bloodshed to come.

I head for the couch, feeling suddenly bone-tired. Mom wants me to attend class today, but it doesn't mean I have to be there early. I close my eyes, wishing Daisy were here with me. We've been apart for a little over an hour, but I already miss her so much. I'm not sure how long I'll be able to stay away.

For the first time ever, I wish I had Phoenix's ability to connect with others via dreams. I sure could use dreaming about Daisy.

My body relaxes against the couch, and I feel the threads of slumber pulling me under. Maybe if I'm lucky she'll invade my dreams nonetheless.

"You're doing everything wrong, mummy boy!" Rufio yells at Morpheus, the small, curly haired kid who somehow ended up in our boat.

"Don't call me that!" He jumps forward, rocking the small vessel and threatening to send us all into the water.

I grab him by his life jacket and pull his ass back on the bench. "Sit down, you idiot, or you'll capsize the boat."

"Can we head back to camp already? This is lame," Phoenix, the cocky blond, pipes up.

"I agree." Rufio throws a piece of bread in the water.

"We haven't found the buoy with the clue yet," Morpheus retorts.

"Who cares about some silly-ass scavenger hunt? That's for low-level Fringes and babies."

I pinch the bridge of my nose, wondering for the thousandth time why I agreed to come to Idol camp. Oh yeah, my mother thought it would be a great opportunity for Rufio to learn social skills, and since I'm his brother, I got roped in too.

"Let's head back," I say. "Your bickering is giving me a headache already."

Suddenly, Morpheus's demeanor changes. His spine becomes rigid, and his tan skin seems to turn paler. He aims his gaze skyward as if searching for something.

"What are you looking at?" Rufio follows his line of vision.

"I don't know. I got a bad feeling all of a sudden."

"Gee, I knew you were a weirdo," Phoenix mutters.

Morpheus doesn't seem to register the mean comment as he hugs himself and shivers.

"Are you cold?" I ask.

"Yes, I'm freezing."

"You're joking, right? It's almost eighty degrees," Phoenix replies.

I'm about to test my telekinetic powers to steer the boat back to shore when my eyes catch dark clouds fast approaching on the horizon.

"Son of a bitch. The weather is turning," I say.

Morpheus stares wide-eyed at the storm. "I knew something was wrong."

The wind and sea change, becoming violent in the blink of an eye. I've never witnessed the weather turn so rapidly like this.

"We need to get out of here!" Phoenix shouts over the howling winds.

"You're a telekinetic, right?" I ask.

He nods. "It's not my major gift though."

"Mine either, but I think if we work together, that should be enough."

A wave crashes against our small boat, flooding half of it. I shake the salty water from my hair and then realize we can't even see the coastline anymore.

"Where's the beach?" Rufio asks.

"We can't possibly have gone that far," Phoenix shouts over the noise.

Heavy rain falls down, creating a gray curtain all around us. Lightning streaks the dark sky, followed by the loud clamor of thunder. The waves are getting bigger and bigger. If we don't get out of the water, we're going to sink.

Morpheus bends forward, folding himself into a tight ball. He makes strange sounds, and I fear he's getting sick.

"If you throw up, I'm tossing you off the boat," Rufio tells him.

He doesn't reply for a moment, but when he finally lifts his head,

I see dark veins coming from under his eyes and down his cheeks. They look like black tears. Freaky.

"What the hell is wrong with you?" Phoenix asks.

"There's an island that way." He points ahead. "That's where we need to go."

I glance in the direction he's pointing at, but there's nothing but a great gray wall. "There's nothing in that direction besides the open sea."

"Trust me. The island is there," he grits out.

Our boat begins to spin, which can only mean one thing: we got caught in a whirlpool. But that doesn't make any sense.

"Fuck! Come on, Phoenix. Help me out here."

I focus my power on moving the boat away from the whirlpool and toward Morpheus's invisible island. Phoenix gets with the program, and together we make the boat move as fast as if it had an engine.

"Guys, you need to add more juice. There's a massive wave coming our way," Rufio warns.

I glance over my shoulder and curse when I see the monstrous wall of water that will for sure crush us.

"We're not going to make it!" Morpheus yells.

I want to tell him he's wrong, but there's no time. The wave catches up with us, sending our boat to the depths of the ocean when it folds on top of our heads. All I feel at first is an intense pressure that keeps me from moving. My body is like a rag doll being yanked around by a rabid dog. Then comes the burning in my lungs. I'm drowning in a sea of bubbles and foam.

I can't see shit, but I have to pick a direction and go for it before the lack of oxygen makes me pass out. I kick my legs with everything I have, and after what feels like an eternity, I break through the surface with a loud gasp. The storm is still raging, and the sea is even more violent than before.

"Rufio! Phoenix! Morpheus!" I yell as loud as I can.

The first bobbing head I see is Phoenix's. I swim in his direction, fucking glad he listened to me and wore his life vest. I reach for the strap and turn him around. "Are you okay?"

His eyes are wide and frightened. The arrogance from earlier is gone. Now he just looks like the kid that he is.

"Yeah. Where are the others?"

"I don't know."

I search our perimeter, seeing nothing but dark waves and small pieces of wood—the remains of our boat.

"Bryce!" Rufio calls in the distance.

I reply, and we play a wicked game of Marco Polo until finally I spot my brother's dark head swimming in our direction. He's dragging Morpheus with him. Thank goodness.

"Is he alive?" Phoenix asks when Rufio reaches us.

"I'm fi-fine," Morpheus replies. "S-so very co-cold."

"Can you still tell us where that island of yours is?" I ask.

In that moment, a cascade of lightning slashes the sky, hitting the beach of a tropical island several times. In the last hit, the face of an angry man seems to appear in the dark clouds. It's gone in the blink of an eye.

"Did you see that?" Phoenix asks.

"Yeah," Rufio replies. "I thought I imagined it."

"Come on. We have to reach the island before it disappears from view."

"This is a mistake," Morpheus whines.

"Shut up, mummy boy. You were the one who told us to get to the island," Rufio retorts angrily.

Morpheus doesn't complain about the nickname like he did before. He keeps repeating, "This is a mistake," all the way to the shore.

8

MORPHEUS

The cab drops Andromeda and me off in front of a huge mansion in one of the best neighborhoods in Hawk City—and also one with the highest prices for square footage in the country. Disgust spreads through my chest like a disease. It's not surprising that this Nathaniel guy, being a demigod, is swimming in riches. Until Daisy came into my life, I never stopped to think about the inequality in the distribution of wealth. My parents weren't rich, but we lived comfortably. I'm ashamed to admit I let my Idol status go to my head and adopted the majority's way of thinking that the only people who mattered were Idols.

Three large security guards—all high-level Fringes—block our path when we approach the gates. I'm quick to assess their levels, confirming what I suspected. They're on the cusp of Idol status. All three are level nine. But you won't see an Idol working security detail. That's not how our world works. I wonder if they're Neo Gods agents.

"This is a private party. Please leave at once," one of them says.

"I'm a guest. Andromeda Belfor," she replies with an air of boredom.

The second security guard glances at the tablet in his hand, and after a moment, he looks at Andromeda, then at me. I don't miss the scrutiny he gives my ensemble.

"I need to see some form of ID," he tells her.

Her aura flares up as her power surges within her small frame. She takes a step forward, revealing her golden chains, which are now pointing at the guy. "Is this identification enough for you?"

The corners of my lips twitch up. It's hard to contain my amusement when three grown-ass men look terrified in front of the force of nature that's Andromeda. I'm fucking glad she's on our side.

"No, that's plenty. Welcome to the party, miss." They part, allowing us to pass.

"What a bunch of dumbasses," she mutters while we're still within earshot.

"Couldn't agree more. Do you think they're with the Neo Gods?" I whisper.

"I have no idea. I haven't met many members, only Nathaniel and a couple of his goons when he kidnapped me."

I stop in my tracks and touch her arm. "Wait? When was that?"

"Not too long ago. Soon after my recruitment, I realized I had made a terrible mistake. I cut off my communication with Nathaniel completely for years. He only started to pester me recently. I guess when he got whiff of the Unmaker."

The darkness inside of me begins to churn. I clench my jaw tight, focusing on keeping my rage under control. I can't lose my shit in front of all these people—that is, not until I discover what Nathaniel knows about my past.

We resume our walk toward the mansion. There are two more suits manning the double doors, but besides a sideways glance, they don't try to block our entrance. Lively music echoes against the smooth walls and high ceiling of the entry foyer. Ahead of us, there's a grand staircase worthy of a classic Hollywood movie. Everywhere I look there are ostentatious displays of excess, from the crystal chandelier to the painted mirror display above the staircase.

Andromeda hisses, clutching at her hand.

"Is he hurting you again?" I ask.

"Yes. We must be late."

On impulse, I take her hand in mine. The power of the Nathaniel's mark feels like burning ice to me. Wisps of shadows sneak around my wrist, slowly snaking around Andromeda's. For once, they're not trying to smother me. On the contrary, they're seeking to counter Nathaniel's power. I sense his presence diminish until the tension in Andromeda's hand eases.

"Thank you. That helped," she says.

"Let's go find the jackass. I can't wait to try my powers on him in person."

"I know where he is now," she grits out.

With shoulders squared, she moves toward the sound of the party. The mansion has a grand ballroom, which is bursting with mostly Idols, but there are also Fringe guests in the mix, which surprises me. Granted, they're on the edge of Idol-hood.

As we move through the crowded space, I sense several stares aimed in my direction. Maybe I should have asked to borrow a suit from Mr. Silverstone. I stick out like a sore thumb in my faded jeans and hoodie, drawing too much attention. When Nathaniel said he was throwing a party, he really meant it. There must be hundreds of people here, and by the amount of bling adorning the female guests' necks, ears, and fingers, this soiree can probably be seen all the way from the moon.

"There he is." Andromeda points at a tall man with light brown hair combed back, busy entertaining a few of his guests.

He has the looks of a charmer with a dazzling smile and

fine features. But it's his dark and magnetic powers that draw his victims to him. I can see it as clearly as day. Oddly, my own powers react to the man, almost as if it recognizes him somehow.

"Hello, brother."

His words echo in my head again. Is he really my brother? If so, what kind of god sired us? Obviously nothing good if I inherited the power to put fear into people's hearts.

Still laughing at his guest's joke, he turns to us. When our gazes meet, I feel like I've been sucker punched. His eyes are nothing like mine, but they look as familiar as if I had been staring at my own reflection in the mirror.

"Excuse me. I must greet some very special guests," Nathaniel says to his friends, then strides in our direction.

For all Andromeda's cockiness, she's tense and a little afraid too. I can easily pick up that type of negative emotion in others since I'm a fearmancer. She knows now that her fate is in the hands of a being far more powerful than she is.

"Andy, I'm so glad you could make it." He smiles broadly, showing perfect white teeth. But his mirth wilts when he glances at her casual clothes. "Tsk. Didn't I ask you to dress appropriately?"

"I'm sorry. Is this not okay?" She glances down, pretending to check her clothes. "Is my ass showing?"

He narrows his eyes briefly, then turns his attention to me and extends his hand. "I'm Nathaniel Wilcox. You must be Morpheus Malek."

I hesitate to take his hand for a second, unsure what's going to happen when we touch. But fuck, I'm not going to let him know I'm wary of him. We shake hands, and when nothing happens, I'm a little disappointed. The feeling doesn't last long. His voice enters my mind, low and dangerous.

"You attempted to help Andromeda just now. I advise you to quit

trying to mess with my recruit. You don't want to get in my way, little brother."

"I'm not your brother. And get the fuck out of my head!"

Nathaniel recoils, a physical reaction to my mental shove. His eyes flash with anger, and I brace for his retaliation.

"You've met Morpheus. What now?" Andromeda pipes up.

Nathaniel's grin slips into a chilling smile. "Now we'll get to know on—" He stops abruptly and diverts his attention to the crowd. "My, oh my. This evening is turning out to be quite magnificent."

I follow his line of vision, finding the source of his amusement right away. Stephan is here, making a beeline in our direction. He took the dress code seriously. He's wearing a perfectly cut tuxedo that makes him look like a movie star. Women turn their heads to watch him pass, but he only has eyes for Andromeda.

"Why is he here?" she asks in a small voice.

"I invited him, naturally. This is a party for the crème de la crème of Hawk City society, after all. What's the matter, Andy? You don't like the surprise?"

Stephan stops near us, sporting the coldest mask I've seen him wear. He spares Andromeda a glance full of loathing that makes me feel bad for her, even if she can't see his glower. She's clearly enamored with the guy.

"Welcome, Stephan," Nathaniel greets him. "I'm delighted you could join us this evening. I know you've been busy these days."

"Yes, extremely busy." His blue eyes become sharper.

No one speaks for a moment, and the longer the silence extends, the tenser the atmosphere becomes. I have no idea what Nathaniel wants, but I didn't come here to witness a staring contest. I open my mouth to get the answers I came for, but then all the lights in the room go out. The crowd lets out a collective gasp of shock.

Immediately, I reach for Andromeda, finding nothing but empty space where she was a second ago. *Fuck!* I search for her signature with my senses, but there's nothing but an endless void. *What the hell is going on?*

A cold hand clamps around my arm, and then Nathaniel's laughter sounds nearby. "Are you afraid, little brother?"

I shove him as hard I can, and he lets go. "Where the fuck am I?"

The absolute darkness begins to lighten into gray until a familiar landscape reveals itself. The island from my nightmares. I'm standing on its sandy beach, and before me, there's the tropical forest that looks innocent enough but hides deadly secrets. Nathaniel is a few feet away from me, looking at the forest too.

"What's this place?" he asks.

"You don't know? You brought us here."

He glances at me with eyes that are widely innocent. "No, I didn't."

A massive cloud formation converges on top of the lush jungle, crackling as bolts of lightning pulse inside. The face of the island god appears before us, filling my chest with dread.

"I never thought I'd see the day you two would meet," the god speaks.

"Who are you?" Nathaniel asks.

Lightning shoots from the sky, hitting Nathaniel square on his chest. The force of the impact sends him flying backward, and he's still caught in the electric current when he lands near the shore.

Damn it. I guess he wasn't lying when he said he didn't bring us here.

I run to where he landed while the island god's laughter booms as loud as thunder behind me.

The veins on Nathaniel's neck strain as he rides the electroshock. His eyes are wide, shining with fear. A part of me wants to help, but then I remember he's been torturing Andromeda for months. Eventually, the tremors stop.

He gasps, bucking his chest. "Motherfucker!"

I turn around, daring to face the source of my torment. "Why are we here?"

"You're here because both of you broke the rules. Now it's time for your punishment."

He sends a massive lightning bolt in my direction, but it's deflected by the dark silhouette of a man that materializes out of thin air. The island god rages so loudly that the noise shakes the ground.

Nathaniel gets back on his feet, bent forward as he clutches his middle.

"Father?" he asks the newcomer.

Wait. Father?

My heart stops beating. I can't breathe.

The man looks over his shoulder, and the only thing from his profile that I can see peeking from the shadows is his fiery eyes.

He lifts his arm, palm facing us, and says, "Go."

My body is yanked back by a great force, and the island of horrors vanishes from my sight. There's a brief moment when I feel and hear nothing, but then I'm back at Nathaniel's party, the sound of merriment suddenly too harsh in my ears after the absolute silence of my trip back. The lights are back on, and all the guests are acting like nothing is amiss. I peer to my left, finding Nathaniel there, looking as astonished I am.

"Who was that man?" I ask.

He rubs his face, not meeting my eyes. "You'd better leave, kid. I think I've had enough of high-octane adventures for one evening." He walks away still slightly hunched.

I should follow him and demand answers now that he's vulnerable, but something holds me back and I don't know what. It's not a premonition, I don't think.

Damn it. This evening turned out be a complete bust. Instead of answers, all I managed was to acquire more questions.

I begin to move toward the ballroom's exit when I remember Andromeda. *Shit. I'm really out of it.* I search my surroundings but find no sign of the lavender-haired girl or Stephan.

Hell. Where did they go?

9

PHOENIX

I wake up with a gasp, panicked. I'm in an unfamiliar room, but that's not the reason my heart is beating so fast that it seems it's going to crash through my rib cage. I had a nightmare, and judging by the sweat on my forehead and the lingering feeling of disgust underneath my skin, I can guess what it was about. I don't dare even think of his name.

After the morning's fiasco with Daisy, I returned to my assigned room. I lay on the bed with zero hopes that I'd fall asleep. I had upset Daisy, and that didn't sit well with me. But I guess I was too exhausted, and my body ended up succumbing to it in the end.

I shove the heels of my hands in my eyes while I try to calm down. *He's gone forever. He can't harm me anymore.* I repeat the mantra in my head until my breathing returns to normal. I wish I could erase all the awful memories still branded in my brain.

My phone pings, alerting me to a text message. Groaning, I reach for it. Maybe it's news from Morpheus or Bryce. My chest feels tight when I see the message is from my mother. I haven't thought much about her since she rescued me from the police station. I caved back then and let her comfort me, but now the old wound is open and bleeding again. She let me suffer all those years at the hands of that monster. I don't think I'll ever be able to forgive her completely.

I toss my phone aside without reading what she wrote. I don't want to deal with her now. She can choke on her guilt for all I care. The best I can do is keep moving forward.

I untangle myself from the sheets and get out of bed. My bedroom shares a bathroom with Rufio's, but it's empty now. I head for it, wincing when I turn on the bright lights. A quick peek at the mirror makes me wince again. I look like shit. Bloodshot eyes, disgusting hair sticking to my forehead, dark circles. *Fuck*. I could be featured in one of those hospital posters for some horrible disease. A shower and shave are top priorities.

The second door opens, and in comes Rufio with messy hair and barely open eyes. He veers for the toilet and, without even acknowledging my presence, takes his dick out and starts to pee.

"Dude. Come on! I was here first."

He yawns and then speaks. "Sorry. Didn't see you there."

"Are you blind?"

"No. I'm so damn tired." He flushes and then nudges me to the side so he can wash his hands.

"Couldn't sleep?"

"No. I slept like the dead."

Jealousy rears its ugly head. Of course he did. Awesome sex will do that to any guy.

"Lucky you." I don't hide the venom in my tone.

My comment seems to fly right over his head. The old Rufio would be shooting daggers at me with his eyes, but there's no change in his demeanor. It's pretty unnerving to be in his presence and feel nothing but a big void where his power used to be.

"What time do you think it is?" he asks.

"I have no clue."

"I think I'm going back to bed."

I watch him drag his feet out of the bathroom with my jaw hanging open. That guy is a completely different person. We've all changed in the past few months; I can't deny that.

I stare at my reflection again.

"Fuck this."

I turn on the shower and wait until the water gets hot enough. Then I take my time under the steamy jets, letting them ease away the tension in my shoulders. After a while, I reach for the soap and begin to scrub every inch of skin ferociously. I feel so dirty that no matter how hard I rub with the soap, it never seems to remove the stain. My skin burns, and it's only when blood tinges the water at my feet that I stop what I'm doing. I scrubbed myself raw. *Fucking fantastic.*

I decide to forgo shaving until I have my shit together. The blade won't cut me, but my hands are the most dangerous things right now.

My mood is down to sewer levels when I exit the foggy bathroom with a towel wrapped around my waist and a second one in my hand to dry my hair. I stop in my tracks when I find Daisy sitting on my bed, waiting for me.

In an instant, her presence infuses me with euphoria. My heart races. Every instinct I have urges me to crush her against my chest, kiss her lips until they become swollen. But I can't do any of those things.

"Hey, Phoenix. We need to talk."

Damn everything to hell. Those are the worst possible words a guy can hear from his girlfriend. It never ends well.

DAISY

It's an effort to keep my eyes glued to Phoenix's face and not let them wander down his chiseled chest that glistens with droplets of water. I shouldn't have stayed in his room when I realized he was in the shower, and now I'm putting my self-control to the test.

His green eyes turn dark under his frown. "Why? Is it because of what I was doing earlier?"

My cheeks become warmer at the memory. Sure, I was mortified to learn he had been spying on Rufio and me, but when the embarrassment faded, only a wicked sense of desire remained.

I clear my throat to get my mind back on track. "No, I didn't come here to talk about that."

He takes a tentative step forward. "So, you aren't mad at me?"

"Not anymore." I take a deep breath to gather my courage. I wish my reason for being here was to give Phoenix a tongue-lashing for his voyeurism. But the topic of this conversation is much more serious than that.

"Daisy, if you don't tell me what's the matter, I'm going to think the worst."

"I'm sorry. This is a hard subject. I wish we didn't have to talk about it at all."

He breaches the distance between us and sits next to me on the bed. There's barely an inch between our bodies, and my desire is to lean into his warmth.

"You can tell me anything, babe. As long as it doesn't involve you wanting to break up with me." He smiles impishly, but I see a hint of fear in his eyes.

"I don't know where you got that crazy notion in your head, but you'd better erase it right away. I'm never letting you go. You're mine."

His face breaks into the brightest of smiles, melting my heart at the sight. "You have no idea how much I want to kiss you right now."

My breathing hitches at the same time my heart does a somersault. "I think I do."

I allow myself to get lost in the depths of his gaze for a while longer, basking in the glorious feeling of his love, but I can't postpone the conversation I came here for. It's too important.

It's an effort to look away first. But I do it, dipping my chin as I release a heavy sigh. "You had a nightmare, didn't you?"

"What?" he asks in a high-pitched voice.

"I think I was pulled into it."

He doesn't say a word for the longest time. I chance a glimpse, afraid of what I might find etched on his face. He's staring straight ahead with his jaw clenched so tight that I can see the strain of his muscles.

"Phoenix?"

"What did you see?" he asks in a tight voice, and my heart shatters.

"Enough." A tear runs down my cheek, even though I swore before coming here that I'd be strong for him.

He dips his chin and stares at his balled fists on his lap. "I don't remember the details of the nightmare, but it left my soul soiled by tar." A shuddering breath leaves his lips. "That monster won't let go of me even after his demise."

My resolution to keep my distance from him until I learn to control my powers shatters like broken glass. I reach for Phoenix's hand, needing to show him through actions how much I love him. He trembles under my touch, then turns his face to mine.

"He *will* be gone, Phoenix. I'll help you extract him like one does poison from a wound. I swear."

Fat tears run down his cheeks. My face is damp too, and the choke in my throat is so immense it feels like I can't draw air in.

Phoenix swings his arm around my neck and pulls me to him too fast for me to stop him. Our lips clash with the intensity of a storm; our tongues mingle, impatient and ravenous, as if the world is ending and this is our last kiss.

My arms circle around his back, and soon we're connected chest to chest. But the headiness I'm feeling isn't only the bliss of pure love. There's a shadow hanging in between us—my powers, trying to unmake Phoenix.

No. I can't let this strange force control me. I won't ruin the life of another loved one.

A groan of pure need comes from Phoenix's throat as he deepens the kiss, pulling me even closer to him. He doesn't seem to notice or care that I'm taking his Idol essence into me. I want to move away and meld myself to him at the same time.

I have to end this one way or another. Using the visualization technique Morpheus taught me, I picture the strands of power coming into me as ribbons. All I need now is a pair of scissors to cut them. But imagining them is harder than I thought. I can't quite make it hold its shape. It doesn't help either when I'm so distracted by Phoenix's tongue and caresses.

With effort, I pull away from his kiss, but we're still touching, which means I'm still stealing from him. He tries to follow my mouth, but I place my fingers over his swollen lips.

"Hold on. I'm unmaking you, and I need to stop."

His green eyes widen a bit. "I didn't feel a thing. I dared to believe you had learned to control your abilities."

"Not yet, but I need your help."

"Anything, babe."

"Don't distract me."

The corners of his lips twitch upward. "I don't know what you mean."

"Right. I'm going to close my eyes, and you're going to remain utterly still."

"Okay."

I watch him for a couple of beats, but not because I don't trust him. It's just so damn hard to not stare at his beautiful face. With a deep breath, I finally close my eyes and restart the exercise. It's a little bit easier to focus now that I don't have his tongue wreaking havoc on my body, but even the touch of his hands is distracting.

Come on, Daisy, you can do it. Think about the reward when you gain control of your powers for real.

The pep talk works. The scissors take shape in my head. Quickly, I use them to snip all the ribbons connecting me to Phoenix. When the last one is cut, the surge of power going into me ceases. He takes a sharp breath in, and my eyes fly open.

"I can sense the difference now. I feel stronger. You're no longer taking my powers away."

"I can't believe it worked," I reply in awe.

Phoenix's mouth splits into a wide smile just before he captures my face between his large hands and kisses me again. I tense, afraid I'm still a thief. But when I feel nothing coming into me, I relax into his arms, surrendering completely to the passion of the moment.

Not only his tongue is hungry—his hands are everywhere, exploring, drawing breathless moans of pleasure from me. I yank the towel that's wrapped around his waist, finding his cock hard and ready for me. My fingers curl around his length, but Phoenix doesn't even allow me one second of fun before he uses his telekinesis to place me in the middle of the bed on my back.

"Hey! I wasn't done."

"Sorry, babe, but I'm on edge already, and any sudden movement could make me explode."

"I want to taste you," I pout.

"Same here." He crawls toward me, peppering my legs with open kisses that set me ablaze. "Thank heavens you're not wearing pants." He lifts my dress and nuzzles my clit with the tip of his nose before licking me through the fabric of my underwear.

I'm unravelling at the speed of light, but I know what I want, and Phoenix is not going to get his way just because he knows exactly what to do to my body to make me lose control. I shut my legs and, pressing my hands on his shoulders, push him back.

"Daisy!" he whines.

"No, I'm not going to be left at your mercy this time. We're both having fun."

"Who said we weren't both going to have a good time?" He arches his eyebrows.

I scooch to the side and then jump out of bed before he can reach over. He does move to follow me, but I wag my index finger at him. "Oh no, sir. You're not getting out of that bed. Lie down."

"But, babe…"

"Lie down, Phoenix. I mean it."

"Fine." He places a pillow under his head and then grabs his cock. "I guess I'll just have to pleasure myself, then."

I narrow my eyes, seeing the challenge in his. "Oh, do you want to play games, sweetheart?"

I pull my dress off and stand in front of him in my panties only. Not breaking eye contact, I lick two fingers and slowly run them down my belly until they disappear underneath the scrap of cotton fabric. Phoenix's eyes bulge from his skull for a second. Then he retaliates.

I fly toward the bed and land softly on top of him in a sixty-nine position. There's no point fighting him any longer. He wins, but there aren't any losers here. Like a greedy little monster, I reach for his cock and lick him from top to base. Phoenix lets out a curse, and then he tears my panties in half. Maybe I shouldn't bother wearing them anymore.

He grabs me by the hips, and then he's between my legs,

torturing me in the best way possible. I'd take my time savoring him like this, but I'm wound too tight; I've been denied him for far too long. My body becomes boneless in a matter of seconds, and then I shatter in orgasmic bliss. Phoenix's release is right around the corner. He's harder and larger inside my mouth. While I'm still riding the waves of pleasure, he climaxes with a loud roar. I drink everything he gives me and don't stop until he makes me.

Feeling the best kind of exhaustion, I collapse next to him with my hand still attached to his semi-hard dick. It seems I can't let go.

I'm still breathing hard when I sense another presence in the room. I lean on my forearms and find Rufio resting against the doorframe of the bathroom. His arms are folded in front of his chest, his expression blank save for the intensity in his eyes.

"Rufio, what the hell, man!" Phoenix yells.

"I just wanted to see what it was like watching Daisy with someone else." His lips curl into a grin. "I concede. It was pretty hot."

He returns to his room, leaving me in flames.

10

BRYCE

I wake with a start, gasping for air. My heart is racing. The TV is on and the lights are flickering. It takes me a few seconds to control the wisps of rogue power that leaked out while I was in the throes of a terrible memory. I take a shuddering breath, rubbing my face. I can't believe I dreamed about the island of horrors. It's been years since those memories plagued my nightmares.

I can't help thinking that their return is a sign that we must prepare for the final showdown with that mystery god who marked us, claiming us for his own army.

Still feeling jittery, I get up and check the time on the microwave's clock. It's fifteen minutes past noon. I've missed half the classes of the day, and now it's lunch break. If it had been any other day, I might have blown school off completely.

I check my phone. There aren't any messages from Daisy or the guys but plenty of missed calls from Mom. *Great.* She must have been busy, or she would have come here to drag my ass to class. I hastily put my uniform on and head out.

This time when I pass in front of Daisy's old dorm room, I don't look or pause. She's not in there, and she'll never come back. As for my stay in Gifted Academy, I hope it's not a long one. Earning a high school diploma never felt more superfluous than it does now that we're on the brink of a civil war.

As I near the main school building, I sense something is wrong. I quicken my steps and burst through the main double doors, ready to face something nasty. I can't really put my finger on the feeling. It's like an ominous cloud is hanging over my head. The hallways are empty, which at this hour is weird as fuck. They should be bursting with students on their way back to class after lunch.

I send a quick text to Toby. It's highly likely that he didn't skip any classes like me. There's no response from him by the time I reach the school cafeteria. Only a few tables are occupied. *Where the hell is everyone?*

The few students present turn to gawk at me. I recognize one of them: Nate, a fire elemental. I'd ask him if something happened, but I'm getting pretty hostile vibes from the guy and his friends. I veer for the buffet, which is currently manned by only one employee.

"Did I miss the lunch crowd?" I ask with a grin, but the Fringe simply looks at me with a vacant stare.

"We only have the vegetarian lasagna left," he says.

"It's okay. I'm not hungry."

The back of my neck prickles, announcing the approach of a few people. I count five different Idol signatures behind me. The Fringe worker steps back, then turns around and runs from the cafeteria. *All right, then.*

Unfazed, I pivot on the spot and find myself surrounded by Nate and his posse. None of them come close to me on the scale of power, but I guess they'd figure ganging up on me would give them a better chance.

I look at them with dispassionate curiosity. "You're in my way."

"What's up, Bryce? Where's the rest of your crew?" a female

voice taunts from my right. The circle of hostile students opens a little, allowing me to see Cherise Blake, Drusilla's old friend.

"What the hell are you doing here? You were expelled."

She twirls a finger around a lock of hair, smiling wickedly. "That decision has been revoked. I'm back, babe."

"We'll see about that," I grit out, then turn to the other idiots. "Move or I'll make you."

They take a step forward, crowding me. "I'd like to see you try. You're outnumb—" Nate begins.

I sling my arm forward, and the five idiots fly backward. Three in the group fall against a table nearby, breaking it into pieces. Two manage to avoid the collision thanks to their gifts. They come at me with all their hatred and might. Both are air elementals, and they combine their powers to try to knock me down by creating a powerful gust of wind. I bend my knees, locking them into position. I'm about to fry those two mother-fuckers when one of them hurls a throwing star at me. I can't redirect the source of my power fast enough to block the weapon. It hits me in the shoulder, piercing through skin and muscle, burning.

Fucking hell. This is a lightning-glass weapon. The Neo Gods have breached the academy.

The realization hits me like a cannonball, adding fuel to my rage. No wonder Cherise is back.

I direct an electric discharge toward the two elementals, hitting them square in their chests. The force of the hit sends them soaring all the way toward the end of the room. I don't care if they live or die.

With a wince, I remove the throwing star, dropping it in my pocket while I prepare to face the other three assholes who I had knocked down earlier. Cherise, so far, hasn't attacked. She seems content just watching. The tallest of the trio has his hands engulfed by flames. *Great. Another elemental.* He throws several fireballs in my direction, which is easy enough to avoid.

But I only realize it was a planned distraction when Cherise finally joins the fight and sends more lightning-glass throwing stars at me.

I avoid most of them through telekinesis, sending them back at her. She's able to evade them all. *Damn it.* My energy levels are dropping fast thanks to the lightning-glass poison in my system. I've been hit in two more spots—my right arm and my left forearm—and each time hurts more than last.

A roar escapes from deep in my throat. I tap every bit of power I have in me, creating a ball of energy bright enough to blind. When the illumination encompasses the entire room, I unleash all my might. There are cries of pain, but they're muffled thanks to the pounding of my pulse in my ears. The blast fades, and so does my strength. My legs give out from under me, and when the room comes into focus again, black dots speckle my sight. At least my adversaries are flat on their backs, motionless.

I don't move from my spot for several beats. A minute later, I catch someone approaching from the corner of my eye. I'm so tapped out that I can't even scan the newcomer's signature. My eyes widen in surprise when I see Renata Pomme, another one of Drusilla's minions, moving toward me. My spine becomes rigid and my hands curl into fists. Unfortunately, I don't have any more juice in me. If she's coming to attack, I can only use my bare hands to defend myself.

"Are you okay?" she asks, surprising the hell out of me. Her eyes are round and devoid of falsehood though.

"I've been poisoned. I need to see Nurse Ellen."

She reaches for my arm and helps me off the floor as if I weigh nothing. She's a level ten Idol, and her main ability is super strength. Toby felt firsthand the power of her gift when she broke his arm while he tried to defend Daisy.

"I thought you were in a psych ward," I say.

"I was for a while. What happened to Drusilla messed me up."

I try not to wince. The island god drove Drusilla insane. She turned against Renata and forced the girl to mutilate herself. And as a final act of lunacy, she compelled Rufio to kill her so she could frame him for her murder. The plan almost worked.

"Why are you helping me?"

She furrows her eyebrows, then glances left and right in a cagey manner. "You guys helped me when Drusilla went crazy. I'm returning the favor."

"Well, thanks. Do you know where everyone is?"

"I can't believe you don't know. There's been a change in the school's administration. Your mother got sacked."

"What?" I freeze midstep.

"It happened earlier this morning. The new principal didn't even let her collect her personal belongings from her office. She was escorted out of the building and off the school grounds."

Shit. Maybe I should have listened to her voice messages or called her back.

"Who is the new principal now?" I ask.

"Mr. Harris. He's an albino freak with pink irises and a mean look about him. The first thing he did was gather all Fringe students and lock them in the auditorium."

Son of a bitch. One of the Neo Gods I met when my father took us to meet his master was an albino man. And now Idol students are armed with lightning-glass weapons. This can't be a coincidence.

"How come Cherise isn't locked down with the other Fringes?"

Renata looks into my eyes, and I read fear in her gaze. "I think Cherise has been recruited by the Neo Gods."

My blood runs cold. "What makes you say that?"

"I overheard her talking with some high-level Fringes

earlier. She was threatening them. Either they joined the cause, or they'd perish with the scum."

Damn it. They're really not fucking around. I'm not even surprised by those developments. We faced Fringes in Hawk City armed with lightning-glass.

My thoughts become consumed with worry. Toby didn't reply to my message. He must be locked down with the rest. I have to get to him.

I steer us toward the auditorium.

"Where do you think you're going?" she asks.

"I have to help those Fringes. They aren't safe."

"You can't help anyone in your current state. You're bleeding and can't even walk on your own."

Fuck. She's right. I need reinforcements. I hope Nurse Ellen is still around. She helped Daisy before, and Phoenix told me her girlfriend was a Norm. But if the Neo Gods took control of Gifted Academy, they must have cleaned house and gotten rid of all Norm sympathizers.

We're halfway to the infirmary when three goons block our path. They're older and not wearing school uniforms. But they're Idols and, my guess, Neo Gods.

"Where do you think you're going?" the one in the middle asks.

"I'm taking him to the see the nurse," Renata replies. "He's hurt."

"Hurt?" The guy to the left snorts. "If he's hurt, then it means he's a Fringe and shouldn't be roaming in the hallways.

Damn. Am I so weak that they're mistaking me for a Fringe?

"I'm not a Fringe," I grit out.

"Then you must be one of those traitors who likes to mingle with the dirt. Leave him to us, girlie."

Renata tenses next to me. I'm totally prepared for her to drop me like deadweight and bail.

"No. I don't care what he does in his spare time. I'm taking him to see the nurse."

"Are you defying me, stupid girl?" the first one snarls.

"I guess I am."

My jaw is hanging to the floor. Renata's one-eighty totally blindsided me. Too bad her bravado will cost her. I'm in no condition to fight three Idols, and I doubt she can take the trio solo.

Their bodies tense as they take on an aggressive stance. I search inside of me for every drop of power I still have. If I can create a bright enough flash, it could buy us time to run away. But before I can summon the strength needed for the feat, an explosion knocks the Neo Gods down and under a mountain of debris. We're not left unscathed. The blast also sends us to the ground.

A gray fog of dust soon makes visibility impossible. It gets into my lungs, causing a fit of coughing.

"Are you okay?" Renata asks, already trying to get me back on my feet.

"No worse than I was before."

"I don't think you're getting medical attention here. We have to go now."

I hesitate, digging my feet into the ground when she tries to steer me toward the exit. "I can't leave Toby behind."

"You're not," a male voice comes from the fog.

A second later, Toby steps into view, followed by my mother and Nurse Ellen.

I stare at them. "You're okay. I thought the new principal had locked all Fringes in the auditorium."

"He did. But I'm no longer a Fringe. I'm an Idol now."

"How is that possible?" Renata asks.

"No time to explain," my mother chimes in. "We need to leave now before they send reinforcements.

"What about the Fringe students?" I ask.

"They're all out. We're the last ones here."

I take a step forward, but my legs falter. I stagger ahead, almost face-planting on the floor if it weren't for Renata keeping me upright. Nurse Ellen comes to assist, and now I'm sandwiched between the two. I've never felt more useless in my life than I do now.

We hurry out of the building, more concerned with speed than stealth since the blast alerted every single Neo God in the vicinity. Mom's car is parked right in front of the entrance, and I wonder how she managed to get back onto campus.

But all my questions will have to wait. Shouts nearby tell me our time is up. The Neo Gods' hounds are loose and coming for us.

11

MORPHEUS

My eyes are bleary when I finally land at the private airport in Saturn's Bay. I had every intention of catching a commercial flight, but Gunther Silverstone insisted on letting me use his personal private jet. Despite having the plane all to myself, I couldn't fall asleep. Too many thoughts bouncing in my head. I may have found a lost brother and my father. Now I don't know what to do with that information.

At least I didn't lose Andromeda at the party after all. She left with Stephan, and I figured they needed the time alone to talk stuff out. It would have sucked balls if on top of my personal turmoil I had to look for her.

There's no one waiting for me when I deboard the plane. I really should have called the guys. I take a deep breath of the afternoon air, which finally has the bite of winter. Then I pull my cell phone out and call the person I need to speak to the most right away: my mother. I've let her keep her secrets for long enough. She obviously knows who my father is, and his connection to the island god. She wouldn't have been able to rescue us from that horrible place all those years ago if she didn't know where to look for us.

She answers on the second ring. "Morpheus? Is that really you?"

"Yes, Mom. It's me."

"I've been worried sick about you. We've been watching the news about Hawk City. What happened in that mall was dreadful. Please tell me you weren't anywhere near it."

"Mom, I'm fine. I just got back to Saturn's Bay, and I was wondering if you could pick me up from the airport."

"The school didn't order a town car to collect you kids? That's absurd. We pay good money in tuition."

"I had to stay in Hawk City a little longer. I caught a later flight and forgot to make arrangements. I'm by myself."

"Oh, okay. Where did you land? At the Intercity Airport?"

"No. I'm actually in a private airport. I'll text you the address."

Fifteen minutes later, Mom's dependable suburban car stops in front of the small waiting area of the airport. I get up, hoisting my duffle bag over my shoulder, and step out before she has the chance to exit the vehicle. She does anyway, circling around the car to engulf me into a mama-bear hug.

"Morpheus, darling. I've missed you so much."

"I've missed you too, Mom."

She eases off, holding me by the arms to look up at my face. "You've lost weight. And you haven't been sleeping much, have you?"

"I couldn't sleep during the flight."

"What about the shadows? Are they—"

"They're under control. Come on. You can ask me all the questions inside the car."

"Oh, okay. I stopped by your favorite fast food restaurant and got you something to eat. You must be starving."

"Yeah, I could eat."

I circle to the back of the car to put my bag in the trunk, then slide into the passenger's seat. Mom is already behind the steering wheel, holding a greasy bag in her hand. The smell of fries and burger fills my nostrils, making my mouth water. I didn't realize how hungry I was until now. Eagerly, I take the bag and dig in.

"Why did you have to stay in Hawk City longer?"

I swallow the big lump of bread and meat in mouth first, buying myself a few seconds to think about what I'm going to say next. I'm determined to get to the truth, but now that I'm about to do it, I find myself tongue-tied.

"I had to meet someone."

"Are you going to elaborate on that?"

I keep staring ahead, not daring to glance at her when I reply, "I met my brother."

"What?" she shrieks, taking her eyes off the road to gawk at me. The car begins to veer toward the next lane, straight into the van occupying that space.

"Mom! Watch the road."

She swerves the vehicle back to her lane and doesn't speak for a couple of beats. "You can't spring something like that on me while I'm driving. I've always suspected Tarek had affairs, but I didn't know about children."

I whip my face to her. "Are you saying he was cheating on you?"

"I never got solid proof, but the signs were there." She sighs heavily, her shoulders sagging. "I can't blame him. I was the one who was unfaithful to him first."

A torrent of emotions crashes against me all at once. Here's the opening to talk about my biological father, but my brain is stuck on the things Tarek, the man who was supposed to be my dad, did to Mom and me throughout all the years.

"Why didn't you leave him?"

"Divorce him? You know that's not an option in our family, Morpheus."

"That's such bullshit. Why stay married to a man who doesn't respect you? Who physically abuses you?"

"He hasn't touched me since the last time you visited."

"Oh, kudos to him," I reply bitterly.

"Let's not talk about your father."

"He's not my father," I grit out.

Mom lets out a loud exhale, but at least she doesn't try to defend him. "You said you met your half brother."

The shadows are churning inside of my chest, reacting now to the rage within me. I'm still so fucking mad about this whole deal with Mom and her husband. I can't believe she's put up with his shit all these years for the sake of appearances.

"Yes, but I didn't mean an offspring of your husband. I'm talking about the real deal."

"What do you mean?"

"You know what I mean, Mom. My biological brother, the son of the man who... sired me. I also caught a glimpse of him. My father. You need to tell me who he is."

She doesn't speak for a long while, and I let her stew on my words without pressing her. I'm not leaving her side until she confesses everything. I'm done staying in the dark about my heritage.

Finally, she signals to exit the highway, but we're nowhere near Gifted Academy. I see then she's heading for a rest stop. *Good.* It's not safe to drive while having this conversation.

"He made me swear I'd never reveal his identity to anyone, not even you," she says.

"My father did?"

"Yes. And I agreed, gladly. I didn't want anyone to know."

"It's too late now. While meeting with my half brother, we were both transported to the island of horrors."

Mom stares at me wide-eyed. "You went back to that place?"

"Yes. The island god brought us there for punishment. You know he marked us all those years ago."

She nods. "I'm sorry I couldn't get to you sooner."

"How did you know where to find us?"

Her eyes are brimming with unshed tears when she looks away, dropping her gaze to her lap. "I had been there before. It's where I first met your father."

"How did you get there?"

"He brought me there. But he showed me a different side of it. He called it Starlight Island."

My jaw slackens while my pulse quickens. "That's the name of the island Norms believe to be a paradise."

"I'm aware of the legend. I don't blame them for thinking that. What I saw was idyllic and peaceful. When I was with your father, I never saw the dark side of the island. I had no idea such a despicable being lived there too."

I pull my hair back, yanking at the strands. "My father stopped the island god from punishing my brother and me. He blocked his blow. He's a god too, isn't he?"

"Yes. Your father is Erebus, the god of shadows and darkness."

My power surges suddenly, coiling violently inside of my chest. My heart is racing while I grapple with the truth. I'm a demigod, then. And my father is not an ordinary god.

"Erebus is a primordial deity," I murmur, still too shocked by the revelation.

"Yes. And I believe the god who has been tormenting you and your friends is Chaos, Erebus's father."

"That son of a bitch is my grandfather?" My voice rises to a shrill.

At once, the invisible lightning tattoo—his mark—burns on my back as if answering my question.

Mom closes her eyes and whispers, "Yes."

I pass a hand over my face. "He wants Daisy gone. Fuck."

"She's special. If he wants her gone, it means she poses a threat to him."

"Daisy is the Unmaker."

I don't see the point in keeping the truth from Mom when our enemy already knows her identity.

"The Unmaker? I thought there had only been one Idol with that power, and she surrendered her gift."

"Daisy is her direct descendant. When Bryce healed her, he awakened the power within her. But why would Chaos want to kill her?"

"Because he's Chaos. He thrives on turmoil and destruction. The more harm he does to mortals, the stronger he becomes."

I rest my head in my hands. "How am I going to keep Daisy safe from him? He's too strong."

Mom touches my shoulder, squeezing it. "You love that girl, don't you?"

I turn to her. "With every piece of my black heart."

"Oh, Morpheus. Your heart is not black. You may be the son of shadows, but you're pure light."

"Am I, Mom? My grandfather is a psycho. My half brother is a villain. As for my father..."

"He was kind to me. He may be darkness, but he knows how to love. Besides, you can't let your heritage define you. You're not evil. You're the kindest person I know." She cups my face, staring at me with undiluted love.

The memory of me lashing out at my former tutor and Daisy coming to his defense pops in my head.

"You're wrong about me. I used to be vile, a bully who took pleasure in tormenting people who were weaker than me."

"Do you still do that?"

I look away. "No, not anymore."

"Why is that, honey? What made you stop?"

"Daisy. She rescued me from the pit of despair. I was so lost before she came into my life." I face my mother again. "I can't let Chaos harm her, Mom."

"You won't. You're a demigod, Morpheus. There's more power in you than you know."

I laugh without humor. "If I can just figure how to tap into all this power, that'd be great. The war for Norms and Fringes has started."

"I know. It's all our community has been talking about. Hard times are ahead of us, but we must endure. Oppressed people don't stay like that for long. Rebellion is inevitable."

"What are you and your husband going to do?"

She gives me a loaded glance. "I don't know about Tarek, but I'm going to fight."

The fire in her eyes surprises me. She's been meek and subdued my entire life, living under the thumb of her husband.

I smile proudly. "I should try to convince you to stay away, but I won't. I'm glad to have you by my side."

12

DAISY

Still in the throes of mortification, I hastily leave Phoenix's room with every intention of taking a very cold shower. But I'm intercepted by Rosie, who comes running into the hallway with her phone in her hand and eyes that are too big for her face.

"The school was taken over by Neo Gods," she blurts out.

"What do you mean?"

Rufio and Phoenix join us in the hallway, but it's Rufio who speaks first. "I just got a text from Bryce. Our mother got sacked, and the new principal is a Neo God."

"Are he and Toby okay?" I ask.

"Toby is fine," Rosie replies. "He didn't mention Bryce."

"Bryce got hurt," Xavier announces as he comes in.

There's a sudden sharp pain in my chest. I press my hand against it, trying to soothe the phantom aching that's just too real. My fear for his safety mixes with guilt. I shouldn't have let Bryce go back to school.

"He didn't tell me that," Rufio replies with an edge.

"He might not have been able to elaborate. He sustained

three wounds from lightning-glass. The poison works quickly. You know that." Xavier gives him a meaningful glance.

Rufio's already pale face blanches even more. Threading his fingers through his hair, he walks away from the group. Phoenix and I lock gazes, and in silent agreement, we both follow him.

"Bryce will be okay," Phoenix tells Rufio. "He's too fucking strong to be taken down that easily."

"Lightning-glass poison can kill any Idol, even the most powerful ones." He turns around. "But I know he'll be okay. My mother will do anything to save her Idol-making machine."

And that knowledge is not comforting in the least. Not the saving Bryce part but what Jodie wants to do with him.

"Are they coming here?" Rosie asks Xavier.

"No. Absolutely not. I don't want Jodie to know this location."

"Good," Rufio says. "You shouldn't trust my mother."

"Am I the only one here thinking that if she can't be trusted, then we shouldn't be following her insane plan to build an army of newly minted Idols?" Phoenix poses the question that's been plaguing my mind since Mr. Silverstone announced his alliance with her.

"Most Idols hate us." Rosie steps forward. "How many do you think will side with the Knights? We need more power on our side."

"There's no guarantee that the Idols Bryce makes will fight for our cause," Rufio retorts.

"I have to go see Bryce," I say suddenly, veering toward the front door.

"Daisy, wait." Xavier comes after me.

"Don't try to stop me."

He places a hand on my arm. "I wasn't trying to. Jodie hasn't told me where she's taken Bryce and all the Fringes she rescued."

"Yet, right? She hasn't told you yet."

"I don't think that's the case. She's still angry that I swept in and took you under my wing. She'll keep their location a secret for as long as she can."

I'm so furious, I could break things. Rage simmers in my gut, ready to be unleashed. If Andromeda were here, she'd be able to find them. But no, I can't think about that traitor now.

"I'll turn Saturn's Bay upside down to find them," I grit out.

Xavier squints while a muscle in his jaw ticks. He's scrutinizing me big-time, but I don't care.

"You're not going traipsing around while there's a reward for your head. That's reckless behavior."

"Newsflash for you: I *am* reckless!" I stomp away before I do something I'll regret later.

To prove my point, I slide the glass door open and step outside. I shouldn't be doing that. Anyone on the beach can see me. Only, there's no one around. I lean against the back of a patio chair, noticing I'm shaking nonstop.

I was short-tempered before I turned into an Idol, but this uncontrollable fury is new. It's clouding my mind. A loud *snap* catches me by surprise. *Shit.* I broke off a piece of the chair with my bare hands.

"Holy cannoli. Did you take steroids or something?"

I turn around, finding Morpheus standing near the sliding door with a small smile on his face. Without hesitation, I run into his arms, almost sending us both to the floor when I crash into him.

"Easy there, girlie." He laughs against my hair.

Curling my fingers around his shirt, I take a whiff of his heady scent. At once, I feel much more centered and in control. He runs his fingers through my hair, making me melt even more. I lean back and stare at his face.

"How did you get here?"

"I called Mr. X, and he gave me the address. My mother dropped me off."

"And was he okay with her knowing this address?"

"I vouched for her. Besides, my mother is an ally. She's going to fight to bring the Neo Gods down."

"I knew I liked her for a reason."

He smiles, showing me his adorable dimples. "You mean another reason besides bringing me into the world?"

I hit his arm playfully. "Yes, another reason." With a sigh, I run my fingers through his curls. "I missed you."

"It's only been a day." He chuckles.

"I know. But I did anyway."

Still amused, he rubs his thumb over my cheek. "You're cute." His mouth comes closer to mine. "I missed you too," he whispers before kissing me in the most tender way possible.

I sink completely into his embrace, trying to mold myself to him. I could kiss him forever, but he's the one who eases off first. "What made you so angry just now? Was it one of those boneheads? Tell me if I need to teach Phoenix or Rufio a lesson."

"We didn't do anything." Phoenix steps out on the patio, glowering in Morpheus's direction.

"I'd rather hear it from Daisy," Morpheus replies.

"We've done nothing to Daisy that warrants complaint. On the contrary." Rufio levels me with one of his trademark intense stares, and my body reacts immediately. A blush creeps up my face, giving me away.

"Hmm." Morpheus narrows his eyes at me. "Is that so?"

I step back. "Enough with the innuendo. What did you find out in Hawk City?"

The mirth vanishes from his face in an instant, and darkness gathers in his gaze. He rubs his chin, turning his attention to the sea. "We should talk inside."

One by one, we return to the cozy living room. Xavier is in

the open kitchen with his ear glued to the phone. Rosie is on the couch with her feet up on the coffee table, distracted by her device as well. She lifts her head when Morpheus slides the door shut.

"Feeling better now?" she asks me.

"A little. But I'm afraid I'm going to get mad all over again." I look at Morpheus.

He takes a deep breath. "There's no sense in beating around the bush, so I'm going straight to it. It turns out Andromeda is not a traitor after all."

"What do you mean? She ambushed Daisy and me," Rosie retorts.

"Are you saying she's not a Neo God agent?" I ask.

"She is, but she also works for the Knights."

"I'll be damned. She's a double agent," Phoenix pipes up.

"Yep. She was recruited by the Neo Gods when she was very young and didn't know any better. Like Rufio and Bryce, she has some kind of mark that keeps her leashed to her... *recruiter*."

The way Morpheus emphasizes the word makes me suspect there's more to the story.

"The mark can't be removed?" Rufio asks.

"Not by Daisy."

"Why not? I was able to remove the block from Bryce's mind." I cross my arms in front of my chest. "Are you saying the Neo God who put that mark on her is stronger than me?"

"Oh, someone's feathers are ruffled." Phoenix laughs.

I spare him a scathing glance before turning my attention to Morpheus again. "Well?"

"Yes, I'd say he's much stronger than you."

"Stronger than a seventeen?" Rufio's eyebrows shoot to the heavens. "Eighteen, then?"

Shaking his head, Morpheus laughs without humor. "No. He's a demigod."

"What?" Xavier approaches, looking so distraught that his tan skin is pale.

"Fuck. How can we hope to win against the Neo Gods when they have a demigod in their ranks?" Rufio complains.

"They aren't the only ones who have a demigod on their side. I learned something else during my prolonged stay in Hawk City," Morpheus replies. "The demigod who's been tormenting Andromeda is my half brother. I'm a demigod too."

Absolute silence descends. We could hear a pin drop. Phoenix and Rufio are gawking at Morpheus with their mouths wide open. Rosie has visibly recoiled from him on the couch, and she eyes him with suspicion.

"Who is your father?" Xavier asks in a raised voice. His eyes wide and a little panicked.

"Erebus."

"You're the son of darkness," he mumbles, passing a hand over his face. "Son of a bitch."

"Yep. Nathaniel knew I was his brother right away, but it wasn't until we were both transported to the island of horrors to face the punishment of the island god that I discovered the truth." Morpheus turns to Rufio and Phoenix. "It was my fault we ended up on the island that day. The island god is Chaos, my grandfather."

Shit. Shit. Shit. Chaos is the *primordial god. If he wants me dead, what can I do?*

A loud roar outside sends my heart straight up to my throat. I turn to watch the sky become dark and menacing in a matter of seconds. Lightning slashes the gray clouds, and in the brief flash of light, I see the face of the terrifying god. Chaos.

13
———

BRYCE

"How many times do I have to tell you not to move?" Ellen barks at me.

"When you stop digging into my arm with that pincer of yours." I glower back at her.

"There are still lightning-glass shards embedded in your muscle. I have to remove everything, or the poison will keep spreading." She pulls out a minuscule piece, then sets it on the tray next to the couch.

Mom's secret hideout turned out to be underneath the school grounds. That's how she was able to return to the building and rescue the Fringe students. She claims she's the only person alive who knows about the location. The knowledge is passed down from principal to principal, but she burned the book with the information long ago. Meaning my father's friend won't acquire the intel.

"Okay, last one," Ellen announces.

Toby comes near and inspects the tray. "How do you know that's the last piece?"

"I've got X-ray vision, kid. Don't you remember?"

He twists his face into a grimace while he rubs the arm

Renata broke. The girl who had been part of Drusilla's posse and dead set on torturing Daisy drops her gaze to the floor.

"I'm really sorry about all the awful things I did to you, Toby."

He keeps staring at her in silence for the longest time. His ginger eyebrows furrow as if he's concentrating hard.

"Okay," he says finally.

"Really? You're going to forgive her just like that?" I ask.

"She *is* sorry. I read it in her mind."

Renata whips her face up, looking at Toby bug-eyed. "You can read thoughts?"

"Well, kind of. I can't read the exact thoughts of Idols, just their intentions. Like I could tell you weren't bullshitting me. With Norms and Fringes, I can actually hear entire sentences. It's freaky as hell."

"Shit, that's a dangerous gift, kid," Ellen chimes in.

"And mega useful to my mother," I add bitterly.

When I healed Toby, he went from Norm to Fringe. As the time passed, his powers increased. Now he's a level ten Idol. I wonder if he'll get even stronger and what that will do to his psyche. A sense of unease lingers inside of me. Still reeling from the aftermath of our showdown with my father in Hawk City, I was quick to agree to help my mother create an army of new Idols. Now, I'm not so sure that's a good idea. We don't know yet if there are any side effects to those I change.

"How is Bryce?" Mom enters the common room Ellen used as a treatment area.

"He'll live. I already dabbed every entry wound with the antidote for the poison."

I watch her closely. There's not even an ounce of emotion in her eyes. As cold as ever. I could have died today, but I'm pretty sure she'd mourn the loss of her weapon more than that of her son. I shouldn't care, but I'm no longer the dispassionate person

I was before. Daisy has woken my heart to love, and now I know I've been denied that my entire life.

"How long until he's completely healed?" she continues her interrogation.

"My advice is to rest for at least forty-eight hours."

"That's too long. We don't have that much time. I'd like Bryce to work on the new recruits as soon as possible."

Ellen stares at my mother as if she's gone crazy. "Asking him to use his gift so soon is not advisable, Jodie. It's foolish."

Mom turns to me. "You've seen what the Neo Gods are capable of, Bryce. You know what they did to Rufio. It's only going to get worse. They're mobilizing their forces as we speak. They'll attack the weak without mercy to draw Daisy out of hiding. We need the numbers."

"We don't even know if I'll be able to make more Idols," I retort, hating that I'm falling for her fearmonger speech.

"One more reason to attempt it as soon as possible."

"Fine. Let's do it now." I get up, but immediately the room begins to spin. *Shit*. I guess I do need more time to heal.

Ellen holds my arm, stabilizing me. "Sit your ass back down. Maybe you can try tomorrow."

I throw my head back, resting it against the couch. "Do you know what the Knights are planning to do?"

Toby's cell phone pings, diverting my attention to him. He must be texting Rosie. I should call Daisy. On the way here, I was only able to text Rufio. I was in too much agony. Plus, I knew that if she heard my pain-laced voice, she'd want to come to Gifted Academy right away.

"Where's my jacket? I need my phone." I look around, finding it draped over a chair nearby.

Mom walks over and retrieves the device from its pocket. Instead of bringing it to me, she swipes her finger across the screen.

"Hey, what are you doing?" I ask.

She doesn't answer, but Toby does it for her. "She's reading your messages."

"That's an invasion of privacy!" I lift my arm and try to use telekinesis to zap the phone out of her hand, but the attempt is too weak. Curse lightning-glass poisoning.

"Just give him the phone, Jodie," Ellen pipes up, but my mother ignores the nurse.

Suddenly, the phone does fly out of her hands into mine, surprising Mom and me. I know I didn't make that happen. I'm completely tapped out.

Mom shoots the nurse a murderous glare. "You'd better stay out of my business, Ellen."

"It wasn't me," she declares.

I glance at Toby. "You have telekinesis too?"

"I didn't do that either." He turns to Renata, who is looking guilty as hell.

My eyebrows arch. "*You* did that?"

"Yeah. My telekinesis is on the weaker side, so I rarely use it."

Shit. This girl is turning out to be quite the box of surprises. Maybe her biggest sin was being too weak to stand up against Drusilla.

Mom turns her ire on her. "How dare you use your powers against me? I won't tolerate that kind of behavior. I'm the top dog here. You either follow my lead or you're out."

I snort. "That will go over well with your new recruits. Respect has to be earned. Snooping on someone's phone is not the way to do it."

"I have to be on top of everything!" she snaps. "Too much is at stake, and not everyone has the drive to see it through until the end no matter the cost."

I don't know what strikes me the most, the manic glint in her eyes or her statement. She sounds unhinged, nothing like the cold and collected woman I used to know. *What's going on here?*

"Everyone needs to chill, okay?" Ellen gets in between us. "Losing our heads won't accomplish anything."

I'm still annoyed when I glance down to see what message Mom was looking at. It's from Rufio, saying that Morpheus just got to the safe house. Nothing from Daisy yet. I can't believe she didn't call. That's not like her.

"I need to get out of here," I say.

"If you're too weak to work, you're too weak to go out. You're staying put," Mom retorts.

"Am I your fucking prisoner now?" I stand on shaky legs, but at least I don't fall back down.

"Of course not. But we're right in the middle of enemy territory. It's not safe to head out in your weakened state."

"How long are we supposed to stay here?" Renata asks.

"We'll know more as soon as I hear back from Gunther." Mom glances at her phone. "He should have called by now. I don't like this."

"I'm pretty sure he's busy trying to fix the mess we left behind in Hawk City," I say. "I'm interested in knowing where my father and his associates are. They have to pay for what they did to Rufio and Daisy."

"What did your father do to Rufio?" Renata glances at me with interest.

Ah hell, please don't tell me she was also a member of Rufio's fan club.

"What he did is not important right now," Mom dismisses the girl in her blunt way. "It would be helpful if you knew the location of the Neo Gods' secret hideout."

"Your husband was careful, but I'm sure it's on higher ground. Possibly inside of a mountain."

"Damn it. That could be anywhere." Mom pinches her chin.

"We need more men on the street. I have to make some calls." She veers for the door.

"What are we supposed to do in the meantime?" Toby asks her. "And how long can we stay down here? How about food, water, medical supplies?"

"You can practice your gift on the Fringes. I want to know if they can be trusted. I'm not turning anyone who doesn't want to fight for our cause into an Idol. As for supplies, we have enough to last a week. I don't plan to stay here that long. This place wasn't meant to run an entire operation or accommodate more than a handful of people. Gunther was supposed to assist with a better location."

"I can't stay here until you figure stuff out, Jodie," Ellen pipes up. "I have a life outside of the academy that I need to get back to."

"I'd prefer if you stayed during working hours, at least. Especially considering Bryce's condition."

Ellen narrows her gaze, no doubt not buying my mother's change of tune. A few minutes ago, she wanted me to start working on the Fringes who are currently waiting in the bigger room next to ours. They can't be comfortable there. There are at least thirty of them, mostly lower levels whose families don't live in Saturn's Bay. The vast majority who escaped took off from campus.

"Sure, that sounds fair."

"That's settled, then." She whirls around and walks out.

"What's going on with your mother?" Ellen asks. "She's acting weirder than usual."

"She's sour because Daisy didn't come back to school."

"She had the right idea." Toby pulls up a chair and drops into it like he's carrying all the weight of the world on his shoulders. "I wish I had gone with her and Rosie."

I yank my hair back in frustration. "Ugh! I hate that I'm stuck here."

"Maybe I can sneak you and Toby out, so you can see your girlfriends," Ellen suggests.

Toby sits straighter in his chair. "Would you do that?"

"Sure. Spending one night out of this place isn't going to change anything."

"Can I come too?" Renata asks, and immediately, I reject the idea. She might have helped me, and Toby vouched for her sincerity, but I'm not ready to trust her or even be friends. I won't forget so easily that she tried to kill Daisy by giving her Silver-voltage.

"No offense, but I don't think either Daisy or Rosie want to see you around."

"Oh." She drops her chin. "I understand."

I sense Ellen's hard stare burning a hole through my face. "What?" I snap. "Do you want me to simply forget everything?"

"No, but you could have been kinder. We could use more of it."

"It's easy for you to say. Miss Regretful there didn't attempt to murder *your* girlfriend by giving her Silver-voltage."

Ellen's face twists into a grimace. Thanks to Phoenix's big mouth, we know her girlfriend is a Norm. She turns to Renata. "Is that true?"

Renata's eyes become wider right before she breaks down into an ugly cry. "I did. There's no excuse for that. I followed along with Drusilla's plan, even knowing what she wanted to do was vile. I was blinded by senseless hate."

"What made you change your mind?" Toby asks.

"It didn't happen right away. But I began to question every-thing when Drusilla went mad and turned against me."

I can't tell if she's truly sorry, or if now that her friends are gone, she's looking for another group to blindly follow. She could have joined the Neo Gods instead. I can't think about it now. Tiredness hits me all of a sudden. I sink against the leather couch and close my eyes.

"That's what happens when you let people walk all over you. Drusilla treated you like dirt," I say.

"I know," she replies in a meek voice.

"I'd better go check on the other students," Ellen declares in a somber tone. Her mood has definitely changed now that she knows what Renata did.

Renata continues to cry, but I'm not in the mood to listen to her pity party, so I tune her out. Glancing at my phone, I press the button to call Daisy.

It rings until it goes to voice mail. *What the hell? Why isn't she picking up the phone?* I try Rufio, Phoenix, and Morpheus, getting the same nonresponse.

"Toby, can you get a hold of Rosie?"

"I texted her not too long ago, but she hasn't replied yet."

Vises of worry tighten around my heart. "Okay, we aren't waiting until nightfall. We're leaving now."

"But we don't know where the safe house is," Toby argues.

"I don't care. I'll drive all over town until I can pick up Daisy's signature."

"Drive what car? And how are we getting out of here without your mother noticing?"

"You can borrow mine," Renata chimes in. "And I'll distract her and Nurse Ellen."

"Okay, that could work," I say.

"There's only one problem. My car is still in the school's garage."

Shit.

"We can't fight the Neo Gods, but I can tell if the coast is clear or not. I can pick up brain waves from pretty far," Toby says.

Not ideal, but I'll take it.

"Let's do it."

14

DAISY

My heart is racing as I stare at the cruel face in the clouds. It vanishes after a second, but the terror it caused in my heart lingers. It's the same nauseating feeling I felt when I dreamed about the island where Chaos branded the loves of my life.

"Did you see that?" I ask.

"That's him. That's Chaos." Morpheus stops closer to me.

"Can he attack Daisy inside the house?" Rosie's voice trembles a little.

"I think he's tethered to the island," he replies without conviction.

The storm is getting larger and moving quickly toward us. "I don't think he's bound to the island anymore," Phoenix pipes up.

"What's going on?" Xavier steps next to me.

No sooner has he asked than a bolt of lightning strikes the beach in front of the safe house, making the floor shake beneath my feet. I jump back with my hand clutching my chest. A knee-jerk reaction. My heart is now stuck in my throat, and quickly, panic starts to take hold of me. I feel powerless and alone, like I'm right back in that nightmare. Heavy rain falls from the sky, and the ocean that had been calm a minute ago becomes turbulent. The waves crash against the shore violently, getting closer and closer to the house.

Someone grabs me by the shoulder, dragging me away from the windows.

"We need to get out of here now!" Morpheus yells.

I finally snap from my stupor and seek Rosie in the room. She's with Rufio, running toward the front door.

"Don't look back," he tells her.

Morpheus laces his hand with mine, and together we run after Rufio and Rosie, with Phoenix and Xavier close behind us. We're a few steps away from the door when a loud boom reverberates against the walls, and a split second later, all the windows facing the beach explode. My time-bending power kicks in on its own, as it usually does when I'm facing mortal danger. The deadly shards of broken glass move at a slower pace, and only a few of them reach us.

Rufio and Rosie are already getting inside the car when we burst out the front door. The rain has turned into hail and drops heavily on us, each piece of frozen rock bigger than the next. Even with my time bending, I feel the sting of the hits. We're all running pretty fast thanks to our enhanced Idol abilities, but Xavier manages to keep pace with us. He almost pulls the driver door off its hinges as he opens it roughly, but he stops briefly to look at the sky.

I don't dare copy him, afraid if I do, I'll get wrapped up again in the terror. Deep down, I know the feeling isn't natural. Chaos has somehow managed to amplify everything that I'm feeling, twisting my emotions against me.

"You can run, but you can't hide. I'm everywhere, I'm everything," Chaos speaks in my mind, making me whimper.

I don't know if Morpheus heard his voice too, but he squeezes my hand tighter, right before he lets go to push me inside the car. I almost fall on top of Rosie, who is already crying. Rufio has his arm wrapped around her shoulders, comforting her, an action that makes me love him even more. It's a sight I never thought possible.

The passenger side door shuts loudly as Phoenix slides into his seat. Hail continues to fall, and the hits against the car sound like we're target practice for a machine gun. Xavier peels out of the driveway, burning rubber as he goes. And yet, we can't seem to outrun the storm. A huge piece of ice drops on the windshield, cracking the glass. Rosie lets out a scream.

"We're okay, Rosie." I grab her hand, and she squeezes so tight it hurts a little.

"Where are we going now?" Phoenix asks.

"I don't know. I'm kind of busy trying to outrun this tempest," Xavier shouts over the loud noise outside.

Suddenly, Morpheus tenses next to me. "Watch out!" he warns.

A second later, lightning strikes a tree ahead of us. Instead of catching fire, it breaks in half and tilts toward the road. It's going to fall right on top of car.

"Don't stop. Keeping going!" I order.

I slow down the massive tree's descent, and we manage to speed past it, missing it by a hair.

"That's fucked up." Rufio twists his neck, looking back.

"We're not going to get far if we don't stop Chaos," Xavier mutters under his breath.

Morpheus shifts his body next to mine, becoming tenser. "Let me out."

"Are you fucking crazy? I'm not letting anyone out," Xavier shouts.

"I'm the only one who stands a chance against Chaos. I can buy time so you can get away."

"No, Morpheus. You can't leave." I grab his arm. "He's going to destroy you."

He stares at me with determination in his eyes. "I have to do this, Daisy. It's the only way."

I open my mouth to argue, but Morpheus reaches for the back of my head and crushes his lips to mine. The kiss is quick and rough. A goodbye kiss. "I love you," he whispers against my mouth, then turns to Xavier. "Stop the car."

To my dismay, he presses on the brakes, bringing the car to a sudden halt. Morpheus is out the door before I can stop him. I start to follow, but Xavier takes off again, and I miss my chance. My vision is hazy when I turn around in my seat to watch Morpheus stand alone on the road, facing the wrath of Chaos.

MORPHEUS

My heart is pounding as I look up at the sky. The clouds morph into Chaos's odious face again. There's a wicked smile there, solely for me.

"You're a foolish boy if you think you can stand against me." His voice sounds like thunder, and I feel it deep in my core.

"I'll fight you until my last breath," I shout.

"Oh, I look forward to it."

He sends lightning my way, but I jump to the side. My pulse is racing as I try to come up with a plan. I'm a demigod, but I have no idea what I'm doing. My father was able to deflect Chaos's strike. Could I do that too? It would have been nice if the guy who sired me had bothered to teach me a few tricks while I was growing up.

Chaos tries to strike me again with more bolts of electricity. I keep jumping from place to place and soon realize the god is toying with me. *Son of a bitch.*

"Use your gifts, Morpheus." A female voice sounds in my

head. It's not my mother's or Daisy's—not that they've ever been able to communicate to me telepathically. *Who the hell is speaking to me, then?*

"He can't see you inside the shadows," she continues.

A rock made of ice hits me in the shoulder, drawing a grunt from me. More rocks the size of basketballs fall down from the sky. It seems Chaos got tired of trying to fry me and now he wants to literally crush me. I have no choice but to heed the mysterious voice in my head. I release the shadows that were already churning inside, letting them cover me from head to toe. I can still see through them, but it seems Chaos is unable to. The frozen rocks keep falling, but nowhere near me. He sends more lightning bolts that also miss the mark.

Okay, I'm now hidden from him, but nowhere close to striking back. I wouldn't know where to start. How does anyone fight a primordial deity?

"You know the answer already, Morpheus. It's in your heart," the lady speaks again.

"Who are you?" I shout in my head, not wanting to give away my location to Chaos.

"Family."

"Family? Are you a demigod too?"

She doesn't answer right away. Meanwhile, I can sense Chaos growing more enraged that he can't find me. His storm system begins to move forward. He's going after Daisy.

"I don't have time for riddles. If you know how to defeat Chaos, tell me now!"

"You already know. What's the opposite of chaos?"

The hail stops. *No.* It didn't stop. Chaos simply got tired of me and moved on. Xavier should be miles and miles away from us by now, but when the clouds stop moving suddenly, I know he's found his next victim.

Since I'm not getting any straight answers from "family," I go after the wrathful god, running so fast it feels like I'm flying.

When my feet don't touch the ground, I look down. My body is gone; I've turned into a big shadow, zooming across the land without bodily restrictions. The feeling is exhilarating and terrifying.

A blast goes off ahead. The horizon turns bright orange as a cloud of flames rises up.

Daisy!

15

―――

BRYCE

The entrance to the tunnel leading to my mother's secret hideout is deep in the forest surrounding campus. It's actually not far from our treehouse. There's a reason no one ever stumbled upon it. It's camouflaged, hidden by a powerful illusion spell put in place by a high-level Idol. Probably a former principal, if what Mom said is true.

Getting out undetected is not a problem. There isn't a soul nearby. We run nonetheless toward the dorm buildings, but not as fast as I would like. I'm still too weak from the lightning-glass poison. We slow down when we reach the path leading to our goal. There's no place to hide from here until we reach one of the buildings.

"Crap. How are we getting to the garage without being spotted?" Toby asks.

"This is the only way. We'll have to make a run a for it," I say.

Renata looks at me. "You can't run fast enough yet, can you?"

She's correct, but her observation rubs me the wrong way. "No, but I'll manage."

"Nonsense. I can carry you."

"I'm not going to let you carry me as if I were an invalid," I grit out.

"So you'd rather we get caught?" Toby asks.

I glower, hating that he's siding with his former bully.

"Come on, Bryce. Don't let your ego get in the way. The people we love might be in grave danger," he continues.

Fuck. His words are akin to a punch to my throat. I'm being a complete idiot right now. "Fine. Let's hurry, then."

Renata offers me her back, and awkwardly, I hop on. She's a tall girl, but I'm much taller than she is, and it feels strange to clutch to her like that, as if I'm trying to climb a streetlight post. She's got a good grip on my legs though.

"Ready?" she asks.

"Toby, do you sense anyone nearby?"

"No. I'm picking up nothing."

"Let's go, then."

We take off. Renata is a little faster than Toby, even with my added weight, and reaches the secondary dorm building first. As soon as he joins us, he pushes us both against the building wall and signals for silence. His spine is tense, and his face is twisted into a worried mask. I wait a few seconds, but I'm too impatient.

"How many can you sense?" I whisper, hating that I can't simply walk out of my hiding spot and face the Idols out there.

I can't even pick up on their signatures. I'm so depleted that I could very well be a Norm right now. Guilt immediately pierces my chest. I may feel this way, but I still have my powers, unlike Rufio.

"Three, at least," Toby replies. "They're about to walk out of the school's building."

"Can you tell me their levels?"

"I haven't got the hang of that yet, but they feel similar to Renata, a little stronger maybe."

"They're definitely twelves," the girl chimes in.

"Are you sure you can't read their minds?" I ask Toby.

"No, but they're restless and annoyed. Like they don't want to do something."

"Maybe they were told to stand guard in case some lost Fringe appears. You can't go anywhere without a car," I say.

"There's the bus," Renata reminds us.

"The bus stop is probably being watched too," I counter. "Okay, we need a plan, stat."

"Can't you summon even a little bit of your powers?" Toby asks.

I lift my fingers and manage to create a sparkle between them. "I don't think I can do whole lot of damage right now."

The sound of a car approaching draws our attention. I press my finger to my lips and wait to hear who comes out. A door opens and shuts, followed by heavy steps on the sidewalk.

"What are you idiots doing here?" my father asks.

My blood runs cold while my pulse skyrockets. If I had all my powers at my disposal, I'd kill him on sight. Rage is making my body shake. I clench my teeth and curl my hands into fists, digging my nails into the softness of my palms.

"We were ordered by the principal to guard the garage's entrance. He thinks there may be Fringes still around, waiting for an opportunity to get their cars and escape."

He grunts. "I wouldn't waste my time with runaway Fringes. I heard my son was here."

There's a pause, and then one of the students replies, "He got into a fight with Nate and a few others and got hurt pretty badly."

"And yet he managed to escape. Pathetic."

"Principal Fa—I mean, Fallon helped him."

"Of course she did. She wouldn't let go of her precious weapon, would she?"

He continues on to wherever he was going, probably to see the new principal, his Neo God buddy. He's gone, but the fury in my body lingers. *Until next time, asshole. You will pay for what you did to my brother.*

"I have an idea," Renata says. "Those guys might not know I helped you escape. What if we pretended I captured you?"

"I'm sure they do know you betrayed them," I argue.

"We don't know that. Besides, I just need to get closer to them to inflict some pain."

"You're going to fight three Idols on your own?" Toby's eyes go round.

"I just have to hit them in key points to make them useless for a few minutes. It should buy you enough time to escape."

I can't believe I'm about to say this.

"If you're going to expose yourself, then you're coming with us. I can't leave you behind to suffer the consequences. My father will destroy you."

She stares at me without blinking for several seconds. *Great. I stunned the girl.*

"Okay. Are you ready?" she finally says.

"Let's get this show started already." I crack my knuckles.

She gets in between Toby and me, taking hold of our arms. Her grip is strong but not painful. We walk out of our hiding spot and put on a show for the three Idols ahead of us. At once, they glance in our direction. Their faces are familiar, but I don't know their names. I was never the social butterfly at school.

"Well, well, well. Look who we got here." The one in the middle smirks.

"Where did you come from?" The second Idol narrows his gaze, watching us with suspicion.

"The forest. They were hiding in their treehouse," Renata replies.

"Bullshit. You helped Bryce escape earlier." The suspicious guy steps closer, and his friends close in. "But Bryce boy here got hurt by lightning-glass. He can't use his powers, can he?"

Fuck. They made us. I knew this plan was idiotic. Then I remember the throwing star I dropped in my pocket earlier. I decided to put my jacket back on with blood and all because of the cold, and now I'm glad I did. The lightning-glass weapon is still there. I stick my hand in it, careful not to cut my fingers on its sharp edges.

When I have a good grip on it, I send it flying straight into the eye of the guy in middle. He lets out a bloodcurdling scream that will alert everyone that something is wrong. Renata lets go of Toby and me and hits the other two idiots in their necks and between their shoulder blades. They drop like flies, unconscious.

"Come on!" I urge, choosing to run instead of letting Renata carry me. We need her unhindered in case she needs to fight others.

The garage is almost empty, and for a second, I fear her car is no longer here. But she makes a beeline for a shiny red sports car, unlocking it. No sooner do we jump in our escape vehicle than several shouts echo around us.

The engine roars, and then we're off. Renata presses the button to open the garage door, which does nothing.

"It's not working." She panics, slowing down.

"Use your telekinesis to make it!" I shout.

"I'm not strong enough."

"I'll help."

I shove every bit of energy into making the damn metal door open, grunting as I go.

"Hurry up! They're coming," Toby warns us.

I feel something sticky come out of my nose—probably blood—and black dots appear in my vision. I must be on the verge of passing out when the damn thing finally budges.

Renata presses the pedal to the metal when the gate is only half open. A loud screech follows as the top of the car scrapes its edge.

Once we hit the road, she pushes the machine to the limit, and my back gets flattened against the car seat.

"The outside gates will be closed too," Toby warns.

"Run over them." I tell Renata.

"Are you sure we'll break through them?"

"Yeah, I'm sure."

Not really, but I can't help her open a second gate. I used all my energy in the garage.

The tall wrought iron gates loom on the horizon. I brace for the impact, but to my surprise, the gate opens as we get near. I glance to my right as we speed by the security check building and catch the security guard, an Idol I don't recognize, salute us. His action gives me hope.

My train of thought is interrupted when the invisible scar on my back starts to burn. *Fuck*. I should have known the island god would return sooner rather than later.

16
———

PHOENIX

"We have to turn back. We can't let Morpheus fight Chaos alone," Daisy tells Xavier.

"I'm sorry, sweetheart. I can't let you do that. He's a god. You can't win in a fight against him," he replies.

"I don't care! Morpheus isn't a god either. Do you think he can beat Chaos?"

"Dai—"

"No, she's right. We can't let Morpheus sacrifice himself," I retort. "Pull over. We're getting out."

"Have you all gone fucking crazy?" Xavier shouts, hitting the steering wheel hard. "I'm not going to risk another life. Morpheus is a demigod. He won't die. You, on the other hand, will."

"You don't understand," Rufio replies calmly. "This isn't about what we can or cannot do. This is about honor. We made a promise to never let each other down. I can't help Morpheus now, but Daisy and Phoenix can."

Xavier takes his eyes off the road for one second to glower at Rufio through the rearview mirror. Two black SUVs stop ahead of us across the road in that moment, blocking our way.

"Shit! Look out!" I yell, and at the same time, I use telekinesis to force our vehicle to stop and avoid a collision.

"What the hell!" Xavier blurts out.

A second later, he pulls a gun from the holster he had hidden underneath his jacket. *Shit, I didn't know he was packing.* But what can an ordinary gun do against an Idol?

"What's going on?" Rosie, who had been mega quiet until that moment, asks.

"Stay calm, everyone," Xavier orders.

Two Idol agents exit one of the first vehicles. But it's not until the driver of the second car reveals himself that my entire body becomes tense. "That's Agent Torrance, the cop who's investigating my father's disappearance. We need to get out of here. Now!"

Tires screech behind us, and without looking, I know our only route of escape is now blocked too. *Damn everything to hell!*

"He's after me. Stay in the car. I'll handle this," I say.

"Bullshit you're doing this alone." Daisy gets out first, garnering a string of curses from me and Xavier.

I follow her, but Xavier stays behind the wheel. He knows that if something happens to Daisy or me, he's the only one capable of protecting Rosie and Rufio. I'd give Daisy a tongue-lashing for her reckless behavior if I didn't have to deal with the asshole cop. How did he know where to find us? I guess Xavier's safe house wasn't safe after all.

"What the fuck is the meaning of this?" I ask. "Are you looking for a second round of ass whooping?"

Agent Torrance's expression twists in rage. He hasn't forgotten the last time we met. I broke free from the cuffs that were dampening my powers in the police precinct's interrogation room and showed him you don't mess with powerful Idols like me.

"This is justice." He pulls out a set of special handcuffs from his jacket. "You either come with me peacefully, or I'll be compelled to use force."

"Why does he have to come with you? Didn't you already interrogate him?" Daisy retorts angrily.

He cocks his head to the side, watching her now with keen interest. I'd be more than glad to sic Daisy on his ass, but I know the nasty tricks he can pull. He's a fire elemental who melted Rufio's car with me in it. And unfortunately, she needs to touch someone to unmake them.

"Yes, but new evidence has come to light." His eyes gleam with malice. "It seems if you're persuasive enough, you can make the most loyal servants babble."

"What are you taking about?" I grit out, doing my best to keep my anger in check. I can't invade his mind thanks to the necklace he wears around his neck containing a vial of my blood. A parting gift from my asshole father to his minion. It's the only thing that can protect someone from my ability.

"Your old butler, Vargas, was all too happy to tell us everything that went down on the evening your father died. So, you see, I'm not only here for you, Mr. Westbrook, I'm here for your accomplice, Miss Daisy Rodale."

His arms shoot forward, and a string of bright blue electricity forms. One of his fucking Tasers. I knew he was going to pull some crap like that. But the zap is moving at a snail's pace. Unfortunately, the cop isn't. He must be wearing a protective vest that makes him immune to Daisy's power. Before he can try something else against her, I tackle him, regretting that I didn't have the time to grab a lightning-glass weapon from our stash in the safe house before we had to escape.

I fall on top of him with my hands wrapped around his neck. I can't use my powers on his mind, but I can choke the life out of him. The sound of shots being fired and the smell of gunpowder hit me all at once. Daisy screams. But I can't take my eyes off the guy underneath me.

"What did you do to Vargas?" I yell.

He tries to pry my hands off his neck to no avail. I'm much stronger than him. His face is turning purple. I'm about to crush his windpipe when a sharp pain in the back of my head knocks me off him. Then comes the shock from the high-voltage current entering my body. He could have burned me to a crisp just now. If he didn't, it's because he needs to deliver me in one piece to whoever is pulling his strings.

My vision is blurry, but I recognize the white-blond Idol with the nasty scar on his face. Delta. He was in Hawk City when Rufio and Daisy were abducted. He's Jonathan Kent's right hand.

"You're scum." He zaps me again, and my muscles spasm. I bite my tongue, trying not to puke. The pain seems to increase each time I'm hit.

In the distance, I hear the sound of Chaos's storm approaching. *Hell.* We're really fucked right now. And Daisy? What happened to her? Did she get hit by a bullet? I turn my face to where she was last, finding her on the ground, cuddling Xavier in her arms. There's blood on the front of his shirt.

Agent Torrance appears in my line of sight, a nasty sneer on his face. "You think you're so powerful, boy. But you're nothing, just a broken piece of shit your daddy liked to play with."

I'm Tasered again by Delta, but I suffer through the excruciating pain in silence. The cop turns around, focusing his gaze in Daisy's direction. He points the Taser in his hand at her, ready to fire. She's distraught. She won't see him before it's too late.

The currents of energy are still coursing through my veins, but somehow I manage to make my muscles work. I jump back onto my feet with a roar, reaching for the back of the cop's vest.

I yank him back at the same time that Rufio yells a battle cry. I turn just in time to see him tackle Delta down, knocking the lightning-glass dagger he had in his hand away. The cop uses my momentary distraction to burn my hand. Reflexively, I let go, which grants him the opportunity to Taser me again. I fall onto my knees while blood pools in my mouth.

Rufio and Delta are rolling on the ground, fighting for dominance. Daisy removed his Idol powers but not his drive. The other agents have drawn their guns, but at this time, they seem content to just watch.

Agent Torrance laughs maniacally. "I'm going to enjoy making you suffer. But first, I'll take care of your little who—"

A gunshot breaks off his tirade. His head explodes in a shower of blood and gray matter, and his body topples forward, lifeless. Across from me, Daisy is standing with Xavier's gun in her hand. She'd look like a statue if it weren't for her out-of-sync breathing. Her eyes are wide and frantic. The other agents turn their weapons in her direction, ready to fire, but they aren't protected from my mind invasion gift like Agent Torrance was. I trap their brains before they have the chance to fire, creating the most horrific scenario I can think off. I send them one of my memories of the island. They drop their weapons to clutch their heads, and then, moaning, they fall to their knees. Then the screaming commences.

Behind me, I hear Rufio's strangled grunt. *Fuck.* For a second, I forgot about him. Delta is straddling him, holding him by the neck while his right arm is pulled back, ready to strike. A blue light sphere grows around his hand. But instead of shooting Rufio, Delta sends his sphere in Daisy's direction.

"No!" I shout.

The energy sphere seems to bounce off an invisible wall in front of Daisy and changes direction, hitting one of the police cars instead. It goes up in flames in a loud explosion, and the blast sends me flying backward. My telekinesis kicks in, and I land on my feet. Rufio is not so lucky; he ends ups a few feet from me, facedown.

I want to check on him, but something else catches my eye.

The weapon Delta had on him. Without pausing to think, I dive for it, then look for Delta. *Shit.* He's making a run for Xavier's car. Rosie is still inside.

I go after him, but before I can reach him, a massive shadow collides with the scum, consuming him entirely in darkness.

17

DAISY

For a moment, I watch the events unfold in front of my eyes as if I'm stuck in a movie that's in slow motion. The gun I took from Xavier is still in my hand. I had no idea there were bullets able to kill an Idol. My ears are ringing now, thanks to the explosion. Xavier is bleeding on the ground after he took a bullet meant for me. Phoenix is frozen as he watches a massive shadow cover Delta from head to toe. Rufio is on the ground facedown, unmoving.

Unmoving.

"Rufio!" I run at breakneck speed, dropping to my knees next to him. I turn him around, and immediately I notice the big gash on his forehead. His eyelids flicker, and then slowly he opens them.

"Daisy. Are you okay?"

"I should be the one asking you that question. What were you thinking, going after Delta like that?"

"I couldn't simply watch you guys fight and do nothing."

The wind picks up speed, howling. Strands of my hair flap around my face, like whips punishing me. I glance over my shoulder, widening my eyes when I see Chaos's storm approach.

"Come on. We have to get out of here." I help Rufio back onto his feet.

Thunder roars in the distance, or maybe it's Chaos's evil laughter. I don't know. We run back to where Xavier is sitting up. He took a bullet to his stomach, and the blood has drenched most of his shirt. He's clutching his midsection, and his face is twisted in pain.

"Can you stand?" Rufio asks.

"Yes," he grunts. "Where's the gun?"

Shit. I left the gun behind. I retrace my steps and collect the weapon, tucking it behind my jeans after I put the safety back on.

Xavier and Rufio have their gazes trained on the dark sky when I return to their side.

"We're out of time," Xavier mumbles.

A strangled cry draws my attention to Phoenix. But the noise isn't coming from him. Delta is the one making those pitiful sounds. He's writhing on the ground while Morpheus stands over him, aloof and almost unreachable. That's him in his true demigod form.

He lifts his face and our gazes meet. His usually warm brown eyes are now glowing like molten lava. He's different and yet the same to me. I take a step forward, only to be stopped by a lightning bolt that strikes the space in between us. Morpheus switches his attention upward, curling his hands into fists.

"You're not going to win, Chaos! I won't let you take Daisy away from us."

In response, Chaos strikes Morpheus next, but somehow he's able to withstand the hit.

"Holy fuck!" Rufio blurts out. "He didn't even flinch."

The clouds gather close together, spinning as they form a massive system. Electricity snaps in the air. I think he's creating a tornado. The wind's howling intensifies, reminding me of a freight train approaching. I feel powerless, unable to stop what's happening.

"*You're not powerless,*" a familiar female voice speaks to me.

"*What can I do against a god?*"

"*There's strength in numbers.*"

I drag Xavier and Rufio with me, running as fast as I can back to the car. But I halt when I get close to Delta, the man who took my parents from me. Rage erupts from my core, making me forget the menace of Chaos for a moment. I want to kill him, pulverize his bones for all the pain he's caused Rosie and me. I can't think about anything else but getting my revenge. It's an all-consuming thought of destruction, of hate.

Then I hear his wicked laughter in my head. Chaos is enjoying this. He wants me to lash out, to strike the bastard. And maybe it's the rebellious streak in me, but I don't want to do anything that gives him pleasure. *Fuck that. Fuck him.*

I glance at the sky and shout, "You want me to kill him, don't you?"

"It's what you want. Don't deny your true nature, Magia. You're the Unmaker, the destroyer."

"I'm not fucking Magia."

Delta stops struggling, and his bugged eyes are unfocused .

"We're taking him with us," I say.

"What? As a prisoner?" Phoenix asks.

"Yes."

"No," Rosie butts in. I didn't even see her get out of the car. She's glowering at me, displaying the hatred that was coursing through my veins just a moment ago.

"We're ending this now. If you can't kill him, I will."

She steps forward only for Morpheus to block her. "Can't you see? If you kill him now, you'll only be giving Chaos more strength. He wants to see us fall into despair and violence."

"I don't care! That monster took my parents from me!" she cries out.

Chaos laughs again. *Damn it.* He's winning.

"Xavier is dying. Would you sacrifice the only parental figure we have left in order to satiate your need for retaliation?" I ask Rosie.

She glances in Xavier's direction and then gasps. "You got shot?"

We only get an angry rumble as warning before Chaos unleashes all his might on us. Dozens of lightning bolts fall at once. A bright light follows when they hit their mark, I just don't know what. It wasn't either of us. When the light fades away, I see a man standing where Rosie and Morpheus were. He's tall and broad-shouldered with pitch-black hair cropped short and golden eyes. His right arm is raised, and vestiges of lightning crackle against his tan skin. When he turns his face to mine, I immediately recognize him. He's Morpheus's father. Erebus.

"It's time for you to go," he says.

I feel a great pressure surround my body, and then I lose sensation completely. My world turns pitch black for a second, sending me careening into panic mode. But as quickly as the darkness overcame me, it fades away. We're now all standing in front of Poppy's Joint.

"Holy hell. What happened?" Phoenix stares at the diner that was like home to me for two years of my life.

"A god happened." Xavier leans forward, hunching his back.

I grab his arm, trying to keep him upright. Rosie comes to assist.

"Why did Erebus send us here?" Rufio asks.

"Maybe he figured this would be a safe enough location for now," Morpheus replies.

Delta, who was also transported with us, groans from his

position on the ground. He still seems out of it.

"What are we going to do with this scumbag here?" Phoenix asks.

Morpheus leans down and yanks a pair of handcuffs from Delta's belt. "We'll cuff him. These are lightning-glass. It will keep him from using his powers on us when he comes out of his punishment."

"What did you do to him?" Rosie asks.

"Put the fear of God in him." He smirks.

Rosie is not amused by Morpheus's quip. Her gaze is trained on Delta, and I'm not sure if I convinced her to forget her revenge. As much as I wanted to give in to the hate, I know it won't make me feel better. The rotten sentiment will only fester like a plague.

Felicity bursts through the diner door, frantic and alarmed.

"Daisy! I can't believe it. It is you." She halts when she takes in the rest of our party. "Oh my God. Your friend's been shot. We need to take him to a hospital."

"No," Xavier says. "No hospitals. I just need to lie down."

Felicity stares at him as if he lost his mind. "You're going to die if you don't get help."

Rufio's spine becomes rigid all of a sudden, and immediately I think Chaos has found us.

"What is it?" I glance at the sky, which is mercifully clear.

"I think I sensed Bryce just now."

"How is that possible? You don't... I mean..." Phoenix rubs his neck awkwardly.

"You can say it. I'm not an Idol anymore. I don't know how I sensed him, but I did. He's nearby."

"He can help Xavier," I murmur. "Does anyone have a working phone?"

"No, my phone is dead," Phoenix replies.

"I lost mine." Morpheus grimaces.

"I didn't have mine on me when we left the house," Rufio

adds.

"Call him from the diner. Come on. I have his number written down in case you haven't got it memorized," Felicity replies.

"Why do you have my brother's number?" Rufio asks.

"Because he wanted us to call him whenever we had blueberry pie on the menu."

Warmth spreads through my chest. Bryce and his love for pie. It might help save Xavier's life.

"And what are we going to do with this son of a bitch here?" Phoenix glances at Delta.

"We'll hand him over to the Knights. He's more useful alive than dead," Morpheus replies.

BRYCE

"Slow down. I think I just picked up on Rufio's signature."

"How is that possible? He doesn't have a signature anymore, and you're weak as hell," Toby replies from the back seat.

"I don't know how, only that I'm sure I did."

"Okay, which direction should I go, then?" Renata asks.

"Downtown."

"Why would your brother be downtown? Do you think the safe house is in the middle of the city?" Toby asks again, getting on my already fried nerves.

"Gee, I don't fucking have the answers, okay? So stop asking," I snap.

"I'm sorry."

I feel like crap now. I shouldn't have barked at him like that. *Damn it, Bryce. Get your head straight.*

A ringtone goes off, breaking the heavy silence. It takes me a moment to realize it's my phone buzzing in my pocket. I fish it out as fast I as I can, frowning when I read "Poppy's Joint" on the screen.

"I'll be damned." I press on the Accept Call button. "Hello?"

"Bryce, oh thank God you picked up."

"Daisy? I've been going crazy with worry. What happened? Are you safe?"

"We are for now. You have to come to Poppy's Joint immediately. Xavier has been hurt pretty badly, and we need your help."

"We're on our way."

"Ask her about Rosie," Toby urges. "Is she unharmed?"

"We're all fine except for Xavier," Daisy answers. "Well, Rufio has a gash on his face."

"It's just a scratch," he mutters in the background.

"How far away are you from here?" she asks me.

"Three minutes, tops."

"Okay. I have to go. I'll see you soon."

The call ends before I can reply.

"You should have told Daisy about your current state," Toby pipes up. "She's hoping you can heal Xavier."

"I know."

"Then why didn't you?" Renata asks.

"Because I *will* heal Xavier," I reply stubbornly.

"How? You could barely walk not half an hour ago," Toby reminds me.

"My strength is returning."

Not a complete lie, but I'm nowhere near recovered yet. If they didn't take Xavier to a hospital, it's because they can't. I'm his only hope, and I won't let him down. I won't let Daisy lose another important person in her life.

Neither Renata nor Toby offer any further argument, but I don't need to read minds to know what they're thinking. I'm delusional, making a mistake. *Fuck, maybe I am, but I'm not going to simply not help the love of my life.*

"I need directions to this diner. I'm not familiar with it," she says.

"Turn right at the next intersection."

She follows my instructions, and less than three minutes later, we park in front of the place where everything started. My heart lurches inside of my chest as the memory of the first time I saw Daisy comes to the forefront of my mind. I couldn't have known how much my life would change that day.

I'm out of the car before Renata has the chance to turn off the engine. "You should wait here."

"Oh, okay. Sure." Her face falls, but I'm not about to walk in there with the enemy in tow.

Toby and I stride together toward the diner's entrance. The neon sign at front says they're closed, but the door is unlocked. I walk in first, scanning the space. The first person I find is Felicity, Daisy's waitress friend.

"They're in the corner in the back," she tells me.

Before I get a visual, I hear Rosie's low whimpering and Daisy comforting her. *Shit. Am I too late?*

Xavier is lying on his back on two tables that were pushed together. The front of his shirt is completely drenched in blood, and his tan skin is ashen, the color of death. But his chest is moving. He's not gone yet.

Daisy turns her head in my direction. A gasp leaves her mouth right before she runs into my arms. I crush her against my chest, relieved beyond measure that she's unharmed. I kiss the top of her head while I drown in her scent.

"I'm so glad you're here, Bryce." She pulls back and gazes into my eyes. "Are you okay? Rufio told me you got hurt."

She drops her eyes as she runs her hands down my chest. "Your jacket. It's covered in blood."

"I got into an altercation with a few Idols. I was outnumbered, and they caught me by surprise."

"They made you bleed. They used lightning-glass against

you.”

I clench my jaw, waiting for Daisy to come to the inevitable conclusion. When her face falls and her eyes fill with tears, I know she did.

“The poison. You can't possibly have recovered from it yet.”

“I'm much better than I was an hour ago.” I glance at Xavier. “I'm going to help your uncle, Daisy.”

A fat tear rolls down her cheek, which I hastily wipe away. “Please don't cry, my love. Everything will be okay.”

I walk around her to inspect Xavier's wound. He got shot in his stomach, and it's a miracle he hasn't died yet. Those are usually fatal.

“Don't look so shocked, kid,” Xavier croaks. “I'm a different kind of Fringe. I heal faster than most.”

“Different or not, you need my help.” I glance at Phoenix, who is sitting nearby, looking positively wretched. “Have you removed the bullet from him yet?”

He faces me, blinking several times as if my voice woke him from a daydream. “No, we didn't want to cause more bleeding or internal damage before you got here.”

“All right. Can you do it now? I have to save all my strength for the healing part.”

He rips Xavier's shirt open, and then with his hand raised above the bullet's entry point, he furrows his forehead in concentration. Xavier grunts, and fuck me, I completely forgot to suggest we give him something for the pain. I'm not sure what though.

It takes a minute for Phoenix to remove the bullet. He had to go slow, and that probably made the experience much more painful. But the damn thing is finally out.

“Is it a normal bullet?” Rufio asks.

“What do you mean, ‘a normal bullet’?” I look at him.

“Xavier had a gun loaded with lightning-glass bullets.”

“Are you shitting me? I thought you could only make blades

with those."

"It's a prototype that Gunther has been working on for a while. Those bullets are difficult to make, impossible to mass produce," Xavier replies.

"I don't know if that's a good thing or not," Rufio mutters.

"It killed Agent Torrance, so right now, I'm glad it exists," Phoenix pipes up.

I shake my head, attempting to regain my focus. I'm going to need every bit of concentration and strength if I'm going to save Xavier from dying in front of us. I place my hand next to the wound. Warmth concentrates on my palm, and then it spreads up my arm. But the light that comes with my healing gift is weak, dim. *Shit.*

"It's not working," Rosie whimpers.

"Shh. Don't distract him," Daisy replies.

She's right, it's not working. There's only one thing I can try. If that doesn't help, then I'll fail.

I close my eyes to search inside of myself for the flame that represents my power. It's small now, but it still flickers brightly. I'm not sure what the lightning-glass poison did to it, but if I use my gift to heal it back to its full capacity, then maybe Xavier will have a chance.

I imagine a bright light enveloping the flame, filling it with more power. It begins to grow and burn brighter little by little, infusing me with hope. As the flame rises, my strength returns. I keep going until the flame itself surpasses the bubble of light.

My hand on Xavier becomes much warmer, and I feel the flow of energy whooshing from my fingertips. I don't dare move a muscle until the entire room is enveloped in a big ball of light. I lose track of time, but slowly, the light begins to fade, my power recedes, and I open my eyes. Xavier's wound is closed, completely healed.

I turn to Daisy, cracking a smile. Then she vanishes from my sight, and darkness takes over everything.

18

———

DAISY

I can't believe my eyes. Bryce, despite being weakened by lightning-glass poison, just healed Xavier completely. Elations surges within me, only to be crushed when Bryce collapses.

"No!" I yell.

Phoenix, who was standing right next to him, stops the fall, catching him in his arms.

"I knew he should haven't done that. He could barely walk an hour ago," Toby says.

"Why the hell didn't you tell me!" I shout.

"How could I? If he didn't try, you would lose your uncle. How could I possibly put you in the position to choose?"

"Maybe he will come back with the smell of a freshly baked blueberry pie," Felicity suggests.

"Those damn desserts aren't magical," Rufio retorts angrily.

I throw him a hard look, hoping he catches the message in my eyes to shut up. Felicity is just trying to help. He does clench his jaw, but he stares right back at me with guiltless eyes.

"Sure, Fefe. We can try the pie. He'll be hungry anyway when he wakes up."

My dear friend hurries back to the kitchen. Poppy's Joint claims their pies are fresh, but the truth is they buy them from a baker and keep some frozen just in case they run out. If Bryce ever finds out, he'll be crushed.

"Where should I put him?" Phoenix asks.

"He can take my place." Xavier slides off the table.

Phoenix sets Bryce there. He's so pale that he looks like a ghost—or a person who already has one foot in the grave. *Shut up, pessimistic thoughts. Bryce is not going to die.* I cup his cheek, which is cold to the touch. "Oh, Bryce. You should have told me the truth. I can't lose you."

His eyebrows furrow together, and a moan escapes his lips.

"How can he build an army of Idols if every time he uses his healing abilities, he collapses like that?" Rosie asks.

"I don't know." I shake my head, fighting the tears in my eyes.

"Do we really need an army of new Idols?" Rufio pipes up. "We have Morpheus, and if we can get more of those special bullets manufactured, anyone can fight."

Xavier's face turns into a grimace. "As much as I would love to put power in the hands of Norms and Fringes, not all of them are honorable. This weapon in the wrong hands could be catastrophic for everyone, us included."

"Getting my brother killed is not an option either!" he retorts angrily.

"I'm not going to die," Bryce replies softly.

His eyes are still closed, but the color has returned to his cheeks. I place a hand against his forehead, exhaling in relief when I don't find it cold to the touch anymore. He flicks his eyes open, searching for my gaze.

"I'm okay, darling."

"Is that Bryce I heard?" Felicity asks from the front of the restaurant.

"Yes, he's awake."

"Great. Just in time for some—"

"Pie," Bryce finishes the sentence. "Blueberry pie." He smiles from ear to ear, and it's an effort to keep my shit together and not kiss him senseless. But with the audience, I don't dare.

"Help me up, please?" he asks. "I'm still a little woozy."

I take his hand and lift him to a sitting position. But sneaky Bryce slings his free arm around my neck and brings my mouth to his. There's no chance I'm going to pull away from the incendiary and heady feeling of being kissed by him. I surrender without putting up a fight and only break apart from him when Xavier clears his throat.

My cheeks are on fire, and for that reason, I keep my head down, refusing to make eye contact with anyone.

"Where should I set the pie?" Felicity asks. "It's piping hot."

"You can set it at this table. I don't think we need to use it as a makeshift bed anymore." Bryce hops off and then pulls up a chair. It's clear he intends to eat the entire pie by himself.

"You baked that pie pretty fast," Rufio points out.

"Well, I just had to warm it up. What's going on with that girl outside? Why didn't she come in?"

"What girl?" I ask.

"The girl in the red sports car," Felicity replies.

I notice the exchanged glance between Bryce and Toby and the sudden tension in both of them. "Who is she?"

"Uh, you're not going to like the answer." Toby rubs the back of his neck.

"Why?" I'm leery in an instant.

"It's Renata Pomme," Bryce replies. "She helped us escape the Neo Gods."

"What? You brought that snake here?" I yell.

"I didn't bring her here on purpose. She was our driver," Bryce replies with a fork in hand, ready to dig into the pie.

"Wait. Is she the one who broke your arm, Toby?" Rosie asks.

He drops his gaze to the floor. "Yeah."

My sister's face turns bright red, and her eyes sparkle with fury. I know that look very well. She turns on her heels and sprints toward the diner's exit.

"Rosie, wait!" I run after her. As much as I'm livid that Renata is here, I don't want my sister to get anywhere near that Idol. As furious as she is, she's still a Norm. Not a match for Renata.

"Ah, shit. Mini Daisy is out for blood," Phoenix pipes up, coming along too.

Once outside, Rosie is already banging on the driver window. "Get out, you stupid bitch!"

"Rosie. What are you doing? She's an Idol," I remind her.

The car door opens and Renata steps out. She doesn't look like she's about to break every bone in Rosie's body though. She seems subdued. Remorseful. *Whatever*. She was part of Drusilla's posse. She tried to kill me with Silver-voltage. I'm not going to pretend she's okay just because she helped Bryce and Toby get out of campus. Too much bad blood to forget.

"I'm out. What do you want?" she asks Rosie.

"This." Rosie pulls her arm back and swings a punch at Renata's nose. Her head snaps back as she staggers against her car.

"Holy shit! Rosie is savage," Phoenix exclaims.

He's enjoying this a lot, but I'm actually mega worried that Renata will retaliate. Things can get ugly pretty quickly.

Renata straightens up, touching her nose. There's no blood there, obviously. Rosie is only a Norm. I notice she's now clutching her hand against her chest and fighting back tears. *Fuck*. I hope she didn't break her hand. Bryce can't heal anyone else anytime soon.

"I suppose I deserved this," Renata says. "You must be Toby's girlfriend."

"You stay away from him," she barks.

"I'm not the despicable person I was before."

I come to Rosie's side, glowering. "We don't fucking care if you've had a revelation. Your job here is done. You can leave now."

"Daisy, maybe we shouldn't be so hasty in dismissing her," Rufio butts in. "We need as much help from Idols as possible."

I glance at him, ready to lash out. But through the red haze of rage, I catch the true meaning of his statement. He can't offer his help, so he's trying to compensate for it. First with the desire to use the Idol-killing bullets, and now accepting Renata as an ally. My anger deflates as clarity shines through.

"How do we know she's not a spy for your father?" I ask.

"She's sincere," Toby replies. "I can't read her thoughts, but I could tell if she were lying."

"We can decide this later," Xavier chimes in. "The most important thing right now is to get off the streets."

"Where are we going now? Agent Torrance knew where we were before. It's possible you have a traitor in your midst," Phoenix replies.

Xavier's gaze turns darker, worried. It's the first time I've seen him unsure of himself.

"What about the Knights? They brought us to a secret location in the woods after we took care of Mr. Westbrook," Rufio says.

No sooner does he bring them up than a black SUV pulls into the parking lot. Every fiber in my body becomes tense. More fucking cops. How did they find us?

Xavier puts a hand on my shoulder. "Relax, honey. I called Gunther a few minutes ago. Those are his associates. They're here for Delta."

Two men wearing a military-style dark uniform and mean attitudes to match their ensemble step out of their vehicle and head our way. I'm blasted immediately by the potency of their powers. They're definitely not trying to hide anything.

"Xavier. You're looking rough," the tallest of them says.

"Getting shot in the guts will do that to a man."

"Where's the prisoner?" the second Knight asks.

"He's inside. We put him in the storage room," Felicity answers.

Both men switch their attention to my friend. One keeps his expression impartial, but the tall one has the trace of a smirk on his lips. "We?"

Felicity's eyes bug out first and then narrow. "Well, I was the one who suggested sticking him in there."

"I hope you did more than lock him in a room, Xavier," the first Knight says.

"Fuck off, Rick. Who do you take me for, an amateur?" Xavier heads back to the diner but stops at the door to look over his shoulder. "Are you coming or not?"

Rick and his friend get moving. Since we already dealt with the reason for us being outside, we should follow them and get back inside too. We've been out in the open for too long.

"What should I do?" Renata asks.

"Leave," Rosie replies angrily.

"Rosie, come on," Toby says. "If I can forgive Renata, why can't you?"

"Dude, just shut up," Phoenix tells him. "You're digging your grave here."

"Clearly Toby has already made up his mind," Morpheus says. "So, it's up to you, Daisy. You were the other one who suffered at her hands. You decide."

I don't need to glance at Rosie to know what she wants me to do. If circumstances were different, I'd tell Renata to get lost. But we aren't in a position to refuse help.

"You can stay, but I'll be watching you like a hawk. Give me one reason to believe you're double-crossing us, I'll unmake you."

Her eyes grow twice their size. I feel horrible for threatening to unmake her in front of Rufio, but I do need to put the fear of God in her heart. If she betrays us, it could cost our lives.

"I'm not going to betray you. I swear."

Rosie pushes Renata out of her way and stomps back to the diner. I fear I might have set back the progress I made with her. First I didn't kill Delta, and now I'm letting Renata into our fold.

Morpheus places a hand on my lower back. "She'll come around."

"I hope so. I can't allow my personal baggage to affect my decisions. I think that's what Chaos is counting on. He wants me to lose control and go on a rampage."

"There's something I need to tell yo—"

The diner door opens again, and out come the two Knight agents dragging Delta between them. He's still handcuffed with a bag over his head.

Rick looks in my direction. "Why are you still outside? There's a bounty on your head, you know."

"Come on, Daisy," Morpheus says.

Renata is the last one to follow us inside the diner. Rosie and Toby were having an argument on the opposite side of the room, but their bickering stops when the reason for their fight comes in.

"You'd better stay away from my sister for a while," I tell her.

Renata rubs her nose. "She has a good hook for a Norm."

We find Xavier, Felicity, and Bryce deep in conversation when we join them. It ceases when we approach the table.

"What's our next move?" Rufio asks.

Judging by Xavier's face, we might not have one yet.

"Gunther doesn't want us anywhere near the Knights' headquarters."

"Why the hell not?" Phoenix asks.

"Because of the pledge we made to Chaos on the island," Bryce replies.

"That was ages ago, and we more than proved we're not working for that son of a bitch," Rufio replies angrily.

"It's not a matter of trust, son. It seems Chaos is using the tattoos you have on your backs to track you."

"That means nowhere is safe," I say.

"No, there's one place, but it's a little unorthodox." He pauses, leaning his forearms on the table and linking his fingers together.

"Are you going to spill, or do we need to tip you over?" Phoenix raises an eyebrow.

"There's an underground group, older than the Knights, that has been preparing for this war for centuries. They're called the Church of the Bold and the Fearless."

"What did you say?" The blood from Rufio's face seem to vanish.

Xavier narrows his gaze. "You've heard of them before."

"Long live the Rinnegati," Bryce mutters. "That's not a church. It's the Norm resistance."

19

DAISY

Since we were transported to the diner by Erebus, we had to split up between Renata's and Felicity's cars. Rosie refused to ride with Toby's tormentor, so they went with Felicity, Xavier, and Morpheus. Which left me no choice but to ride with the girl. I don't trust her, no matter what Toby said.

Phoenix is riding shotgun, and I'm sandwiched between Rufio and Bryce. We haven't spoken since we left. I have a thousand questions, but I refuse to ask them in front of her. She already knows too much. The most burning question is how Bryce and Rufio know about the Church of the Bold and the Fearless.

Xavier didn't elaborate on where we were going, but the drive takes hours. By the time we arrive, it's already late in the night, and the world is pitch black outside. We're out in the boonies. The car's headlights reveal a welcome sign that says "Church of the Bold and the Fearless Campgrounds." The little I can see shows a place that looks like the perfect setting for a horror movie. Everything is shrouded in darkness save for the lonely lamppost in front of a large cabin.

Two men with long gray beards are waiting for us. They're dressed like hippies, wearing loose tunics and pants above sandals. It's hard to believe they're part of any resistance.

"That's the drunk guy from the bus," Rufio says, breaking the silence.

"You've taken the bus?" Renata asks with a hint of surprise in her tone.

"Yes," Bryce replies coldly.

It seems only Toby truly believes in her redemption.

We get out of the car and meet the others in front of the rustic building.

"Greetings, my friends." One of the hippies opens his arms. "I'm Harry, and this my brother Artex. Welcome to the Church of the Bold and the Fearless."

"Harry, thank you for granting us sanctuary," Xavier replies.

"We couldn't say no to the reason this all started." Both men glance in my direction, making me uncomfortable. Their intense gazes seem to imply that I was somehow responsible for their organization. But that's impossible if they've been around for centuries.

"Long live the Rinnegati," both brothers say in unison.

That's what Bryce said in the diner. It's the motto of the church, it seems. Rinnegati was the last name Magia's descendants adopted. It means renegade. Fitting, since that's what she did.

"Now, come, friends. You must be weary from your journey. We have prepared supper. Let's fill our bellies and get to know one another." Harry motions for us to follow him inside the cabin.

"I'm not sure I want to get to know them too much," Rufio whispers to me.

The interior of the main cabin is as rustic as the outside and in need of some heavy cleaning. Spiderwebs are in every corner, and the furniture is covered in a film of dust save for the main table in the middle of the room, which has been cleaned. There's a spread of sandwiches, drinks, fruit, and even a large steamy bowl of soup in the middle.

"I know it's not much, but it was the best we could put together on such short notice." Harry glances at me.

"You don't live here?" Phoenix asks.

"Oh no. We only use this building in the summer when members of our church come from all parts of the country. My brother and I have a camper parked near the lake. Your bungalows are there too. But eat before the soup gets cold."

"It looks amazing. Thank you," I say.

He nods happily and then points at the bench. "Sit, sit."

I glance at Morpheus, who is looking curiously at me. He then lifts his shoulder in a boyish shrug and takes the bench seat across from where Harry pointed. I follow Morpheus's lead, and soon we're all seated at the table, digging into the food the curious men have prepared for us.

There's not much talking while our mouths are busy, but soon the food is gone and our bellies are full. It's time to get some answers.

"What exactly is the Church of the Bold and the Fearless?" I ask.

The two brothers exchange a glance, and then Harry answers, "We're dedicated to preserving the memory of our patron, Magia Rinnegati, and fighting for justice."

"So, you're the Norm resistance," Bryce says.

"I suppose we are." Artex smiles.

"How come we've never heard about you until now?" I ask.

"We've always been extremely careful while we waited."

"Waited for what?" Phoenix reaches for a piece of bread and sticks it in his mouth.

"For Daisy's return."

"I'm completely lost," Felicity pipes up. "Why would you be waiting for her return?"

"You're in her company and don't know?" Harry's bushy eyebrows shoot to the heavens.

"She hasn't been brought up to speed yet," Morpheus explains. "You knew Magia's descendant would come back and regain the powers she lost?"

Both men nod. "Yes, it's been foretold that the Unmaker would return to bring balance to the world. For hundreds of years, we've been preparing for war."

I swallow the huge lump in my throat. *War.* I knew it was where we're headed, but now that it's finally happening, I don't know if I'm strong enough to see it through. Bryce, who is sitting next to me, reaches for my hand under the table and squeezes it. Our eyes lock, and we exchange a silent message. He's got my back.

"What do you mean, you've been preparing for war?" Rufio asks.

Harry narrows his eyes. "I remember you. You were on the bus headed downtown. You were going to Unearthly Desires. I hope now that you've found Magia's heir, you're on the path to enlightenment."

Phoenix begins to laugh and ends up choking on his drink. I drop my eyes to the table, wondering what Harry and Artex would do if they knew I worked at that strip joint and that the owner is sitting right next to them.

"Yeah, Daisy set me straight," Rufio says in a tone that's filled with double meaning.

Jerkface. He's only making my mortification worse.

"How many followers do you have? And are they ready to fight?" Xavier thankfully brings the conversation back on track.

"We have around one hundred followers in the Saturn's Bay area, but our chapter in Hawk City has about four hundred. Our numbers doubled since the disaster at the mall."

"We were there," I say.

"We know. You were on the news. We're ready to follow you, Daisy, and change the world."

Shit. Follow me? I'm not ready for that kind of responsibility. I'm not a savior.

"No offense, but five hundred Norms won't change anything. We're dealing with powerful Idols, and they mean to exterminate your kind," Rufio retorts.

"You mean *our* kind." Harry pierces him with a hard stare.

Rufio's face turns into stone. He doesn't blink or seem to breathe. After a moment, he says, "Yes, our kind."

"We have the Unmaker and her counterpart." Harry glances at Bryce. "The Maker. We can't lose."

"How do you know about me?" Bryce asks.

"It's been foretold. You found each other, as was meant to be."

It seems all their explanations will boil down to "It's been foretold." *Great.*

"Wait. Do you expect Bryce to turn your followers into Idols?" I ask, fearing that's the case.

"Oh no, child. That's not something we take lightly. To mess with the natural order of things is against our philosophy. What I meant is that your union will bring forth the God-killer. No Idol on the planet can withstand the God-killer's wrath."

"What do you mean, 'from their union'? Like Daisy will have a child with Bryce who will have superpowers?" Rosie asks, wide-eyed.

If the conversation wasn't already getting awkward, Rosie had to open her big mouth.

"Well, that we don't know. But anything is possible." Artex shrugs.

I stand suddenly, too tired to handle all the stares and assumptions about my life. "I'm ready to retire. It's been a long day."

"Of course. If the ladies are ready, I'll show you to your bungalow."

"Hold up. Daisy isn't staying with us?" Phoenix asks, and I want the floor to open up and swallow me whole. If those guys think a strip club is bad, imagine if they discover I have four boyfriends.

"I'm afraid I don't understand the question," Harry says.

"Don't mind him. He's just being overprotective," I reply.

"Oh, don't worry. Your bungalow is right next to the ladies'." Harry smiles.

"Besides, this place is safe. No one can find it unless they're meant to find it," Artex adds.

"Not even a god?" Morpheus asks.

Harry's face splits into a secret smile. He turns to Xavier. "You didn't tell them why this place is so special?"

"I didn't have the chance." Xavier stands. "Maybe we should show them before we go to bed."

"All right."

Harry and Artex each take a lamp from the counter and head out using the cabin's back exit. The path from the building splits into two a little ahead. One goes down the hill toward the lake and the bungalows that I can see as mere silhouettes bathed in moonlight. It's so serene and beckoning.

The other direction leads into the forest, which is far less appealing. The brothers take that route. *No surprise there.* The light from the lamp casts spooky shadows as we go. Rosie, who is still mad at Toby and giving him the silent treatment, steps closer to me. She won't talk to me either, but I'm not getting death glares from her anymore.

The walk is quiet; no one seems to want to talk much. I doubt the dark forest is making them as uncomfortable as I am. It's not fear of the dark. I just hate nature. It's stupid to feel this way. I'm no longer a Norm. If some wild animal decides to attack us, I can defend myself, and yet I can't shake off the feeling.

Mercifully, the forest thins out after a few minutes, opening into a clearing at the foot of a mountain. A few yards away, the large mouth of a cave stares at us. Strangely, it's not dark inside. There's illumination coming from within. Immediately, I begin to feel weak, and the guys all grunt in discomfort.

"What is this place?" Bryce asks, rubbing his forehead.

"This is where lightning-glass is mined," Harry explains. "It was Magia who first discovered the material back in Italy, and the secret was passed down through the generations. This particular source was discovered in the sixties."

Phoenix hugs his middle, leaning forward. "Fuck. I feel sick to my stomach."

"Yeah, me too," Renata chimes in.

Morpheus crosses his arms and casually takes a few steps closer. "So, it affects Idols, but how can you be sure it will prevent a god?"

"Is it affecting you?" Phoenix asks.

"Why would he be immune to the cave?" Artex peers at Morpheus more intensely.

I elbow Phoenix's arm to make him shush. He was about to disclose that Morpheus is a demigod. I don't care that these guys are supposedly the Norm resistance. I don't know enough about them to start spilling all of our secrets. And it's probably the reason Morpheus has been toning down his powers.

"Yeah, it's affecting me." Morpheus frowns, peering at the cave through narrowed eyes.

"Why does being near raw lightning-glass affect them this way?" Rufio asks.

"The crystals emit a gas that's toxic to Idols. The stronger the Idol, the more it affects them," Artex answers.

"So, it would be really uncomfortable to a god or a demigod?" Bryce rubs his chin, deep in thought.

Phoenix pulls the front of his sweater up to cover his nose. "Are we getting poisoned by standing so close to the cave?"

"No. Poisoning only occurs when lightning-glass enters the bloodstream. But staying here too long will make you feel horrible."

"That's why you said we would be safe here, because of that cave. But that means we can't stay at the bungalows tonight," I say.

"They're far enough. Did you feel anything before?" Harry asks.

"No, just now," I admit.

"Back up." Bryce lifts his hand. "If the fumes from the cave only affect us when we're near it, how are they protecting the camp from invasion?"

"The fumes rise up, creating a miasma around the area, like a dome. It repels Idols, even if they don't know the reason."

"I didn't sense repulsion when we got near," Phoenix says. "Did anyone?" He glances around our group.

"A little," Renata confesses in a small voice. "But it passed quickly, so I didn't think much about it."

"We should return to the bungalows," I say. "There's no sense standing here and suffering."

"Hold on. I have a question," Rufio pipes up. "If the fumes affect Idols, who does all the mining?"

"Who do you think, boy? We do." Harry stuffs up his chest.

"But you said no one comes around here." Rosie joins the conversation.

"I said no one comes to the campgrounds during winter, and it's true. But there are volunteers working the mines during the day. Now that the war has started, we need as much lightning-glass as possible."

My forehead begins to throb, no doubt because of the fumes. "Can we go now?"

"Shit. I'm sorry, Daisy. Is it getting really bad?" Rufio steps closer and begins to rub my back.

Goose bumps form underneath my jacket where Rufio touches me, even through the layers of clothing. The friction also causes heat that spreads through my limbs and between my legs.

"A little," I murmur, a bit out of breath.

He laces his fingers with mine and tug me toward the forest. "Let's go, then."

I feel Harry's and Artex's gazes burn a hole through my face. *Shit.* Do Rufio and I look too cozy for their morals? I don't pull my hand from his though. I'm not going to let some zealot freaks dictate how I should live my life.

We don't wait for them to guide us back. The path in the forest is pretty obvious now that my eyesight has adjusted to the gloom. However, it's clear the brothers want to remain in charge. They hurry ahead of us and then lead us the rest of the way.

The first bungalow is where I'm staying with Felicity, Rosie, and Renata. *Ah, crap.* I wonder how that's going to work. Rosie still won't even come close to the Idol girl. Harry unlocks the door, which squeaks as it opens. He walks into the dark and then pulls the switch of the light bulb dangling from the ceiling. There are three bunk beds with exposed, stained mattresses. They're probably lumpy too. Fancy, this place ain't, but I've slept in worse locations.

I glance at Renata, who has probably never slept anywhere but five-stars hotels. Surprisingly, she's not looking at anything with revulsion but rather with detached curiosity. Maybe she isn't as bad as her other friends were. But whatever.

"The linens are in this closet," Harry points out. "They're clean, but perhaps a little dusty."

"It's fine. We really appreciate the hospitality," Felicity replies.

He nods. "I will leave you to get settled. You all look like you need a good night's rest."

No sooner does the man leave than Rosie strides toward one of the bunk beds. "I'll take the top."

Felicity veers toward the closet and winces when she opens the door. "Clean, he said?" She pulls out one gray sheet and shakes it open, creating a cloud of dust.

Rosie starts to sneeze, and I'm close too. Once Felicity is done shaking off the dust from the fabric, I can see it's actually white, not gray.

"I wonder what he considers filthy, then?" I say.

"Well, did you pay attention to their clothes? It looked like they hadn't been washed in months." Renata scrunches her nose.

"Well, maybe they can't afford the laundromat. Not everyone in the world swims in money," Rosie retorts.

"I'm sorry. I didn't mean to offend anyone."

"It's best if you don't make comments, girlie. You're out of your element here," Felicity says.

Her tone isn't as harsh as Rosie's was, but she's not keen on sharing the roof with Renata either.

"Let's make the beds and go to sleep. We have a long day ahead of us tomorrow," I tell them.

20

DAISY

Getting comfortable enough to sleep took a while, but I know I've finally succumbed to slumber when I find myself in the cozy chalet in the mountains that Phoenix brought me to once in his dreams. Snow is falling outside, just like the last time. He's waiting for me in front of the crackling fireplace. When he looks over his shoulder, the bright smile that splits his face makes me all fuzzy and warm inside.

"Hello, love. Sorry to invade your dreams again."

"Don't be sorry. It's a welcome invasion."

I breach the distance between us, immediately seeking the comfort of his embrace. His arms snake around my back as his head dips. His lips are warm and taste like apples. I lean into him, tilting my head to the side to deepen the kiss. Quickly, my body responds to our proximity, and yearning hits me hard. I want our clothes gone so I can connect to him skin to skin.

But he pulls back, leaving me bereft. "I didn't come here for sexy times. You need to wake up."

My eyebrow furrows. "Why? What's going on?"

"Impromptu secret meeting. Join us by the lake shore in five minutes."

The dream disintegrates like a beautiful sandcastle destroyed by the sea. I wake up to a void that smells faintly of mildew and old furniture. I'm back in the old bungalow with the lumpy mattress. However, my lips still tingle from kissing Phoenix in the dream, and desire dances around my hips, teasing my sex. I'm so turned on right now it's not even funny.

At first, I see nothing. It's pitch black inside the room with the light turned off and the windows shut. I wait a minute for my eyesight to adjust, then slowly swing my legs to the side of the bed and get up.

I slept with my street clothes on because this place is too dirty and cold to undress. But I'm barefoot save for my socks. Blindly, I get to my knees and search for my boots. I know I left them by the side of the bed last night. When I find them, I grab the pair and get ready to leave. I'll put them on outside. But the jacket is another story. I have no idea where it ended up, and I'm not going to look for it in the dark and risk bumping into something.

I check on Rosie first. She's on her belly, her favorite sleeping position. The steady rise and fall of her back tell me she's out cold. Felicity took the bunk bed across from us for herself. She's snoring, which means she won't wake up until morning. Renata is the only wildcard here. I don't know her sleeping patterns, so I can't figure out if she's in deep slumber or not. She took the third bunk bed, the farthest one from us.

Well, there's nothing for it. I have to move if I want to get out of here.

Walking on my tiptoes, I veer toward the door. The old wooden floor creaks as I put weight on the boards, making me wince. Renata sighs in her sleep, slinging her arm across her face. I freeze and wait for one, two seconds before I continue. I finally make it across the room, but now comes the hardest part. The door hinges are old and mega noisy. We also latched the door last night.

Holding my breath, I slide the latch to the side slowly. It clicks as it releases, and I hold my breath. Renata mumbles something in her sleep. It's too incoherent for me to understand. She rolls toward the wall, curling into a ball. I wait another beat, and when the room remains quiet, I open the door. I can't do anything about the noise besides hoping all my companions remain in dreamland.

My heart is beating a little faster, and my stomach is twisted in anticipation by the time I'm finally out of the bungalow. It must be the exhilaration of doing something sneakily. I put on my boots first, then hurry down the steps toward the path down to the lake. Before I reach the end, four shapes appear in my field of vision. My boyfriends. It seems like forever since we all hung out together after our relationship solidified. I'm not sure how the dynamics are going to work out. If my heart was beating fast before, now it's racing.

"Hey," I say. "What's going on?"

Bryce turns to me, his expression solemn and hard. "I need to tell you what happened at school."

"Oh." I'm a little disappointed. I think after the sexy dream with Phoenix, I was expecting something else. "It couldn't wait until tomorrow?"

"I don't think tomorrow we'll have much time."

"Why not?"

"I'm sure Harry and Artex will be banging on your door at the crack of dawn," Morpheus replies. "I wish we didn't need their help. They rub me the wrong way."

"I don't like or trust them either," Phoenix adds.

"Same here," Rufio chimes in. "It's like they don't see you, Daisy. They have you on a pedestal."

"We don't have much choice in the matter. If their organization is providing lightning-glass to the Knights, we have to work with them," I say.

"Daisy is right. We have to collaborate with them, even if they act a little strange," Bryce pipes up.

"You're just saying that because those weirdos think you and Daisy together will bring forth the God-killer," Rufio retorts.

I raise my hands. "Guys. Please don't argue. We'll keep our shields up when we're around them. It's the best we can do." I focus on Bryce. "Now tell me what happened at school."

"My mother got fired, and the new principal is a Neo God member, high up in the ranks. Rufio and I met him when those fuckers put the mind gag in our brains."

"I can't believe she didn't see that coming."

"She got cocky and thought she was untouchable. She forgot that my father's connections run much deeper than hers."

"So, we lost Gifted Academy to the Neo Gods. Is that what you're saying?"

"Yep. The first mandate from the new principal was to lock down all Fringe students. To what purpose, I don't know. He also armed some of the students with throwing stars made of lightning-glass."

"I'd really like to know who is supplying those weapons to the Neo Gods." Phoenix kicks a loose pebble.

"Well, the Knights had a mole, and they lost a transport of weapons. Gunther told me before I left to attend Nathaniel's party." Morpheus's tone drips with contempt.

Oh yeah. With all the running for our lives, I forgot about that other hand grenade ready to detonate. I hope the Silver-stones can handle Morpheus's asshole half brother.

"Okay, but one lost transport wouldn't account for the number of weapons we've seen in the hands of Neo Gods and

Fringe gangs," Rufio rebuffs. "They must be getting their supply from someplace else."

"Do you think maybe they've found another source of raw lightning-glass?" I ask.

No one speaks for several beats. It seems my question has dropped like a bomb.

"If they did, then they also have Norms working for them. I can't think why any Norm would do that," Bryce says.

"Maybe they're been forced to." Phoenix crosses his arms.

Hell. Norms working as slaves for the Neo Gods? The idea alone brings bile to my mouth.

"This is only going to get worse, isn't it?" I say, feeling miserable.

Morpheus squeezes my shoulder. "Yes, but we're going to win in the end."

I look into his eyes, afraid of the answer I might find there. "How do you know? Have you foreseen it?"

He shakes his head. "No. I haven't had any premonitions in a while. It seems now that I've mastered my gift and unlocked my demigod powers, I've lost the sight."

"Anyway," Bryce interjects. "Back to the events that happened at school yesterday. We were able to free all Fringe students the new principal had locked down. The majority took off, but some stayed behind with Mom."

"What do you mean, they stayed behind?" I ask.

"There's a secret facility right under the school grounds."

"Your mom took me to a secret chamber once, but it was high up, not underground. I thought that was it."

"I guess not."

"How was she able to get there if the school was under the Neo Gods' control?"

"There's a tunnel that leads there. The entrance is hidden in the forest by a powerful camouflage spell."

Man, and the surprises keep piling up.

"Why is she keeping those Fringes with her?" I ask, but I can already guess the reason.

"They don't have anywhere to go since their families are from out of town, but she also wanted me to change them into Idols."

"Assuming they want to be changed into Idols. Did she ask them?" Rufio poses the question that was also in my mind.

Bryce gives him a droll stare. "Do you think she cares about what they want? Convincing them to become Idols in the aftermath of their ordeal would be child's play for her. No wonder she wanted me to work on them right away."

"But you got hurt and couldn't do it," I say, relieved that Jodie's plan was thwarted.

"And then when Toby and I tried to reach you and couldn't get through, we knew something bad had happened. We snuck out, disobeying my mother's orders. She must be furious right now."

"Let her be furious." Rufio snorts.

Feeling restless, I break away from their circle to pace in front of the lake. "We need to rethink your agreement with your mother."

"What do you mean?"

"You can't start making Idols left and right. I think the reason it drains you so much is because you're not meant to do it."

"I've only done it three times, to save your life and the lives of your loved ones." He sounds defensive. "Are you saying I shouldn't have done it then?"

Shame takes me over. *Yeah, I'm being a hypocrite.*

"I don't think that's what Daisy is saying at all, bro," Phoenix comes to my defense.

Ignoring him, Bryce continues. "Does that speech have anything to do with what Harry said about the natural order of things?"

"A little, but most importantly, it has to do with your health. I won't stand back and watch you suffer, not even if that could win us the war."

"Creating more Idols is not going to win us the war," Morpheus says solemnly.

"How do you know?" Phoenix asks. "You haven't had a vision in a while."

Morpheus meets his gaze. "True. But I know who's behind all this mess."

"Chaos," I say.

He nods. "He's not the only one to blame. The gods made a clusterfuck of things when they mingled with mortals and created the demigods and Idols. All Chaos did was pit us against one another. Destruction and violence are what give him power."

"I thought he was bound to his island though. The war between Idols and everyone else has been raging for centuries," I say.

"I think I know what happened, and why he wants to destroy you."

"Come on, dude. Don't leave us hanging," Phoenix urges him.

"It was Magia. I think that when she returned her gift, she weakened Chaos to the point he became bound to his island of horrors. But with the growing amount of violence and the impending war, he's gained strength again."

My throat closes up as the gravity of our situation bears down on me. I don't want to sink into despair, but it's pretty hard when the odds of winning against Chaos are slim.

"Those are a lot of assumptions there, Morpheus," Rufio rebuffs.

"Shit, the antique book. I completely forgot about it." I smack my forehead. "Do you think it has information useful to us about Chaos, Magia, and these foretold events everyone keeps talking about?"

"Are you speaking of the book that told you how to block me from invading your mind?" Phoenix asks.

"Yeah. I left in my dorm room."

"I'm afraid your room has been ransacked by now by the new principal. He has a master key," Bryce replies somberly, my mood sinking to the pits of despair. There goes the slim hope that I could find a way to restore Rufio's powers.

"Another god spoke to me when I was battling Chaos," Morpheus resumes his story. "She told me the only way to win against him was to be what he's not."

"What other god?" I ask, remembering the woman's voice that spoke in my mind.

"A woman. She didn't say who she was, only that she was family."

Phoenix snorts. "With the way those gods liked to fuck around, that narrows down to nothing."

Morpheus sighs out loud. "I know."

"Okay, but can we assume that the goddess speaking to Morpheus and Daisy are the same person?" Bryce asks.

"She spoke to me in riddles, refused to give straight answers. Annoying as fuck," Morpheus replies.

"Same with me," I tell him. "What did she tell you?"

"That the key to beating Chaos is to do the opposite of what he wants. We have to be his opposite."

"She told me there's strength in numbers." Phoenix gives him a droll look. "Not very helpful, I know."

"Your dad showed up twice now to save you from Chaos. Why can't he just appear when Bad Grandpa isn't trying to kill you? Answers would be extremely helpful." Rufio folds his arms and glances at the lake.

Frustrated, I find a boulder near the shore and sit down. Maybe if I gaze at the serene waters, I'll get a revelation.

Rufio approaches—I know it's him because of the lack of powers. He massages my shoulders for a moment and leans close to my ear. "It will be okay, babe."

I was already melting at his touch alone, but when he kisses me on the neck just below my ear, I dissolve completely. The fire that Phoenix started in the dream reignites. Rufio keeps peppering my skin with open kisses, leaving a trail of goose bumps. I don't want to think about our problems anymore. I just want to spend a worry-free evening with the men I love. I close my eyes, but I can still sense when Bryce and Morpheus close in.

Someone drops in front of me, parting my legs. The flux of energy that flows into me has Bryce's signature. He runs his fingers up my legs, stopping just inches from my sex. Then he kisses me between my breasts, and everything becomes intense fast. My eyes fly open as heat creeps up my cheeks. Morpheus and Phoenix are standing behind Bryce, utterly still, but the desire in their gazes can't be missed. Morpheus's eyes are actually the color of liquid gold now.

Bryce lifts his face to mine. "We want to be with you, Daisy."

"All at the same time?" I squeak.

"Why not?" Phoenix smiles. "You're our girlfriend."

Deep down, I knew our relationship would evolve to this. It's the natural course of things. But the old me who couldn't have ever dreamed of being involved with four incredible guys at once is balking at the idea.

"If you don't want to or you're not ready, it's okay," Rufio whispers softly.

The two occasions where he and Phoenix took turns playing the voyeurism card comes to the forefront of my mind. It was a little embarrassing, but also hot as hell. My pussy throbs, already on board with the idea of a sausage party. My head is the problem.

"I'm afraid," I confess.

"Afraid of what, darling?" Bryce looks into my eyes.

"That I'll fuck it up."

Phoenix chuckles. "Impossible."

"You can't know that. This is all new to me."

"Do you think we've done this before?" Bryce asks, fighting a smirk.

I push him back, then get back on my feet. "I don't know."

Phoenix chuckles. "We were never willing to share a girl before you came into our lives."

"Oh," I say like an idiot.

Bryce steps closer, invading my personal space. His intentions are clear; he wants to restart things. I press my palm against his chest, halting him. I can't believe I'm about to say this when my heart feels like it's about to leapfrog out of my chest.

"I'm game."

21

DAISY

"But not here. We're not going to have an orgy out in the open where anyone can catch us."

Morpheus glances in the direction of the bungalows. "We can find a place to go."

Bryce laces our hands together. "Come on, love."

My heart is hammering in the confines of my chest as we make our way back up the path. With each step closer to the bungalows, it drums faster. I'm on the verge of a heart attack while we wait for Phoenix to work the lock of the building farthest from Harry and Artex's trailer.

Opening an empty bungalow is child's play for him. He probably didn't even have to concentrate. He goes in first, not bothering to turn on the light. We walk in the dark, and in the dark we stay. We don't want to let anyone know we're here.

"What hap—" I'm attacked by a hungry mouth that covers my mine. Phoenix captures my face between his hands as his tongue pries my lips open.

Not that I offered any resistance.

A pair of strong arms circles my waist from behind, pulling me flush against a wall of solid muscle. Rufio's. His erection presses against my ass while his hands unbutton and unzip my jeans.

I go from nervous and unsure to horny as fuck in the pitter-patter of a heartbeat. Rufio's fingers disappear under my panties, and when he finds my clit, my legs turn into jelly. If I weren't sandwiched between him and Phoenix, I'd collapse on the floor. My jeans roll down my legs of their own accord—which means either Phoenix or Bryce is using telekinesis to get me out of my clothes.

Suddenly, Phoenix and Rufio are yanked from me. The loss of support makes me lose my balance and fall right into Bryce's arms.

"Oops, careful, babe." He laughs.

"What the hell, Bryce!" Phoenix complains. "I wasn't done."

"You were hogging her," Morpheus says as he takes Rufio's place behind me.

"Boys, don't fight. There's enough of me for everyone."

Arching my spine, I stretch my arm, reaching for the back of Morpheus's head. His lips find my neck and then my ear. When he captures my earlobe between his teeth, it sends a zing of pleasure straight down to my core.

A wanton gasp escapes my lips, followed by Phoenix's and Rufio's grunts.

"Damn it, we need a big mattress," Phoenix declares.

I hear the sound of furniture getting pushed around, but my eyes are closed, and all my senses are distracted at the moment.

Bryce is kissing down my belly, going exactly where my need is greatest. I don't think I've ever been this hungry before. When he places a kiss on my pubic bone, I throw my head back, moaning like a cat in heat.

"Fuck if that's not the most beautiful sound I've ever heard," Phoenix breathes out, his voice tight with want.

I thread my fingers through Bryce's hair, yanking at the

strands as he dives into my folds, unraveling me with his tongue.

Morpheus grabs the edge of my sweater and pulls the fabric up, helping me out of it. I took my bra off earlier before I went to bed, so the cool air turns my already hard nipples into pebbles. Rough hands cover them, different hands. Two fingers pinch my chin and turn my face to a pair of soft and ravenous lips. The taste of cinnamon fills my mouth as Morpheus's tongue dances with mine. Soon my head becomes light and my body tingles. I'm spinning on sensory overload, and I don't know anymore who's touching what part of me, but I'm surrounded by all of them. Well, I know Bryce is still busy in between my legs, as the pressure keeps building and building down below.

But greedy me wants more, so much more. I pull away from the kiss and breathlessly say, "If someone doesn't fuck me right now, I'm going to combust."

"I got this," Morpheus whispers against my lips.

Just then, Bryce sends me soaring into outer space. I cry out, clutching his shoulder as the climax hits me suddenly. Morpheus's arms go around me, covering my breasts as he kisses the back of my neck. The waves of pleasure keep coming, shattering me into pieces.

Bryce finishes his torture by placing a kiss on each of my inner thighs. Then he unfurls from his lower position, and not a second later, Morpheus lifts me in his arms.

"Where are we going?" I ask.

"Not far."

Two steps are all he needs to reach the mega mattress that Phoenix and Rufio put together.

A bubble of laughter floats up my throat.

Rubbing the back of his neck, Phoenix says, "I know it's not great, but it's the best we could do with the limited resources available."

"Hey, this is camping, not a five-star hotel," I say. "You can put me down now, Morpheus."

He drops me at the edge of the four mattresses they pushed together to make one. I doubt they'll stay like that once we start... *Oh God.* My brain is trying to ruin everything again by thinking too much. I put a lid on it and let my emotions take control. I prefer where they're headed.

I'm still wrapped in Morpheus's arms, so I untangle from them and walk to the middle of our love nest. My eyes have adjusted to the gloom, and I can see that so far, no one is ready for me.

Pouting, I put my hands on my hips. "How come I'm the only one naked here?"

I swear to God, I've never seen four guys undress so fast. One blink of the eye and I'm surrounded by the most gorgeous, sexiest men I've ever met, all wearing their birthday suits and rocking raging erections. My mouth waters.

"Dude, if you don't make your move, I'm going in." Phoenix tells Morpheus.

He walks over, watching me with eyes that glow golden in the dark. His shadows aren't present, but his demigod essence is radiating from his body in luscious waves. I can feel them against my skin, caressing, probing. I don't know if I'm imagining things or if Morpheus has learned a few new tricks.

He reaches for my hair, running his fingers through the strands. "What do you want me to do, Daisy?"

Oh shit. Does he want me to spell it out? Before I lose my nerve, I pull him to me, gripping the back of his head and sealing my lips to his for a searing kiss. I let the furnace that was brewing in my center expand until I'm burning from the inside out.

We fall to the mattress together in a tangle of limbs. His erection is already pressing against my entrance, but instead of thrusting inside of me, he turns me around and lifts my hips off the mattress. In this new position, I can have my fun with all of them at the same time. I don't need to say anything out loud. Our minds are connected, our desires in sync.

A condom wrapper is torn. I'm glad someone here is thinking straight, because I'm not. Holding on to my hips, Morpheus hammers into me all the way to the hilt. I cry out from the pain and pleasure. Rufio drops to his knees in front of me while Bryce and Phoenix position themselves on each side of me. Rufio grabs a fistful of my hair, tilting my face upward. Our gazes lock, and for a fleeting moment, his eyes turn electric blue, just like when his Idol powers used to flare up.

Did I imagine that?

Something uncoils inside of me, not desire but the hint of knowledge, a secret that was buried deep my mind and is just now coming to the surface. But my thought gets scrambled again when Morpheus hits me in my special place, and another wave of orgasm wrecks my body.

***

RUFIO

Daisy hesitates for a split second, getting a strange glint in her eyes. The emotion is fleeting and disappears when she climaxes again. Still in the throes of passion, she curls her fingers around my shaft and licks its length. I forget her peculiar reaction at once and give in to the sensations. I tighten my grip around her hair when her mouth replaces her hand, wrapping around my cock, sucking and licking.

"Fuck me," I breathe out, holding her head in place with both hands.

Bryce and Phoenix each let out grunts of pleasure when she gives them attention. A little bit of telekinesis powers comes into play, and Daisy is able to maintain her all-fours position without actually needing to brace her hands on the mattress. They're kind of busy whacking off my brother and Phoenix.

There's a constant jostling of her body thanks to Morpheus pounding behind her. It only serves to amplify the pleasure of her tongue against my sensitive skin. I don't want to succumb too soon to the sensation, but Daisy is a fucking magician with her tongue.

The first one to lose the battle is Morpheus, who lets out a guttural cry as he tosses his head back, shaking all over. Phoenix and Bryce are the next ones to fall, and soon the air become impregnated with the scent of sex.

But I hold on, the last guy standing. Bryce, Phoenix, and Morpheus have already collapsed on the mattress. *Wimps.* Daisy looks at me from under her eyelashes, sassy, naughty. She's challenging me. *All right, then. Accepted.*

I pull away and she whimpers. "Rufio, I wasn—"

Grabbing her by the shoulders, I pin her against the mattress. She falls on her back with me between her legs. My cock teases at her entrance, but I don't go in, not yet.

"You weren't what?" I ask.

"Finished," she answers.

A rueful smile blooms on my lips. "You got that right." Lifting my face, I say, "Someone please toss me—" The condom packet hits my forehead, then falls between Daisy's breasts.

She brings it to her mouth and tears it with her teeth. "Should I help you do it?" she asks in the sexiest tone, almost causing my undoing.

"Better if I do it myself."

I've never put on protection so fast in my life. Once I'm wrapped up and good to go, I hook my arm under her thigh and lift her leg over my shoulder. Then I slide in, grinding my teeth as I focus on not coming prematurely. My balls are tight, ready to explode.

I know the guys are getting busy again. Their grunts

become loud, and so do the sounds of cocks receiving hand attention. I mean, watching Daisy getting fucked is almost as good as doing it yourself. Who knew voyeurism could be so hot?

Daisy captures my face between her hands, bringing my lips to her hungry mouth. She's the devil with her tongue in every way that counts. My cock is getting harder, and no amount of butt cheek clenching can save me now. She releases my face, and her nails find my back. I lose my shit when she digs them in, leaving her mark. A primal scream comes from deep in my throat as I empty myself into her sheath. She destroys me in the best way possible, only to put me back together better than I was before.

I become utterly still, my face hiding in the crook of her neck after the final thrust. My ears are ringing, and they don't stop until I roll off her and stare at the ceiling. I'm out of breath, and I don't think it has anything to do with the fact that I'm now a Norm. She brought me to this stage of complete exhaustion before, when I was me.

No one speaks for several minutes until Phoenix does the honor of breaking the silence.

"Fuuuuck," he blurts out.

We all chuckle because he managed to capture in one word exactly the mood of this moment.

"Well, I don't think I can walk now." Daisy laughs.

"We'll take turns carrying you," Bryce replies.

"That could result in more mind-blowing sex though," Morpheus adds.

"No complaints on my part." I sling my arm to the side, a thoughtless movement. A second later, the mattress I'm lying on disappears, and I hit the hardwood floor with a thud. "What the hell!"

"What happened?" Bryce asks.

The light in the bungalow turns on, and I find myself surrounded by ashes.

22

BRYCE

"Holy fucking shit!" Phoenix gets up slowly, staring at the mess surrounding Rufio with his mouth agape and eyes that are bugging out of his skull.

I step closer to my brother, not daring to believe what I'm seeing. "Who did that?" I ask, turning to Daisy. "Was it you?"

She sits up, curling her knees up to hug her legs. "Do what? Turn the mattress into dust? When did I ever have that power?"

Rufio jumps to his feet, brushing the soot from his body. "That was my gift."

I watch him closely now, scanning for any signs that he might have somehow recovered his powers. After a few seconds, my hope deflates. He's still an empty shell.

"Dude, are your powers returning?" Phoenix asks.

Rufio's eyebrows furrow, and then he shakes his head. "No. I feel nothing, not even a spark of power. I don't think I did that."

"Well, someone must have done it." Morpheus glances at Daisy. "It could have been you, darling."

Her eyes become rounder. "If I did that without knowing, then I'm a menace." She buries her face in her hands. "Ugh. I can't believe this. As soon as I get one deadly gift under control, I develop another."

"We don't know that's what happened." I send a glower in Morpheus's direction. At least he has the decency to show remorse for his outburst.

A loud knock on the door cuts off our discussion.

"Daisy, are you in there?" Xavier asks.

"Shit," she whisper-shouts, getting back to her feet. "Where are my clothes?"

"I'm going to assume that you're in there with your... *boyfriends*."

Damn. Is Xavier going to play the pissed-off father role now? I hope not.

"I'll be out in a second," she says.

"Turn off the light. We've got company."

I kill the lights at once. We definitely don't want those religious freaks privy to what we did here. I don't think they're open-minded enough to approve of our dynamic.

"Shit. What's that supposed to mean?" Phoenix asks. "It can't be morning yet."

"It doesn't matter. Just hurry up and get dressed," Daisy urges.

A minute later, we're ready to face the music. However, the voices of several people trickle inside the bungalow. It seems when Xavier mentioned we had company, he wasn't simply referring to Harry and Artex.

"What's going on outside?" Rufio opens a window shutter a fraction and peers out. "Fuck. I think word got out that Daisy is here."

"Who is out there?" she asks.

"Judging by their attire, I'd say members of your church."

"It's not my church," she grits out, crossing her arms in front of her chest.

"They're heading to the lake, but there's no chance we can sneak out without being seen."

I glance at Morpheus. "We need your handy shadow trick, Morpheus."

"I'm on it. Stay close to me." He opens the door slowly and walks out first.

There's a group of people walking past us, but no one glances in our direction. When they're out of earshot, I say, "Maybe we should stay hidden and find out what's going on first."

"Yeah, I agree," Daisy replies.

Maintaining close distance, we head down to the lake, where a group of thirty people has gathered around the hippie brothers. Thankfully, not every single member of the church has come here. We stop a few feet from the edge of the perimeter.

"Where's Magia's descendant?" one eager woman at the front asks. "Where's the Unmaker?"

"I know you're all excited to meet her, but she's been through a lot and needs to rest," Harry says.

"We should double down our efforts at the mines," a man speaks, followed by murmurs of agreement.

"Yes, that's something you should all be doing right now. Return to the mines. We need as many lightning-glass weapons as you can produce."

"But who is going to fight with us?" someone else asks.

"The Knights will," Xavier answers, walking through the crowd until he reaches the hippie brothers' side.

"Can they still be trusted?" the first woman asks. "A week ago, our warehouse on the northside was ransacked. No one else was supposed to know that location besides the Knights."

"There's been a breach," Xavier announces. "But the mole has been dealt with."

His confession doesn't lessen the tension among the crowd.

They're jittery, suspicious. I hope the Knights' setback doesn't cost us their support. We need them to mine lightning-glass.

"Don't let troublesome thoughts plague your mind, my friends," Harry says. "The Unmaker, the Equalizer, is here. Have faith in her. Go now and let your hard work ease your worries."

Slowly, the crowd disperses. We move out of the way as fast as we can. Getting caught spying on them won't help with their trust issues.

They're almost at the top of the path where it diverges into the forest when Rosie comes down with hurried steps followed by Felicity and Renata.

"Has anyone seen Daisy?" she asks, loud enough that the church members overhear and stop in their tracks.

Son of a bitch. She had to go and open her big mouth in front of all these strangers. I know she's young, but I'd expect a higher level of maturity from her considering the type of life she led.

"Have you never taught your sister common sense?" Phoenix whispers to Daisy. "Why is she asking about you in front of all these strangers?"

"She must be freaking out. Give her a break," Daisy mutters, but I catch the edge in her voice. She's also unhappy about Rosie's outburst.

"She's not in the bungalow resting?" Artex asks, arching both eyebrows.

"No. We woke up and she was gone," she replies.

Toby joins the group, rubbing his sleepy eyes and sporting crazy bed hair. "What's going on?"

"Daisy is missing." Rosie crosses her arms.

"Oh, come on, Rosie. Seriously?" Daisy mutters under her breath.

"Let's not jump to conclusions. I'm sure she isn't missing," Xavier replies.

"The guys aren't in the bungalow either," Toby declares. "They must be together. Maybe they went on an exploration trip."

"In the middle of the nig—oh." Rosie's mouth rounds as understanding finally dawns on her.

"A little dense there, huh?" Phoenix quips, earning an elbow shove from Daisy.

The newcomers are still waiting at the top of the path, probably wondering if their help will be needed for locating Daisy.

"I think we need to come out of hiding before they form a search party," I say.

"But if we show up out of thin air now, they'll know we were spying on them," Phoenix replies.

"Let's return to the camp's main cabin. We can always say we went in search of food," Rufio suggests.

"Okay, let's hurry, then."

Even knowing that I'm going to piss him off royally, I pick up Rufio and throw him over my shoulder.

"Bryce," he hisses. "What the hell!"

"Sorry, bro. You're too slow."

He shuts his pie hole, but only because making a bigger fuss would give our location away. We run at Idol speed, reaching the camp's main building in a heartbeat. After making sure the coast is clear, Morpheus lifts the shadows that hid us.

I set Rufio back on his feet but step away quickly when I see the ill intentions flashing in his eyes. He wants to punch me.

"You're an ass," he grits out.

I open my mouth to reply when his blue eyes flash with an electric spark that I've always associated with the flaring up of his powers.

"What the fuck!" I blurt out.

Catching my tone, the others stare at my brother. "What is it?" Daisy asks.

Rufio's eyes are normal again, and there's no change in his aura. He's still a Norm. Maybe I imagined the whole thing.

I shake my head. "Nothing. It was nothing."

Phoenix veers toward the cabin, disappearing inside the building in the next second.

"Where are you going?" Morpheus asks.

"Since we're here, might as well look for food. I'm starving."

Daisy's stomach grumbles, which results in her getting the cutest pink shade on her cheeks. "I could eat."

Unable to resist, I sling my arm around her shoulder and kiss her on the temple. "Of course you could after that marathon."

"Oh my God. Can we please not talk about it?"

"Why not? It was amazing," I say.

"Well, I don't know. I guess I need to get used to it."

"You sure have to, babe," Phoenix says from inside the cabin. "This will be the new normal."

He didn't waste any time and has already raided the cabin's fridge and dumped everything edible on the counter. Sadly, it's not much.

Morpheus inspects the loot with a frown. "I think going out for breakfast is in order."

"We can't leave. Your grandpa is still looking for us," Rufio retorts.

Daisy takes a seat at the table, leaning her elbows on it and resting her chin on her linked hands.

"Are you tired, love?" I ask.

"A bit."

I stand behind her and massage her shoulders, which are tense as fuck. "Tell me if I'm hurting you."

"No. This is nice."

"There's enough ingredients here for one sandwich." Phoenix looks at Daisy. "We're out of butter and mayo. Is that okay?"

"Oh, don't worry about me. I don't need to eat right now." She waves her hand dismissively.

Phoenix's face twists into a scowl. "No dice, babe. You've got to eat. All those folks outside are depending on you to save the day."

She drops her face to the table with a groan. "Don't remind me."

"Knock, knock," a woman in her midforties, wearing a long paisley print dress, calls from the entrance. "I hope I'm not interrupting anything."

Daisy's spine becomes stiff in an instant as she raises her head off the table.

"Who are you?" Rufio asks bluntly.

Gee, brother. Take it down a notch.

"I'm Ophelia Sparks, leader of the northern chapter." She walks in, grinning from ear to ear as her gaze sets on Daisy. "I'm beyond honored to finally meet Magia's descendant. We've been waiting for your arrival for centuries."

"Hi, nice to meet you," Daisy says in a small voice.

Ophelia glances quickly in Phoenix's direction. "Oh, I see you're making a sandwich. I brought groceries if any of you young fellas want to help unload the car."

There's a moment of tension when none of us move or reply. We don't want to leave Daisy alone with this stranger.

"I'll go. Come on, Rufio." Morpheus waves him over.

Grumbling, my brother follows him outside but throws a glower toward Ophelia. Subtle, my brother isn't.

The woman approaches the table and stops across from Daisy. She doesn't say anything as she stares with a stupid grin on her face. *Gee, these people are weird.*

"Please, sit down." Daisy points at the seat.

"Oh, thank you. Thank you very much."

"How long have you been the leader of your church?" Phoenix asks, walking over to the table.

She crinkles her forehead. "Oh, for about ten years now, but I've been a member of the church since I was a little girl. My parents were also members. As a matter of fact, our involvement with the church goes back to when it was first established."

"You're kind of a superfan of Magia, then?" Phoenix grins wickedly. He's mocking her, but the fact flies right over her head.

She cocks her head to the side. "I suppose you could say that."

Morpheus and Rufio return carrying several bags between them. Since the kitchen counter is occupied with the mess left behind, they dump all the groceries on the table.

"Wow, you got a lot of food there," Daisy says.

"Harry called and told me you'd be staying at the camp for a while."

The mood inside the cabin changes drastically. Now we're all staring at the lady with a frown.

"Why did he say that?" Daisy asks.

"We can't let you wander off before we have a solid plan. The Neo Gods are searching for you, child."

"We had plans to meet up with the Knights," I say.

She looks at me in surprise. "Oh, I don't think that's wise, son. Haven't you heard? The Knights are crumbling."

23

DAISY

"What do you mean, they're crumbling?" My voice rises in pitch while my pulse quickens. Without the Knights, there's no hope for us.

"I don't know the details, but Gunther Silverstone told us to cease distribution of lightning-glass weapons until further notice. We had to change the locations of our factories in the middle of the night, and we all got new burner phones."

"What about this place? Who knows about it?" Bryce asks.

"Only members of the church, Xavier, and the Silverstone family."

"They had a mole, but he told me they had eliminated that threat." Morpheus begins to pace, troubled. "Why is he taking those extra precautions?"

"Do you think they had another leak? Andromeda?" I ask. He told me she's a double agent, but what if she's playing both sides?

He shakes his head. "No, it's definitely not her."

"If the Knights had a spy in their midst, what guarantee do you have that you also don't have traitors in your church?" Rufio asks Ophelia, not hiding his aggressive stance.

She arches her eyebrows, glancing at him with round eyes. "Our members are devoted to Magia. They'd never betray her."

My heart feels heavy, consumed with worry. I wish I could believe her words, but I've learned that betrayal can come from where you least expect it. Also, her declaration that we must remain here for an undetermined amount of time doesn't sit well with me. I didn't evade being used by Jodie Fallon only to fall under these people's control.

"Daisy!" Rosie bursts through the door, followed by Toby. "Where have you been?"

"I couldn't sleep, so I met up with the guys and we decided to come here in search of food."

Her face becomes flushed as her embarrassment takes over. "Oh, I got worried."

I'm annoyed with my sister for saying whatever she felt like in front of strangers, but I'll deal with her later.

Ophelia rises from the table. "I'd better leave you kids to eat in peace and see if Harry and Artex have everything they need. We're expecting a big turnout later today."

"Wait, more people are coming here?" Phoenix raises his eyebrows.

"Oh yeah. Harry sent word that we need more workers mining the cave."

"Is it wise to draw so much attention to this place?" Bryce asks. "Someone might be followed."

"Oh, have faith, young man. The power of Magia is on our side."

She leaves the cabin with a bounce in her step and not a hint of concern. I wait until I know for sure she's not within earshot before I speak. "We can't stay here."

"Oh, I'm glad you think so too," Rufio replies. "These people are nuts and completely out of touch with reality."

"It's extremely concerning that they're not even considering the possibility they might have a mole." Morpheus rubs his chin, staring out the open door.

The sky is no longer pitch black, which means we have to make a decision quickly before people start arriving.

"If it makes you feel any better, Xavier doesn't completely trust them either," Toby says.

"Dude, of course it doesn't make us feel better." Phoenix throws his hands up in the air.

"He asked me to listen to the thoughts of the newcomers, and also of Harry and Artex. I didn't pick up anything malicious from them. The group who arrived is definitely one hundred percent on board with assisting Daisy in defeating the Neo Gods."

"That's good to know," Phoenix replies.

"But," Toby continues.

"Oh fuck, there's always a but," Rufio mutters.

"Their devotion to Magia is almost obsessive. I fear that if Daisy does anything they don't agree with, they might turn against us."

If I wasn't already worried about them, I would be now. My heart feels like it's being squeezed by a boa constrictor.

I hug my middle, feeling completely at a loss. "What should we do?"

"Shh. Someone is coming," Morpheus warns us.

A minute later, Xavier comes in, but he didn't come alone. I sense Renata's signature just outside the cabin. Felicity must be with her too.

"Ophelia told me you were eating breakfast." He eyes all the groceries that are still inside the bags. "I see you didn't start yet."

"When can we leave?" I ask.

His eyebrows scrunch together, and his lips form a thin flat line. "I can't get a hold of Gunther, and with Chaos out there looking for us, I'm not sure we can—not just yet, anyway."

"We can't stay here," Morpheus says, dead serious.

"You're concerned about Magia's followers."

"They aren't followers, they're fanatics," Bryce rebuffs.

"And delusional," Rufio adds. "They aren't in the least concerned about a breach or being followed here."

"I know. I've tried to make Harry and Artex see reason, but they do believe the mine and the miasma caused by the lightning-glass fumes will be enough of a deterrent."

"Not if the enemy is one of them." Phoenix snorts.

"I don't want to piss them off and lose our source of lightning-glass, but we do need a plan. We can't stay here for much longer," I say.

There's also the fact that I want to interrogate Delta. Maybe I can get him to tell us where the Neo Gods' secret headquarters is. And there's also the matter of the antique book that could be in the hands of the new principal, and I need it. *Shit.* I should have kept that tome with me at all times.

"I have an idea," Rosie pipes up.

"This ought to be good," Phoenix whispers mockingly.

Rosie narrows her eyes in his direction but decides to ignore the jab. *Thank God.*

"What if we got our hands on some of the lightning-glass in raw form and load the trunks of our cars with it? Do you think it will create enough fumes to form a protective barrier around us?" she asks Xavier.

"But it affects us. We won't be able to fight," I say.

"Well, it will affect anyone trying to attack us as well." She shrugs.

"That's not a bad idea," Xavier mutters. "But we also need a safe place to stay."

"I'll call my mother. She'll help us," Morpheus replies.

Felicity comes into the cabin in a hurry, interrupting our meeting. "Harry and Artex are coming this way."

"Thanks, Felicity," Xavier says, then turns to us. "Try to keep your true feelings concealed around any church member. And Rosie, no more outbursts in front of strangers. That was irresponsible of you."

She shrinks into herself as she dips her chin. "I'm sorry. I just panicked."

The old me would offer her a comforting remark, but I can't keep babying her. She could have landed us in big trouble earlier.

She glances at me, then at Toby, who also doesn't say a word. No surprise there; she's been acting like a total ass toward him because of the Renata deal. Her lower lip quivers, and I fear waterworks are not far behind. We're saved from a scene when Harry and Artex stop by the entrance and stick their heads inside.

"Good morning, folks. Ophelia told me you're having breakfast," Harry says.

"Well, we didn't even start yet," I say.

"Oh, no worries. We just came by to see if you're finding everything to your satisfaction. There was a bit of worry earlier when the young one thought you had disappeared."

"Everything is fine. And no disappearances. We just got hungry early." I force a fake smile.

"Ophelia gave us a tongue-lashing when she saw your accommodations," Artex says. "You will have better mattresses and sheets tonight."

"Oh, you shouldn't trouble yourselves." Hopefully we won't have to spend another night.

"It's no trouble at all," Harry pipes up. "Oh, by the way, I've scheduled an assembly in an hour so you can meet everyone. They're beyond excited to meet you, Daisy."

"Great. I can't wait," I reply with false enthusiasm.

The brothers finally leave us alone, talking animatedly as they go. As for me, I have gremlins in my stomach, which make me lose my appetite.

"What's wrong, babe? You look whiter than a ghost," Phoenix asks.

"I hate being in the spotlight."

The corners of his lips twitch upward, and his eyes dance with amusement. "Really? I'd never thought you were crowd shy."

Oh God. He's thinking about my brief foray as a stripper. I'd throttle him if we were alone. For now, I settle for a death glare.

Xavier squeezes my shoulder. "Don't worry, sweetheart. We'll be by your side."

"That's perfect, actually." Rufio claps his hands, getting a crazy intense look in his eyes. "The mines will be empty during the assembly. Rosie, Felicity, and I can take that opportunity to scavenge some raw lightning-glass for our escape plan."

No one objects to Rufio's idea, but I can't shake off the feeling that bad things are coming our way.

24

DAISY

I force breakfast down my throat, despite my stomach twisting in knots. I can't afford to turn down food. With the way our situation keeps changing and with our imminent break away from camp, I have to keep up my strength.

Once everyone has their bellies full, Felicity begins to pack all nonperishable food items in bags.

"What are you doing?" Phoenix asks.

"If we're planning on going on the run again, we have to be prepared. Don't just stand there gawking. Help me pack. I'll drop this off in our bungalow before we head to the mines."

"Good call, Fefe," I say.

Bryce places his hand on my lower back and asks, "Ready to meet your fans?" There's a small smile plastered on his lips, but his eyes aren't playful.

"Sure."

Rufio bumps Phoenix to the side. "Go on. I'll help here."

"What about me?" Renata asks. She's been so quiet during the entire time that I almost forgot she was here.

"You can't come to the mines with us, so I suppose tag along with Daisy." Rufio shrugs.

She glances at me, projecting an insecure aura that I hadn't been able to pick up until now. Rosie's animosity toward the girl hasn't decreased much though. She's filled with hate, just like I was before I joined Gifted Academy. But as much as it would be easier to cling to the dark feeling, I know deep in my heart that's not the way. If I want the world to change, I have to start with me.

"You can come, Renata. We could use extra muscle," I tell her.

She smiles from ear to ear, and the gesture illuminates her entire face. "Thank you."

Rosie makes a disgruntled sound in the back of her throat, but I ignore her. Toby steps closer to her and tries to give her a kiss on the cheek, but she turns her face away. His expression becomes crestfallen, and redness spreads through his cheeks. Shaking my head, I let out a heavy sigh. If Rosie doesn't change her attitude, she might end up losing her boyfriend.

Wanting to get this circus show over with, we head out. Xavier is a little ahead of us, and I'm sandwiched between Phoenix and Bryce. Morpheus is right behind me with Toby and Renata.

"I know it goes without saying, but it's best if you don't flaunt your polyamorous relationship to the world," Xavier says.

"We won't," I reply meekly.

Xavier seems cool about me dating four guys, but I still want to crawl into a dark space. I'm not embarrassed that I love them, but the idea that my uncle knows what we were up to the night before makes me uncomfortable.

"I'm sorry about Rosie," Toby tells Renata. "She's been through a lot at the hands of Idols."

"I can't begin to imagine. But it's okay. I deserve her harsh treatment. You, on the other hand... What was your sin?"

Oh boy. Dangerous territory. I wonder if Toby will answer

that question. I'd like to believe Rosie was able to see past his new Idol status, but maybe deep down she can't. What does that say about my relationship with her? When I think we're making progress, she does a one-eighty on me.

"For starters, I forgave you." Toby laughs without humor.

"Rosie is young. You can't expect her to get over things as quickly as the rest of you," Xavier pipes up.

Maybe he's right. She was so young when we lost our parents, and I was a poor replacement. My eyes burn, but I fight the tears and the morose feeling festering in my chest.

Down the hill, a small conglomeration of people is slowly forming as the workers trickle down from the mines. There's a little stage made out of wooden crates that wasn't there last night, and Harry and Artex are standing next to it.

When the brothers catch our approach, their faces split into joyful smiles. Soon, the rest of the crowd turns in our direction, and the infectious feeling of euphoria spreads through them. My face is ablaze with so many eyes on me, all appraising and expectant. *Fuck. What if I end up saying the wrong thing and disappointing everyone?*

The crowd parts to let us through, but their murmurs of awe quickly become a smothering blanket. My throat begins to close up, and getting air into my lungs is harder now.

"You're just in time. Most of the workers have come down," Harry says.

I glance at the gathering, counting way more people than I did last night. "Did more people arrive?"

"Oh yeah. Ophelia rented two busses to bring every single member of her chapter here. Everyone is excited to meet you."

"Oh? And how many are here now?" I ask.

"About sixty, but we're expecting a hundred more to arrive by nightfall."

"One hundred?" Phoenix asks, surprised. "That's more than what you said were in the Saturn's Bay area."

"Yes, yes." Harry bobs his head up and down. "But we have members who are scattered in other states."

My panic is growing, but I can't let anyone see how distressed I am by the news. "Is everyone here?" I ask. "I'd like to address them now."

Artex and Harry stretches their necks to take in the crowd. "Hmm, I think so," Artex replies.

"Okay then." I step on the stage, and it's clear to me that the brothers wanted to say a few words beforehand by the way their foreheads crinkle. But if I'm to lead these people, I can't let others speak for me.

"Hi, everyone. My name is Daisy Rodale. I'm so glad to finally meet you all. I just learned recently about my heritage, and until a day ago, I had no idea Magia, my ancestor, had so many dedicated followers."

"We love you, Daisy!" someone shouts in the crowd, and immediately Bryce's, Phoenix's, and Morpheus's demeanors change. I don't need to glance in their direction to know they aren't happy about the outburst.

"I hope to deserve your dedication," I add quickly.

"We are here to serve you," a woman near the stage says. "Show us how."

I open my mouth to reply, but Harry quickly jumps onto the stage and speaks over me. "The best way to serve Magia is to continue your work in the mines and make as many weapons as possible."

"What about the prophecy?" someone asks.

I switch my attention to Xavier with a question in my eyes. *What prophecy?*

"Yes, yes. We're getting to that soon. But now—"

My spine becomes rigid when I pick up a different Idol signature approaching. I glance at the path, and my jaw drops when I spot Jodie Fallon striding down to us, accompanied by another member of the church, if I were to guess by his attire.

"Son of a bitch," I mutter.

"What is it, child?" Harry looks at me.

"I thought you said no one would be able to find this place," Bryce grits out.

Harry follows my line of vision. "She's with Brother Orion. Is there a problem?"

"We shall see," Xavier answers.

Jodie glances briefly in Bryce's direction, but her hard stare settles on me. "You've been difficult to track, Daisy."

"That was the point," I retort. "What are you doing here?"

"Well, since I can't reach anyone via phone, I had to track you down the old-fashioned way."

Xavier jumps onto the stage, stopping next to me. "We weren't trying to be off the grid, Jodie. There've been complications."

"Oh, you got that right. The Neo Gods have declared open season against Norms. They've attacked several Norm schools, burned them to the ground. The number of casualties is still unknown."

My blood runs cold. "They went after children?"

"Don't sound so surprised, Daisy. The Neo Gods are vile. Of course they would strike where it hurts the most. You can't hide anymore. We have to strike back now or risk losing the war."

The crowd begins to speak all at once, agitated and frightened. I guess we won't need to sneak out of campus now. I turn to Xavier. "We must get ready."

"Calm down, folks. Calm down," Harry urges the crowd. "We knew dark times were ahead of us, but let's not allow the awful news to deviate us from the master plan."

"What the hell are you talking about?" Bryce asks angrily. "They should be alarmed. They should prepare. We have to stop the Neo Gods before they kill more innocent people."

Harry shakes his head. "No one is going anywhere."

"What? Are you out of your mind?" I yell, not holding back my fury.

"Your friends can go, but you and the white-haired boy must stay," Artex replies calmly.

"Why?"

"The prophecy," Morpheus replies bitterly. "They want you to make the God-killer."

25

RUFIO

I grind my teeth as I try to make as little sound as possible creeping through the forest. Unfortunately, my companions sound like a pair of rhinos stomping behind me. I glance over my shoulder and hiss, "Could you please make less noise? We're trying to be inconspicuous here."

"Sorry," Rosie mumbles under her breath.

I pause suddenly when I hear voices getting nearer and raise my hand, signaling for them to do the same. We're not on the path, but any sudden movement might give away our location. We definitely don't want to be caught going to the mines. I pay attention to the topic of conversation, hoping to get some intel about our hosts, but the two guys walking down the path are talking about a game they watched last night.

We don't move until their voices fade away. Then we continue our trek slowly, a pace I set to compensate for my companions' lack of grace. When the forest begins to thin out, we stay hidden behind some bushes and pause to make sure the mines are truly empty.

"What are we waiting for?" Rosie asks.

"I want to be certain those guys we saw were the last workers coming from the cave."

"I don't hear anything," Felicity pipes up. "It'd be nice to have Idol super senses."

I grind my teeth, irritated that her comment reminds me of what I've lost. If I don't think too much about it, I can pretend everything is fine. At least Daisy isn't here to see the truth on my face. I don't know want her to feel guiltier than she does already.

"Just wait another minute," I say.

Even without Idol senses, I can tell Rosie and Felicity are not very patient. I'm on edge too; the sooner we get this mission underway, the sooner we'll be done. But ruining the entire operation because we jumped the gun would be stupid.

"Okay, the place has been quiet for a while," I say after a few minutes have passed. "Let's go."

I sprint toward the mouth of the cave, but I stop just at the entrance, flattening my body against the stony wall to slowly stick my head inside. Thanks to the illumination, I can see the tunnel goes on for miles. I go in first, careful to not make any noise. Sound carries here. Along the way, I spot axes and picks meant to cut the rocks. But so far, no sign of lightning-glass. I wonder what it looks like in its raw form. We walk for about a minute until I have my answer. The uneven rocky surface gives way to a deep blue quartz-like material that shines under the dim light. My jaw drops as I move closer.

"Wow. It looks like a starry sky," Felicity murmurs.

I touch the wall, still in awe that something so beautiful can be deadly to Idols. Was this material on Earth from the beginning of time, or was it put here by another capricious deity?

"Hey, Rufio. Over here," Rosie hisses. "I've found something."

Felicity and I stride toward her. She's standing in front of a pile of rough-cut lightning-glass stones.

"Bingo," I say.

"They're so big." Felicity wraps her arms around one and tries to lift. "Ugh. It weighs a ton too. I might be able to only carry the smaller ones."

I attempt to grab the one she couldn't, and to my dismay, I struggle with it too. "Shit. This is not good. We're going to need more than three small stones, and making this trip several times is not an option."

"They must be transporting the stones somehow." Rosie glances around.

"Right. Let's see if there's a mine cart somewhere," I say.

We veer farther down the tunnel, and it takes another minute to find a wheelbarrow. I push forward slowly, but the progress back to the lightning-glass stones is too noisy, and it echoes loudly against the high walls of the cave. There's nothing for it though. We just have to work quickly and get out of here. I start with the largest stones, trying not to grunt as I lift them into the barrow. *Fuck, I hate being a puny Norm.*

After the bottom of the cart is covered with the larger stones, Rosie and Felicity fill the gaps with the smaller units.

"It's enough. We don't want to make the pile too high or we might lose some on the way back," I tell them.

"Can you push the load?" Felicity asks.

My normal reaction would be to give her a droll stare, but in my new state, who knows if I can actually lift this shit? I take a deep breath before I go for it. My muscles strain with the effort, but I clench my teeth and suffer in silence. Once I begin to move, it becomes easier. But the racket of the wheel and stones bouncing against the metal barrow is making me anxious. I'll feel better once we're out of the cave. Sweat pools on my forehead, and my breathing is already coming out in bursts. *Jeez, I think I need to add physical conditioning to my daily routine. I'm so weak, it's not even funny.*

When I see the mouth of the cave get near, it injects me

with a burst of strength. I quicken my pace, eager to get out of this place. But thanks to my lack of Idol powers, I don't notice we're no longer alone until two miners block our way.

"Where do you think you're going with those rocks, lad?" a man with a ginger beard rasps in a thick Scottish accent.

"Uh, Harry asked us to help while you were busy at the assembly. You know, we can't waste any time," I reply.

The man rubs his beard, watching me through slits. "Harry asked you, huh?"

"Yeah, he did," Felicity replies.

Scottish man glances at his companion. "What do you think, Stone?"

Stone, who is a short and wiry man with thinning hair and eyes that are too big for his gaunt face, replies, "Harry would never send strangers into the mines without training. I'd say they're lying, Wallace."

The Scottish guy turns to us, and judging by the fury raging in his eyes, I'd say we're in trouble.

"I knew it! You're thieves. Sound the alarm, Stone."

Ah fuck. We can't have that.

Without a second thought, I break into a run, pushing the wheelbarrow as fast as I can. I hit the big Scottish guy before he can move out of the way. The impact sends him to the ground, but I lose some of my load in the process. He lets out a roar as one of the bigger pieces falls on his leg. From the corner of my eye, I catch Stone making a beeline to the forest to no doubt sound the alarm. But Felicity and Rosie run after him.

The waitress catches him first by jumping on his back. The momentum sends both of them down. I'd go after to help, but the seconds I was distracted cost me. Wallace tackles me to the ground, knocking the wind out of me. Stunned, I don't offer resistance in the beginning, which gives the burly man the advantage. He straddles me and curls his fingers around my neck. Adrenaline finally spurs me into action, but as hard as I fight the man, I can't pry his hands off my neck. Dark spots are already speckling my vision from the lack of oxygen. Desperation makes me search inside of me for my Idol spark. A foolish hope. There's nothing but an empty void there.

Suddenly, Wallace's hold on me slackens, and he falls to the side. My vision is blurry, but when it returns to normal, I find Rosie peering down at me, holding a smaller lightning-glass stone in her hand.

"Are you okay?" she asks.

I rub my neck, finding it tender to the touch. "I will be in a moment," I croak.

Felicity joins us and then offers me her hand. "That was close."

"I know. Thank you." I look beyond them, searching for Stone. I find him down, unmoving. "What did you do to him?"

"The same thing I did to that guy over there." Rosie points at Wallace. "Knocked him unconscious." She tosses up the stone in her hand, catching it again with dexterity. "These are good in raw form too."

"We have to move. It's possible someone overheard the ruckus." I straighten the wheelbarrow and then fill it up again.

"Wait. We can't just leave these guys here," Felicity says. "The moment they're found, or they come to, they'll sound the alarm."

I curse under my breath. She's right. *Shit.* I drop the wheelbarrow and run back to the cave. "Stay here. I'm going to look for a cord to tie them up."

I'm lucky that there are a few rolls of cord right at the entrance. I return to the girls as quickly as I can, but the laborious work of dragging the passed-out Norms out of the open takes time. We move them to the forest and tie them up to a tree that's concealed by heavy shrubbery.

"We have to gag them," Rosie says.

"I know." I take off my jacket and then rip off strips of my T-shirt.

Rosie and Felicity giggle.

"What's so funny?" I ask, irritated.

"Your shirt's like a girlie crop top now. You look hilarious," Rosie replies.

"Hahaha. Yeah, it's hilarious. Quit laughing and help me here." I toss a strip in their direction, not caring who catches it.

Two minutes later, we return to the abandoned wheelbarrow and reload the stones as quickly as we can. When we finally veer toward the forest, my anxiety levels have risen through the roof. And to think Daisy lived most of her life like this, afraid of what or who was going to harm her and her sister. I feel so wretched now that I'm walking in her shoes, not because I'm sorry for my fate but because I'm ashamed of how badly I treated Norms and Fringes in the past.

Letting depression take hold of my emotions won't help me, so I push it to a far corner of my mind and focus on the task at hand. It's a little hard to navigate uneven ground, but it's the only way we can be sure to not get caught. By my calculations and the steepness of the terrain, I'd say we're about halfway to our final destination: the campgrounds' parking area. We have to load the stones into Felicity's and Renata's car trunks and then return to the assembly. Eventually, those mine workers will be missed, and a search party will be sent out. We can't be anywhere near here when they're found.

The forest is thinning out, and the best part is I don't hear a sound coming from up ahead. Hopefully the parking lot is truly deserted. I begin to let myself believe everything will turn out okay when cold dread licks the back of my neck, sending ripples of worry down my spine.

Bryce is in trouble.

26

BRYCE

"What kind of nonsense is that? Make a God-killer? There isn't such a thing!" I yell, losing my temper.

"Bryce...," Mom starts.

"What? Did you know about this?" I laugh without humor. "Why am I asking? Of course you knew."

"I don't understand. How can we make a God-killer?" Daisy asks Harry, who is watching our meltdown with amused curiosity.

If he makes some kind of asinine comment, I'm going to wipe that fucking grin off his face with my bare hands. I know I'm blowing up faster than normal. I can usually control my emotions better. I guess I should say "could." It's been a while since I've turned into a short-fused person like Rufio used to be.

Artex rubs the back of his head, getting flustered all of a sudden. "Well, the prophecy doesn't spell out the details of how. We've always assumed it was talking about the conception of a child."

I pinch the bridge of my nose and count to ten in my head.

"Let me get this straight," Phoenix butts in. "You want Bryce to knock Daisy up and then wait for their child to grow up to then fight the Neo Gods. Is that your master plan?"

"Uh, we've always assumed that was the purpose of their child. To free us all from the oppressing hands of the Neo Gods and the evil deities they answer to," Ophelia replies.

"But by then it will be too late. The Neo Gods will have decimated the entire Norm and Fringe population," Daisy argues. "We can't wait!"

Xavier hugs her sideways, taking a protective stance. His expression leaves no room for doubt. Anyone who tries to harm or force Daisy into anything will feel his wrath. And not the wrath of a level six Fringe. Xavier is now an Idol, probably level twelve. Things have moved so fast that it didn't even occur to me to scan his powers, plus the guy masks them on a daily basis. But not now. He's broadcasting his abilities to everyone.

"You healed him, didn't you?" Mom whispers to me.

"Yes," I hiss.

"Perhaps we should rethink our plan," Ophelia muses. "Maybe Daisy ought to fight the Neo Gods before she can fulfill the prophecy."

Her suggestion meets with approval from half the people in the audience. Even Artex seems unsure how to proceed now. Not his brother Harry. There's a crazy glint in his eyes that doesn't give me comfort. Well, dealing with one fanatic Norm won't be a problem. The issue is the rest of the assembly that's on his side.

"When you said the deity the Neo Gods answer to, who were you referring to?" Morpheus asks.

"A name was never mentioned, but we suspect it's a primordial god," Ophelia answers.

I lock gazes with Morpheus, and I can almost read his mind. The prophecy must be speaking about Chaos. It has to be.

"We should wait until the leaders of the other chapters arrive and put it to a vote," Harry declares.

I'm about to blow the guy to smithereens, but Phoenix steps in front of him, invading his personal space. "There's no vote. You have no say over our lives. I don't fucking care how long you've been worshipping Daisy's ancestor. We're leaving now, and that's final."

Toby slinks closer to me and pulls on my sleeve to get my attention. "We shouldn't be going head-to-head with Harry. I'm picking up a lot of bad intentions from the crowd. They're armed to the teeth with lightning-glass weapons, including throwing stars."

"Fuck." I search the crowd, noticing immediately the change in their demeanor. If they're all armed, they can overpower us easily. There are too many of them.

In the distance, I see Rufio running toward us, followed by Rosie and Felicity. He looks agitated, and he's also missing half of his shirt. Either he knows we're in trouble or he's running away from some. *Hell and damn. How the fuck did we go from the frying pan into the fire?*

"Phoenix, calm down." Morpheus pulls him back.

"Yes, you'd better cool your jets, boy," Harry replies in a cold voice.

Rufio has finally reached us. He's out of breath and sweating like a pig. "What's going on? What is she doing here?" He glares at Mom.

"I came because the Neo Gods attacked, and we need every Idol on the streets fighting them off, not holed up in some camp in the middle of nowhere."

"They won't let us go because they want Bryce and Daisy to make a baby first," Renata adds.

How can anyone hear that and not think the idea is ludicrous?

"What?" Rufio, Felicity, and Rosie say together in high-pitched tones.

"This has to happen," Morpheus declares, and at first, I think I heard him wrong, but when I catch his gaze, there's a plea there for me to follow along. But unfortunately, I'm the only one who caught Morpheus's silent message. Phoenix's feathers are ruffled, and he's ready to blow.

"Let Morpheus speak, bro," I tell him.

"Yes, of course it must happen. I'm glad at least someone in Daisy's party can see the light," Harry pipes up.

"It will happen, but there's something you're missing. A very important detail," Morpheus continues.

Harry sharpens his gaze, rubbing his long beard. "What detail?"

"In order for conception to occur, Daisy and Bryce must be united by the infinity band first."

My stomach bottoms out. I know what he's doing; he's trying to buy us time, because only an Idol who is more powerful than the couple can perform the ceremony. Meaning Morpheus is the only one who can do it. But it's not fair that his vision will come to pass in order to trick some fanatics. I love Daisy with all my heart and soul, and yes, the idea of an infinity band vow doesn't scare me now as it did when I first learned of Morpheus's vision. But the circumstances are making me nauseated. This will be the most important moment of our lives, and now it's been soiled by these fucking hippies.

"What's that?" someone in the crowd asks.

"It's a powerful magic binding. It lasts for all eternity," Ophelia replies. "It makes sense that it must happen first."

"There's only one problem," Harry butts in, looking as amused as a prickly bear. "We need an Idol more powerful than Daisy and Bryce, which means more delays."

"No delays. You have someone more powerful than both of us standing right in front of you," I say.

Harry furrows his bushy eyebrows. "Who?"

Morpheus steps forward, letting go of the damper he had on his powers. "Me."

Gasps echo all around us as they realize Morpheus is in reality the most powerful being they've ever seen in their entire lives. A demigod.

Harry and Artex shuffle backward until they literally fall off the stage, a fact that gives me great satisfaction.

"You've deceived us," Harry babbles.

"A necessary precaution. I'm Daisy's guardian. Therefore, if I suspect any of you have any ill intentions toward her or her party, you *will* regret it."

"Oh snap," Toby mutters under his breath. "Lots of cursing popping around."

"Do we need to run?" I ask in a whisper.

"No. Morpheus's power display has made the most aggressive ones wary. They won't dare attack now. But they aren't happy."

"That's absurd. We have no intentions of harming Daisy. She's our savior," Ophelia retorts, clearly offended by his remark.

Morpheus's tough-as-nails expression doesn't waver. "You've been warned. The ritual will take place tonight. I suggest you return to your duties in the mines."

"Why at night and not now?" Harry asks.

"This is the way. Don't argue with me."

Artex's eyes widen, and almost immediately he clutches his brother's arms. I can sense Morpheus is using his fearmancer gift on the weaker link of the duo.

"Listen to him, Harry. We should definitely listen to him," the man says.

"Fine. We'll reconvene here after sunset."

The crowd disperses, but their footsteps are slow and lacking enthusiasm. It makes me wonder how many are truly working the mines voluntarily.

"I must finish cleaning up your bungalow. We can't have a demigod sleeping in filth," Ophelia declares, bolting up the path with three other members.

"Do you need anything for the ritual?" Artex asks through a shaky voice. Morpheus hasn't released his grip on him yet. *Good.* I wish it were Harry who was suffering, but his time will come.

"No, just peace and quiet. I don't want anyone bothering us until nightfall."

Harry grunts, openly glaring at us. "As you wish."

He and his brother soon depart, and it's not until they disappear from our sight into the forest that Phoenix whirls around and jumps on Morpheus.

"What the hell was that all about?"

"Phoenix, babe, relax. It's all going to work out." Daisy touches his back.

"So, what's your plan?" Rufio butts in. "Surely you're not going to wait until nightfall to escape this camp from hell?"

"Of course not. But I had to get rid of that mob before they turned against us."

"If we displease those fools, we can say goodbye to our supply of lightning-glass weapons," my mother pipes up.

"Are you saying those religious freaks have complete control of all the lightning-glass mines?" Felicity asks.

"I believe so," Xavier answers in a somber tone.

"That was fucking smart." Rufio crosses his arms.

"I guess we'll have to make do with the stock we have now," I say.

"Where's the rest of your shirt?" Renata looks closely at Rufio.

"I had to improvise."

"Did you manage to collect lightning-glass in its raw form?" I ask.

"Yeah, but we had a problem. Two miners caught us in the act, and we had to fight them off."

"What happened to them?" Daisy stares at the trio, wide-eyed.

"We knocked them out," Rosie replies. "Then we hid them in the forest gagged and bound."

Xavier rubs his face. "They'll miss those workers. We can't linger."

"I'm sure they'll be guarding the parking area," Phoenix says.

"I have a plan for getting rid of any watchdogs they have, but first we must have a place to go," Xavier replies.

"I'll call my mother," Morpheus says. "She has connections in the Fringe community."

"They confiscated my phone before they allowed me into the camp, but..." Mom bends over, and retrieves a small device attached to her ankle and hidden under her pants. "I came prepared."

Morpheus quickly takes the phone from her hands, but a string of curses follows.

"What is it?" Daisy asks.

"There's no service."

"What? That's impossible. That should work in the most remote areas. It's a satellite phone."

"It's the miasma. I bet it's interfering with the connection," Toby chimes in.

Xavier exhales loudly, resting his hands on his hips. "I guess we'll have to call her after we get away from here."

27

MORPHEUS

I follow Xavier's line of sight, catching him staring at Harry and Artex's trailer. "They didn't go that way."

"No, but I need to borrow some clothes from Harry first."

"What for?" Phoenix asks. "Even if you had a wig and fake beard, you couldn't pass for the man."

Daisy grimaces, fleetingly glancing at Jodie first before switching her attention to Xavier.

"Don't you get your panties twisted in a bunch, Daisy. I know about his secret," Jodie deadpans.

"I'll explain how I plan to disguise myself as Harry later. Toby and Morpheus, you two come with me. Everyone else should return to their bungalows and stay put."

"What about the miners we left in the forest?" Felicity glances in the mountain's direction.

"It'd be nice if one of you could scramble minds, change memories," Rosie says, surprising me.

"Mind alteration is forbidden, against the law," Jodie replies.

"That didn't stop Dad from using Sweepers to save my ass," Rufio retorts bitterly.

"There's no sense wishing for something we don't have. Let's get going before the brothers return. The plan is to be far away from this place when those miners are discovered." Xavier steps forward.

Toby follows him, but I stop briefly to talk to Daisy. "Are you okay?"

"I will be once we're on the road. I can't believe they turned out to be evil like that. Is there anyone we can count on?"

"You can count on us." I glance in Jodie's direction. "Well, most of us."

Our former principal narrows her eyes to slits but doesn't offer a retort to my barb. She really can't say anything in her defense that won't sound like a half-baked excuse.

Daisy pecks me on the cheek, making me forget the woman in an instant. I'd grab her face for a proper kiss on the mouth, but Xavier and Toby are almost at the trailer. "I'll be back."

I hurry after them using my Idol speed—not the supersonic, bodiless demigod kind. I'll save that for emergency situations.

"All right. What are we doing here?" I ask once I stop next to them.

"Can you use your gift to conceal us? I don't want anyone to know what we're up to."

"Sure."

I barely need to concentrate to bring forth my shadows. In the blink of an eye, they cover the three of us, concealing us completely from curious glances. "It's done."

Xavier tries the door, finding it locked.

"Maybe we should have asked Phoenix to tag along too. He would be able to open that for us," Toby says.

"No need. I can do it," Xavier replies.

A second later, we hear the lock turn.

"Have you always possessed telekinesis, or is that a new perk from Bryce's work on you?" I ask.

"A new perk. I've never wished to be an Idol, but I can't complain." He opens the door slowly, maybe afraid there's an alarm or booby trap. We know there's no one inside.

I'm the last one in, closing the door softly. "Phew. It reeks in here."

"Are you surprised?" Toby scrunches his nose in disgust as he peruses the messy interior. The small kitchen sink is full of dirty dishes, and there are piles of trash and clothes scattered everywhere. "This place is a pigsty."

"You said you need clothes, right?" I lift one garment that I could have mistaken for a burlap sack. It's so dirty, it's stiff.

Xavier covers his face with his arm. "God, I'll throw up if I have to wear that. Let's look for something less filthy."

"Maybe he keeps his clean clothes in a closet." Toby veers toward the end of the trailer where a small bunk bed is pushed against the wall.

"If there is one," I mumble to myself.

I knock into some boxes, sending them to the floor. Several lightning-glass daggers and flying stars spill from one of them. "No clothes, but these could come in handy."

"Let me see that." Xavier picks up the box and searches inside. "Son of bitch." He pulls out a plastic bag filled with bullets.

"Are those made of lightning-glass?" I ask.

"I'm betting they are. Fuck. These guys are not playing around. We have to get out of here."

"I think I found something that doesn't smell like someone died in it." Toby returns to the main room, holding a yellowed tunic and loose brown pants.

Xavier sticks the bag with the bullets in his jacket pocket, then grabs as many daggers and flying stars as he can from the floor.

"Are you changing now?" Toby asks.

"No, let's get—"

"Hey, are you done in there?" Phoenix asks from outside. "Harry is coming this way."

"Shit!" Xavier puts the weapons back in the box I dislodged, deciding to take the whole package with him. "Open the door, Toby."

Toby and I go out first on high alert. Phoenix is bouncing on the balls of his feet, filled with jittery tension as he stares ahead. I can see his powers are engaged, ready to be unleashed. Xavier stops next to me, closing the door of the trailer with his new powers.

"Are we still invisible to the world?" he asks.

"Yes. But we need to stick together."

We move as fast as we can, and when Harry finally reaches the door of his trailer, we're already near our bungalow. I hope he doesn't notice one of his boxes is missing. Hopefully he won't see anything is amiss in that mess.

I don't dare to breathe easily until we're inside. Everyone is here, and the room feels much smaller.

"What do you have there?" Bryce points at the box in Xavier's hand.

"Weapons." He pulls the plastic bag from his jacket, setting it on top of the box. "And bullets. It seems they weren't difficult to manufacture after all."

"Lightning-glass bullets?" Jodie arches both eyebrows, moving closer to the bag.

"Yes, Jodie. But don't get any ideas. I'm not giving you any," Xavier retorts.

"Why did Mr. Silverstone believe they were difficult to mass produce?" Daisy asks.

"I believe he's been lied to," Xavier replies. "More and more, I suspect the members of this church don't want equality at all.

They want all Idols gone, either by the stripping off their powers or death."

"That's horrible," Felicity mumbles. "We can't go from one oppressing race to another."

"We won't. Not if I have anything to say about it." Daisy curls her hands into fists, getting into warrior mode. *Damn, I love this side of her.* I'd pull her into my arms and kiss her senseless, but now is not the time for bold, romantic gestures.

"What's next?" Rufio asks.

"We head to the main building and pretend we're going there to eat. It will give us a chance to scope out the parking area," Xavier explains.

"And then what? Fight and flee?" Rosie asks.

"I'd like to avoid a confrontation. It will most likely draw attention we don't need," he says. "Now, can I please have some privacy while I change into my disguise?"

When no one moves a muscle, he makes a circular motion in the air with his hand. "Turn around."

"Oh, sorry," Felicity says, getting red-faced.

Xavier's transformation doesn't take that long, maybe two minutes tops, including the change of clothes.

"Okay, I'm ready. How do I look?"

I turn and can't help dropping my jaw. "Son of a bitch."

"Holy fucking shit!" Phoenix exclaims. "What kind of power is that?"

"Xavier is a Morph. A rare ability, but quite handy," Jodie replies with an air of arrogance.

"Okay, stop gawking already." Xavier looks at Toby and me. "Let's get this shit show over with. Besides the stench, these clothes itch like crazy."

"What should we do with these weapons?" Renata asks.

"Divide them among yourselves, but no bullets for Jodie."

"You're beginning to piss me off, Xavier." She glowers at him.

"Beginning? Damn, I guess I'm not doing a good job, then."

With a clench of her jaw, she turns to the others. "Careful not to cut yourselves with the sharp blades. I don't have the antidote for lightning-glass poison with me."

As we predicted, the parking lot area is heavily guarded. There are at least six big fellows standing at attention, all carrying visible guns that I now know are loaded with bullets that can end my friends. I don't know what being hit by one will do to me, but I'm not about to volunteer for a test. I'm not immune to the fumes in the cave, so I have to assume those bullets will also hurt me.

Xavier stops before they see us and turns to Toby. "Any information you can pick up from those men, now is the time to tell me. Names would be useful."

Toby stretches his neck out to take a peek at the guards. "I got one name. Peter. I'm not sure who's called that though."

He grumbles. "Okay. It's better if I don't speak much."

The watchdogs visibly tense when they see our big group approach. The largest of the lot, a burly man with skin as dark as coal, steps forward. He doesn't look like a hippie. In fact, none of them do. Those men are militia. *Fuck.*

"Harry, what are you doing here?"

"I have to feed these kids. Teenagers are always hungry," Xavier grumbles.

The watchdogs relax their stance a little, but the big guy is still watching us intensely as we enter the building.

"What else did you learn from those men?" Xavier asks Toby.

"They've been ordered to shoot anyone who tries to steal Daisy away from camp."

"I'm so angry right now, I could break things," Daisy grits out. "They're as bad as the Neo Gods."

Rufio moves to the window, which, thanks to the grime, provides us some privacy. "Their eyes are trained on the building. How are we going to take them down?"

Xavier veers toward the kitchen and takes food out of the fridge, setting it on the counter.

"Are you going to eat now?" Toby arches his eyebrows.

"No, I'm setting up the scene in case someone comes in."

"The cars are loaded with lightning-glass. Let's hope that's enough to deter Chaos," Rufio says.

"Or that those goons didn't mess with them," Felicity adds.

"Since we're here, should we try to find a landline phone?" Renata pipes up.

"No, we have to focus on getting out of here," Rufio retorts.

"I have a plan," Phoenix says. "I can trap those motherfuckers' minds into an insane nightmare from inside the building. They'll be helpless."

"Do it," Xavier tells him. "Everyone else, get ready."

Phoenix joins Rufio by the window and doesn't move for a minute or so. He lets out a grunt after a while.

"What's wrong?" Daisy asks.

"I can't reach their minds. It's like they have a shield."

"They can't possibly have a vial of your blood." Daisy steps forward, looking troubled.

"I won't be surprised if they do." Phoenix moves back, rubbing his forehead.

"I don't think so. They must be wearing vests that protect them from Idol power," Rufio replies.

"If they're immune to Phoenix's powers, they'll be immune to all of us," Jodie helpfully observes.

"Not all of us," I say.

"Shit!" Toby exclaims, staring wide-eyed at the front door.

"What, kid?" Xavier pulls his arm.

"They've found the missing miners and—"

"Fuck, they're coming." Rufio steps away from the window, holding his lightning-glass dagger ready.

The front door is kicked open, and the real Harry fills the

frame, holding a shotgun in his hand. His eyes immediately zero in on Xavier.

"Look at what we have here. One of the shapeshifting snakes. I thought you had been hunted to extinction."

"Clearly not," Xavier grits out.

"That needs to be fixed." Harry takes aim and fires.

I move at the speed of light, jumping in front of Xavier to take the bullet meant for him. I expect a fiery pain to pierce my chest, but all I feel is a sting. Harry curses and then prepares to fire again, but Xavier yanks the gun from his hold using his new gifts and aims it at the son of a bitch's head. Harry clearly isn't wearing a protective vest like his mercenaries.

"You were saying?" Xavier asks.

His goons storm the small space, weapons ready to fire. I don't waste any time. I turn my dark gift on them, wrapping their hearts in the ultimate sense of dread. There's resistance, but their protective attire is no match for my demigod powers. They drop their guns and then fall to their knees.

Harry spares them a pitiful glance but seems unaffected by their predicament. "Go ahead. Kill me. You can't stop what's coming. We will rid the world of the poisonous existence of Idols, even your sweet, darling Daisy."

Xavier tenses even more, and I know exactly what he intends to do, but the gunshot will alert the others that something is amiss. I swing my arm forward, sending a slingshot of shadows in Harry's direction. It hits the center of his chest, making him collapse on the ground. He struggles for a moment, clutching his left arm, before he stops moving altogether.

"What did you do to him?" Toby asks, bug-eyed.

"I gave him a sudden heart attack."

"What about them?" Rosie points at the four men writhing on the floor.

"They can die too, for all I care." Xavier lowers the shotgun and then pulls a dagger from inside his jacket pocket. Quickly, he slashes the necks of all of them with such precision that no speckles of blood get on his clothes.

I glance at Daisy, worried that her guardian's actions might have terrified her. But neither she nor Rosie seem affected. I guess they've seen far worse in their lives.

"Weren't there six men outside?" Felicity asks.

Shit. She's right.

"We need to hurry. The missing guards must have gone down to alert the others," Bryce says.

Phoenix heads out first. "The coast is clear."

We run out of the building straight toward our cars, which are pretty much useless. Their tires have been slashed.

"What now?" Rosie asks.

"I can fix that." Jodie raises her hand, and the tires inflate back to usable condition.

"What about the holes in them?" Rufio asks.

"I can keep them full for a while."

Our group splits into the two vehicles, but I don't make a move. We can't let those fanatics have access to lightning-glass, but the only way to stop them is if we blow up the mountain.

Bryce looks over his shoulder. "Morpheus, aren't you coming?"

I hesitate for second. I could try to do it, but what if I can't?

"Yes," I reply finally.

I jump in Felicity's car, which is the only one with a seat left. Unfortunately, Jodie Fallon is also here.

Great. This going to be a hella fun trip.

28

DAISY

"How many lightning-glass stones did you stuff in the trunk of the car?" I ask Rufio, trying to suppress a yawn. This tiredness is not normal.

"Not nearly enough to fill the space. It turns out they weigh a ton, and I couldn't carry more than one load."

"No wonder you looked winded when you came to the assembly," Bryce comments from the front seat.

"Yeah, perks of my new reality," Rufio grumbles. "Well, at least I'm immune to the fumes." He glances at me. "How are you, Daisy?"

"Tired, but so far, no headache yet. I hope it's enough to deter Chaos. We're in no condition to fight him now, especially so close to those lunatics."

"Renata, stay close to Felicity's car. I don't know how long my mother can sustain her gift or how far her reach is," Bryce says.

"Okay."

Rufio sinks against the car seat, pressing a closed fist against his forehead. "Fuck, I'm so tired of running for our lives. We need a break."

"I hope they don't come after us." I glance back, but the road behind us is deserted.

"I'm glad we didn't have to go through Morpheus's ritual," Bryce says offhandedly, and even though I don't think he meant anything by it, I feel the sting of his remark.

He doesn't want to be linked to me through all eternity. I get it. It's a huge commitment.

"Dude, why not? I'd do it." Phoenix links his hand with mine, and when I glance at him, he winks.

"You misunderstood me. I'm not saying I don't want an infinity band with Daisy, I just didn't want to do it to appease those motherfuckers."

The ache in my chest eases off, and I finally dare to ask, "What is that vow, anyway?"

"It's a commitment that lasts forever, even after death. You'd be linked to Bryce through all your lives, if you believe in such a thing," Rufio replies tartly.

"But Daisy is involved with you, Phoenix, and Morpheus. How would that work?" Renata asks.

"It doesn't matter. We're talking hypothetically here. I don't need an infinity band to show how much I love her," Bryce replies.

My face becomes hot, a reaction that it seems I will never cease to have when one of them professes their love for me in front of others. It's stupid considering how far we've gone in our relationship.

I notice we begin to slow down, and I see the brake lights on Felicity's car are on. "What's going on?"

"I don't know. I'm just keeping pace with your friend."

Soon, a couple of buses pass by us, going toward the camp. They're filled to capacity, but I can't make out who's inside.

"Shit. Were those more fanatics?" Phoenix asks.

"It seems so," Rufio replies. "We left just in time."

We pick up speed again, but after ten minutes on the road, Felicity takes the next exit.

"Where is she going?" I ask.

We find out soon enough. Felicity parks in the busiest fast food restaurant that comes up on the street.

"We can't possibility be stopping to eat. We're too close to the camp," Rufio says.

"I could eat." Phoenix shrugs. "Burgers and fries, who can pass that up?"

"Do you have a hole in your stomach or something?" Rufio angles his body forward to glare at him.

"Dude, I haven't eaten in hours. It takes a lot to keep this sexy machine running."

I shake my head, trying my best to keep my grin from showing. We're not out of the woods yet, but Phoenix's humor, as inappropriate as it is, infuses a warm feeling in my chest.

"They're getting out of the car. Let's see what's going on," I say.

Bryce is the first to reach Xavier, who has changed back to his true self and has also ditched Harry's clothes.

"What's up?" Bryce asks.

"We're acquiring new transportation. Our vehicles are too recognizable, and Jodie won't be able to keep the tires inflated for hours on."

"Not a lot of good choices here." Phoenix looks over the parking lot, which is filled with small vehicles that are most likely older than us.

My eyes land on two station wagons, the best cars in the lot which could accommodate our large group, but they usually belong to people with children. I won't steal from a family.

Just then, a company van pulls up. Two men in uniform get out and head into the restaurant.

"I think that will do," Xavier says. "It's best if we drive in one vehicle."

"I'll need help unloading the lightning-glass stones from our trunks," Rufio says.

"Bryce and I can do it from afar. We just need Morpheus's camouflage skills." Phoenix stretches his arms forward with his hands linked together, cracking his knuckles in the process.

The wind suddenly picks up speed, sending chills down my spine. I glance at the sky, noticing with a sinking feeling in the pit of my stomach that those clouds are getting together, dark and ominous, in an unnatural way. *Shit.* That must be Chaos.

"We have to move, folks!" Xavier warns.

Morpheus's expression changes, turning veiled and almost inhuman. His eyes glow like liquid gold again as the shadows gather behind him. With a motion of his arms, the shadows expand, creating a massive shield that covers all of us, including our target vehicle.

Without missing a beat, Bryce and Phoenix get to work, each one focusing on a car. They pop the trunks open and then send the big pieces of lightning-glass stones floating across the lot toward the open back of the van.

The loud rumble of thunder above makes me jump on the spot. Rufio pulls me to his side and kisses me on the cheek. "He's not going to harm you. We won't let him."

"As much as I love hearing that, I can't let you be my knights in shining armor. I'm not a damsel in distress."

Rufio smirks while his eyes dance with amusement. "I know you aren't. You're our firecracker, our slayer queen. But we'll never stop wanting to protect you."

"All right, everyone. Let's move," Xavier commands.

With his hand on my lower back, Rufio nudges me forward. I'm much more powerful than he is now, but that doesn't change his protective stance. I get into the van after Rosie and Felicity, but they get in the back seat, closer to the lightning-glass rocks, whereas I'm instructed to sit near the front. Rufio slides in next to my sister. I'm now sandwiched between Bryce and Phoenix, while Toby and Renata sit across from us, an arrangement that must not be pleasing to Rosie. I glance at her, and sure as shit, I find her throwing daggers with her eyes at the back of Renata's head.

Morpheus is the last one in. He pretty much jumps inside and slides the door shut with a bang. "Go. Go! The owners of the van are coming back."

Xavier, who already had the motor running, presses the pedal to the metal, burning rubber. The sudden acceleration sends me forward since I didn't buckle up yet. But Bryce and Phoenix reach out, keeping me in place.

"You'd better put your seat belt on, darling." Phoenix fumbles around the space between our bodies, looking for the seat belt but also copping a feel in the process. His antics only serve to wake my body.

"It's okay. I can do it myself." I try to be stern, but it's impossible to stay mad when I look at his gorgeous face. *Ugh. Why does he have to be so pretty?*

Xavier buzzes the horn, almost giving me a heart attack.

"Son of a bitch. Is that fucker blind?" he yells.

"What's going on?" Rufio asks from the back seat.

"It's like they can't even see us," Xavier continues. "Stupid idiots."

"Oops!" Morpheus says. "I still have us concealed by shadows. My bad."

He doesn't blush, but the sheepish expression he's sporting now is adorable. If only we didn't have to save the world.

"Where are we going?" I turn in my seat as much as the constraints of the seat belt allow.

Jodie passes over her cell phone to me. "My phone is working now, but the signal is weak. You should try contacting your mother, Morpheus."

I take the phone from her, then pass it to him.

"If the signal is weak, that means the lightning-glass is

working." Bryce slings his arm across my shoulders, casually placing his hand on my forearm. He caresses me absentmindedly, but I'm all too aware of his touch.

"And Chaos is not on our tail." Renata looks out the window. "My parents must be freaking out. It's been days since Gifted Academy got taken over by Neo Gods."

"Maybe you can call them after Morpheus is done with the phone," Toby suggests.

"No!" Xavier and Jodie say at the same time.

"I'm sorry, kid, but there's no way to know your parents haven't sided with Neo Gods or aren't under their surveillance. We can't risk it," Xavier adds in a softer tone.

"I know." Renata drops her gaze to her lap.

"Mom?" Morpheus speaks into the phone. "Are you there? I can't hear you very well."

"Put the call on speaker," Phoenix pipes up.

The signal is breaking up, and we can't make out the words Mrs. Malek is saying.

"You're too close to the fumes. Trade places with me," I say.

We make the switch, which gives Bryce and Phoenix unhappy puppy faces. I roll my eyes. Boys.

"Morpheus, I've been worried sick about you," her voice comes out more clearly now. "I saw on the news that cops were killed near the safe house."

"Yes, they came for Phoenix. Mom, we're on the run and need a place to stay ASAP. We need your help."

"I was afraid that would come to pass. I made calls after I dropped you off at the safe house. How far are you from Saturn's Bay?"

"Three hours, at least," he replies.

"I'll text you an address. Please, stay far away from Norm neighborhoods. It isn't safe."

"How is the situation now?" I ask.

"Oh, is that you, Daisy?"

"Yes, it's me."

"Not great. The Neo Gods came out in full force. They also had help from Fringe criminals. Those poor children." Her voice cracks at the end, making me choke up.

Tears gather in my eyes, brought forth by a mix of sorrow and rage. Unmaking those bastards is not enough. I want them nuked from the face of the Earth.

Rosie whimpers softly behind me, earning Toby's attention. He turns in his seat but doesn't make a comment.

"It's okay, honey. They're going to pay for all their sins," Felicity comforts my sister.

"Yes. Yes they will," I say.

29

PHOENIX

After three gruesome hours without breaks inside a crowded van, we finally arrive at the destination Mrs. Malek gave us. It's in an industrial area, but judging by the conditions of the buildings, we're not in Idol-controlled territory. The painting is fading on some facades, but it's not so completely terrible that I'd suspect those buildings belong to Norms. I don't really think they can afford to own anything.

Xavier parks in front of a warehouse with faded gray walls. There's a ramp leading to a great rusty metal gate in the loading area and a door next to it that almost blends in with the wall. No signs of any kind. The parking lot is completely empty too.

"Where are we?" I ask.

"We're in Flaunders, east of downtown," Xavier replies. "I thought most of these warehouses were abandoned."

"Why would they be deserted?" Daisy asks.

"Sometimes a business area just dies for no obvious reason," Jodie pipes up.

Rufio snorts. "Yeah, right. There's always a reason, and you bet your ass Idols are behind it."

"Excuse me?" Jodie says with a stern motherly tone.

"Oh, drop the act, Mother. Like you can expect respect from me."

I whistle. "Boy, that escalated fast."

"Everyone quit bickering. You're giving me a headache," Xavier grumbles.

"It could be the fumes," Renata replies. "I've had one for the past hour."

"I'm going to text my mother and tell her we're here," Morpheus says from next to me.

He had to trade places with Daisy so he could use the phone, and we never switched back. Another reason I'm sour.

A minute later, his mother walks out of the building through the small door. The wind is howling outside, which makes me wonder if it's a natural occurrence or if Chaos has followed us here. Mrs. Malek's curly hair is flapping wildly around her face while she tries to keep her jacket closed. Thanks to the light color of the fabric, it's easy to spot the bloodstains on her sleeve. Morpheus notices that too. He curses, then turns into dark smoke, vanishing through the crack in the window in the blink of an eye.

"What the hell was that?" I ask.

"He's embraced his demigod side." Daisy reaches for the door handle, but I open it for her with my mind. She glances at me and smiles. "Thanks."

My heart goes to a hundred in an instant. *Damn, I have it bad for this girl.* I follow her, but considering her attention is now riveted on Mrs. Malek, I try to ignore my naughty thoughts. Morpheus has shifted back into a solid human. He's Chaos's grandson all right. That was a freaky trick he pulled.

"Mom, are you okay?" Morpheus stares at his mother's clothes.

"Yes. This isn't my blood. I've been helping with the wounded. Come inside quickly."

"Any chance you can open the loading gate for us? We have

cargo that shouldn't be left outside," Xavier says from inside the van.

"Yes, of course. We don't want any vehicles parked here anyway."

We all head inside and discover a world that looks like it came straight from a war movie. Part of the warehouse floor has been converted into a makeshift hospital where wounded patients lie on blankets and mattresses on the floor. It makes me sick when I realize that most of them are children.

Daisy gasps, covering her mouth with a closed fist. I start toward her, but the sound of my name being called out stops me in my tracks. I turn toward it and find my mother making a beeline in my direction.

"Phoenix, oh thank heavens you're okay." She pulls me into an embrace. I'm too stunned to react, so I just stand there like a wooden pole.

"What are you doing here?" I pull back, wrestling with the conflicting emotions bouncing around in my chest. The little boy in me wants to lean into the comfort of her embrace, but the jaded person I am now can't let go of the pain.

"I tracked Shereen down when I couldn't locate you. I heard about that awful cop on the news."

"Yeah, he got what he deserved. But are you helping the Norms and Fringes now?"

She jerks her head back as if my question offends her. "I've never shared your father's ideals about them."

Hearing her speak about him makes me nauseated. The latch holding the dark memories of my abuse cracks right down the middle. If I don't focus on something else, it will split open. I turn to Mrs. Malek. "What can we do to help?"

"Please get settled first, and then look for Ellen. She'll tell you what to do."

Bryce steps forward, looking grimmer than ever. "Point me at your most critical cases."

Daisy's and Rufio's faces blanch. Bryce has not fared well after healing the dying. But how could we look at all these hurt people and not try to help?

"There's one little boy, not much older than two, who's in bad shape. We don't think he'll last much longer," Mom says. "I'll take you to him."

Bryce and Daisy follow my mother, and because I can't stay too far away from the love of my life, I do too. I avoid glancing at the people along the way, but not because I lack sympathy. I'm afraid if I do, I'll break down. I'm hanging on by a thread already. Their pain is getting to me; it's making me remember my own. Another fissure on the latch. *Fuck.* I grind my teeth harder.

When Mom stops next to a little kid who has more than half of his body covered in burns, my legs falter. Daisy makes a distressed sound, covering her mouth with her hands.

"Those motherfuckers," Bryce grits out.

"How? I thought they'd attacked the schools. He's too young," Daisy says.

"I don't know. He was found underneath his mother on the sidewalk near one of the attack locations. She died trying to protect him."

"So he's an orphan?" I ask through the lump in my throat.

"We don't know. His father might be looking for him."

"He's so quiet," Daisy murmurs.

"I think Ellen might have given him sedatives," Mom replies.

Bryce kneels next to the kid, placing his hand above his chest. Immediately, a bright glow comes forth, illuminating the area. The boy disappears underneath the halo. Bryce doesn't move a muscle. The only indication that he's working hard is the furrow of his eyebrows. I step closer to Daisy, linking our hands together. She squeezes mine tightly, but I don't know if she's aware that she's doing it. I'm not sure how long Bryce maintains his healing powers at full capacity, but when the light fades, it does quickly, and he tumbles sideways soon after. I try to stop him with my powers, but my mother reaches him first.

"Oh no. Bryce." Daisy lets go of my hand and crouches next to him.

"He's out cold. Is he okay?" Mom asks me as she cradles him in her lap.

"I hope so. Healing weakens him."

Bryce stirs and mumbles incoherent words, but his eyes remain closed. The boy he healed, however, is awake now.

"Mommy?" he asks in a tiny voice. "Where's Mommy?"

Ah hell. Now we have to tell him he'll never see his mother again. My heart tightens to the point that it might shatter into tiny fragments. I sit next to him, careful not to scare the poor kid even more. There's not a single scar left on his body, but his big hazel eyes are filled with fear as he stares at me.

"Hey, buddy. How are you feeling?"

"You're one of the bad guys."

Fuck. It didn't even occur to me to mask my powers. "I'm not a bad guy. I'm on your side."

"But you're an Idol."

I wince. Hell, we do have a terrible rep. "Yes, but not all Idols are bad."

He keeps watching me with unblinking eyes for a moment, and then he switches his attention to the others. "Do you know where my mommy is?"

"No, honey. What's her name?" Daisy smiles kindly at him, but her eyes tell a different story. They're bright and sad.

"I think Daddy calls her Margaret."

"Do you know your last name?" my mother asks.

He pinches his eyebrows together and then shakes his head. "I can't remember."

Rufio and Morpheus find us, and by their solemn expressions, I gather they have bad news.

"What is it?" I ask.

"Xavier wants to hold a meeting," Morpheus replies. "But I think we should wait until Bryce recovers."

"I'll be up in a second," he mumbles, his eyes still closed.

"How are you feeling?" Daisy caresses his cheek.

"Like I've been running on fumes for days."

"Speaking of fumes, do you think the lightning-glass stones we brought will be enough to keep us hidden from Bad Grandpa?" I ask Morpheus.

"Nope. I can sense him getting closer. It's why Xavier wants to talk. There might be another away to hide us from him."

"Who is Bad Grandpa?" The kid Bryce healed sits up, rubbing his eyes. His blond hair is still covered in soot and dried blood. I guess Bryce's abilities don't include cleanup.

"My grandfather," Morpheus replies.

"Why is he bad?"

"Because he's old and grumpy," Bryce butts in, finally getting back up. He massages his temple and then tries to suppress a yawn.

"I don't have a grandpa or grandma." The little boy glances down, his shoulders slumping forward. He looks so vulnerable and alone, I want to hug him and tell him everything will be okay.

"You're not missing much." Morpheus shrugs.

"What's your name?" Rufio asks the kid.

"Theo."

He scrunches up his nose, and a second later, he sneezes, which sends him flying across the room.

"What the fuck!" Rufio yells.

Bryce and I both throw our arms forward, but I'm the only one who actually does stop Theo from a nasty fall. Bryce is still out of juice. I bring him back to us. More precisely, back to my mother's arms.

"Are you okay, Theo?" She cradles him like he was her own child. I imagine that's how she used to be with me before my father did what he did.

The fissure on the latch in my brain spreads in different directions like a spider web. One more blow and I'll drown in my dark memories.

"I sneezed and flew," he says in awe. "I was never able to do that before."

"No, but I think things are going to be a little different from now on," Bryce replies.

"Different how? Do I have superhero powers?" His eyes become as round as saucers.

He has no idea.

"Didn't you just heal him?" Morpheus asks Bryce.

"Yeah."

"Wow, so the change is happening faster." Morpheus passes a hand over his face.

"It seems so, but the side effects are getting harder too. I feel awful."

"Don't even think about healing anyone else today," Daisy tells him sternly.

"I don't think I could even if I wanted to. I'm numb inside; I can barely feel my power in my core."

I trade a worried glance with Rufio. It's hard to tell if we're thinking the same thing. I do wonder if when Bryce heals someone, he's actually transferring some of his powers to that person. If that's the case, how long until he has nothing left?

The rumble of thunder reverberates across the warehouse's high ceiling, getting our full attention.

"Crap. I think Chaos found us," I say.

30

DAISY

Bryce has to rely on me for support as we walk toward the warehouse section that has some office space. Morpheus is ahead of us, body coiled tight with tension. It's like he's carrying the entire weight of the world on his shoulders. It can't be easy knowing a relative is hell-bent on killing everyone you know. What a group of damaged people we are. I lost my parents in a horrible way, and the loves of my life have to contend with terrible ones. At least Mrs. Malek loves Morpheus unconditionally, and it seems Phoenix's mother is trying to make amends for her past mistakes.

Morpheus stops in front of a door that has a lit sign above it that says "On Air." It strikes me as odd. But when I enter the room, I understand the reason for it. We're actually inside the radio station *The Freaks*. A huge poster showing off the hosts is the first thing I see, hanging at the far end of the wall. Then there are all the other famous bands' posters, concert T-shirts in frames, and even a guitar mounted on the wall. The actual studio where they broadcast their show is sectioned off in a soundproof room in the left corner. The half-glass panels for walls allow visitors to peek inside. One of the hosts is in there, wearing big earphones and making sure Norms and Fringes still have their source of entertainment despite the tragedy that has struck our town.

"Am I dreaming, or are we actually inside a radio station?" Phoenix asks.

A man with salt-and-pepper hair and a wrinkled tan face approaches, sporting a tentative smile. I recognize him from the poster, I just don't know which one of the hosts he is, Travis or Morty.

"Hi, I'm Travis Ross. You must be Daisy."

"Yeah. These are Bryce, Morpheus, and Phoenix, and I suppose you've already met the rest," I say.

"Yes I have. Please take a seat. Your friend looks a little worn out." He points at the empty leather couch. There are three in the room, and with the current seating arrangement, I can see the battle lines are still firmly in place. Rosie and Felicity occupy one, Jodie and Renata another. Toby and Xavier are standing, clearly not wanting to pick sides.

"Where's my mother? We're running out of time," Morpheus asks. "I can sense Chaos looming right above us. I don't think the few pieces of raw lightning-glass stones we brought are doing much to deter him."

"She'll return shortly," Travis assures Morpheus.

"Okay, I'm so confused. Can someone explain to me how a Fringe radio station got involved in the fight against the Neo Gods?" Bryce asks.

"Morty and I have always been involved in fighting oppression. It's the main reason we started the station more than thirty years ago."

"But why this warehouse?" I ask.

"We've only been here for the past few months. We piss off too many powerful Idols to remain in one location for too long." He lifts his shoulders in a casual what-can-you-do shrug.

"But a warehouse?" Phoenix presses.

"It belonged to Morty's parents. It was abandoned for years since most businesses in the area either went bankrupt or moved to greener pastures. We figured if we moved here, we wouldn't have to change locations so soon. But then the war broke out, and our location became providential."

"Too bad we brought a vengeful god to you," Renata remarks, earning an immediate glower from Rosie.

"You make it sound like we did it on purpose," she snaps.

Renata stares in Rosie's direction, clearly surprised. "I didn't mean it like that."

Mrs. Malek comes in, interrupting what was sure to become a useless argument. She's followed by the blind Zions who assisted her before when Morpheus couldn't yet control his powers.

"You asked them to come here?" Morpheus widens his eyes.

"Don't fret, young man. We're not the enemy," one of them replies.

"Shereen, I didn't know when you said you were getting help you meant them." Xavier watches the duo with suspicion.

"Who are they? Priests?" Renata asks Jodie.

"Something like that," she answers but keeps her shrewd eyes locked on the newcomers.

"How are you going to help us deter Chaos?" Morpheus asks.

Both men turn toward the sound of his voice. I know they're blind, but they do have an uncanny ability to make you feel uncomfortable under their unseen scrutiny. Kind of like how Andromeda makes me feel. I haven't thought about her in a while, but I wonder what's going on in Hawk City with her and the Silverstones. The fact that we haven't heard from them in so long is troublesome. And what about Delta? Were the Knights' agents able to get information from him? *Hell*. We lost precious time in that camp of deranged fanatics.

"I see you've finally reclaimed what the shadows took. You've accepted your legacy," one of the Zions says.

"Wait a second," Rufio butts in. "Did you know he was Erebus's son?"

Mrs. Malek drops her gaze to the floor. "Yes, they've always known."

A deafening rumble above us sends my adrenaline levels through the roof. If Chaos decides to strike now, what will happen to all those wounded people?

"You'd better start talking," Xavier intervenes. "We're on borrowed time here."

"Morpheus needs to fully embrace his demigod status."

"I thought I did that already. Still, I can't win against Chaos. He's a primordial god."

"You don't need to win against him. We just want to become invisible to him. And that's your specialty, boy," one of them replies.

They look so similar, it's hard to tell them apart. Their white hair is cropped short, and they seem to be about the same age. The only difference is that one is slightly taller than the other.

"Sorry to interrupt, but an introduction would be appreciated," Travis says.

"I'm so sorry. Where are my manners?" Mrs. Malek replies. "These are brothers Ismael and Iago."

They bow their heads, and then the one named Ismael says, "I sense distrust in your heart. You don't need to fear betrayal from us."

Travis scowls at the duo, but he doesn't offer a retort.

"Do you want Morpheus to cover the entire building in shadows and keep that up for an indefinite amount of time?" I bring the conversation back on track.

"You sound surprised, child. He's a demigod; he's capable of unbelievable things, just like you were once before."

"Me?" I squeak. "Do you mean Magia?"

"Yes, naturally we meant her," Iago replies.

"But Magia was an Idol. Even if she was the Unmaker, she didn't have infinite abilities," Xavier pipes up.

The Zions crinkle their foreheads in deep frowns. "What gave you the notion Magia was an Idol?"

"Uh... wasn't she?" Phoenix crosses his arms in front of his chest, watching the Zions through slits.

"No. Magia was a demigod, just like Morpheus," Ismael replies.

"Well, not like Morpheus," Iago butts in. "She was the daughter of Eris and an Idol, unlike Morpheus. And she also had better control of her abilities."

"Rub it in, why don't you?" Morpheus glowers at the duo.

"Hold on." I raise my hand. "Who is Eris?"

"Eris, also known as Strife, is Nyx and Erebus's daughter," Xavier replies almost to himself. His eyes are troubled, unfocused.

"Whoa. So Magia and Morpheus were related?" Phoenix glances at Morpheus and me. "Dude!"

"Quit looking at me like I've suddenly become a perv," Morpheus grits out. "Even if that's true, Daisy is not Magia."

I rub my head, trying to get rid of the headache that's already brewing.

"If she was a demigod, how could she have turned into a Norm?" Rufio asks.

"Because she asked Gaia for a favor, and Gaia can do just about anything," Mrs. Malek replies.

I'm still reeling from this revelation, and judging by Jodie's stupefied expression, she also didn't know about that detail. However, another thunderclap draws our attention to our priority, which is to hinder Chaos.

"Okay, tell me what I must do." Morpheus turns to the

Zions. "You can give us a lecture about my messed-up side of the family later."

"To fully embrace your demigod powers, you must give up your humanity completely," Ismael says.

No.

The blood seems to drain from Morpheus's face. "I'm not sure I want to do that."

"You don't have a choice. Your attachment to your Fringe lineage is keeping you from unleashing your true potential. It's either that or Chaos will level this place to the ground," Iago counters.

"What's going to happen to Morpheus if he gives up his humanity? Will he turn into a complete asshole?" Phoenix asks.

"That, we can't answer," both men reply in unison.

Resting his hands on his hips, Morpheus dips his chin low, staring at the ground. His shoulders hunch forward as he lets out a heavy exhale. Even though I'm terrified at the possibility that he might become someone as cold as Chaos, I can't lose faith in him now. I step closer and lift his face to mine with the tip of my finger.

"You're not going to change. I believe in you," I say, looking deep into his eyes.

"How can you be so sure?"

"Because of the light I see shining here." I press my palm against his chest. "It's stronger than any darkness."

He reaches for my face, cupping my cheek. "You're too good for this world, my love. But for you, I'll try to stay the same. I promise."

"I have no doubt you will." I smile to mask my fear.

Every single deity we've come across has left a bad impression on us. Even the woman who spoke to me in my mind wasn't very nice. I mean, would it kill her to give me straight answers?

Was that Eris? And is it possible she was also speaking to Morpheus? It makes sense it's the same goddess since she's linked to us both. But if she's Strife, she can't have good intentions. Should we even trust her?

Morpheus turns to the Zions. "I'm ready."

31

MORPHEUS

For safety reasons, the Zions and I move to a different part of the building, far away from our group and the wounded. My mother and Daisy wanted to come, but if I'm to give up my Fringe part, my humanity, I can't have either of them nearby. They're my weakness, and I don't need any sage Idols to tell me that.

Like Travis mentioned, it's providential that their radio station moved to such a massive building. Toward the back, there's nothing but empty boxes and industrial shelves collecting dust.

The silence during the trek here has already gotten to my nerves. To distract myself from what I have to do, I ask, "What's the deal with your impairment? Were you both born blind?"

"No. Blindness was our vow when we joined the brother-hood," Ismael replies.

"Oh, I've only met one Idol who's blind. She's a level eighteen, but she was born that way."

"You must be speaking of Andromeda Belfor, Nathaniel's daughter," Iago says casually.

Wait. What?

I shake my head. "I must have misheard you. Nathaniel can't possibly be her father. That son of a bitch has been torturing her for months."

"And have you never heard of fathers mistreating their offspring before?" Ismael raises a bushy eyebrow.

He must know my adoptive father is an asshole, but somehow I don't think he's only talking about him. I suspect they also know about Phoenix and what Maximus Westbrook did to him. If that's true, what else do they know?

The lights in the warehouse begin to flicker suddenly, and then I hear Chaos's evil laughter in my head, loud and painful. It feels like my skull is going to split in two.

"Ugh!" I bend forward, clutching my head.

The walls and floor begin to shake, and the howling of wind is a clear indication something horrible is happening outside. I can't believe Chaos hasn't unleashed his wrath on us yet.

"We've delayed this for too long. You have to let go of your mortal anchors," Ismael urges.

"I don't know how to do that," I say.

"*Yes, you do, Morpheus,*" the familiar female voice tells me. "*You've taught Daisy before, haven't you?*"

"*Eris, you're back.*"

"*Oh, so those old farts already told you about me. Pity. I wanted to do the grand reveal myself.*" She laughs.

"*You had plenty of time to tell me you were my half sister.*"

"*True, but it's no fun letting go of all the secrets at once. What about the suspense, the buildup?*"

The screeching noise of metal being twisted interferes with my mind-to-mind conversation. I look up, noticing the roof is shaking terribly and the beams keeping it in place are compromised.

"Morpheus, have you done what we told you?" Ismael asks.

"Trust me, I'm trying, but I need some guidance here. I don't know how to cut my ties with my human side."

"Oh, little brother, you're a little slow, aren't you?" Eris asks, amused.

"And you're a huge bitch, aren't you?" I retort.

"Ouch. Was that supposed to be a comeback?"

"If you're not going to help, get out of my head. You're distracting me."

"I should let you fail, but you're lucky my vendetta against Grandpa is bigger than you. If you want to cut your ties with your weaker side, you have to let go of your sweet mommy and Daisy."

My heart shrivels into a dried-up muscle. *"I won't give them up."*

"Oh, you're so dramatic. Not give them up forever. If you're still you when this is over, you can come back to them."

"What do you mean, if I'm still me?"

"Oh, darling. Once you experience life as a demigod, you won't desire to return to a mundane life. Why do you think Nathaniel is messed up in the head?"

"Honestly, I don't know. But I'm nothing like him."

"We shall see. Now listen closely, because I'm not going to repeat myself. Imagine a ribbon that's tying you to your mommy and Daisy. Now picture a big-ass pair of scissors and cut those ribbons. Presto."

"Oh, come on. It can't be as simple as a visualization exercise."

"It worked for Daisy, didn't it?"

"He can't do it, Eris. Your plan to piss me off is not going to work," Chaos says loudly, not in my head. "You bet on the wrong horse."

My head doesn't feel so heavy, and I realize it's because Eris has left my mind. Either she left of her own free will, or Chaos sent her away. It doesn't matter. She left me with one piece of advice, and I guess I have to make it work or go bust.

The Zions begin to chant in a foreign language and burn sage. Do they hope to ban Chaos from the premises with that?

Only a mountain filled with poisonous fumes was able to keep the god at bay.

"What are you doing?" I ask.

"Helping you find your center. You must connect completely with your demigod powers," Ismael replies.

"I'm going to enjoy tearing your little lover limb from limb. Her sacrifice all those years ago will be for nothing," Chaos says.

"Why do you hate Magia so much?" I ask him to buy time.

"She betrayed me, just like her father did. It's no surprise. The apple doesn't fall far from the tree."

Lightning strikes the ceiling, punching a hole through it to land a few feet from me in a shower of sparks. I jump back, and a second later, another lightning bolt hits the spot where I was.

"But I guess lightning does strike the same spot twice." He laughs.

The Zions continue chanting, but I can tell they're getting nervous. Everyone is counting on me, but I remain clueless about what to do. I close my eyes and try to focus, even though it's damn hard when I know Chaos is above me, ready to strike again at any second. Despite that, I turn my attention to my powers. If I don't master them, then I can say goodbye to Mom and Daisy for real. Their images pop in the forefront of my mind. They're both looking at me with undeniable love and pride, something I've always craved from a different person.

I don't picture a ribbon like Eris suggested; I simply turn my back on them, shattering my heart. But the raw power inside my core vanquishes the pain as it takes over my entire being. It spreads though my body like liquid euphoria. With their explosion, the shadows come forth. I don't become them like I did before, but I can't feel my body anymore either. It's almost like I'm in a different plane and mundane things such as hunger, thirst, and aches no longer matter.

With the full awakening of my powers also comes the

awareness of Chaos's reach. I thought he had escaped from the island and followed us here. But that's not true. He's still tethered to that piece of land in the ocean; only his conscience is free to torment us.

I finally change into my smoky form and zoom upward, traveling through the ceiling without breaking it to pierce the storm created by Chaos. He screams in rage as wisps of darkness attempt to reform the angry clouds. But I slash them with the whips that sprout from my ethereal wrists.

I can play this game forever, but that's not the plan. I just want to hide the building from him. Now that I know he's not free, I can meet him for our final showdown later. I turn my attention to creating the biggest shadow I've ever conjured. It grows in size at alarming speed, covering the warehouse in a matter of seconds. Once I know it's invisible to Chaos and to the mortals too, I glance at what's left of his pitiful storm. I zap the nimbus with a flick of my wrist, drawing another roar from him.

My lips curl into a victorious grin, but my amusement is cut short when I sense another presence nearby.

"Well done, little brother. You kicked Grandpa's ass." A young woman with hair as black as midnight and skin so white it's almost translucent is hovering a few feet from me.

"Eris, I see you've finally decided to show your face."

"Oh, you think I was hiding before?"

"Weren't you?"

"No, silly. You simply couldn't see me because you weren't a true demigod yet."

"What happens now?"

"Now you decide what you want to do next. You can return to those people below, or you can wreak havoc with me. You know, sibling bonding." She smiles like a psycho.

I glance down, and with just a mere thought, I can see Daisy pacing back and forth, worried sick about me. My roommates attempt to console her, but they can't take the worry from her heart. My mother is sitting next to Rosie and Felicity, also distressed. I should return and ease their mind, but I don't have an ounce of desire to do so. I know I should care, but I can't get in touch with those feelings.

"They're waiting for me," I say. "I should go back."

"True, the old you would most definitely do that. But you're not that weakling Fringe spawn who needed magical bracelets to control your powers. You're Erebus's son. A demigod. You're more than the cage you were raised in."

As if sensing I'm spying on her, Daisy glances up. When I look into her eyes, I feel something stir in my chest, a spark.

"Come on, Morpheus. There's so much I want to show you," Eris insists.

I glance at her with dispassionate curiosity. She's my sister, and yet I don't feel a thing. What I do care about is the knowledge she possesses. But there's something else I have to take care of first.

"You said you wanted to wreak havoc together, right? I just so happen to know exactly where we should start."

32

DAISY

We're already on pins and needles, but when a loud explosion on the north side of the building shocks the entire structure, I'm out of the radio station in a flash. Phoenix runs after me and stops me from going after Morpheus.

"Let me go!" I try to break free from his hold.

"No. You're not thinking straight. If you run after him, you might ruin any progress he's made."

Rufio and Bryce soon join us outside.

"You don't know that!" I yell through angry tears.

"He's right, honey," Bryce says.

Phoenix pulls me toward him, crushing me against his chest. "Morpheus will be okay, my love. He's immortal."

"I know, but I can't help worrying about him." I pull back so I can glance at Bryce and Rufio too. "About all of you. You'll be the death of me."

Rufio's and Bryce's expressions turn into scowls.

"Look who's talking. You're one reckless woman," Rufio retorts.

"I'm not!" I yell stubbornly, knowing very well it's a lie.

Phoenix grabs my other forearm, forcing me to glance at him. His eyebrows are furrowed together, and his lips are nothing but a thin flat line on his face. "Never talk about dying in front of me, darling. *Please.*" He wipes my wet cheeks dry. "I love you so, so much. I can't bear the thought of losing you."

"You're not going to lose me."

"Is everything okay?" Travis asks from the open door.

"Yes," Bryce replies.

The man's gaze travels across the expansive room, perhaps searching for damage to the building.

Phoenix becomes stiff in my arms when he looks over my shoulder and says, "Mom?"

With hurried steps, she reaches us, holding Theo in her arms. "What was that noise? The children are frightened."

"It's Chaos," Phoenix replies.

Her green eyes become rounder. "He's found us? What can we do?"

"Morpheus and the Zions are working on something. Don't worry, Mrs. Westbrook. It will be all right." Bryce smiles through the heartfelt lie. He can't possibly know we'll be okay.

Her gaze darkens. "Call me Leticia. I don't want anything to do with that name anymore."

"I can protect you all now that I'm a superhero," Theo chimes in.

Bless his heart, the kid is adorable. No wonder Phoenix's mom won't let go of him. Maybe he reminds her of Phoenix when he was little.

The rest of our party trickles out of the studio and forms a circle around us. Xavier opens his mouth to say something but seems to become tongue-tied when his eyes land on Leticia.

Felicity glances at the ceiling. "The storm has grown quiet. Do you think Morpheus succeeded?"

She's right—the noise from the thunder and wind has ceased.

"He must have," Bryce pipes up. "Not that I had any doubt he would."

Yeah, but at what cost?

"The Zions are coming back," Rufio points out.

I follow his line of vision and see the old men in their red and gold robes making their way to us. They're alone.

"Where's Morpheus?" Mrs. Malek asks the question that was on the tip of my tongue.

I'd meet them halfway, but I'm afraid the news they have for us isn't good. Phoenix, probably sensing the tension in my body, pulls me close to him, keeping his arm wrapped around my shoulders.

My heart is stuck in my throat when the Zions finally reach our group.

"What happened out there?" Rufio is the one who asks first.

"Morpheus was able to ascend to demigod form," Ismael replies.

"Does that mean he managed to conceal the warehouse from Chaos?" Xavier asks.

"That would be the case." Iago nods.

"So, where is he?" I ask.

"That, we do not know. We didn't speak to or see him after he did what he had to do," Ismael deadpans.

I'm getting seriously pissed at them. How can they stand there so peacefully when we don't know where Morpheus went?

"Do you think he simply abandoned us now that he's uber powerful?" Renata asks.

"No," I say. "He wouldn't. If he left, he must have a reason. He'll come back."

The conviction in my tone is more to convince myself than anyone else. He'll come back to me. He has to.

Xavier pinches the bridge of his nose, exhaling loudly. "Now that we don't have Chaos breathing down our necks, let's assess our situation." He turns to Travis. "What do you know about the Neo Gods' attacks?"

The man grimaces, then switches his attention to Leticia and Theo. "Maybe we should have this conversation back in the office."

Understanding dawns on her face. We shouldn't remind Theo of those terrible events.

"Before you go, we're in dire need of medical supplies and food. When can we expect a delivery to arrive?" she asks.

"I don't know. Everyone is scrambling at the moment, and we also don't want to lead the Neo Gods here."

"Maybe we can get supplies," Renata suggests. "We have the van."

"Yeah, a stolen van. If you want to get arrested, be my guest," Rosie retorts.

"I don't think the police are worried about grand theft auto at the moment," Bryce replies. "We could go on a supply run."

"No, you kids are going to stay put," Xavier butts in. "And don't forget you have to recover, Bryce."

"I agree with Xavier. I'm sure there will be more people coming in who need healing," Jodie adds.

"If Bryce is up for it tomorrow, he can help Ellen with some of the other kids. Theo was the gravest case, but there are other children who could use your help."

Jodie turns her face into a scowl. "If they're not in mortal danger, then we should let them heal naturally."

Bryce glowers at her. "Why? Because if they're kids, even as Idols you can't use them in your army?"

Her eyebrows meet her hairline. "That's absurd. Of course that's not the reason. I'm only thinking about the toll healing has on you."

Yeah, like we believe her. I seek Toby's gaze, our very own truth teller. As if reading the question in my eyes, he shakes his head, confirming what I already knew. Jodie is full of shit. I wish she had never found us.

"Fine, we can rest for a day, but you can't expect us to stay hidden here while the world outside burns," Rufio pipes up.

"No, but I also don't want anyone running into a dangerous situation unprepared," Xavier fires back.

"Plus, we should give Morpheus a chance to come back," I say.

"Well, don't count on him returning." Jodie snorts. "He's a demigod. His priorities aren't the same anymore."

"Don't you dare judge him by your moral standards," I snap.

"What about Delta? Since you didn't let me kill him, shouldn't the Knights have gotten information from him already?" Rosie asks.

"You've apprehended Delta?" Jodie widen her eyes. "And you handed him over to the Knights without interrogating him first?"

"We didn't have the means to drag his sorry ass along while we were trying to escape. I did what I thought was best," Xavier replies angrily.

"Maybe we should find out if they have new information," Toby says hopefully.

"I wouldn't count much on the Knights getting anything out of that fu—I mean, guy," Phoenix replies, glancing apologetically at his mother for his almost slipup in front of Theo. "Bryce and Rufio had blocks, and only Daisy was able to breach through."

I can't believe that didn't occur to me until now. "I have to go see him."

A shadow crosses Xavier's eyes. I'm afraid he's going to say no, but he knows we desperately need information on the Neo

Gods. If I can find their secret hideout in the mountains, even better.

"I'll make the call," he replies finally.

Travis, who had been listening to the exchange silently until now, chimes in. "There's a secure line you can use in the studio."

"Thank you. I'll do it right now."

"Maybe you should also try to reach Mr. Silverstone," Toby suggests. "We've heard nothing from him for a while."

I don't need to read minds to know the lack of news from Gunther is weighing heavily on Xavier's shoulders.

"Things are chaotic in Hawk City as well. There have been several attacks in Norm neighborhoods," Travis replies somberly.

"Also schools?" I ask.

"No, not schools, but just as devastating."

"And let me guess, the Idol police are doing nothing to deter those terrorists." Rufio's eyes seem to flash bright blue for a second, but I must be imagining things.

"Not with the chief of police being a top dog in their organization," I reply, remembering vividly that he was one of my targets. Too bad I didn't have the chance to take him down.

"The cops here aren't helping either. The Neo Gods' hold is deep in every branch of the government," Travis says with a deep frown.

Felicity hugs her middle, appearing smaller. "How can we win this war, then?"

"Just kill the big bad," Theo replies calmly.

"The big bad?" I ask, amused by his statement despite our dire situation.

He nods. "Yeah. If you kill the main villain, then his followers will fall too."

"Where did you learn that?" Leticia asks.

"From cartoons." He shrugs.

"That's actually not a bad plan." Bryce rubs his chin.

"Okay, but who is the head?" Phoenix asks.

Bryce and Rufio trade a glance, but it's Rufio who replies. "The master."

33

DAISY

There was nothing to do but learn as much as we could from the situation and then come up with a plan. After we heard from Travis, Morty, Ellen, and her Norm girlfriend—who also happened to be a teacher in one of the schools attacked—we now know most of the attacks were carried out by a team of two high-level Idols and five or six Fringes. Every single one of the attackers was armed with lightning-glass weapons, but only the Idols had protective vests.

The meeting took around two hours, and then Ellen showed us around and introduced us to the other volunteers who were helping with the injured. None of them were Idols, which didn't surprise me.

The majority of the wounds were burns and glass cuts, and I could tell it killed Bryce that he couldn't heal them yet. It was hard to look closely at those poor children and teens and maintain a serene expression. I was torn between blind rage and the deepest sorrow.

While we were helping Ellen, Xavier snuck out with Travis, Mrs. Malek, and Leticia to get the supplies. We couldn't risk exposure, but it was apparently okay if the adults did. That rubbed me the wrong way, but I was too tired to fight Xavier about it. They came back safe, and that's all that mattered.

Nighttime has fallen with no sign of Morpheus yet. We've all settled for the evening in an area separated from the makeshift hospital by a pile of empty cardboard boxes. Comfort is not to be found, since every single mattress and sleeping bag are being used in the hospital. Our hosts offered the leather couches in their studio to Mrs. Malek, Leticia, and Felicity. No one bothered to offer Jodie the courtesy. It seems her reputation preceded her.

But they didn't want the perk, and it took much insistence from everyone to make them accept the offer. Theo, who has grown attached to Phoenix's mother, also slept with them. As for us, we're making do on the floor, turning our jackets into pillows and trying to ignore the cold bite of the hard surface. It's still better than the bungalows in the camp from hell.

Rosie has thawed out toward Toby—finally—and is cuddled with him in a corner. Both fell asleep within minutes. Renata picked a spot as far as possible from us to avoid another conflict. No one can say she isn't trying. We're by no means friends, but days of running for our lives together has created some type of bond between us. I no longer resent her for all the awful things she did in the past. Rosie is another story.

I'm sandwiched between Rufio and Phoenix. They went down pretty fast too, but I can't sleep. Worry gnaws at my insides, carving a hole in my heart.

Bryce said he was going to use the restroom, but that was ten minutes ago. I suspect he's with the children in the hospital. He knows better than to try to heal anyone now, but he can also be stubborn as hell. Since it's not likely I can sleep, I decide to go look for him. Getting up without stirring my human blankets is difficult, and for a moment, I think Rufio is waking up. But aside from mumbling in his sleep, he doesn't do anything else.

On my tiptoes, I mince away from our sleeping camp and veer toward the makeshift hospital. The place is dim; the only lights are from the small lamps on the walls. Ellen is awake, doing her rounds, but there's no sign of Bryce. *Strange.* Maybe he did go to the restroom.

I turn around before Ellen sees me and chastises me for not resting, but I don't return to where the others are. My feet take me to the back of the warehouse where Morpheus went with the Zions earlier in order to ascend to his demigod status.

The word demigod leaves a stain in my mind. I can't believe Magia was one who chose to become mortal. I wish I knew why she did that when the vast majority of her kind are selfish and capricious. And why that important fact is not common knowledge. Even those religious freaks believed she was an Idol. I wonder if that antique book I got from the school's librarian had that information. But if it did, I'm sure Jodie would have known. She wouldn't have told Mrs. Wilkins to give me that book without knowing exactly what it contained. It's a pity that it's now probably in the hands of the new Neo God principal.

But we have the Zions, who seem to possess a plethora of knowledge. I didn't have the chance to grill the brothers today, but tomorrow that's my top priority. I'm glad they decided to stay.

I finally reach my final destination. This section of the warehouse is completely separate from the used area by sheet metal walls that go all the way up to the ceiling. The entrance is an opening big enough to allow a truck through. The sliding door is half open, but inside is not as dark as I expected it to be.

It's much colder here than it was in the main section of the warehouse though, and the reason is the huge hole in the ceiling. There's a charred spot right below it, and my guess is a lightning bolt struck here. That must have been the awful noise we heard earlier. Moonlight is pouring through the gap, creating a small silvery area. I stand under it, glancing at the starry sky.

"Oh, Morpheus. Where are you?" I whisper.

My question meets with silence, which only makes the choke in my throat grow larger. I drop my head in my hands, fighting the despair that's beginning to take hold of me. Tears prickle my eyes, but if I let them fall now, I don't think I will ever stop bawling.

I hear footsteps approach, and a split second later, I sense Bryce. I turn around just as he's within reach. We both freeze for a moment with our gazes locked. A thousand thoughts are exchanged in that single glance, and then I don't know who attacks whom first. I'm in his arms and my fingers are in his hair, making a mess out of it. I'm not kissing him; I'm devouring his mouth as if he's the only sustenance I need.

We fly out of the spotlight, disappearing into a dark corner. My back meets the wall while Bryce presses his body against mine. Our hands become impatient, eager, as they try to get us out of our clothes as fast as possible. My jacket and top go first; then my jeans are the next to disappear in the darkness. It may seem like we're two careless teenagers who can't go a day without sex, but that isn't what this is about. After the cruelty we saw, the ordeals we've gone through, connecting skin to skin is the only way we can feel human again.

We haven't stopped kissing since we started, but when I feel Bryce's erection press against me, I tense, pulling away. "We need protection."

Bryce's eyes are glowing, giving him an even more other-worldly appearance. Hooded like that, they're sexy as hell.

"Do we?" he whispers, giving me pause.

"Yes, Bryce, we do. I'm not on the pill."

"I know, but what about the prophecy? What if the only way to truly end this war is to vanquish Chaos?"

"Are you saying you believe our child would be the God-killer?"

"I don't know. It makes sense. And Morpheus had a vision about us being linked by the infinity band. What if our meeting was preordained?"

"Preordained? I'm not sure about that."

"I never told anyone this, but I wasn't headed to Poppy's Joint that night we met. I didn't even know it existed before I parked in front of it."

"But you said you came in because we're notorious for our pies."

He shakes his head. "I got that from your poster on the window. I was driving aimlessly that night. Don't get me wrong. I wanted pie."

"How did you know where to go, then?"

"I had a vision of the place. It popped into my head unbidden. And somehow, I was able to find it without getting lost even though I had never been there before. It was as if a greater force was leading me there."

My heart is beating much faster now while I'm grappling with Bryce's revelation. My mind whirls as it tries to connect all the pieces in this gigantic puzzle.

"Why didn't you tell me before?"

"I didn't think it was important. But then there were other details, such as how Gunther knew exactly how long to keep me locked away until you were in mortal danger, or how he and my mother knew I'd be able to heal you. I think a demigod or even a god is feeding them this information."

"And you think all that means those crazy fanatics were right about the God-killer?"

He caresses my cheek. "I just think it's not a theory we should ignore."

I bite my lower lip. "But what if it's bullshit? I'm only eighteen. I'm not ready to... procreate. Besides, the world is crazy right now. It'd be irresponsible to bring a child into it."

He sighs against my lips, the hot air tickling my skin. "You're right. We shouldn't be reckless about this. Besides, I think if I knocked you up, Xavier would have my balls."

"Yeah, I think he would."

Bryce steps back and then picks up his jeans from the floor. "This is the last one." He pulls a wrapper from the back pocket. "Maybe we should have asked Xavier to buy us more condoms."

Heat rushes to my face. "They risked their lives to get essential supplies."

"Well, I consider avoiding teen pregnancy essential." He smiles cheekily.

"I think Phoenix's humor is rubbing off on you."

"Maybe." Bryce tears the package with his teeth without breaking eye contact, then rolls the condom down his shaft. I'm still in the same spot with my back pressed against the wall when he cages me in by bracing his forearms on each side of my head. "Where were we?"

I reach for his fine ass and pull his hips against mine. I'm so wet that he slides halfway in even in this awkward position.

"About here," I murmur.

He grabs my hips, lifting me off the floor. I wrap my legs around him, hooking them at the ankles behind his butt, which grants him easy access for a home run. He fills me completely while searing my mouth with an ardent kiss. I dig my heels against his ass, squeezing him, which elicits a grunt from deep his throat.

"Damn it, babe. Why do you always have to feel so fucking amazing?"

"Would you rather I didn't?" I pepper his jaw with kisses.

"Hell no."

There's no keeping the pace slow with us because the urgency from before has returned with a vengeance. Bryce pistons in and out of me like a man on a mission, quickly turning my body into mush. The delicious pressure between my legs builds up quickly, and I'm glad my mouth is currently busy or I'd scream from the top of my lungs. It feels so good, and I obviously have zero control of my body.

Bryce's grunts become louder as he increases his tempo. In this empty area, our lovemaking sounds, even if muffled, echo too noisily. I begin to worry Xavier is going to bust us, but my mind scrambles when the wave of cosmic orgasm finally hits me. Accidentally, I bite Bryce's lower lip, drawing blood. *Man, I'm savage.*

Bryce follows suit in the next minute, abandoning my mouth to hide his face in the crook of my neck. His body spasms almost violently as he empties himself in me, warm and sleek.

Huh?

I push him back with such force that he loses his balance and staggers back. "What's wrong?"

Ignoring him, I glance at the mess that's trickling down my legs. "Bryce!"

"What?"

"Look!" I point at it. "What the hell happened to the condom?"

He glances at his dick, which is still at half mast but also bare save for the ring of rubber around the base. "It broke."

"How could it break?" My voice rises to a pitch, ringing around us.

"Shhh. Do you want to draw everyone here?" he hisses.

"Fuck, fuck, fuck. This can't be happening." I pull my hair back, yanking at the strands. Then I begin to jump in place.

"What are you doing?"

"Helping gravity."

"Do you think that will work?"

"I don't know, Bryce. I'm freaking out here, can't you see?" I grab my discarded shirt from the floor and clean myself to the best of my ability.

Bryce steps closer and takes the shirt from my hand. "Let me help you."

He drops to his knees and runs the cloth up my legs, sending tingles down my spine. *Damn it.* I'm not supposed to get aroused when there could be millions of sperm traveling up to my womb.

"Maybe I could lick it clean," he says with a smile.

I hit his shoulder. "Bryce, come on. This is serious."

His grin wilts to nothing, and finally his expression reflects our predicament. He unfurls from his crouch, looking incredibly guilty. "I'm sorry, Daisy."

"You didn't do this on purpose, did you?"

He quirks both eyebrows. "Of course not. How can you even ask?"

I shake my head, dropping my gaze to his neck. "Shit. I know you wouldn't do it. It's almost like we jinxed ourselves by talking about making a God-killer."

"Maybe we did." He steps back, running his hand through his hair. "Or maybe we have zero control over our lives, and this was supposed to happen."

I hear voices just outside, and that prompts me into getting dressed. There's nothing we can do about our situation in this moment. Bryce offers me his shirt since mine is unwearable now.

"Daisy?" Ellen calls from the entrance.

"Hey, Ellen."

"And Bryce. I'm not going to ask. I just came by to let you know that Xavier is looking for you, and he doesn't seem happy."

Crap. "Okay. Thanks."

Her silhouette disappears from the door, but before I can take a step forward, Bryce takes my hand, halting me. "I want you to know that whatever happens, I'm here. We'll face it together."

Tears fill my eyes as several emotions compete for space in my chest. I'm remorseful for accusing him of tampering with the condom, afraid we did make a god-killing baby tonight, and filled with unmeasurable joy that this amazing guy loves me so much.

I rise on my tiptoes to kiss him softly on the lips. "I know. But first, we might have to face my pissed-off uncle."

34

MORPHEUS

With my unrestrained demigod powers, arriving at my destination took a mere thought. Eris, my half sister, tagged along, but I could have come without her. I returned to the Church of the Bold and the Fearless camp to take care of loose ends. Those motherfuckers tricked us, tried to kill us. They deserve what's coming for them. From my vantage point, I can see the miasma surrounding the area, but I can't glimpse past the smog. However, the discomfort I felt when I was inside the cave isn't present now.

"Why did you bring me here?" Eris asks.

"There are very wicked people down there who deserve punishment."

"Oh, you're taking the wrathful god approach?"

"When it comes to those people, yes."

"I love that you're fully embracing your dark side, brother." She scrunches up her nose. "But this place reeks!"

She's right. The miasma does have a smell. I didn't notice before, but maybe it's because I wasn't a true demigod yet.

"You know why that's the case?" I quirk an eyebrow.

She slings her arm over her nose and glowers at me. "Obviously. I may be your half sister, Morpheus, but I'm a full-fledged god, not a halfling like you. There's a lightning-glass reserve down there. One of Magia's last acts of rebellion before she turned her back on her legacy."

"What do you mean?"

"Magia was a difficult child, stubborn as hell. I should know, I gave birth to the brat. She hated the way Idols treated Norms and Fringes, so I gave her the power to unmake them."

"She wasn't born with it?" My eyes widen.

"No. She did use her gift to punish Idols who misbehaved, giving me great pride. But Chaos soon set his eyes on her, wanted to use her to further his wicked games of war. He tricked her into unmaking innocent Idols, including the man she had fallen in love with. When she found out, she was heartbroken, and the rage consumed her."

The vision I had of Daisy and Bryce linked to some mysterious people from the past comes to the forefront of my mind, and with it, the certainty that Bryce is a descendant of the Idol Magia loved.

"Bryce Kent is related to that Idol," I say.

"Yes. He is." Eris lets out a loaded sigh. "Chaos's meddling cost their relationship. He loves to see his family suffer. That's why he killed Magia's father too."

I narrow my eyes. "Let me guess: that's why you're hell-bent on getting in his way."

She smiles in a chilling manner. "Naturally. I'm Strife; I wouldn't be helping to bring peace to the world if it wasn't to hurt that son of a bitch."

"So, gods can fall for mortals," I mutter.

She tilts her head to the side. "Of course we can. Where do you think all those demigods and Idols come from? It isn't always about lust, you know?"

"Hmm." I gaze into the distance.

"You're still in love with Daisy, even if you're a little numb to the feeling. You're adjusting to your powers, and they've taken over completely. Once you get used to them, you'll be back by her side in the blink of an eye."

I should feel relief, but the only emotion churning in my chest is the all-consuming desire for retaliation.

"Right now, all I care about is destroying every source of lightning-glass in the world, starting with the one below us."

"Why would you want to destroy them? Magia created them so Norms and Fringes could protect themselves from Idols."

"Her intentions were good, but unfortunately, once Norms and Fringes have a taste of power, they want everything for themselves. Humanity is rotten regardless of which side they're on."

"Chaos's prison is weakening. If the war keeps raging, he'll be set free, and then there won't be a world for any of the races."

"It's why I have to destroy him first."

"He's a god, Morpheus. Even bound to the island, he's still more powerful than you. Our father couldn't take him down, and he tried several times."

"But Magia's sacrifice weakened him, didn't it? It's what tethered him to the island."

"How do you know that?"

"A hunch." I shrug, not wanting to get into details about the bits of information Chaos let slip during our interactions. "Why else would he be obsessed with killing Daisy?"

"Good hunch."

"What about the prophecy that Daisy and Bryce can create a God-killer? Is that true?"

Eris grimaces and then tries to hide it, but too late. "The prophecy was a mistake."

"I don't follow."

"Do you want to destroy shit or what?" she tries to change the subject.

"I want you to tell me the truth, Eris. Can Daisy and Bryce create the God-killer?"

"Yes." She crosses her arms. "Yes, they can. But the Fates didn't tell me how."

I frown. "The Fates?"

"Shortly after Magia's mortal life ended, I made a mistake and went to see them. All gods know not to mess with those psychos, but I was grieving and not thinking straight."

"What happened?"

"What do you think happened? They sealed Daisy and Bryce's fate with this insane destiny by creating the prophecy of the God-killer."

"According to the lore, whatever destiny the Fates give to someone can't be altered, but it usually has terrible consequences for the bearer. What's going to happen to Daisy and Bryce?" My voice rises, sounding like thunder.

"I don't know. No one does."

The shadows manifest, circling around me like a dark tornado. The rage in my core expands at the speed of light. I want to wreak havoc in the world, destroy everything in sight. And I'll start right now. I zap downward, piercing through the miasma with ease. I sense Eris is following me, which means Chaos could have done the same if he hadn't been stuck on that island of horrors.

It's the middle of the day, so the miners are working at full speed in the cave. I come by the camp's administration building first, and the first person I recognize is Artex, giving orders to men dressed in dark uniforms to load a truck with several wooden crates. I know exactly what is in those boxes. More lightning-glass weapons. I also notice there are way more people in the camp than before. The parking lot is full, and there are several tents near the bungalows.

My first act as avenging demigod is to strike every single soldier down below with mind-shattering fear. They drop the boxes they were carrying and then collapse to the ground. Their hearts will give out in a minute or so. I save Artex for last. He aims a shotgun in my direction and fires, but in my dark smoke form, the lightning-glass bullet simply goes through me without causing any damage.

But before he has the chance to reload, I become corporeal again and hammer into him, sending him backward. He loses the gun, crashing against a tree nearby. I leap forward, landing right in front of him.

"Hello, Artex. Miss me?"

"Get away from me, you freak."

"I warned you if you tried to harm Daisy, you would feel my wrath. Well, I'm here keeping my word."

"I'm not afraid of death."

"Oh, you will be."

I get into his head, knowing exactly what he fears the most. It seems the hippie fanatic is afraid of dogs. Shadows slither from my wrists, taking the shape of two hellhounds by my side. Artex's eyes turn round as he attempts to get back up, but he can't get traction on the ground to lift his body. My creations growl, ready to attack, which results in Artex soiling himself.

"No, no. Stay away from me," he begs.

My lips split into a grin. "Sic, boys."

Snarling, they pounce, disappearing inside the man. But to Artex, those monsters are tearing him apart for real. He thrashes on the ground, trying to protect his body from the vicious attack that's only happening in his mind.

"That was absolutely brilliant, brother. Very creative." Eris stops next to me.

"Come on. We have a mountain to blow up."

"And how do you plan to do that? As far as I can tell, you've only inherited the shadows from Daddy, not his ability to control storms or fire."

"I can make those fanatics do it themselves. They must have explosives around."

She rubs her chin as if in deep thought. "That would take too long, and honestly, I bore easily. I can help you speed up the process."

"In exchange for what?"

She shrugs. "I don't know yet. I'll think of something."

"Yeah, like I'm going to fall for that BS. You either help me without asking for anything in return or you can simply leave. I don't care either way."

"You're feistier than I expected."

"Don't tell me you never spied on me."

She waves her hand dismissively. "Yeah, a few times, only to see if you had finally figured out you were a demigod."

Artex's shrieks cease, and then he goes utterly still. I had already forgotten about him. His eyes remain wide open but are now unseeing. *Good riddance.*

I head to the forest, and it's only when I'm halfway down the path that I remember I could have zapped to the mountain. I suppose it'll take a while to get used to my new reality. Eris seems fine to tag along in this manner. *Damn. This whole situation is surreal.* Not too long ago, I thought I was a freak, a weakling because I needed magical bracelets to contain my powers. And now I'm strolling through the woods with a god next to me.

The moment of self-awareness lasts just a minute before I hear commotion ahead. By the tone and words used, my guess is that more hired soldiers are coming up ahead.

"How did you end up here?" Eris asks.

"Well, we had to go somewhere to hide from Chaos. This was the only option presented to us at the time. You have the uncanny ability to simply disappear at the worst times."

"I had no choice. Chaos was on my case, trying to suck me back to his island. That's something you have to be careful about. If he pulls you there, it's a bitch to get out."

"He already did that once," I grumble.

The forest is thinning out, so I mask my presence simply because I want to observe those motherfuckers first before I nuke them all. There is a group of mercenaries armed with assault weapons overseeing the mine workers, who are mostly members of the church. A woman comes out of the cave, pushing a barrow filled to the top with lightning-glass rough stones. She looks familiar. It takes me a second to recognize her as the person who was in charge of getting our accommodations more comfortable. Ophelia Sparks was her name. She doesn't look happy now.

"You're too slow," the mercenary says. "Our team is expecting a delivery by the end of the day."

"We're doing the best we can, but most of these people aren't strong enough to work for countless hours. We didn't sign up to be slaves, especially for the likes of you."

He backhands her on the face so hard it sends the woman to the ground.

"Boy, if Grandpa could see this. He'd love it," Eris pipes up. When I don't comment, she asks, "You're not having second thoughts, are you? I mean, some of those miners *are* innocent."

I glance at her. "There are no innocents here. They would have killed us all if we hadn't escaped."

"Okay then. So, what's your plan?"

"Can you tell me how many workers are in the mines?"

"Yes, but so should you. Come on, Morpheus. It's time to stretch your demigod powers."

I close my eyes, blocking out all the noise from the people in front of us. I let my awareness expand, searching for the low humming essence of those Norms. To Idols, they feel like empty shells. But that's not true. They just don't shine as bright as the others. I count at least fifteen people in there, which should be easy enough to manipulate. Fear can motivate people into doing the craziest shit.

I form the thought in my mind, and then I send it to theirs. In an instant, panic takes hold of them. They drop their tools and go in search of something to deter the monster they've awakened from the bowels of the cave. They don't flee, simply because doing so would be worse. Their only hope for survival is blowing up the cave, sealing the monster inside.

Quickly, they place every single unit of explosives they can find against the walls of raw lightning-glass. The location is perfect, since it's deep enough in the cave. Once the explosives go off, the entire ceiling will collapse on top of them. I just need to give them a final nudge, but I hesitate.

"What's the matter, little brother? Can't pull the trigger?" Eris asks maliciously.

I'm a demigod; I shouldn't be plagued by human morals, but I am. The biggest sin those people have committed was being weak sheep who blindly followed two fanatics. Do they deserve to die for it? And could Daisy forgive me for killing them so cold-bloodedly?

I ignore Eris and change tactics. I allow those miners to flee the scene. They're out in less than a minute, and immediately the hired guns begin to bark at them. Those are the ones who don't have one ounce of innocence in them. I can see their rotten hearts; I can read their amoral thoughts. I capture their conscience in my powers, twisting their reality, giving them no option but to go into the mine and carry out the mission.

Released from the compulsion that kept them inside the cave, the miners run away as fast as they can.

"Oh, Morpheus. You took pity on them." Eris laughs.

The explosion keeps me from replying. It shakes the ground violently. The blast would have sent us both flying back and debris would have torn us apart if we were mortals. A cloud of dust takes over the clearing, quickly covering us both.

"Do you know where the other lightning-glass reserves are?" I ask.

"Yes."

"Let's go, then. I want them all gone by the end of the day."

"Are we really doing this?" Eris asks.

"Yes. At least I am."

35

DAISY

There's no hiding what Bryce and I were up to from Xavier considering I'm wearing Bryce's shirt, and most likely my face is red and my lips are swollen. I find my uncle pacing at the edge of the hospital, alone. I'm relieved that I won't have to listen to his sermon in front of the others.

He stops moving and drops his eyes to my feet; then his gaze slowly travels up the length of my body. His shrewd eyes narrow to slits, and his jaw is clenched tight. When he switches his attention to Bryce, his expression doesn't improve. At least it doesn't get worse.

"You were looking for me?" I ask.

"Yes. I should chastise you for not resting, but I'll save that for later. I have news about Delta."

My heart skips a beat, and then it becomes tight as hell. "Were the Knights able to crack him?"

"No. And that's why I came looking for you. We're running out of time. We have to find the location of their headquarters, and the only person who was able to remove the blockage from Bryce's mind was you."

"I'll do it. Are we leaving now?"

"Yes, but I don't want to make a big deal out of it."

"I'll come with," Bryce pipes up.

Xavier shakes his head. "I'm sorry, son. You can't come."

"Why the hell not?"

"Isn't Chaos tracking you through the tattoo on your back?"

Bryce grimaces and then drops his gaze to the floor.

"Who is coming with me? Only you?" I ask.

He nods. "It's better this way."

"No. I'm coming too," Rufio declares from behind Xavier.

"If you were eavesdropping, you know why you can't come."

"I'm no longer marked." He pulls up his T-shirt and turns around. "Go ahead, Daisy. Touch my back."

I glance briefly at Bryce, and then I press my fingers between Rufio's shoulder blades. Nothing happens. "How is that possible?"

He pulls his T-shirt down and faces me. "You probably removed his mark when you unmade me."

I swallow the sudden lump that forms in my throat. If I was looking for a silver lining in this situation, I found it. But I can't voice my thoughts out loud.

"Fine. You're no longer a human tracking device for Chaos, but I still don't think you should come. It's not safe out in the streets," Xavier retorts.

Rufio flares his nostrils, glowering at him. "You think that just because I'm a Norm, I can't defend myself?"

"He's not saying that at all," I butt in. "And I do think you should come."

"Daisy—" Xavier starts.

"No buts. Facing that monster won't be easy for me. I want Rufio there."

"You should bring Toby too," Bryce suggests. "It's always handy to have a mind reader when you want to get information from someone."

"He wouldn't be able to read Delta's thoughts if he has a block in his mind," Rufio points out.

"Maybe not, but it won't hurt to learn what goes on in the heads of those Knight agents."

I get exactly what Bryce is implying. If the Knights were breached, who knows how many traitors they still have in their midst?

Xavier pinches the bridge of his nose, sighing heavily. "And how do you propose we get Toby without waking your sister in the process?"

We all glance in our sleeping camp's direction. Rosie and Toby are still entwined. Her head is resting on his chest, and he has his arm around her shoulder.

"I can separate them by levitation," Bryce says.

"Ugh. Fine. Do it. But if Rosie wakes up, under no circumstance is she coming with us."

"You don't need to say that twice," I reply. "I doubt she's given up on getting revenge."

Bryce lifts his arm, furrowing his eyebrows in concentration. There's a visible strain around his mouth. His nostrils flare, followed by a grunt. A few seconds pass, and when Toby doesn't budge, he lowers his arm. "Fuck!"

"You still haven't recovered. Don't push yourself," I tell him.

"This is maddening." He yanks his long bangs back with a jerky movement.

"I can try, but I might fuck this up," Xavier says. "I haven't gotten the hang of telekinesis yet."

"What are you doing?" Jodie finds us.

Fucking great.

There's a moment of silence. Naturally, no one wants to include Jodie in anything.

"We need to talk to Toby but without disturbing Rosie," I say.

"What do you want to talk to him about?" She eyes me suspiciously.

With a sigh, Xavier replies, "We're going to meet some Knight agents, and we want Toby to come with us."

Her cunning eyes become wider. "You're going to see Delta, aren't you?"

"I'm not telling you anything, Jodie. Now, if you're done interrogating us, I have a job to do."

"You're going to mess up. Allow me." She twirls her fingers, and a soft breeze stirs. It travels toward Toby and Rosie to gently move them apart. Controlling the air, Jodie brings Toby to us. He curls into a ball, which disrupts the bed of air keeping him hovering above the ground and causes a premature fall. Or maybe Jodie just dropped him on purpose.

"What the—" He jerks to a sitting position, searching his perimeter for danger.

"Shhh. Keep your voice down," I say.

"How did I get from there to here?" He rubs the arm that took the brunt of the fall.

"We didn't want to disturb Rosie." I offer him my hand.

He glances at our small gathering, leery. "What's going on, guys? Why the cloak-and-dagger attitude?"

"We're going on a secret mission, and we need your special skills," Xavier replies.

His eyebrows shoot to the heavens. "You want me to mind read? You know I can't do it properly if they're Idols."

"But you can get general vibes, can't you? On a scale of one to ten, how pissed off do you think my mother is?" Bryce asks casually.

"Uh..." Toby glances briefly in Jodie's direction, getting flustered at the speed of light. His cheeks are so red, it looks like he's wearing blush.

"How amusing." She glowers at Bryce.

"Eleven," Toby replies. "Who's coming on this mission?"

"Just you, me, Xavier, and Rufio," I say.

"Is that... wise? I mean, Xavier and I are newly made Idols, and Rufio is..." Toby's cheeks become even redder.

"You can say it, Toby. I'm only a Norm." He crosses his arms in front of his chest, twisting his face into a grimace.

"That's insane. I should come, at least. You need more protection," Jodie butts in.

"And I already said you're not coming. That's final, Jodie." Xavier stares her down.

She throws her hands up in the air. "Fine. Be my guest. I hope you don't get caught by the Neo Gods."

"Oh, I wouldn't mind if they crossed our path." Rufio's eyes take on a dangerous glint, and I swear they flash brighter for a second.

"I would," Xavier retorts. "All right. Get ready. We leave in five minutes."

RUFIO

"Daisy, can you check if Jodie is truly not following us?" Xavier asks from the driver seat.

"Can't you look yourself?" I pipe up.

"Rufio, cut it out," Daisy chastises me.

I've been picking on Xavier since we left the warehouse. Yeah, I'm still pissed that he didn't want me to come because he believes I'm a deadweight. If I'm being honest with myself, the anger is also aimed at me. Most of the time, I think the team has no use for me, but I can't live my life in self-pity.

"She's the most powerful Idol in this car, and her reach is greater," Xavier replies calmly, but I don't miss the underlying irritation in his tone.

"My mother is not going to follow us," I rebuff.

"It doesn't hurt to be careful," he grumbles.

"I'm not sensing her at all." Daisy glances at the side mirror. "And there's no car behind us."

"Where are we going?" Toby changes the subject. I'm not sure if he's trying to defuse the tension or not, but he's got my attention.

"To one of the Knights' secret locations."

"Is it that cabin in the woods Gunther Silverstone brought us to?" Daisy asks.

"No, a different place. They've had to make several changes in the last few weeks. Still, I'm not sure who to trust in their group, to be honest."

"Have you heard from him?" I ask.

"No. His radio silence is worrying me."

"You don't think he was captured or killed, do you?" Daisy asks in a high-pitched voice.

"Let's hope not."

Xavier's reply doesn't comfort me, and clearly it doesn't comfort Daisy either. Even without my Idol senses, I can tell she's tense as hell.

"When Morpheus returns, maybe he can connect with his half brother?" I suggest.

"Do you believe he'll come back?" Toby asks.

"Yes," Daisy and I reply in unison.

She turns in her seat to look at me. "You really think so?"

"Yes, sweetheart. He'll come back. He loves you too much to stay away."

Xavier grumbles. "Can you please not do the gushy thing in front of me? I'm still getting used to my niece dating four guys at once."

I snort. "That's pretty rich coming from the man who runs a strip club and allowed said niece to work there."

"Kid, you're lucky I'm driving. But keep smart-mouthing me and you will get the ass-whooping of your life."

Toby giggles but tries to hide his amusement when I award him a murderous glance.

"Rufio has a point though," Daisy comes to my defense.

"May I remind you that I didn't want to give you the job? You begged me for it, and I saved you from humiliation in the end."

"Good times," I mutter.

"I don't need any reminders." She glances out the window, crossing her arms in front of her chest.

My memories of that night are fuzzy, but what I do remember is bittersweet. I hated Daisy blindly back then. I can't believe I harbored such ugly feelings, and now I can't live without her.

I press my hand against my leather jacket, feeling the hard shape of the lightning-glass dagger I stuffed in my pocket. Let everyone think I'm harmless just because I don't have my Idol powers anymore. If anyone tries to harm Daisy, I'll gut them like the pigs they are.

"What's your take on Phoenix's mother?" Toby asks. "She looks so young. When did she have him?"

"I haven't made up my mind about her, to be honest," Daisy replies. "I know what that monster did to her, but at the same time, she didn't try to help Phoenix."

"You don't know she didn't, honey." Xavier is quick to come to Leticia's defense.

"Someone is smitten," I tease.

"I'm not smitten," he replies with indignation.

"Yes you are." Daisy laughs. "Totally."

"I don't want to hear another word about that nonsense. And don't go spreading rumors either. We're in the middle of war. There's no time for ridiculous gossip."

"It's not gossip if it's true. Besides, I think romance is exactly what we need in times of war."

"Yeah, I know you do. I hope you're being careful." Xavier throws Daisy a meaningful glance.

She seems to sink against the leather seat, becoming smaller. "Of course we are. Jeez."

"And I trust I don't even need to have this conversation with you, Toby," Xavier continues.

"What? Oh my God, Mr. X. You don't have to worry about Rosie and me."

I smirk, taking great pleasure in watching the guy squirm in his seat. I bet his face is in flames right now.

"How much longer until we get to the secret location?" Daisy asks, ripping my amusement to shreds.

Delta killed her parents on the orders of my father. Now she has to face the motherfucker, probably get into his head. I wish I could do that for her, take away the burden. But all I can do is stand by her side and be anything she needs me to be.

"Another ten minutes."

"What did they say when you talked to them?" she asks in a small voice.

"They tried everything, but they couldn't break him."

Her powers flare up suddenly, violent and angry. "But I can, and I will."

36

RUFIO

This might be a different location, but the vibe is the same as the other secret hideout. Another cabin in the woods, far away from civilization. The building is not large by any means. Maybe there are two bedrooms max. If they're using torture—which I'm sure they must—Delta's screams could be heard from outside. Not that there's anyone around to hear it.

"This is it?" I ask.

"That's the address." Xavier turns off the engine but keeps the headlights on.

No sooner does he reply than an agent exits through the front door. He lifts his arm to shield his eyes from the glare, preventing us from seeing his face. When he stops next to the driver window, I find he's not one of the agents who came to Poppy's Joint.

"Xavier, we've been waiting for you," he says in a thick French accent.

"Who are you?"

"Marlon Boucher. Gunther sent for me." He peers inside the car, immediately taking note of Daisy. "I see you've brought the Unmaker. Good, good." He switches his attention to the back seat. "But who is the Norm?"

"The name is Rufio Kent," I grit out.

Marlon's eyebrows arch. "You're Jonathan Kent's son. I'm sorry. I didn't know. Terrible thing he did to you."

The man steps back to allow Xavier to open the door. But Toby, Daisy, and I don't get out immediately. I turn to Toby. "What do you think? Can we trust that guy?"

"I don't know. His mind is completely blocked off from me. It's like he has a shield. I can't even get a read on his true disposition."

"Fucking fantastic," I mutter.

"Are you armed?" Daisy asks me.

I pat my jacket pocket. "You bet. Don't worry, babe. I'll keep my eyes trained on him."

Toby reaches for the door handle. "We'd better get going before he suspects we're talking about him."

The air is much cooler in the forest. I'd close off my jacket, but I want easy access to the lightning dagger in the inside pocket. I have another blade attached to an ankle holster, flying stars in my side pockets, and I also grabbed a few small rough-cut lightning-glass stones.

Once out of the car, I step close to Daisy, and together we follow Marlon, Xavier, and Toby into the cabin. Nothing inside screams that this place is a holding facility. It's a cozy little cabin with rustic furniture, a small kitchen, and a narrow corridor that leads to the bedrooms.

Another agent comes from that direction, and this one I recognize. He came to collect Delta from the diner.

"Castro, have you made any progress?" Xavier asks the man.

"No. The block inside his mind sends him into shock every time we get close to getting information. Not even Marlon was able to breach it."

"Why are you singling him out?" I ask.

"Because breaking through people's minds is my specialty." He smiles in a cocky way.

"Clearly you're not very good," I retort.

The man narrows his eyes but then shakes his head, laughing as if I'm not worth a reply. *Asshole.*

"I can breach Delta's block," Daisy says.

"Are you going to unmake him?" Marlon quirks an eyebrow.

Lifting her chin, she says, "Yes."

There's no hesitation on her part. She's putting on a tough front, but I know how much this situation is affecting her.

"Let's go, then. We're running out of time." Castro veers toward the corridor.

Daisy glances in my direction, saying without words that she needs me to come with her. But I also read guilt in her eyes. I don't know what more I can do to make her stop feeling that way.

"I'll be by your side the whole time, my love."

"I know, but maybe it'll be too hard for you to watch."

I grin. "Not at all. It will give me great pleasure to watch you punish that son of a bitch."

Xavier, who had followed Castro ahead of us, stops in his tracks and looks over his shoulder. "Daisy, are you coming?"

"Yeah."

Marlon waves his arm in a flourishing gesture. "After you."

Daisy steps in front of him, but the man cuts in front of me, following close behind her. I have every intention of pushing him out of my way, but Toby grabs my jacket sleeve. I tense on the spot. He must have sensed something.

Daisy, Xavier, and Marlon disappear through a door, and my instincts are telling me to hurry up, but I have to find out what Toby picked up first.

"Speak fast," I tell him.

"I just sensed something dubious from Marlon. He lied to us when he said he couldn't breach Delta's mind."

"Why would he do that?"

Toby glances at the front door. "Shit. We're not alone here. I sense at least five more Idols closing in on the cabin."

The small hairs on the back of my neck stand on end. Pulling my lightning-glass dagger from my pocket, I whirl around. "This is a trap."

I run toward the room Daisy disappeared into, but when I try to open the door, it won't budge. *Fuck!* Kicking the damn thing doesn't help either.

"Daisy!" I yell.

There's no response, which makes me more desperate. My eyes burn, filled with tears of frustration. *I'm a fucking weakling, and I failed her.*

"Let me try." Toby pushes me out of the way, but he can't bring the door down either.

Our time is up. The front door bursts open, and in come the Idols Toby sensed. Surprisingly, they aren't carrying lightning-glass weapons like I expected.

"Stop right there," the man at the front commands.

I take a step forward with my weapon ready. "Make me."

The asshole steps aside to allow a familiar person to enter.

"Soren. Motherfucker. Where the hell have you been?"

"Where is Daisy?" he asks with urgency.

"Trapped in that room. Toby and I couldn't break through."

"Shit. It's because Castro is in there. He's sealed the room from inside."

"Are you saying there's no way to get in?" My voice rises to a shrill.

"Yes, that's exactly what I'm saying. Is Daisy there alone?"

"No, Xavier is with her."

"Then let's hope they realize this was a trap before the worst happens."

DAISY

The knots in my stomach twist more savagely when my eyes land on Delta. His arms are cuffed behind the chair, and his blond head is dipped low. The door closes behind me with a resounding click, sounding final. Rufio has yet to come in, but I can't wait for him. My feet move of their own accord, bringing me closer to the monster who murdered my parents in cold blood.

He lifts his ugly face, boring into me with the weight of his hate-filled stare.

"I knew you would show up sooner or later."

"Why do you look so smug? Do you know what's going to happen to you?"

He laughs in a carefree manner. "Hmm, let me guess. You're going to unmake me so that asshole over there can get the location of our headquarters."

"That's right. But I don't need Marlon to get the intel. I can do it myself."

I reach for his head, but he swiftly jumps from his seat, free from his restraints, and pushes me back. I crash against Xavier, and we almost end up on the floor. Marlon and Castro untangle us, but before I can use my powers against Marlon, he throws a lightning-glass net over me, dampening my powers.

Fuck. Not again.

Rufio pounds against the door, screaming my name. Xavier is also rendered powerless by the other agent.

"What the hell are you doing?" he yells at Castro.

Delta laughs maliciously. "You're fools. Do you seriously believe Idols would side with Fringes and Norms? Only the mentally unstable would pick a race of insects over their own."

Marlon's grip on my arm is painful, and the net is cutting off my connection to my powers. But looking at Delta's glee, watching him take pleasure in our precarious situation, brings forth all the pain he caused Rosie and me. With it comes undiluted hate. I don't try to fight it. I let it expand like a dark stain in my soul because it's infusing me with renewed power. The strength in me doesn't come from Magia, the Idol. It comes from Magia, the fucking demigod.

I pull back the arm Marlon is holding and toss him across the room. Delta's smug expression contorts into a fit of rage. He conjures up a sphere of blue energy, but instead of sending it in my direction, he tosses it in Xavier's. *Son of a bitch*. He wants to kill every single member of my family in front of me. But the sphere crashes against the net and dissolves into wisps of harmless electric current. The lightning-glass annulled the blast.

"You're one stupid motherfucker." I jump on him, sending him crashing against the chair with my hands wrapped around his head.

Delta grunts as he tries to fight me off, but I'm much stronger than he is. My gift surges within me, more powerful than ever before. But as I pull Delta's power into me, I also get the ugliness in his heart. I'm privy to his depraved thoughts. He was the one who suggested they begin their attacks at the Norm schools. He used to torture his victims before killing them. He's the scum of the earth, and taking his powers away is not enough. He needs to fucking die.

He tries to not make a sound as I unmake him, even though I know it's painful. I dig my fingers harder against his temples, crushing his skull. Then he screams. My vision is blurry and tinged in red. There's no power left in him, but I keep applying pressure, keep squeezing, until finally his skull caves in and his head explodes in my hands like a watermelon, splashing blood and gray matter all over me.

Someone calls my name, but the sound seems to be coming

from afar. All I can hear is the sound of my heavy breathing coming out in bursts. Then strong arms hug me from behind, pulling me tight against a hard chest.

"Daisy. Fuck. You're okay," Rufio says, but he's wrong, so very wrong.

37

PHOENIX

I slept like the dead. Didn't even dream, which is too bad because I wouldn't have minded dreaming about Daisy since we have a tendency to share them and they're hot as sin. Without opening my eyes, I stretch my arm, finding nothing but the cold floor. Still groggy, I peel my eyes open and discover Daisy is gone. *Damn, she's already up and didn't wake me?*

I sense a pair of eyes staring at my back, and when I look over my shoulder, I find Theo standing super close, staring at me.

"Hey there, buddy. What's up?"

"Did you know you snore?"

I lean on my elbows, then cover my mouth with a fist as I try to hide my yawn. "I do?"

"Yeah. Mega loud."

Rubbing my eyes, I sit up. Then I run my fingers through my hair. It's pointless. It's so dirty, only water and shampoo will make it manageable again. I rub my scruffy jaw and wonder if Daisy likes the rugged look.

"What time is it?" I yawn again. I can't believe how tired I am.

Theo shrugs. "I don't know."

Rosie minces toward me, sporting some terrible bed hair. "Where's everyone?"

"I don't know. I just woke up."

"Toby's gone. Where could he be?"

"Maybe he went to the restroom. Speaking of which." I jump to my feet because one, I gotta pee, and two, there's no sense in sitting around and trying to guess where everyone went. I'll just go look for them.

Theo decides to follow me, and I wonder if he's potty trained already. I don't see the volume of a diaper under his pants, so I hope he is. The small restroom only has one stall and a urinal. While I'm busy doing my thing, Theo decides he has to use the bathroom too. That answers my earlier question. But when he doesn't leave the throne, I go investigate.

"Are okay, buddy?"

"Yeah. I'm done dropping a deuce."

I snicker, almost choking in the process. "Dude, who taught you to say that?"

"My dad."

"Well, if you're done, then hop off."

"I can't. You have to wipe my butt."

"Uh, come again?"

"I can't do it. My arms don't reach that far." He demonstrates by stretching his arm and twisting his torso.

I step back. "Oh no, no. I'm not wiping your butt, dude. No way."

He shrugs and jump off the toilet seat. "Okay."

"What are you doing?" I ask when he reaches for his pants.

He glances down and then back at me, sporting the cutest frown. "Getting dressed."

"Oh, for fuck's sake. I can't let you walk around with poop all over your butt."

He gasps, widening his eyes. "You said a bad word."

"Ah, hell. I did. Sorry."

"It's okay. I won't tell your mommy."

"Thanks, buddy. Now come on. Let's get you cleaned up."

Five minutes later, half of which I spent washing shit off my hands, we're finally on our way back to find everyone. We meet with my mother first, but her attention goes straight to the kid.

"Theo, where were you? I've been searching for you everywhere."

"I was with Phoenix. I had to go poo. He wiped my butt."

I throw my head back and groan. "Go ahead, say it a little louder so everyone can hear it."

"You helped him in the bathroom?" Mom watches me with eyes that are filled with amusement and surprise.

"Yup. Didn't have much choice in the matter. Have you seen Daisy?"

"I believe she went out with Xavier."

"What do you mean, she went out? Where?" I raise my voice. "I thought we were supposed to stay put because it was too risky to go anywhere."

"Calm down, honey. I'm sure Daisy is safe. Toby and Rufio also went with them."

"What the fuc—I mean, what the fudge? Why didn't they wake me?"

Bryce walks out of the room to my right, eating a doughnut. Naturally, if there's anything with sugar in the area, Mr. Sweet-tooth is the first to find it.

"Relax, bro. They'll be fine. Have a little faith," he says.

"I can't believe you're okay with this."

His carefree expression changes swiftly. "I'm not okay. I would have gone with them if I could. But you and I have a target on our backs. Chaos is tracking us through our tattoos, remember?"

Almost as if the son of a bitch can hear us, the tattoo between my shoulder blades begins to burn. I'm so fucking angry, I could destroy things. I settle for stealing Bryce's breakfast. Using a bit of telekinesis, I pry the treat from his fingers as he was about to take another bite, then stuff the whole thing in my mouth.

"What the hell, Phoenix!"

"Bryce! Language." Mom looks meaningfully in Theo's direction.

His remorseful expression makes me laugh, but since my mouth is full of doughnut, I end up choking on it.

"Serves you right," he pipes up.

Theo pulls on my sleeve. "I'm hungry."

"Come on, honey. Let's get you something to eat." Mom takes his hand and steers him into the room Bryce walked out of earlier.

I swallow the huge lump of food and ask, "Do they have coffee in there? I could use a pick-me-up. I'm so fucking tired."

"Yeah, there's some." Bryce's line of vision follows my mother and Theo. "It seems the little kid has stolen your mom's heart."

"Yeah," I reply, trying not to let the resentment take hold. I wish I'd had that kind of relationship with her when I was little. All my memories are tainted with pain. "We haven't heard anything about his father yet?"

"No. But I don't dare hope he's alive. There have been many losses among Norms."

My dark mood plummets completely, and it would have continued its spiraling descent into a pit of despair if I didn't sense Daisy's approach just then. Bryce's spine becomes taut too as he whirls around, facing the front of the warehouse. A minute later, the larger gate opens, and the van we stole drives in. Another car follows. A quick scan reveals there are Idols inside, including a familiar signature.

Bryce and I head toward the vehicles using our Idol speed. Xavier and Toby are the first to exit, but when Daisy finally follows them, my stomach bottoms out. She's covered in blood.

"Daisy!"

We're by her side in a flash but refrain from touching her.

"Are you hurt?" Bryce asks.

She shakes her head, not meeting his eyes.

"She killed Delta with her bare hands," Rufio answers for her.

Rosie comes running and then collides into Toby. A bunch of mushy nonsense leaves her mouth, but I block her out.

Soren and four other guys join our circle, looking grim as fuck.

"Is anyone going to tell us what happened? Did you manage to get the Neo Gods' headquarters location?' I ask.

"Yes," Daisy replies, lifting her face. "I got that from Delta."

"We came back to acquire weapons and strategize," Xavier adds.

I crack my knuckles. "Awesome. I can't wait to inflict some pain."

"You're not coming with us," Daisy says, then looks at Bryce. "None of you."

"The fuck we aren't," Bryce retorts. "I don't care about Chaos. I'm not going to let you head out again to fight those men, Daisy."

"It's not wise, Bryce. We've talked about this," Xavier butts in.

"No offense, Mr. X, but we need every man on this operation. You went alone last night and almost died," Soren replies.

"What?" I ask loudly.

"It was a trap. Two of the agents were traitors. They had

killed one of their own, Rick, and wanted to do the same to Daisy," Toby explains.

My nostrils flare as fury erupts from the pit of my stomach. "I hope you killed them all."

"Yes. They're gone," Daisy replies with a vacant glimmer in her eyes.

Damn it. She's not okay.

Felicity, who joined us at some point, steps forward, pushing Bryce and me out of the way. "Let's get you out of those filthy clothes, hon."

She steers Daisy away from us, and my instinct is to follow, but Bryce puts a hand on my arm. "Give her some space."

I'd bark at him if I didn't read the sorrow in his eyes. It's killing him too to stay away from her.

"Is Daisy going to be okay?" Soren asks. "We're going to need every single person on deck when we storm the Neo Gods' headquarters. Going without the Unmaker would be a blow."

"I'll go talk to her." Rosie steps away from Toby.

Xavier gets in her away, leaning down. "Please try not to put more burdens on your sister's shoulders."

Rosie twits her face into a grimace. "I won't. I promise."

DAISY

I let Felicity take my clothes off and then wipe the grime off my skin as if I'm watching the scene from far away. The numbness has taken over, and I don't know how to snap out of it. My entire life I fantasized about killing Delta, and now that I've gone and done it, there's no sense of joy or vindication. I'm empty.

Rosie comes into the office space that Travis and Morty let

us use. She watches me in silence for a moment, but I'm sure she has a lot of questions.

"Go ahead. Ask away."

"Did you really kill him?"

"Yeah. I did."

"You didn't want to kill him before. What made you change your mind?" There's no accusation in her tone.

I take a deep breath, letting my shoulders drop.

"Rosie, give Daisy a break," Felicity chastises her.

"No, it's okay, Fefe. I don't mind talking about it. Maybe it will help."

"At least get dressed first."

And by getting dressed, she means put on the oversized hoodie with *The Freaks* logo. We raided their merchandise closet. There's still blood on my jeans, but we don't have a replacement for them.

Finally dressed, I sit on the leather couch, folding my legs underneath me. "My plan was to only unmake him, but when I was inside his head, I saw every single atrocity he committed in his life. It was horrible. Then the realization hit me that he wouldn't stop his evil ways even if he didn't have any powers. Unmaking him wasn't enough. So I snapped and crushed his skull with my bare hands."

"Holy shit, girlie." Felicity widens her eyes. "No wonder you had so much gunk on your clothes."

"Why do you feel guilty now?" Rosie asks.

"I don't think guilt is what's swirling in my chest. I feel numb."

"It's understandable, sweetie." Felicity pats my shoulder. "To end a life, no matter how despicable that person was, is a heavy burden. It marks your soul forever."

"Well, I don't care about my soul." Rosie lifts her chin angrily. "Give me a lightning-glass dagger and I'll gladly end as many Neo Gods as I can find."

"I wish you didn't feel that way, but you'll get your chance sooner rather than later," I reply bitterly.

Before she can reply, the foundations of the building begin to vibrate and the lights flicker.

"What the hell" I jump to my feet while my heartbeat accelerates.

Looking at the ceiling, Rosie asks, "You don't think it's Chaos, do you?"

Expanding my senses, I attempt to guess who—or what—is approaching. All I see is a great mass of darkness. *Shit.*

I run out of the office and almost collide with Bryce. "What's going on?" I ask.

"We don't know, but something powerful is coming our way. We'd better brace for an attack."

Just then, the lights go out completely. The patients in our hospital shriek in fright. Ellen and the other volunteers attempt to calm the children down, but it's pretty hard to do that when we're shrouded in darkness. Monsters love the dark.

38

DAISY

The lights return just in time for us to see a great vortex of black smoke build up near the ceiling. My body is as tense as a coiled spring, while my heart feels like it's a fucking freight train. Bryce's powers are also engaged to the max as he stares upward. The vortex converges down, not too far from where we're standing. Slowly, a shape takes form. The shadows recede, and Morpheus appears in front of us in his demigod form.

"What the fucking hell!" Bryce yells my exact thoughts.

I can't believe I didn't recognize Morpheus's signature. My heart demands that I run to him, but my brain is commanding me to stay put. And when another shape materializes next to him, a woman with pale skin and jet-black hair, I become even more leery.

"Morpheus, you son of a bitch." Phoenix strides toward him. "Did you want to give us a heart attack? What kind of bullshit entrance was that? We thought you were Chaos."

The woman smirks and glances at Morpheus. "I told you they wouldn't recognize you."

Her tone denotes intimacy, which awakens the possessive side in me. "Who the fuck are you?"

She arches her eyebrows, looking surprised. "Oh my. You don't recognize me?"

"Should I?"

"Daisy." Morpheus takes a step forward. "This is Eris, my half sister."

Magia's mother. *Shit.* My anger deflates, but not completely. I'm still mad as hell at Morpheus for taking off. "Where have you been?"

"I had to take care of something important."

"And you couldn't tell us before you vanished?" Rufio steps next to me, glaring openly at Morpheus and his companion.

"No."

"Don't mind Morpheus. He hasn't completely adjusted to being a demigod yet. He'll be a cold asshole for a while," Eris pipes up.

He furrows his eyebrows, and his eyes, which were glowing like molten gold, return to normal. "Am I still acting like that?"

"Yes," everyone replies in unison.

"Morpheus!" Mrs. Malek pushes through the crowd to get to him.

She, unlike me, doesn't hesitate to pull her son into a hug. He tenses for a second but then returns the gesture.

"I was so worried about you," she says, easing off to look at his face. Then she does something wholly unexpected. She pinches his arm. "Don't ever do that to me again."

"Ouch! Mom, come on." He steps back, rubbing the spot.

"No way he felt that," Phoenix whispers to me.

Mrs. Malek glances over her shoulder. "Oh, he felt it."

Oh, motherly powers. Good to know someone can keep him in check, even if he's a demigod now.

"Sorry to interrupt the party, but we have an attack to plan." Xavier approaches our group.

"An attack? Where?" Morpheus asks.

"We have the Neo Gods' headquarters location," I say.

"Then tell me and I'll take care of it."

"Alone?" My voice rises to a pitch.

"Yes, alone. Don't look at me like that. I've just destroyed every single lightning-glass mine in the world. I can level another mountain to the ground and bury Neo Gods with it."

"You did what?" Soren pushes through the small gathering to reach the front.

"You heard me."

"Hold up." Rufio raises his hand. "I must have misheard you."

"Am I not speaking English? I destroyed all the lightning-glass reserves."

"Why would you do that?" Jodie asks. "We needed those weapons."

"Exactly. My father spent years to gain the trust of the leaders of the church, and you're saying you fucking blew everything up?" Soren yells.

"I'm sorry that Gunther's work was in vain. But destroying the reserves had to be done." Morpheus glowers at him.

"Why?" I ask.

"Because they would do more harm than good in the long run. Surely you can see that. Those religious freaks had made an alliance with mercenaries. Their goal was to end all Idols, not only the Neo Gods."

"You had no right!" Rufio takes a step forward, shaking with fury. "Norms deserve a way to fight. You just took that option from us!"

"I'm sorry, Rufio."

"Bullshit! You're not sorry. You did it because you don't fucking care about anyone else now that you've mastered your demigod powers. You're just as bad as Chaos," Rufio spits out.

"I'm nothing like him." Morpheus takes an aggressive stance, moving forward.

Fuck. This is escalating too fast. I jump in between them with my arms raised. "Stop it! We can't start to fight among ourselves."

"As far as I'm concerned, Morpheus clearly stated which side he's on, and it's not ours," Rufio replies.

"You're acting like a spoiled brat. It's not my fault you don't have your powers anymore," Morpheus rebuffs.

Damn it. That comment hurt. It's not his fault; it's mine.

Ellen marches in our direction, almost spitting fire from her nose. "You two!" She points a finger at Rufio and Morpheus. "If you can't behave, get out. You're scaring the children."

Bryce pulls Rufio back. "Come on, bro. You need to calm down."

"Let go of me." He jerks free from Bryce's hold, and for a second, dark veins appear on his face.

"Rufio, your face," Bryce points out.

"What?" he snaps.

The veins are gone, but if Bryce saw them too, then I didn't imagine it.

"You had markings, just like when your powers used to manifest," I tell him.

Jodie peers closely at her son. "He can't possibly be regaining his powers, can he?"

I glance at Eris, who must know more about Magia's powers than anyone else. I notice she too is looking at Rufio with rapt attention.

"Is it possible for an unmade Idol to recover their powers?" I ask.

"No. It's never happened to any Idol Magia unmade. There's no reason to believe it would be any different with him."

"My powers aren't returning. I'd know otherwise," Rufio adds.

"Something is definitely happening to you. Remember when that mattress you were lying on simply turned into dust?" Phoenix chimes in.

Heat creeps up my cheeks remembering that night. God, he'd better not keep talking about it.

"Okay, I'm bored," Eris says. "I'm gonna go."

She vanishes in the next second, leaving me annoyed as hell. I didn't have the chance to interrogate her.

Morpheus is suddenly by my side. He can obviously move much faster than us Idols. "Daisy, I need that address."

"I'm not giving it to you."

He narrows his eyes to slits. "Are you serious?"

"Yes, dead serious. This is not your personal fight, Morpheus. We should be working as a team."

"Why, when I can deal with the Neo Gods in the blink of an eye?"

"Cocky much?" I raise an eyebrow.

"No, just realistic."

"I liked you better when you didn't know about your heritage. You're an ass now."

I turn on my heels and stride away. I'm too fucking pissed to have a reasonable conversation with him. I'm being petty and immature by not giving him the address, but he can get it from Xavier anyway. I don't realize I'm crying until my nose gets stuffed up.

I head for the restroom, hoping it's empty. I just need a moment alone to calm down. But apparently that's not in the cards for me. When I enter, Morpheus is there, waiting for me. Naturally, he can now appear and disappear at will.

"Why did you follow me?"

"Because you're angry, and I want to understand why."

"Were you always this thick, or is being obtuse a trait of your demigod status?"

His eyes darken and his shadows coil around his body. "That was a low blow, Daisy."

"Was it? I mean, you must know why I'm angry. You left without saying a word, made the decision to destroy all the lightning-glass reserves without talking to the rest of us first, and now you want to go on a solo mission again. Did I miss anything?"

"Yeah, you damn well missed something." He flies across the room to invade my personal space. "I've done all this to protect everyone. You saw what those fanatics were up to. Lightning-glass weapons in the hands of criminals could be devastating. It was the right call to make."

"Maybe. But you should have talked to us first instead of letting your ego take over."

"My ego..." He steps back, threading his fingers through his hair. "That wasn't it, Daisy. I wanted to make those assholes pay for trying to hurt you."

"Did you?"

"I didn't kill every single person in the camp if that's what you're asking. I'm not a monster."

Guilt pierces my chest. "I'm not saying you are."

"Really? Could have fooled me."

"Morpheus." I step closer. "I don't want to fight with you."

The angry storm vanishes from his eyes. "I don't want to fight with you either."

"Then stop being so stubborn."

His eyebrows shoot to the heavens. "I'm being stubborn? Pot, meet kettle."

My anger returns. It's clear we can't have a normal conversation right now without arguing. I turn around before I say something I'll regret, but Morpheus doesn't allow me to take a step. He's in front of me, blocking my path.

"Don't walk away from me."

"Like you did?" I lift my chin in defiance.

His eyes are once again otherworldly, and the power radiating from him vibrates against my skin. Goose bumps break out on my arms, and crazy enough, wisps of desire curl around the base of my spine.

His brows furrow while regret shines in his eyes. "I'm sorry." He reaches for the back of my head, tangling his fingers in my hair. "I shouldn't have left. I was… overwhelmed. I still am."

His confession deflates my anger. With a sigh, I move closer to him and cup his cheek. "Let me help you."

He leans down, pressing his forehead against mine. "I don't know how anymore."

Rising on my tiptoes, I bring my lips to his. His response is immediate. He twists a lock of my hair, keeping my head in place while he invades my mouth with his tongue. My skin tingles all over, a reaction that's completely new and exciting. My powers respond to his, flowing through my veins effervescently.

I'm suddenly floating on air as light as a feather. I latch on to his body, wrapping my legs around his hips. Our clothes vanish like magic, and with the barriers gone, Morpheus's erection teases my center.

"How did you do that?" I ask against his mouth.

"I'm not sure, to be honest. I just wanted our clothes gone, and poof."

"You'd better learn how to bring them—" My back meets the wall, and Morpheus slides all the way in, scrambling all my thoughts.

He captures my lips again, unraveling me completely as his tongue teases mine. My head is light, as if it's filled with cotton candy. Euphoria makes me feel like I'm high. Maybe I am. Kissing Morpheus is like tasting the nectar of the gods, literally.

He's moving between my legs, unmerciful, and with each trust, it becomes harder to maintain my grip on reality. I'm slowly but surely becoming detached from body, untethered to the constraints of the physical world. I know I'm forgetting something, but I can't fathom what.

Our bodies are slick, our breathing coming out in bursts but in sync. I'm terribly close to release, and I know Morpheus is too. When it finally hits us, it's like we turn into smoke, quickly mixing together to become one.

39

MORPHEUS

I'm not sure how it happened, but somehow during our lovemaking, I was able to peer inside Daisy's mind. It happened naturally, as if we were connected not only physically but on a spiritual level too. I didn't mean to snoop around, but the knowledge I wanted was right there in front of me. I couldn't avoid learning the location to the Neo Gods' headquarters.

Daisy can't be angry at me for that, but she can and will be furious that I took off alone to do what I said I would. There's absolutely no fucking sense or reason to risk everyone's lives when I can destroy the place alone.

Getting to the Sapphire mountain range where the secret hideout is took me no more than a mere thought. If we had come by car, it would have taken an hour. Another argument for why my coming alone was the right call.

Then why the hell do I feel so guilty about it?

I'm standing in front of the side of a mountain. There's a narrow road that leads to a dead end, which means the entrance is there, hidden. I narrow my eyes, and with ease I can see the shape of a steel gate underneath the stony wall. It's reinforced by lightning-glass, a precaution in case someone tries to use their powers to forcibly open it.

Expanding my awareness further, I count around fifty people inside the facility, which has three levels. The majority of the Neo Gods are on the first level, right on the other side of the gate. I'm concealed from the security cameras, and I'll remain like that until I can strike everyone in one fell swoop. For that, I want to be on the other side so I can witness their reaction when they die.

I let the shadows consume me, taking their form, and then I zap through the cracks of the hidden entrance. When I rematerialize, I keep the shadows around me and observe the motherfuckers who will soon become dead meat.

They're busy loading trucks and vans with assault weapons and explosives concealed inside black boxes, and part of their uniform includes vests that I'm sure protects them from Idol attacks. There are no Fringes in the mix, meaning this is a high-level operation. I can't imagine what kind of destruction was next on their agenda, but it's clear they don't intend to rely on their powers only. This is war.

I'm about to unleash my wrath on them when the elevator at the far end of the room opens and an ancient creature walks out. He oozes power despite his age and the fact that he requires a cane to move. One of the soldiers turns his attention to him, saluting the man as if he was a general.

"Everything ready for phase two?" the old man asks.

"Yes, Master. All explosives have been loaded in the trunks."

"Good, good. I don't want one brick left standing in any of the Norm and Fringe neighborhoods."

"Fringes too? Jonathan's orders were to concentrate on Norm-populated areas," the soldier argues.

"Yes. That was the original plan, but there have been new developments."

I wonder if he's referring to me destroying all the lightning-glass reserves.

"We'll lose the Fringe support if we turn against them now."

"They have served their purpose. And yours is not to argue with me. There's no sense delaying the inevitable. It's time for the Idol race to reign supreme."

His hatred snaps my self-control. I've heard enough. It's showtime.

I pull the shadows into me, revealing myself.

"Is it though?" I cock an eyebrow.

Several curses erupt among the soldiers, but none of them attempt to attack. They can't while they're trying not to soil themselves. I have everyone present in my grip save for the old fuck. The one they called master.

Slowly, I make my way to him, grinning. The man holds his cane with both hands, stooping over it. He watches with me with curiosity but not fear.

"So, you're the one behind all this," I say.

He lifts his chin higher, defiantly. "I was expecting you."

"Oh? Is that so?"

"He told me my life would end at the hands of a traitor."

I narrow my eyes to slits. "Who did?"

"The god I serve, the one who shall be free before this is over. Chaos."

I grab the man by his neck, lifting him off the ground and letting my shadows slither free to cover the vermin's body. "You're one of his minions, then."

The old man begins to laugh. "Just like you are."

"You're wrong. I serve no one."

"Ah, the arrogance of the young. Go ahead, kill me," he goads.

There's no fear in his eyes, only malice. I feel like he's manipulating me to do something I shouldn't.

"What's the matter, Fringe scum? Can't do it? It must be the blood of that whore mother of yours."

My rage takes over, clouding everything. I squeeze his throat harder, crushing it as if it were made out of butter. His blood spatters, covering my hand right before I drop him. He flops on the floor like a fish out of water. I watch him with detached curiosity as he slowly suffocates in his own blood.

The head of the Neo Gods is dead, and yet I don't feel an ounce of satisfaction. This was too easy. And Jonathan Kent isn't here. Killing him would have been way more interesting, but Rufio or Bryce probably want the pleasure for themselves. It doesn't matter. Without his boss and resources, smoking him out will be only a matter of time. I glance around, noticing I killed every single soldier around while the master was distracting me. *Damn it. Who's going to set up the explosives now?*

Someone behind me shouts, and then a scorching blaze comes barreling my way. I turn into smoke, rising out of its path. Two more Neo Gods have come out of the elevator and boldly decided to attack me. I should end them on the spot, but their arrival is providential. I have a final task for them.

I land in front of the trucks filled to the brim with explosives, and then I tone down my powers.

"It seems you missed," I taunt them.

Both Idols are fire elementals, level thirteen and fourteen respectively. I don't know if pretending to be an Idol will fool them, especially considering the carnage I already left in my wake.

"Where are your accomplices?" the tallest of the duo asks.

I shrug. "Gone."

"So they left you behind, huh? They should have checked the rest of the facility. Can't expect much from a bunch of dumb fucks."

His companion glances at the crumpled form of their boss, surrounded by his own blood. "They killed the master."

Both men twist their expressions in anger before attacking me with everything they've got. *Perfect.* Their fireballs converge, becoming a beauty of destruction. Like before, I turn into smoke and zoom out of its path. It hits the trucks that were behind me, setting off a massive explosion that pulverizes not only the Neo Gods' facility but also the entire mountain. I continue my ascension to avoid the cloud of debris that quickly forms.

I may not have felt anything when I killed the master, but my ethereal body tingles all over as I watch the entire mountain collapse. But my moment of pleasure is short-lived. I sense his dark presence behind me too late and can't avoid being swallowed whole by Chaos's cloud of doom.

DAISY

I wake up alone in the restroom fully dressed. My ears are buzzing, and my head feels light. I'm not sure what exactly happened. Everything is foggy, almost as if I've been dreaming and can't remember the details.

I came here to run away from Morpheus, but he followed me. *Did that really happen?* I get back onto my feet and turn to the mirror. Besides my tangled hair, there are no other visible signs that I just had sex. That is, until I step closer to the sink and become painstakingly aware of the throb between my legs. I didn't dream it, then.

With the realization come a million questions, but the most important one is: Why did Morpheus leave me?

"Daisy?" Phoenix asks from outside the restroom. "Are you okay?"

"Yeah. You can come in."

He does, followed by Bryce and Rufio. They scan the small space, maybe to be sure I'm truly alone.

"Where's mummy boy?" Rufio asks.

"Mummy boy?" I crinkle my forehead.

"That's what Rufio used to call Morpheus before we became friends. It used to piss him off to no end." Phoenix glances at the ceiling. "If he's not down here kicking his ass, he's definitely left the building."

I run a shaky hand through my hair. "I don't understand why he left in a hurry again. Unless..." I glance at the guys. "You didn't give him the address to the Neo Gods' facility, did you?"

"We haven't seen Morpheus since you stormed off and he followed you here," Bryce replies.

I laugh without humor. "I thought he'd come back for good. I guess he has truly become one of those asshole deities."

My heart breaks as I utter those words. I wanted to believe we wouldn't lose him once he embraced his demigod status.

"Don't be sad, love. Maybe we just need to give him more time." Phoenix pulls me against his chest and kisses the top of my head.

"You're right. It has only been a day." I curl my fingers around his shirt, melting a little in his embrace.

"If we want to catch those sons of bitches before they launch another attack, we need to go now," Rufio urges, making me tense again.

I ease out of Phoenix's arms and stare at Rufio and Bryce. "Let's go, then."

Outside, I immediately sense the high tension in the air. Xavier glowers at me from across the room. *Shit*. Disappearing for a quickie with my demigod boyfriend probably didn't go down well with him. We're in the middle of a war, after all.

I try to come up with something to say, but everything sounds like a half-baked excuse.

"We're ready to go. We've only been waiting for you," he says.

Mortification makes my face hot. "I'm ready."

From the corner of my eye, I catch Rosie shoving a lightning-glass dagger in a thigh holster. It's clear that accessory came from the Knights.

"You're not coming with us," I tell her.

"Don't even try to keep me here," she retorts. "Xavier already tried."

"Tried?" I quirk an eyebrow at him.

"Yeah, but like you, Rosie is another stubborn child. I don't have to time to argue. If she wants to fight, so be it."

"Exactly. Why can't I fight for those I love?" she adds, glancing at Toby.

The lights in the warehouse once again begin to act strangely, flickering on and off. For a second, I think it's Morpheus returning, but the signature I pick up is not his.

Eris.

She appears in the middle of the hospital, frightening some of the children who were up. Ellen strides toward her, ready to tear the goddess down with a string of insults.

"What are you doing here? Get the hell out!" Ellen points in our direction.

Eris's lips twist into a grin. "Sorry. I miscalculated."

Miscalculate, my ass.

She saunters in our direction, swinging her hips from side to side as if she were a model on a catwalk. When she appeared before, she was wearing regular clothes—a pair of dark jeans and a vintage T-shirt. Today she's going for the seductress vibe, wearing a low-cut snug black dress with slits on both sides of the skirt that go up almost to her hips. Her long silky ebony hair sways with the movement, and her ruby lips curl in a knowing grin.

I check my guys to make sure they're not falling for her

games, but mercifully, their expressions are suspicious, as they should be. Soren's jaw, on the other hand, is hanging loose, and I can totally picture his tongue rolling out cartoon-style. *Dumbass.*

"What are you doing here?" I ask.

Her grin vanishes when her attention switches to me. "I came to warn you that what I feared has happened. Chaos took Morpheus to his island."

40

DAISY

Everything else takes a back seat, including raiding the Neo Gods' headquarters. Our top priority now is to save Morpheus from Chaos.

"You must take us there," I say.

Eris shakes her head. "Absolutely not. If I take you, Chaos will trap me too. He's been trying to put me in a cell for centuries. I'm not going to make it easy for him."

"You must! It'll take days to get to the island by boat, and that's assuming we can find it again," Mrs. Malek argues.

"I'm not taking you there, but there's another way to get to Starlight Island fast." Eris looks pointedly at Jodie. "Come on, darling. Tell them about our arrangement."

All eyes turn to Jodie, who has gone whiter than a sheet of paper. Her eyes are trained on Eris, wide and unblinking.

"Mother, what the hell is she talking about?" Bryce asks.

Jodie swallows hard, amplifying the visible tension around her mouth. "When William died, I vowed to avenge his death. Eris came to me and proposed a deal. She would help me bring the downfall of the Neo Gods and kill Jonathan in the process in exchange for my assistance."

"Assistance with what?" Rufio asks angrily.

"With anything she needed."

"Son of a bitch," Phoenix mutters.

"Don't look so shocked, guys. In comparison to Chaos, I was a pretty good boss. I helped more than I asked for stuff in return. Who do you think told Jodie Daisy was the descendant of Magia destined to receive her powers? Or that Bryce had the ability to make Idols?"

"Oh my God." I hug my middle, remembering the conversation Bryce and I had last night. He was right. We've been nothing but puppets this whole time.

"That's messed up," Soren pipes up.

Eris turns to him. "Maybe, but your father benefited greatly from the intel I gave Jodie."

"No offense, but can we deal with this revelation later? We have to rescue my son. How do we get to the island?" Mrs. Malek asks.

"I gave Jodie a portal-key in case Chaos ever managed to capture me. It's still in your office, isn't it?" She raises an eyebrow at her.

"Yes, which presents a problem since I no longer have access to it."

"I guess you'll just have to find a way to retrieve it, then." Eris shrugs.

"But the school has been overrun by the Neo Gods," Renata chimes in.

"I can get you inside the campus, but I'm sure Chaos has his sight trained on it. I won't be able to linger."

"That's fine," Xavier says. "How many can you tele-transport to Gifted Academy?"

Her eyes flash with amusement. "All of you."

One moment we're in the warehouse, and in the next we're standing right in front of Gifted Academy's main building. Eris is nowhere to be seen.

"Fuck! A little warning would have been nice," Phoenix complains.

"Shit. We're out in the open. Let's look for cover," Xavier commands.

We scramble, splitting into two groups. I head for the right with Bryce, Phoenix, Rufio, Toby, Rosie, and Renata. Soren, the rest of the Knights, Jodie, Mrs. Malek, and Xavier veer for the left.

"Man, it would be nice to have Morpheus's concealing powers right about now." Phoenix tries to become smaller by hiding behind the shrubbery next to the building.

A moment later, a group of students exits the building. They're relaxed and chatting animatedly, which means they don't know we're out here. Maybe the security cameras didn't catch us after all. They stop suddenly when Jonathan Kent turns a corner. I tense for a split second before my brain grasps that he's wearing the same clothes Xavier was.

"Damn. Your uncle is good, Daisy," Phoenix whispers.

"Mr. Kent. How did you get here so fast?" one of the guys asks.

Crap. So Bryce and Rufio's father is around. That's not good for us at all. Bryce's anger flares like fireworks. He wants to make his father pay for what he did to Rufio, but we can't deviate from the plan, which is to get to Jodie's old office and retrieve the portal-key. Too bad we don't know what it looks like. *Damn, Eris didn't give us a second to get organized.*

"Where are you going?" Xavier asks instead of replying.

"We were headed to the gym."

"Fine. Get going, then."

The guys look at each other and then shrug. *Phew, those aren't the sharpest tools in the shed. We got lucky.*

Bryce steps out of his hiding spot and aims his index fingers at the two security cameras mounted near the entrance. A current of electricity whooshes from them, and I want to tell him not to fry them, only it's too late.

"You shouldn't have done that," Rufio tells him.

Bryce glances at his brother with a frown. "I shouldn't have done what? Change the feed to run in a loop?"

"Oh, I thought you had destroyed the feed altogether." Rufio shrugs, earning an eye roll from Bryce.

"Please. This is not my first rodeo."

"Come on, guys. Let's go before we bump into anyone else." Xavier waves us over.

"Do you think school is still in session, considering the current events?" Toby asks.

"It's hard to tell," I say, trying to suppress a yawn.

"Shit, you didn't sleep at all last night, did you, honey?" Phoenix glances at me.

"No. But it's okay. I'll rest when this is over."

If the school is operating as if nothing is amiss, then the students should be in class at this hour. Bryce takes the lead, tampering with the security feed of every camera along the way. My heart is beating savagely in my chest, and if this were a movie, there would be an ominous soundtrack in the background. The tension is high in our group, and in hindsight, maybe we shouldn't have come all together. It's easier to be inconspicuous in a smaller party. Too late now.

We're moving as fast as we can, but not at Idol speed because of Rosie and Rufio. Suggesting they be carried wouldn't fly with either of them, plus it would hinder whoever had the load. Bryce flattens his back against the wall when we reach the final corner that leads to Jodie's former office.

Toby pushes forward until he's right next to Bryce. "What are you doing? We can't go that way."

"Why not?"

"Are you seriously not registering all the Idols that are standing in front of the principal's office?"

"No."

"They must be masking their signatures," Jodie chimes in.

"I'll draw them from there," Xavier says.

"No." I grab his arm. "What if one of those Idols is the real Jonathan Kent?"

"Why can't he simply change into someone else?" Renata suggests. "Maybe a teacher?"

"I'd have to know what the person looks like, and besides Jonathan, there's no one else I know."

"I have a better idea," Soren pipes up. "We'll split into two groups. My team will drive those people away from the principal's office."

An evil laugh echoes behind us, raising the small hair on the back of my neck. "Oh, that would have been genius if only you had the foresight to watch your backs," Cherise says, standing only a few feet away from us flanked by four guys. Those numbers wouldn't be bad if the bitch didn't have a gun in her hand aimed at my head.

Rufio and Phoenix step in front of me, creating a proactive shield. *Damn it.* Why do they think their lives are worth less than mine?

"Oh, isn't that nice? Daisy has gotten herself a human shield. You know what I love about guns? There are six bullets in it. One for each—"

Before she can finish her tirade, Soren charges her, sending her careening down the corridor and taking two of her goons in the process. She fires the gun, missing Soren by a mile, but it alerts the other Neo Gods to our presence. Shouts of alarm echo in the hallway, and I foresee the situation getting much worse in the next few seconds. Rosie's eyes have a wild glint in them as she holds her dagger up with trembling hands. *Shit.* I knew it was mistake letting her come.

The other Neo Gods join the fray, and then it's a matter of avoiding getting hit by their powers and their lightning-glass weapons. There are too many people fighting in this confined space. Freezing time without affecting everyone is impossible. But when one of the Neo Gods tosses a throwing star in Phoenix's direction, I freeze the weapon mid-trajectory, stopping its motion completely. Phoenix turns around, plucks the star from the air, and shoves into the Neo God's eyes.

Someone grabs my jacket from behind, immediately turning it into ice. The cold blast continues on. If I don't break free, I'll become an ice statue. With a grunt, I twist my arm back and yank the person off me. It's a short brunette not much older than Rosie. Her age and innocent-looking face don't give me pause. Her eyes are filled with hatred and rage. It's me or her.

I reach for her head, digging my fingers into her temple. She grabs my wrists, trying to freeze them, but my powers are engaged. I feel nothing besides a lick of frost against my skin. She screams when I begin to unmake her, too caught up in her pain to fight my hold. Her legs give out from under her, but I keep my grip despite her fall. The sound of fighting fades to the background. My ears are buzzing with euphoria. Only when the girl's eyes roll back in their sockets do I let go. She's empty. My work is done.

It takes me a moment to regain my focus, and when I do, I can't find Rosie and panic. Soren yells "Duck!" and since I don't know who he was talking to, I bend forward. The explosion happens across from me near where Rufio was standing. Dark smoke fills the hallway, only to be dissipated a second later by Jodie. I finally get a visual of Rosie fighting side by side with Renata and Toby farther down the corridor. I don't miss the fact that her "nemesis" is trying her best to protect my sister. Maybe Rosie will finally get over her hatred.

Everyone is giving their all, but the longer we stay here, the higher the chances we'll be overwhelmed. I'm sure Neo God reinforcements are coming.

No sooner does the thought enter my mind than I sense evil approaching. I turn toward the menacing presence while my entire body locks into aggressive mode. Jonathan Kent is here, looking smug as shit with a victorious grin on his odious face. He thinks he has us pinned down. Well, he can underestimate us all he wants.

I take a step forward only to be blocked by Bryce and Rufio. Anger quickly bubbles up my throat, but then reason prevails. This is not my fight. It's theirs. I stand back and let them deal with their father.

"I knew brains weren't your forte, but I confess you coming to Gifted Academy shows a new level of stupidity from you two."

Bryce lets out a battle cry and attacks. His energy blast hits Jonathan's chest and fizzles into nothing. The son of a bitch is wearing a protective vest.

"Nice try." He smiles.

The awful screech of metal bending catches my attention. The lockers lining the hallway are twisting out of shape, turning into clumps of distorted steel. Rosie and Renata scream as they're trapped by the deadly shapes.

"No!" I leap in their direction, ready to pry them loose with my bare hands, but Renata breaks free first and is already helping Rosie.

My ears pick up the sound of a blade cutting through air. I turn just in time to freeze a piece of sharp metal that Jonathan sent my way. More shouts echo in the hallway, coming from behind the man. We're seriously outnumbered here, so the only way out is to find the portal-key to Starlight Island.

Jodie pushes Bryce and Rufio out of her way, bracing to deal with her husband herself. "Go! I've got this."

The man laughs. "Really, Jodie. You're going to play the martyr now? Do you think that will buy your sons' love and respect?"

Without breaking eye contact with Jonathan, she yells again. "I said go, damn it!"

It's clear that neither Bryce nor Rufio intend to obey, but when my gaze drops to her hand, I understand then what Jodie plans to do. Phoenix, who is now next to me, has his eyes trained exactly where mine were a second ago. We look at each other, and then, without words, we know what to do.

Using telekinesis, he sends Bryce and Rufio back all the way to the principal's office corridor. I urge everyone on our team to follow them, freezing our opponents to the best of my ability. My trick only works on those who aren't wearing protective vests. Unfortunately, the Neo God presently fighting with Xavier is a massive albino who is unaffected. Xavier has a lightning-glass dagger in his hand, but the man is able to easily avoid his attacks.

I spare one fleeting glance in Rosie's direction to make sure she's out of the fray before I zoom around the man and fling two throwing stars at his ankles. He lets out a roar, arching his back. Instead of using the moment of distraction to stab his opponent, Xavier kicks him in the nuts, bringing him to his knees. Then, with chilling precision, he slashes the man's throat. I guess that's his MO.

Wordlessly, he grabs my arm, and together we run to where our group has gathered. I notice Soren is the only one left on his team. *Damn it.*

"Everyone to the office!" I yell.

Rosie, Toby, and Renata run ahead with me close behind. Toby skids to a halt as we near the office's door, holding his arms wide. "Wait!"

His warning is too late for Renata, who, thanks to the momentum, crosses through the threshold without pause. A loud gasp follows, which twists my stomach into knots. Something awful has happened. I mince forward slowly, letting my awareness expand. Renata is on the floor, clutching her middle.

Standing before her with a bloodied lightning-glass knife in her hand is Bethany Walkers, Jodie's former assistant.

"No!" I kick the woman in the stomach, sending her sprawling across the reception area.

She releases her weapon, but the deranged smile doesn't disappear from her face. "If I had known you would become the Unmaker, I'd have killed you the moment you stepped foot in here."

Bryce walks in, his body crackling with barely contained rage. "You'd have been struck down if you had tried. But don't worry, I can take care of that now."

A bolt of white energy whooshes from Bryce's outstretched hand, hitting Bethany in the middle of her chest. She cries out for a moment, but her agonized moans fade into nothing as her body fries to a crisp. I've never seen Bryce unleash that kind of deadly power before.

The entire building shakes on its foundation when the grenade in Jodie's hand detonates. Bryce looks over his shoulder, shock etched on his face.

"Mom," he murmurs.

I step closer and touch his cheek. "I'm sorry, babe."

He peers into my eyes. "I can't believe she did that."

"Come on, kids. Don't let her sacrifice be in vain," Xavier urges us.

I lace my hand with Bryce's and steer us into the principal's office. Immediately, I seek out Rufio. His gaze is downcast, and his shoulders are hunched forward. I can't begin to imagine what he must be feeling right now.

"Does anyone know what the portal-key looks like?" Phoenix asks, drawing my attention to him.

"No," Rufio replies.

"It must give off some kind of energy," Soren replies.

"What about Renata? She's been stabbed by lightning-glass," Rosie says.

"Don't worry about me," the girl replies weakly.

Bryce starts to go to her, but Phoenix stops him. "You can't do it, Bryce. We need you on the island."

"I can't simply let her die," he argues.

"It wouldn't work, son," Xavier interrupts. "Only the antidote against its poison will help Renata now."

I doubt there's any at Starlight Island, which means the girl is doomed. It's clearly the conclusion everyone in the room has come to judging by their grim expressions.

"We need to find the portal-key." Mrs. Malek veers for the big desk and begins to look inside drawers. But an object on it catches my attention. It's the pyramid-shaped paperweight I threw at Phoenix on the day he cornered me here. It drew blood.

Son of a bitch.

No ordinary object would have been able to hurt him like that unless it was made out of lightning-glass... or something else god-made.

I run to the desk and take the object in my hand. A small light flickers inside as a low vibration sends tingles up my arm.

"I think I found it," I say.

41

DAISY

The portal-key took us to the idyllic beach of Starlight Island in the blink of an eye. When I touched the object, I knew exactly what I had to do to open the portal. Maybe it unlocked a memory from Magia. Anyone connected to the portal-key—even indirectly—would be transported to the island.

The place looks exactly as it did in my dream. This is where Morpheus was as well, when I invaded his memories by accident. Warm waves lap at my ankles, and a soft summer breeze caresses my skin. Despite the picturesque beauty, there's something awfully wrong in the atmosphere. A wicked presence humming underneath the white sand.

I take stock of our group, noticing with relief that everyone made the trip. Renata doesn't look great though. Mrs. Malek is offering her support since the girl can't even stand upright on her own anymore. The bloodstain on her shirt has already changed to dark brown, almost black. I'm not sure if at this point the antidote can help her.

I catch Bryce looking in her direction too, which makes my anguish grow. I wonder if what Xavier said about the antidote being the only thing that could help Renata is true. If Bryce can bring me back from certain death, then surely he could heal Renata. But if he does that, he'll be too weak to fight against Chaos.

I bite my lower lip, deciding to keep my suspicions to myself. The guilt over Renata's death—if that comes to pass—I'll carry alone.

"What now?" Soren asks.

"We look for Morpheus," I say.

Phoenix stares hard in the direction of the jungle. It looks unwelcoming even under the bright sunlight. Ironic that Chaos's prison would be in such a beautiful place.

Rosie ambles forward. "Oh my God. This is just like the legends said. This is indeed paradise."

"What are you talking about?" Toby glances at the wall of verdant but oppressive trees and then back at her. "You think an ominous jungle is paradise?"

"What jungle?" Her forehead crinkles.

Apprehension runs down my spine. I trade a worried glance with the guys and then move next to Rosie. "What can you see?"

"She must be looking at the village. When Erebus brought me here, that was the view from the beach," Mrs. Malek explains.

"But why is Rosie seeing the village whereas we're all seeing the jungle?" Rufio asks.

"Wait. Something is happening." Toby points at the distance.

Like magic, the jungle shimmers and then fades away, allowing me to see the village too. "What in the world?"

"We should go there. Maybe they'll have an antidote for Renata." Rosie walks ahead without pause.

"No! Nobody move," Bryce interjects. "It's probably a trap."

"I've been to the village. It does exist," Mrs. Malek tells us.

"Well, the jungle is gone. We only have two options. Stay here and wait for Chaos to find us, or head to the village and try to find Morpheus," I say.

Rufio shakes his head. "Morpheus won't be in the village, Daisy."

"Well, he has to be somewhere!" I snap.

In my distraction, I can't stop Rosie from sprinting ahead. She's almost at the edge of the village. *How the fuck did she get there so fast?*

"Rosie! Wait up." Toby scrambles to follow her.

I try to follow too, but it feels like I'm walking through quicksand in slow motion. I can't get traction. Everyone else seems to be suffering from the same problem.

The village vanishes again, and the jungle takes its place. The tops of the trees begin to sway as if something large is making its way through. Rosie is on a collision path with it.

Raising my arm, I try to freeze her, but she keeps running without pause.

"Someone stop her!" I yell.

"I can't move!" Soren shouts in frustration. "Something is messing with my gift."

The trees and shrubbery at the edge of the jungle part for a giant were-worm. Its flower-shaped mouth opens, revealing long sharklike teeth. Rosie finally stops, looking up at the monster in front of her. She screams in horror right before the giant worm strikes. She vanishes before our eyes as the monster swallows her whole and disappears into the sand.

"No!" I drop to my knees with my arm outstretched. My ragged scream comes from deep in my chest, raw and filled with agony. "Rosie, no."

Toby clutches his head, staring at the gaping hole the worm left behind.

The sky turns pitch black as Chaos's storm gathers above

us. His evil laughter echoes in my ears, whipping my already bleeding soul raw.

The ground begins to tremble, announcing something terrible is coming our way. A rough pair of hands lifts me up. Rufio's. "Come on, Daisy. We have to get out of here."

"I can't leave. We have to go after Rosie."

"She's gone, my love. She's gone."

I pull free from his grasp. "No! Don't say that. I won't give up on her."

A patch of sand explodes in front of us as the were-worm returns, roaring savagely. The sight should propel me to run in the opposite direction. But something inside of me snaps. Rage and pain erase my self-preservation instinct. Instead, I face the beast with shoulders squared and my bare fists as weapons.

"Give me my sister back, motherfucker!"

The monster shrieks in response, a sound so high-pitched it hurts my ears. The giant worm coils its body back, preparing to strike. I brace for the impact, not knowing how I'm going to avoid those sharp teeth. It stops midmotion when a net of electricity wraps around it. Bryce is at the opposite end of that string of energy. The white-blue light from his blast emphasizes the strain on his face. He's giving everything he has to kill the beast. It coils and thrashes violently, screeching loudly.

But as it dies, more worms erupt from the sand, quickly surrounding us. The wind is howling viciously. My hair flaps wildly around my face, blocking my visibility even more. Nevertheless, I sense when one of Chaos's creatures approaches me from behind. I whirl around and then jump as high as I can out of its path. It hits the spot where I had been standing, and then it slithers away into the sand.

A path opens up for me, allowing me to see Rufio attempting to protect Mrs. Malek and Renata on his own with the help of two lightning-glass daggers. They look puny and pointless against the beasts that are fast approaching them.

No. I won't let those monsters take him from me too.

With a war cry, I break into a run. I've recovered from the lethargy from before. Maybe it's the fury propelling me. Or desperation. Either way, I have no idea how I'm going to stop those monsters from devouring them or me. All I know is I have to try.

***

MORPHEUS

I regain consciousness bound to a giant tree trunk in a jungle I know all too well. It's Chaos's preferred territory, where he lets his beasts wander free to terrorize anyone who is unlucky enough to venture in. Seven years ago, that was us.

I push against my restraints, surprised when the vines break easily. The drop is ten feet, which I can't stop from happening. *What the hell!* I search inside my core for my newly awakened demigod powers. They're there, alive and kicking, but also trapped behind an invisible force. This didn't happen when I was here before.

Duh, Morpheus. You're in his prison. Of course he tampered with your ability to break free.

I must be deep in his realm. It doesn't matter. I'll find a way out of here. Daisy and my friends need me.

"Hello?" I call out. If there are monsters here, I'd rather face them now.

My voice echoes in the emptiness of the forest. It's quiet, eerily so, just as it was when we ventured here seven years ago to battle for our lives. Little did we know that surviving Chaos's wicked games would bind us to him. Suddenly I realize I haven't felt his mark on my back in a while. Does it mean that by ascending to demigod status, I broke free from his shackles?

With careful steps, I begin my exploration. Sweat dots my

skin, and I'm painfully aware of my heart beating in staccato rhythm. Little rays of sunlight are able to penetrate the thick canopy, but they do little to change the grim sensation that hangs in the air. I hear the crack of a twig snapping behind me, which spikes up my adrenaline levels. My heart is stuck in my throat as I whirl around, ready to fight whatever creature is coming.

There's a dark silhouette of a man hidden partially behind a thick shrub. His breathing is coming out in bursts, as if he's been running for miles. I swallow the lump in my throat, knowing without a shred of doubt that this is one Chaos's fiends. And here I am without access to my powers and no weapon on me. His eyes glow an unnatural fiery red, and his fingers are contorted into claws. With a roar, he breaks into a run straight at me. Without my ability to smoke out of the way, I brace for the impact. It's not until he crosses a ray of light that I recognize him.

"Stephan?"

My words have no impact on him. He leaps to tackle me, and at the last second, I finally snap out of my surprise. I jump out of the way, pivoting so my back is no longer to him. Stephan staggers forward thanks to the momentum but recovers fast.

"How did you get here, and what the fuck happened to you?"

There's no sign of recognition in his eyes. He's gone berserk. And worse, he's in possession of his powers, unlike me. He rips a massive tree out of the ground and hurls it at me with the strength of a giant. It happens too fast, and I can't get out of its path. A large branch hits me in the stomach, sending me flying back. I hit my head on a boulder when I fall, getting stunned for a moment. Stephan flies in my direction, carrying in his hands a large piece of rock. He raises it above his head with the clear intent of smashing my face with it.

Before he has the chance, a dark mass of smoke collides

with him, removing him from my line of vision. I get back up, trying to ignore the throbbing in the back of my head. I touch the sore spot, and my fingers come away smeared in blood.

Stephan is now pinned to a tree nearby by a man dressed in black from head to toe. He looks over his shoulder, clearing the shadows that were covering his face before.

"Erebus," I murmur.

"Hello, son."

"How did you find me?" I mince toward him.

"You're my son. I'll always find you. I sensed the moment Chaos whisked you here."

Stephan keeps trying to break from the hold Erebus has around his neck.

"What happened to him?"

"He's been bewitched by Chaos. I don't know how he got here, but I know why. Nathaniel and Andromeda are on the island, and he came after them."

"Andromeda is here? Is she in danger?"

"Everyone on this godforsaken island is."

"Can you help him?"

Erebus faces Stephan. "Possibly."

He touches his forehead, and immediately Stephan stops struggling. A moment passes before his eyes are no longer glowing nor his expression contorted in rage. When his gaze returns to blue, it's confused.

Erebus releases him and steps back.

"Who are you?" he asks, covering his neck with his hand.

"I'm Morpheus's father."

My spine goes taut as I whip my attention to him. Several emotions swirl in my chest, but the strongest one is satisfaction. I don't know him at all, but I'm happy that he claimed me.

Fuck. Am I that starved for acceptance from a father figure?

Stephan then acknowledges my presence. "What are you doing here?"

"I could ask you the same thing."

He threads his fingers through his hair while his gaze darkens. "I came after Andy. I have to find her before Nathaniel fucks things up."

I open my mouth to demand a better explanation, but the ground begins to shake, and the forest turns much darker as the rays of sunshine disappear.

"Chaos. Something is happening," Erebus says.

"Andy," Stephan murmurs before taking flight. He disappears in the gloom of the jungle in the blink of an eye.

"We have to help him," I say.

Erebus visibly tenses and then levels me with an intense stare. "We will, but not by going after him."

"What do you mean?"

"The destiny the Fates laid upon you and your friends is about to come to fruition. You must prepare."

"The creation of the God-killer, but for that we need Bryce and Dai—*no*. They're here, aren't they?" Fear grips my insides, twisting them savagely.

"Yes, they came to rescue you. We need to act quickly and stop Chaos before he gains too much strength. He's about to break free from the island."

"How the fuck do we stop him? How can Bryce and Daisy create a God-killer in such a short time?"

"With your help."

My eyebrows shoot to the heavens. "My help?"

A myriad of absurd scenarios flashes through my head, and none of them are something I want to take part in.

"They must be linked by the infinity band, son. Just like you saw in your vision." He pauses, cocking his head to the side as if he's trying to listen to something in the distance. "Blood has been spilled already. We're running out of time."

"Whose blood?"

He steps into my personal space, grabbing me roughly by

the shoulders. "Don't you get it, son? The stars have aligned so you can finally defeat Chaos. Everything that's happened to you and your friends was preordained."

"What the hell are you talking about?"

"Your friendship with the Kent brothers and Phoenix, your meeting Daisy and falling in love with her, it was all part of it. The five of you had to form an unbreakable bond for the impossible to come to pass."

"Are you saying we were all pieces on this damn gameboard of the gods?" I shout.

Regret shines in his eyes before he glances away. "We're all pieces. I'm sorry."

"Was that why we were lured to this place when we were kids? So Chaos could have fun with us?"

"No, he wanted to destroy you. He too knew about what the Fates had done. He couldn't, so he thought to control you instead."

I press a closed fist to my forehead, trying to hold back my anger. "I get Daisy's, Bryce's, and my role in the prophecy. But what about Rufio and Phoenix? How do they come into the equation?"

"Daisy and Bryce are the Maker and the Unmaker, opposites. You're the link. When their powers unite, they'll forget who they are. They'll turn into pure energy for a moment, dangerous and unstable. They'll need a tether, a reminder of their humanity, a heart. That's Phoenix."

"What about Rufio?"

"Isn't it obvious, son? Rufio, the Idol born with the power of destruction, now an empty shell. He's the vessel. He's the God-killer."

42

MORPHEUS

"How can Rufio become the God-killer?"

"Don't ask me, son. But whatever the Fates decide, it will pass, no matter how crazy it is."

My heart becomes tight all of a sudden. I press a closed fist against my chest, trying to massage the phantom pain away. Cold dread licks the back of my neck, and then I see the vision of the beach. It's swarmed by were-worms, Chaos's preferred beasts, and they're attacking my family.

"No!"

"You've seen them too. They need your help, son."

"I can't help them if I can't reconnect with my powers," I shout, frustrated.

"You can break free from the shackles Chaos put on you like I did. Have faith, Morpheus. It's your destiny."

I point a finger at his face, shaking with anger. "Don't fucking talk about destiny to me. I don't want to hear another word."

Erebus's eyes flash bright orange while the shadows gather around his frame. "Sticking your head in the sand is not going to solve your problems."

"The boy is weak," Chaos's disembodied voice echoes in the forest. "That's what you get from procreating with scum."

"My mother is not scum. You're the disease in this world."

Chaos laughs. "Your insults mean nothing to me. You'll never be able to save your loved ones. Just take a seat and enjoy while I obliterate them one by one."

The image of Rosie running straight to one of his monsters and then being devoured by it fills my mouth with bile. That's the blood spilled that Erebus mentioned. *Motherfucker*. My heart aches for Daisy, knowing how hard she fought to protect her sister. Chaos needs to be stopped.

The wrath swirling in the pit of my stomach erupts like a volcano, taking over my entire being. I hear a distinct *snap* inside my core. The block Chaos placed around my powers broke, and my gift is unleashed. My roar echoes in the jungle, raw and savage, before I become the dark.

PHOENIX

I've just torn a giant worm in two using telekinesis when I hear Daisy's war cry. Rufio, Mrs. Malek, and Renata are surrounded by the monsters, and Rufio is their only line of defense. *Fuck.* He doesn't lack gumption, only the means to fight them.

From the corner of my eye, I catch Toby having trouble with a worm of his own. He's found a broken tree trunk that he's using as a club. But I can tell he's running out of steam. I can get him out of danger and then run to assist Daisy and Rufio, but then Xavier joins Toby, and together they impale the beast.

A blur zooms across the white sand, piercing through the worm that was flanking Renata and Mrs. Malek from the left. Soren erupts from the other side of the beast, covered in gore. Savage. My appreciation for the Silverstone grows.

Daisy is still in trouble though. I run at breakneck speed toward her. She's slowed the worms' advance, but not by much. They seem to be partially immune to her gift. *Damn it.* Following Toby's example, I acquire a piece of wood, but mine comes straight from the jungle. Drawing the tree to me takes more effort than normal. It seems everything is much harder here. Chaos is not fucking around. But neither am I.

The tree becomes a spear in my hand. I leap over the closest worm and shove my improvised weapon into the back of its ugly head. It jerks with a roar, sending me off its back. It squirms violently as it dies, and I almost get hit by its tail. I roll off to avoid a deadly blow, then jump back to my feet, ready to face another monster. But just then, the tattoo between my shoulder blades begins to burn. The pain is excruciating, debilitating.

In the distance, I hear Bryce holler as he drops to his knees. Heavy rain falls down on us and then come the fucking lightning bolts, striking the beach in rapid succession. Eventually, it'll hit one of us. *Fuck.*

No sooner do I think that than one falls right where Rufio was standing. It misses him when a shadow pushes him off.

Morpheus!

No, that's not him. It's Erebus. He reaches for Daisy and Rufio, gripping their arms roughly. He's saying something, but I can't hear the words. Regardless, I don't fucking like what I'm seeing. I take a step toward them only to be blocked by lightning striking my path. I glower at the sky, doing my best to ignore the burning pain in my back. Chaos's ugly face forms in the clouds, his green eyes glowing with malice. I flip him off, then run.

Bryce joins me, but before we reach Daisy and Rufio, we're swept off our feet by a giant tornado that appeared out of nowhere. The pressure is immense as the wind tries to tear our bodies into pieces. *How the fuck are we getting out this one?*

DAISY

"No!" I pull my arm free from Erebus's grasp as I watch a dark tornado engulf Bryce and Phoenix. They disappear from my view immediately, while in the background, Chaos laughs.

"Let go of me, fucker!" Rufio struggles to break free.

Erebus steps back, releasing him. "Go after them. Now!"

Rufio's eyes are frantic when our gazes collide. If that's dangerous to me, it's suicidal to him. But I know he won't stay behind. My eyes are burning already, knowing the outcome of our act, but nothing will deter him. I offer him my hand. He squeezes it tightly, and together we run toward the tornado.

The howling of the wind is deafening, and the debris swirling around the vortex is deadly. I force us to a halt right before we get sucked into it and hug Rufio, using my body as a shield.

"I love you," I say next to his ear, not knowing if he can hear me at all through the noise.

He curls his fingers around the fabric of my jacket and replies, "Till the end of time."

The tornado catches up with us, lifting us off the ground in an instant. The force of the wind is tremendous, and it tries to rip us apart. But I hold tightly to Rufio, refusing to let go. Suddenly, the pressure eases off, and the noise of the howling wind fades. We're in the middle of the tornado, inside the eye of the storm.

I sense their presence before I get a visual. Bryce and Phoenix are flying near us, slowly coming closer. They're unharmed and I could weep for joy, but we're so not out of the woods yet.

Still holding on to each other, Rufio and I stretch out our arms, reaching for Bryce and Phoenix. I curl my fingers around

Phoenix's hand and yank him toward me as Rufio does the same with Bryce. We form a circle, suspended in air as if we're a group of skydivers. How long until Chaos realizes we're in a safe location inside his wicked twister?

"What now?" Bryce asks.

"Now we kill him," Morpheus says, approaching us from above.

"Morpheus!" I exclaim. "You're okay."

My heart fills with joy despite our dire situation.

"Fuck a duck. Are you doing this?" Phoenix asks.

"No. My father is keeping Chaos distracted while we do what we have to."

"And that is?" Rufio asks.

"Daisy and Bryce must be linked by the infinity band, and then they make you a God-killer."

"What?" we all ask in unison.

"I don't have time to explain. Just follow my lead. Daisy and Bryce, get in the middle of the circle. Quickly!"

I do what he says, unsure of how this will play out. It's the only chance to get out of this alive though. Bryce and I join hands and wait for Morpheus to continue. He's joined our group and, together with Rufio and Phoenix, reforms the circle around us.

He closes his eyes briefly and starts to chant in a foreign language. As the strange words pour out of his mouth, I sense a new type of energy surround us. It tingles against my skin, connects me to Bryce more than ever. Morpheus's eyes fly open, glowing a warm yellow that reminds of the sun. My skin gets warm, and then the sleeves of both my jacket and Bryce's catch fire. Only they don't burn.

Now our forearms are bare, and on them, peculiar symbols glow the same color as Morpheus's eyes. Gold energy billows from my wrists and Bryce's, forming a lasso around our joined hands. I lose the sensation of my body, almost as if my soul detached from it. Bryce and I are soaring above the circle below, still linked through our hands but now also through our essences. He's glowing like a star, so beautiful and radiant. He smiles at me, making me burst with joy.

"We're finally together now for all eternity," he says.

"For all eternity," I repeat in awe.

Our spirits inch closer, meeting in the middle. His ethereal face leans into mine, and when he kisses me, an explosion of lights takes place. We're enveloped by a vortex of raw, primal magic. I close my eyes to feel every single emotion coursing through me. The moment only lasts a few seconds before we're jolted back into our bodies as if the elastic band connecting us to them stretched too far.

My eyes fly open at the same time that the tornado becomes violent again. Bryce is torn from my hands. Our circle breaks, and each one of my soul mates disappears from view.

BRYCE

The time Erebus bought us is up. The ritual of the infinity band must have alerted Chaos of what we were up to. My body is spiraling out of control. I'm tossed around like dirty laundry inside a washing machine. Pieces of debris hit me, and every time they do, it sends me in a different direction. I can take those blows, but my brother can't.

"Rufio!" I call out. "Where are you?"

I hear no response besides the deafening howling of winds going at two hundred miles an hour. Then Chaos gets into my head.

"You're too late. He's dead."

"No!"

"Your little vow means nothing. You can't defeat me. Nothing on this planet can. I'm everything and nothing. I'm the void."

"Bryce!" I hear Daisy's voice. It's muffled but strong.

The link of the infinity band flares up, and I use it to guide me to her. She collides with me in the next moment, going so fast that she almost slips through my hands.

"We have to find the others, but especially Rufio," she says.

"I know. I can do it. Don't let go of me."

"Never."

I close my eyes and focus on the connection I've always had with my brother. I thought my ability to sense him was linked to our powers, but it didn't go away after he was unmade. It's hard to concentrate when there's so much noise in the background and Chaos keeps laughing perversely in my head, the sound akin to nails against chalkboard.

I'm giving my all, stretching my awareness to the max, when a burst of power enters my body, enhancing my reach. It's Daisy, infusing me with her energy. Together we go much farther into the mayhem until I sense Rufio's life force, close to the ground. He's not alone. Phoenix and Morpheus have found him.

"I see him. Let's go!" I shout over the cacophony.

We fly downward, swerving left and right to avoid the shit that's inside the vortex. I have a visual of them, but before we come within reach, a bolt of lightning arcs down the funnel and hits Rufio straight on.

"No!" I shout, or maybe Daisy does. I don't know.

His body convulses as the energy blast crackles around his body. Morpheus and Phoenix keep holding him, but Rufio's head already hangs low, and the charred hole in his chest is unmistakable.

As if our thoughts are also connected, Daisy and I reach our arms forward and attempt to pull the energy from the lightning blast from Rufio. The electric current converges back to the point of impact and then shoots straight to us. The blast is jarring, and it makes all my muscles spasm. I end up biting my tongue, drawing blood in the process, but those sensations are nothing compared to the raw agony of not sensing Rufio's essence anymore. I feel Daisy's pain as if it were my own, which is amplified by her still-raw feelings over Rosie's passing.

Everything is so rotten; it has to end.

Chaos has to end.

RUFIO

I'm in a tunnel made of light. The translucent walls keep rushing by, becoming a blur. There's a bright glow ahead, beckoning me. I want to answer the call, but something holds me back. I glance down, noticing a gold cord wrapped around my waist. It's taut, keeping me in place as my body is sucked forward.

Something is coming to me, and at first, I can't make out its shape. As it gets near and the brightness fades, I see my mother floating in front of me. She's washed-out, transparent.

"You have to go back, Rufio. You aren't done with your task yet."

"What is this place?"

"An in-between."

"So, I'm dead?"

"Not yet. You must return to the island and do what I couldn't."

The cord yanks me back, but I can't leave, not yet. There are so many things I want to tell my mother, so many questions I didn't get to ask.

"What about you? Can't you come with me?"

Her expression falls. "Oh no, darling. I can't come. I've completed my mission. My time is done."

My eyes burn and I don't understand why. I'm so fucking confused. There was a time when I loved my mother unconditionally, but I've hated her for too damn long. And yet my heart is breaking, knowing if I go, I'll never see her face again.

"Go now, Rufio. Your brother needs you. The whole world needs you."

"I'm sorry, Mom."

"I know you are. I am too. Tell your brother I love him. I love you both. Now go." She lifts her hand, palm facing forward, and creates a gust of wind that sends me back.

The tunnel begins to move again, this time in reverse. I lose the feeling of my body for a moment as I'm sucked into a vortex. And then I'm back in the middle of Chaos's hell. But instead of being half dead, I'm filled with a primordial power that runs through my veins with the strength of lightning and the fury of thunder. I release it, and it emerges from my body in beams of light. His odious laughter ceases abruptly when a ray of pure energy pierces through his darkness. Instead of being consumed by the void, it cracks it down in the middle.

"You won't defeat me. I am everything."

"You're nothing."

"If I end, your friends die. The love of your life dies."

"You're a liar."

I give everything I have, and the first crack multiplies to thousands, spreading rapidly through his mass. He roars savagely, the sound like an earthquake destroying an entire city. But there's nothing he can do to save himself.

I'm the God-killer.

43

DAISY

It's done. Chaos's malevolence has vanished in the aftermath of an explosion of pure energy, leaving me in the vacuum. Bryce's hand slipped through my fingers, and now I'm floating in the middle of nowhere, suspended in time and space. It's neither dark nor light. It's nothing. But my powers, my ability to unmake Idols, is flowing out of me unrestrained, and I don't care.

I'm not sure how long I stay floating, disconnected from everything and everyone. It feels like I'm slowly fading. But then a featherlike touch brushes my cheek, infusing my body with warmth. The beautiful face of Phoenix appears in front of my eyes. He tells me to come back to him, kickstarting my heart once again. I hadn't realized it stopped beating.

I begin to spin rapidly while I regain the feeling in my body. Tingles spread all over my skin, eradicating the numbness from before. My mind is whirling as my scrambled thoughts try to come together into something that makes sense.

The crash comes suddenly, leaving me breathless. My eyes fly open, but almost immediately I shut them again, unable to handle the brightness. I swing my arm over my face, covering my eyelids. It feels good to be solid once more. Warm sand cushioned my fall, or maybe that didn't happen for real. The impact was only in my head, just like in a dream.

"Daisy, my love!" Phoenix brushes a strand of hair off my forehead. "Are you okay?"

I uncover my eyes and slowly open them. Phoenix is hovering above me, blocking the sun. His face is shadowed, but it's impossible to miss the frown marring his forehead.

"I'm okay now."

He helps me to a sitting position, allowing me to see the aftermath of our battle. Only there's nothing to see but the peaceful white sand beach. The monsters are gone, and the jungle that felt foreboding and evil is not as dense or dark. It's normal.

Bryce, Morpheus, and Rufio walk over, coming from different directions. My heart expands, finally released from the barbed wire wrapped around it. I jump to my feet, glad my legs are stable enough to hold me upright. Phoenix's hand is on my lower back though. My boyfriends surround me, and for a moment, all we do is stare at one another in awe.

"Is it truly over?" I ask.

"Yes, I killed him," Rufio says.

"I thought you died," I reply through a choke.

"I almost did. But then my mother sent me back. She told me I wasn't done with my mission."

"You saw Mom?" Bryce's eyebrows arch.

Rufio nods. "I'll tell you more later."

It's impossible to miss their sadness. Morpheus steps closer to Rufio with eyes narrowed. "Your powers. They're back."

Rufio's brows furrow. He presses his hand against his chest, dipping his chin. "Shit. You're right. I hadn't noticed it until now."

"Daisy!" Xavier is running toward us. There's a gash on his

forehead that bled and dried. His clothes are torn in some spots, but other than that, he's in one piece.

He pushes the boys aside and engulfs me in a bear hug. "You're okay. God. I thought I had lost you too."

I hang on to his last word. *Too.* Rosie. It wasn't a nightmare. She's gone.

I suppress a gasp, burying my face in his chest. But I can't fight the tears that are burning my eyes and drenching my face. I broke my promise. I didn't keep her safe.

Guilt and shame take me over. I pull away from Xavier's arms, avoiding eye contact with him. Slowly, I head toward the edge of the jungle, to the exact spot where I last saw my sister. My heart is heavy and bleeding again. My throat constricts, making it hard to breathe.

I'm almost at the end of my trek when the jungle parts, revealing the peaceful village I saw before. Children run freely near the small lake the village surrounds, laughing and splashing water around. I see a familiar blonde head in the middle of the fun.

"Rosie!" I take a step forward, ready to break into a run, but Eris appears, blocking my way. Her hair is as black as ever, but today she's wearing white clothes, and her face isn't so pale.

"You can't follow your sister, honey."

"Why not?"

"She's gone beyond the veil. She's at peace now."

Eris steps to the side and allows me to see Rosie running toward our parents. They look exactly as they did seven years ago; the only difference is that they're happy, worry-free. They hug Rosie fiercely. The vision pulls at the strings of my heart. Jealousy mingles with yearning. I miss them so much.

The village disappears, shimmering out of sight. I wonder if I truly saw that or if it was all a figment of my imagination.

"Where did they go?" I wipe my wet cheeks with my fingers.

"Mortals aren't meant to see Starlight Island until they're

ready to become part of it. I let you see, hoping it would ease the pain in your heart."

"The pain will never go away."

Eris eyes shine with empathy. "I know."

"How could you possibly? You're a god. Immortal."

"But not without feelings. It broke my heart when Magia chose a mortal life."

I turn away, unable to withstand her stare. Magia was her daughter, and I'm her descendant. So I'm related to Eris, but I can't summon an ounce of emotion toward her, and that makes me feel guilty.

"You'd better return to your boyfriends. Bryce is about to do something foolish."

I whirl around. Bryce is kneeling next to Renata, who somehow hasn't passed away yet.

"We've defeated Chaos. He can try to heal her now."

"Oh, Daisy. Can't you see? Every time Bryce heals someone, he's shaving off years of his life. If he keeps it up, he won't live past thirty."

"No," I breathe.

"You can stop it, you know. You could take away his ability to heal."

"Do you mean I could unmake him?"

"No. Just that part of his gift."

I shake my head. "I can't do that to him. It's wrong. Besides, we're the same level. He can block me."

"There's always a way around that." She shrugs. "If you change your mind, I can help you."

I watch her through narrowed eyes. Now that her arch-nemesis is gone, she has no reason to spare us her mischievous ways. She's Strife, after all.

"I'll pass. Thanks," I snap.

She rolls her eyes before vanishing. I glance back where the magical village was, feeling the sharp pang in my chest.

"Daisy?" Toby calls out.

He's walking over, and seeing his devastated expression is akin to a steely knife piercing my chest. He loved Rosie so much, and he didn't even get to see her at peace like I did.

"Are you okay?" I meet him halfway.

His eyes are filled with tears. He shakes his head, trembling from head to toe. I pull him into my arms, and then he breaks down. His cries are desperate and heartfelt. It amplifies my own sadness. I don't hold back. I let it all out, knowing this is the first step of the long recovery process, even if deep down I know this wound will never heal completely.

MORPHEUS

"Should we go after her?" Phoenix asks.

"No. Daisy and Toby need time to process their feelings," I say.

From the corner of my eye, I catch Xavier staring at the ocean with a fisted hand covering his mouth. My mother steps close to him and places a hand on his back in support. They remain silent for a long while, just looking ahead. My eyes begin to prickle, forcing me to look away. I can't become overwhelmed by my emotions. I need to remain strong for Daisy.

I sense Erebus's presence near the jungle. He's watching Mom from the shadows, and for the first time, I wonder if he ever loved her.

"*Yes I did. I still do,*" he answers in my head.

"*I didn't know you could read minds,*" I reply, annoyed.

"*I can when you ask me a question directly.*"

"*Did she love you back?*"

He doesn't answer right away, but when he does, it's not what I expect from a fucking god. "*It's complicated.*"

I snort, earning questioning glances from Rufio and Phoenix. I raise my index finger, asking for a moment.

"Well, her husband is a piece of shit. If you still love her, maybe you should do something about that."

"What makes you think I'm better than him?"

"I know you are."

"Hmm."

"Shit. Is that Andromeda and Stephan?" Phoenix points in the distance.

I glance toward the duo, who are walking toward us with difficulty, clutching each other. Stephan looks worse for the wear, with lacerations all over his face.

"What are they doing here?" Soren takes off to meet them halfway.

I want to know as well, since I didn't have time to ask Stephan why Nathaniel brought Andromeda here. But Daisy and Toby are finally heading back to us, and that gets my undivided attention. They veer in Bryce's direction, who's sitting next to Renata, hugging his knees with his head hanging low. She's asleep but alive. Bryce was able to heal her, which means he must be on the verge of passing out.

The ground shakes suddenly, and the small hairs on the back of my neck stand on end.

Xavier and Mom let out gasps of terror. I follow their line of vision, getting caught in their distress. A giant tsunami wave is fast approaching the island. It'll hit us in less than a minute. My stomach bottoms out. *Fuck!*

"You need to go," Erebus tells me. *"Now that Chaos is gone, there's no need for this island anymore."*

"What about the village?"

"It doesn't exist on this plane. It won't be affected."

"Can't you send us back like before?"

He sighs heavily. *"Yes. So can you."*

"I don't know how, and we don't have time for me to learn!"

"Fine. I'll do it this once, but you have to practice, son."

"I need a teacher," I say, hoping he knows I'm talking about him.

"We'll see. Now gather your friends."

"Come on, guys. Form a circle." I wave them over with urgency toward where Bryce and Renata are.

"What are you doing?" Soren asks.

"Getting us out of here." I look in the distance, locking gazes with my father. He nods, and a moment later, we're standing in front of Poppy's Joint.

It's still in one piece, even though it's smack in the middle of Norm territory. I can't believe it survived the destruction and looting whereas every single building in the vicinity was raided. When a beacon of light shines over the diner's neon sign, I recognize the deity responsible for the preservation of this place. Gaia.

44

DAISY

Five days have gone by, during which I didn't leave my assigned room in Xavier's real home except to eat. Without Chaos at our backs, and with the Neo Gods' movement pretty much extinguished, there was no need to go to a safe house.

Begrudgingly, Xavier procured a second queen-sized bed to squeeze in the room so I could sleep with all my boyfriends. Then he muttered something about obtaining noise-canceling earphones stat. We did sleep, but we also made love a lot. I guess his grumpiness was kind of warranted.

I wake up on the sixth day of my reclusion, knowing it's time to face the world. I'm literally surrounded in the middle of the bed by the loves of my life, which means I can't get up without waking them. Bryce and Rufio are on each of my sides, sleeping at ninety-degree angles from me so Phoenix and Morpheus could get a piece too. Bryce's arm is across my breasts, and Rufio's curls around my waist. Morpheus and Phoenix are using my legs as pillows.

I squirm, trying to get my upper body free, but the slight movement disturbs Phoenix's sleep. With his eyes still closed, he kisses my thigh and then slowly slinks upward. My sex clenches in anticipation. I know where this is going. But I'm suddenly antsy to find out what's going on in the world. Mind-blowing sex will have to wait.

I press my hand against Phoenix's shoulders, stopping his caresses. He lifts his head and glances at me through half-open sleepy eyes. "What?"

"I have to use the restroom."

"Oh." He slides off me and then, using his gift, pushes everyone else off me too.

There are groans of complaint, but I don't stay in bed long enough to hear them all. I jump off and then hide in the bathroom. I do have to pee, but it's not an immediate need. Instead, I put on the bathrobe that's hanging behind the door, then sneak out through the adjacent guest room that also connects to the bathroom. The pink décor makes it quite obvious this was supposed to be Rosie's bedroom. A terrible ache flares in my chest, almost turning me into a sobbing mess again. It's like this every morning. I wake up happy, and then I remember that Rosie is gone, and the pain becomes fresh again.

Fighting back the tears with a clench of my jaw, I head out. Xavier is sitting by the kitchen counter, nursing a coffee mug while he stares at his phone with a stupid grin.

"What's on that phone that made you so happy?" I ask, making a beeline for the coffeepot.

"Nothing." Embarrassment washes over his face. He turns the phone facedown so I can't peer at the screen. Very suspicious.

"Riiight. How is Leticia doing?" I smirk.

Xavier opens and closes his mouth without saying a word. I shake my head and grab a cup to pour some coffee.

"She's fine. Still helping Ellen with the injured. We've now moved them to a proper hospital."

"Oh, that's good to know. And what about Theo? Any luck finding his father or other relative?"

Xavier's face falls. "Not yet. I'm beginning to fear we won't find anyone to claim him. He's staying with Leticia for now."

I close my eyes, trying my best to keep my shit together, but it's so hard when I hear about more deaths and more kids left without parents.

"Anyway, Leticia and I are going out to dinner tonight."

My eyebrows arch. "Oh? Is this your first date?"

"Yes, but I'd like to keep that between us. I don't want Phoenix to know yet."

My amusement grows by leaps and bounds, making me forget the pain in my chest. "And why is that? Are you afraid he's going to give you grief?"

"No. I just don't want to give him leverage over me. I'd like to be able to bust his balls about you for a little longer."

I snort. "Oh my God."

"Anyway. How are you feeling today?"

The question is loaded and brings forth the darkness. "No better than yesterday, or the day before. I miss her so much." I stare into my cup of coffee.

"I know, honey. I do too."

I could say something ugly to him, like he can't possibly miss someone he didn't know or spend any time with. But hurting Xavier won't make me feel any better.

"What's going on in the world? Is it still in shambles?"

Xavier's gaze turns hard in a flash. "Wow, I can't believe those boys managed to keep their mouths shut. I'm in awe."

I frown. "What do you mean?"

"I didn't want to say anything while you were recovering, but there've been new developments."

I move closer to the counter, clutching the mug tighter. "You're making me nervous."

The doorbell rings, interrupting our conversation. Xavier

moves to rise from his seat, but a second later, Felicity's voice echoes in the entry foyer. "Hello? Everyone still asleep here?"

She joins us in the kitchen, carrying bags of delicious breakfast food. I smell bacon, cheese, sausage, and pancakes. My stomach grumbles, but I won't let food distract me from Xavier's imminent revelation.

"Hi, hon. It's nice to see you up so early." She smiles kindly at me.

"Yeah," I reply half-heartedly.

The guys slowly trickle down from the bedroom, drawn by the smell of food. They're always hungry. Bryce stops behind me, wrapping his arm around my waist to lean his chin on my shoulder. "What do we have here?"

"I brought everything we have on the menu," Felicity replies.

"Including pie?" Bryce asks hopefully.

"Pie is not breakfast food, bro." Rufio reaches for a bag.

Bryce steps around me. "Whatever. Hand me one of those."

"Will you boys wait until I can unpack everything? Geez," Felicity says, exasperated.

I cut my eyes to Xavier. "What were you going to tell me?"

Everyone freezes, and a sudden tension fills the air.

"Somehow when Chaos was vanquished, all the Idols not on the island were unmade."

I feel the blood drain from my face. "What?"

"We don't know how it happened, but the reports keep coming in. Every single Idol hospital has been overrun with people freaking out that they can't use their powers anymore."

"Oh my God. I did that."

Xavier narrows his eyes. "Oh no, honey. No one is blaming you for it. It was most likely Chaos's last evil act."

I pinch the bridge of my nose. "It wasn't him. It was me. I lost control of my powers for a while. They were unbound."

"Is it that bad if Idols don't have powers anymore?" Felicity asks. "Now everyone is equal. Isn't that what the Knights wanted?"

"But not *everyone* has been 'normalized,'" Rufio replies. "I've recovered my powers, and everyone in this room still have theirs."

"Theo hasn't been unmade either, and he wasn't on the island," Xavier chimes in.

"Maybe because he was turned into an Idol by me," Bryce replies. "We don't yet know if the entire Idol population has lost their powers."

Morpheus, who was quiet till now, glances at me. "No, they have. This was all part of the destiny the Fates bestowed upon us."

"How do you know that?" I ask.

"I've been talking with my father." He shrugs.

"Dude, you didn't tell us you're hanging out with Erebus," Phoenix pipes up.

"I didn't want to make a big deal out of it."

I pass a hand over my face. "If they hated me before, now I've truly become anathema."

Phoenix pulls me into a side embrace. "Those who knew the identity of the Unmaker are either your friends or dead. No one will harm you, babe."

"I'm not worried about that. I just feel so wretched. Not all Idols were evil, and now they were punished along with the bad."

"Daisy, this was preordained. There was nothing you could have done that would alter the course set by the Fates. Don't feel guilty about it. It wasn't your fault," Morpheus says.

I glance around the room, noticing immediately that they all agree with him. I get what he's saying. We're nothing but pawns on the gameboard of the gods. But that doesn't make me feel better.

I take a deep breath, pushing the feeling aside for now. "All right. There must be tons of things to do. Where do we start?"

EPILOGUE
DAISY

Two months later

"Daisy, come on. Let us in," Phoenix whines.

"No. And if you keep asking, you're sleeping in the guest room," I reply as I continue my pacing, staring at the various white sticks on the counter.

It's been two months since Bryce and I had the condom accident, but with everything that happened in the aftermath of Chaos's defeat, I didn't notice I hadn't gotten my period until today. Then it was panic mode galore. The guys went out and bought every single pregnancy test on the market.

Now my stomach is in knots as I wait for the damn results. In the end, the God-killer didn't turn out to be a child Bryce and I conceived, but that doesn't mean I'm not knocked up. *Fuck.* I pull my hair back, yanking at the strands. I can't be pregnant. I'm only eighteen. Plus, Xavier will kill me.

A faint pink line begins to appear on the first test. I hold my breath until it turns magenta. But it remains single, which means the test is negative. I wait until the other results come in, and when they all display the same thing, I breathe out in relief.

Then I open the bathroom door and yell, "I'm not pregnant!"

Relief washes over Bryce's, Rufio's, and Morpheus's faces. Only Phoenix seems disappointed.

"Come again?" Xavier asks from the now-open door, looking absolutely livid.

My face becomes as hot as lava. I couldn't be more embarrassed, and if I had Morpheus's gift, I'd use it to run away from my uncle's wrath.

"Daisy, why did you believe you were pregnant?" he asks in a low voice. "I thought you were being careful."

Bryce jumps from his seat on the bed, standing in between Xavier and me. "We are, Mr. X. We totally are. We had an accident a couple of months back. You see, the condom, uh... broke."

I cover my face with my hands. *Someone kill me now.*

"Uh, hello? Why is everyone in the kids' room?" Leticia asks.

I uncover my face and notice she's touching Xavier's shoulder in an intimate way. Phoenix notices it too and narrows his eyes. *Oh man, they haven't come out to him yet about their relationship.*

He rises from the bed slowly. "Mom, what's going on between you and Mr. X?"

Xavier still makes all the boys call him by Mr. X. It was his way to try to maintain the façade that he's the boss of the house. I appreciate him stepping into a parental role, but I've been on my own for too long. I do indulge him though, since we're all living under his roof. It's a temporary arrangement until Bryce and Rufio can touch their parents' money. Phoenix gave his inheritance to charity.

Most of the public schools are still closed after the attacks, and none of us were inclined to return to Gifted Academy or enroll in a different private school. For now, we're studying at home and helping with rebuilding our new world. We've been volunteering at the hospital too. Well, we all have besides Bryce. I told him the toll his healing ability has on his life force and begged him not to heal anyone anymore. I can't bear the thought of losing him in only a few years.

Leticia trades a glance with Xavier, then replies, "Why don't we all go into the living room?"

The moment we step outside, Theo, the little boy Leticia adopted, comes running and crashes into my legs. "Daisy! I've missed you."

I pick him up, squeezing him tight. "I've missed you too, little man. What have you been up to?"

"I've been learning new tricks."

The front door opens, and in come Toby and Renata, plus a new addition to the team. Theo's eyes bug out when he sees what's in Toby's arms.

"Puppy!"

He wiggles free from my hold and flies toward the dog. Toby sets the puppy down, and now we won't have to entertain that kid for hours.

"Hey, guys. It's been a while." I take turns hugging them both.

To say Renata and I have come a long way is an understatement. She's the living proof that people can learn from their mistakes and change. She and Toby have become fast friends, and she's helped him a lot to deal with his grief.

"So, who else is coming tonight? Can we expect to see the Silverstones and Andy?" Toby asks.

"No, they're too busy in Hawk City. They won't come down here for another couple of weeks," I reply.

"So, are you going to answer my earlier question or what?" Phoenix glowers at his mother and Xavier.

"Well…" Leticia looks at Xavier. "Should I tell them, or do you want to?"

"No, go ahead, honey."

Honey? Oh, dear.

"Xavier asked me to marry him, and I said yes!" she squeaks, showing us her sparkling engagement ring.

"Oh my God. Congratulations!" I say.

"What?" Phoenix replies a second later. "How can you be engaged? You barely know each other."

"We've been dating for a while," she replies.

"Behind our backs?" His voice rises to a shriek. "And you have the gall to give us grief over Daisy's pregnancy scare?" He points a finger at Xavier.

"Phoenix!" I yell. "What the hell!"

"Dude. Seriously?" Morpheus makes a what-were-you-thinking gesture with his hand.

He glances sheepishly at me. "Oops, sorry, babe."

I throw my hands up in the air. "Ugh. Never mind. Let's eat dinner before I die of embarrassment."

Xavier's phone rings, killing the tense moment. Leticia walks over to Phoenix and touches his face. "Are you mad at me? I didn't want to say anything until I knew it was serious."

"No, I'm not mad at you. I'm mad at him for busting my balls about Daisy all this time when he was sneaking around with my mother."

Leticia giggles like a schoolgirl. She's a completely different person from when I first met her. "He makes me happy, honey. I didn't expect I'd ever get the chance for that."

Phoenix's expression softens. "If he makes you happy, then I am too."

They hug, and fuck if a tear doesn't roll down my cheek.

"Guys, sorry to ruin the evening, but Felicity has an emergency at the diner. The fridge isn't working, and I need to find someone to fix that ASAP."

"What's the problem?" Bryce asks. "Maybe it's something I can help with."

"I don't know if it's an electrical problem, but you know you can't display your powers in public."

We all groan in resignation. It's been confirmed that the entire population of Idols and Fringes have lost their powers. Some blame the Unmaker, but other theories have surfaced, such as they were punished by Gaia for being so wicked. Regardless, we can't flaunt our gifts or they'll suspect I'm the Unmaker, and then I'll have a target on my back again.

"If the fridge isn't working, what's going to happen to all those frozen pies?" Bryce asks.

"You know about them?" I arch my eyebrows.

"Yeah, I caught Felicity with a load of them. It's no biggie." He shrugs. "They're still delicious."

"Okay, we all know where Bryce is going with that. Let's all go to the diner and have dinner there," Rufio suggests.

"It sounds good to me," Renata chimes in.

"Me too," Toby agrees.

"Super. Let me get my jacket."

***

Since there was no need anymore for Xavier to pretend to be Poppy, his solution was to retire the old man. He posed as the new owner who kept everything the same. No one suspected a thing.

He was able to find a technician to fix the fridge, but even so, Bryce claimed the integrity of the frozen pies had been compromised. His so-called logical solution was to bake and eat them all. At least he shared one with the rest of us.

I excuse myself from the table to use the restroom, but when I return, I stop at a distance and observe my new family for a little bit. I can't believe all that has happened to me in such a short period of time. I've found the biggest love in the world with four amazing men. My own magnificent four. I've made new friendships that will last a lifetime. I have Xavier, the protector and father figure I didn't know I needed. And now with him marrying Leticia and, my guess, adopting Theo, everything is coming into place. The only person missing in this picture-perfect scenario is Rosie. I miss her so damn much every day, but slowly, I'm learning to cope with her absence. Knowing she's reunited with my parents helps.

Bryce is laughing at something Theo said when I catch his gaze. His smile changes from amusement to a sexy grin that makes my toes curl inside my shoes. Then he winks at me, turning me into a puddle. Soon, Rufio, Phoenix, and Morpheus notice where his attention is diverted, and hell and damn, I'm literally on fire under their scorching gazes.

"You'd better get back to your seat, girlie, before you orgasm where you stand," Felicity jokes.

"**O**kay, I don't want to go home right now," Rufio pipes up from the shotgun seat.

"Why not? I'm dying to get Daisy out of her clothes." Phoenix squeezes my thigh.

"Do you seriously want to perform an orgy under Mr. X's roof right after the pregnancy test incident?" Morpheus asks.

"No," I say with regret. "Definitely not."

I'm burning with desire, but I really don't want to get it on tonight where Xavier can hear us.

"I have a suggestion," Bryce says from the driver seat.

"I'm listening," I say.

"Isn't Unearthly Desires closed until further notice?"

"Yeah." I narrow my eyes. "You want to go there?"

"Why not? It has couches."

Phoenix rubs his hands together. "And stripper poles. Oh, I like this idea very much. How about a lap dance, babe?"

I turn my face to glare at him properly. "Really?"

"What?" he asks with innocent, round eyes.

"Don't try to make him understand, love." Morpheus shakes his head, grinning.

An idea forms in my head. "Okay, sure. Let's go there."

"Uh-oh. I don't like that tone." Rufio turns in his seat. "You're plotting something, aren't you, my little demon?"

"Maybe." I smile.

It's strange to be at Unearthly Desires at this late hour and see the neon sign turned off and the parking lot deserted. The windows have been boarded up to avoid looting and break-ins. Getting the alarm disabled and the door unlocked is child's play for Bryce. Although Xavier's told us several times to not use our powers out in the open, there's no one around here.

Once inside, Bryce turns on all the stage and bar lights but keeps the overhead ones dimmed. I take a seat in front of the main stage, propping my legs up on the table and linking my hands behind my head.

"All right, guys. Here's the deal. To get some love tonight, you'll have to earn it."

"I knew you were up to no good." Rufio points his finger at me, trying to keep a serious face, but the upturn of his lips gives him away.

"That's right, babe. I'm a bad girl tonight, and I want to see you all strip for me. Work that pole."

They trade glances and, with a collective shrug, hop on the stage. Bryce turns the music system on. *What do you know, the boy has moves.*

It's funny to watch them dance at first, but then it gets really hot. *Fuck.* It's no fun to simply sit back and not participate. I jump from the chair, already yanking at my clothes.

"Wait, Morpheus. You're doing that move wrong, babe. Let me teach you," I say with a grin.

I join them on the stage, hoping Bryce didn't accidentally turn the security cameras on because tonight, I'm not holding anything back.

*** THE END ***

Not ready to say good-bye to this world yet? Read Andromeda and Stephan's story in **RECKLESS TIMES. Available now.**

DAISY & RUFIO
GIFTED ACADEMY

ALSO BY MICHELLE HERCULES

Paranormal Romance:

Dark Prince (Blueblood Vampires #1)

Wild Thing (Blueblood Vampires #2)

Forgotten Heir (Blueblood Vampires #3)

Reckless Times (Gifted Academy #5)

Contemporary Romance:

Wonderwall (Love Me, I'm Famous #1)

Sugar, We're Going Down (Love Me, I'm Famous #2)

Wreck of the Day (Love Me, I'm Famous #3)

Devils Don't Fly (Love Me, I'm Famous #4)

Love Me Like You Do (Love Me, I'm Famous #5)

Catch You (Love Me, I'm Famous #6)

All The Right Moves

Heart Stopper (Rebels of Rushmore #1)

Heart Breaker (Rebels of Rushmore #2)

Heart Starter (Rebels of Rushmore #3)

Reverse Harem Romance:

Wicked Gods (Gifted Academy #1)

Ruthless Idols (Gifted Academy #2)

Hateful Heroes (Gifted Academy #3)

Broken Knights (Gifted Academy #4)

Lost Horizon (Oz in Space #1)

ABOUT THE AUTHOR

USA Today Bestselling Author Michelle Hercules always knew creative arts were her calling but not in a million years did she think she would become an author. With a background in fashion design she thought she would follow that path. But one day, out of the blue, she had an idea for a book. One page turned into ten pages, ten pages turned into a hundred, and before she knew, her first novel, The Prophecy of Arcadia, was born.

Michelle Hercules resides in Florida with her husband and daughter. She is currently working on the *Blueblood Vampires* series and the *Rebels of Rushmore* series.

Join Michelle Hercules' Reader Group:
https://www.facebook.com/groups/mhsoars

Connect with Michelle Hercules:
www.michellehercules.com
books@mhsoars.com